Praise for the

"[An] unwaveringly superb series about a ~~young~~ tested Maine game warden ... The prose is as sharp as an arrow and so lyrical that it sometimes borders on poetry."

—Associated Press

"Maine writer Paul Doiron has demonstrated he is a master at crafting compelling mysteries." —*Maine Sunday Telegram*

"No list of Maine mysteries would be complete without Paul Doiron." —*Bangor Daily News*

"[Doiron] keeps getting better." —*New York Journal of Books*

"Brilliant." —*The Globe and Mail*

"Paul Doiron is shaping up as the Tony Hillerman of the east."
—*Toronto Star*

"A uniformly strong series that has quietly taken its place among the very best outdoors-based crime dramas." —*Booklist*

"Few writers can combine a poet's appreciation of nature with the tension and twists of a great thriller, but Paul Doiron does it with ease." —John Connolly, *New York Times* bestselling author of *The Unquiet* and *The Wrath of Angels*

"Doiron has gotten it all magnificently right: a hell of a good mystery, beautifully drawn landscape and characters so evocatively written they follow you off the page ... The guy can write."
—Nevada Barr, *New York Times* bestselling author of *The Rope*

Also by Paul Doiron

Skin
and
Bones

And Other Mike Bowditch
Short Stories

Paul Doiron

MINOTAUR BOOKS
NEW YORK

First published in the United States by Minotaur Books, an imprint of St. Martin's Publishing Group

SKIN AND BONES. Copyright © 2025 by Paul Doiron. "The Bear Trap" copyright © 2014 by Paul Doiron. "Backtrack" copyright © 2019 by Paul Doiron. "Rabid" copyright © 2018 by Paul Doiron. "The Imposter" copyright © 2020 by Paul Doiron. "Skin and Bones" copyright © 2022 by Paul Doiron. "The Caretaker" copyright © 2021 by Paul Doiron. "Snakebit" copyright © 2023 by Paul Doiron. "Sheep's Clothing" copyright © 2025 by Paul Doiron. All rights reserved. Printed in the United States of America. For information, address St. Martin's Publishing Group, 120 Broadway, New York, NY 10271.

www.minotaurbooks.com

The Library of Congress Cataloging-in-Publication Data is available upon request.

ISBN 978-1-250-38212-2 (trade paperback)
ISBN 978-1-250-38213-9 (hardcover)
ISBN 978-1-250-38214-6 (ebook)

Our books may be purchased in bulk for promotional, educational, or business use. Please contact your local bookseller or the Macmillan Corporate and Premium Sales Department at 1-800-221-7945, extension 5442, or by email at MacmillanSpecialMarkets@macmillan.com.

"The Bear Trap" published previously by CriminalElement.com.

First Edition: 2025

10 9 8 7 6 5 4 3 2 1

This one is for my readers

Contents

Introduction

As is often the case with fiction, this collection began in serendipity. I never consciously set out to write short stories to fill in the untold history of my Mike Bowditch novels. But then one morning, some years ago, I got a phone call from a Maine game warden who had an exclusive for me.

The date was April 4, 2013, and only hours earlier Sergeant Terry Hughes had arrested a semilegendary criminal named Christopher Thomas Knight (a.k.a. the North Pond Hermit), who had terrorized the Belgrade Lakes area for decades. Knight claimed to have lived in almost total isolation for twenty-seven years in a hidden camp, subsisting entirely off food and other items he burgled from vacant homes and cottages. Both Hughes and I understood that once it got out, this unbelievable story would be an international phenomenon—which it proved to be.

"You have to write a book about this!" Hughes said.

I considered his request and still ask myself, "What if . . . ?" when I contemplate the enduring bestsellerdom of *The Stranger in the Woods*, the book journalist Michael Finkel eventually wrote about Knight. But I knew I wasn't the man for the job. I doubted I could get Knight to speak with me and wasn't inclined to trust what he said if he did. Although he suffered from mental illness and was nonviolent, the hermit tested my willingness to sympathize with him—he'd harmed hundreds of people for his own selfishness, regularly stealing from a summer camp for disabled children, among other bad acts—and I didn't want to contribute to the romanticization I rightly predicted would come his way.

But the principal reason I chose to let the true story pass from my hands was that I understood that I am a writer of fiction to my very bones. And so instead of sitting down to collect facts and interviews, I let my imagination loose. I had created a character in *The Poacher's Son* named Charley Stevens, a wry and wizened retired warden who'd obviously had many adventures before meeting my protagonist, Mike Bowditch. "What if Charley had pursued a hermit of his own as a rookie officer?"

Two weeks later, I had completed "The Bear Trap"—my first story—and then in 2017, my publisher asked if they could bring it out as a digital e-short and audio. The success of "The Bear Trap"—and frankly the creative boost I experienced from composing it—encouraged me to write more stories.

In addition to fleshing out the past lives of my supporting characters, I realized I could connect the gaps between the novels. (The last story in this collection, "Sheep's Clothing," picks up roughly where my fifteenth book, *Pitch Dark*, leaves off.) I often have the disembodied feeling of standing outside the work I have created, and I have been as curious as anyone to know what Mike and his friends were doing while my authorial attention wandered.

Mostly, I wanted a chance to play. These short stories allowed me certain freedoms I couldn't otherwise have explored within the parameters I had set for my Bowditch novels. Here, I could tell a tale in Charley's voice ("Backtrack") or describe Mike from the perspective of an omniscient, slightly haughty narrator ("Snakebit"). And I could riff on a few of my literary influences—Poe in "Skin and Bones" and Conan Doyle in "The Caretaker," to give two examples—along the way.

Although the order of this collection roughly corresponds to the events of the Mike Bowditch saga, I would discourage longtime readers from focusing on which adventures happened precisely when in the larger chronology of Mike's life. Instead, I hope these stories will be embraced with the same (wicked) playfulness that fueled their writing. My fondest wish is that someone who has never read a word of mine will pick up this volume and enjoy these eight tales on their own terms: as windows—some cracked, others tinted—into the wildness that is Maine.

The Bear Trap

The wind moved across the surface of the lake like breath upon a mirror. In the stern of the canoe, Charley Stevens dipped a paddle to bring us around again over a submerged field of weeds. We were fishing for early-season pike. Charley was a retired Maine game warden—thirty years in the service—and the best woodsman I'd ever met.

The evening before, I'd happened to remark that I'd never caught a northern pike on a fly rod before. Charley had sat upright in his chair, as if the notion offended his sensibilities, and said I needed remedial schooling if I were going to have any future at all in the Warden Service. It was my first year on the job, and every day I was learning how little I actually knew about my new profession.

And so, here we were, at dawn, on a distant body of water I knew only by name.

"How do you know this place, anyway?" I asked.

"Oh, this was my first district when I was a new warden, back from the war." The canoe rocked gently, almost like a cradle. "Of course, it's changed a lot since those days."

I waited for him to go on, but he pressed his lips together and squinted across the lake toward a mist-blurred line of trees.

In my experience, retired wardens loved nothing more than

to tell tales about their escapades in the North Woods. I was always having my gullibility tested by some gray-haired joker who believed the point of spinning yarns was to see how many lies he could pass off as the truth. Charley's approach to storytelling was to casually mention some brush with death he'd had as if it were a humdrum matter of no particular interest. That very morning, on the drive over, I was shocked to hear him let slip that he'd spent months in Vietnam as a prisoner at the Hanoi Hilton, in the same cell block as John McCain. I wanted to believe the old geezer, but I had been raised a skeptic.

I reeled in my line. "How has it changed?"

He raised the dripping paddle toward a point of land where the pines had been cleared to make way for a cedar-shingle mansion. "Do you see that monstrosity of a domicile? There used to be a boys' summer camp on the far side of it. Maybe it's still going. A lot of them closed. I don't know how many nights I spent staked out in the puckerbrush, trying to nab the damned hermit who kept robbing the place."

"Wait," I said. "What hermit?"

He frowned. "I thought you wanted to hook a pike."

"I do."

"I can't believe you didn't hear about it in warden school. But I guess it's ancient history to the current generation."

"Come on, Charley. Tell me."

He sighed, his breath shimmering in the chilly air. Then he set the paddle across his knees and nodded in the direction of the trapper's basket at my feet. "Pour me a cup of coffee from that thermos. I bet it's still hot."

⁓

Charley's field training officer was a chain-smoking former Marine by the name of Nash. He was a veteran of Peleliu and Okinawa, who said he could no longer recognize the country he had fought for in this land of psychedelic rock and long-haired hippies. Sergeant Nash believed the men of Charley's generation were soft—why else were they getting their asses handed to them by a bunch of yellow midgets in black pajamas?—and he did nothing to hide his cynicism.

When Charley showed up on the first day of work, not wearing his service revolver, Sergeant Nash threatened to write him up for dereliction of duty. Charley explained that he didn't think Maine game wardens needed to go everywhere armed; some situations called for wearing a gun and others didn't. Mostly, being an effective law enforcement officer came down to being skilled in the art of persuasion, of laying out the choices a man had before him: to make things better for himself or worse. The legendary sheriff Buford Pusser—whose life story had recently been dramatized in the movie *Walking Tall*—had faced down the Dixie mafia with just a stick. None of these arguments persuaded Nash, who told his new warden to strap on his Smith & Wesson or hand over his shiny new badge.

Sergeant Nash spent that first morning subjecting Charley to a lengthy diatribe on the Maine Warden Service's decline in admissions standards while he pointed out his favorite places to spy on scofflaw fishermen. The sergeant never seemed to have met an innocent man. The world he described seemed to be one populated by either empty-headed dope fiends and toothless poachers or by criminal masterminds.

When Nash told his young charge that a bearded wild man was living in the woods of central Maine; that this mysterious figure traveled only by night, venturing out from his hidden lair to rob lakeside camps of their canned goods, propane tanks, and blankets; that he had burglarized hundreds of properties over the years but had only been glimpsed twice, the first time by a couple of amorous teenagers who thought they'd found privacy on a cabin porch, the second time in the headlights of a speeding car that came flying around a bend; and that this backwoods phantom had been eluding authorities since the Eisenhower administration—Charley had reason to be skeptical.

"Maybe I'll be the one to catch him," said the young warden.

"Keep dreaming." Nash pressed a new cigarette to his lips.

Even after he'd begun patrolling his district alone and started introducing himself around the lakeside villages, Charley wondered if this so-called hermit was a collective joke the community was playing on its new warden. Everywhere he went, he discovered a new piece of the legend. At Stinson's Store, some wag had sketched a wanted poster, depicting a bearded, bespectacled creature named Sweet Tooth. The reward for the burglar's apprehension was listed as "a cool million" dollars.

"Why do you call him Sweet Tooth?" Charley asked Mott Stinson.

The storekeeper, who had been slicing tomatoes for Italian sandwiches, wiped his hands on his apron, leaving marks like bloody fingerprints. "Well, he has pretty unusual tastes in food," the old man said. "He'll take peanut butter and maple syrup, but he'll leave behind cans of tuna fish and vegetable soup."

"Peanut butter and maple syrup?" Charley peered again at the poster. "Are you sure it's not a bear?"

"Oh, he's human, all right. People leave notes for him. 'Take all the food or clothing you want, but please don't take the power tools,' and damn if he doesn't oblige. He cleaned me out of paperbacks a few years ago. Tell me what sort of animal reads Travis McGee."

Soon Charley began to receive calls himself from burglarized camp owners, and sure enough, the stories the victims told him were bizarre, if not borderline comical:

"He took all of my husband's underwear and the writing desk from the guest room. When he left, he locked the door behind him."

"He broke the faucet climbing in through the window above

the kitchen sink and then ransacked our liquor cabinet. Took everything but a fifth of tequila."

"*He stole the batteries out of my camp radio—but then left the radio. I figured he must already have one of his own.*"

"*All he took from our place was a big stack of* National Geographic *magazines.*"

In his first year, Charley counted nearly a hundred thefts. Most were reported in the springtime, when the owners returned to Maine to open up their camps and realized that someone had been sleeping in their beds and eating their porridge, so to speak. On each call, he would inspect the crime scene for evidence, but the hermit seemed to wear gloves and walk without ever leaving a footprint. The closest Charley got to him that first summer was when he stumbled across a cache of household goods expertly hidden in a ravine cave. Beneath a green tarp was a neat little dugout area with a dirt floor swept clean of needles and a row of twenty-pound propane bottles rigged together and connected to a propane light. There was a folding director's chair and a plank bookshelf on which were arranged alphabetically a series of books, including an impressive collection of Travis McGee mysteries. Charley decided this must be the hermit's personal library, although the *National Geographic*s were nowhere to be seen.

He spent a few bug-bitten nights lying on his stomach nearby, watching the cave, but only encountered a single raccoon that wandered onto the scene to sniff the propane tanks.

The general consensus, when Charley addressed the members of the lake association at their annual meeting, was that the hermit was a nuisance but not a danger. Sweet Tooth never robbed a building while its owner was at home, and he had passed up many opportunities to steal cash, jewelry, and firearms. A few people—newcomers from out of state who had recently purchased their properties—stood up to tell their stories with fear in their eyes or anger in their voices. Charley had the sense that they came from urban neighborhoods where the term *crime wave* didn't provoke smiles. He felt slightly sorry for these frightened city people who carried their fear like so much overweight luggage.

The incident that changed Charley's mind about the hermit was the third time he robbed the boys' camp. It was a damp, drizzly morning in early April, months before the first campers were due to arrive. The director—a prematurely bald young man by the name of Lafontaine—met the warden at the mess hall, with his hands thrust into his raincoat pockets and an expression of utter defeat on his smooth pink face.

"He took everything this time," said Lafontaine.

"Can you be more specific?" said Charley.

The camp director indicated the broken latch where the hermit had jimmied the door. He escorted Charley across the vast, echoey cafeteria, with its pine floors and war banners hanging from the rafters, and brought him into the kitchen. He showed off cupboards in which round circles in the dust revealed where huge cans of food had formerly been. He opened the door to a walk-in freezer and waved his hand at the frosted shelves like a magician's assistant gesturing at an empty box where the magician had just vanished into thin air. "I bought four hundred and fifty dollars' worth of food yesterday, and that bastard got away with all of it. What's he going to do with eight pounds of hot fudge?"

Eat it, Charley supposed, but the despair in Lafontaine's voice kept him from making a glib comment. He knew that the camp catered to disadvantaged children from big cities who had never heard a loon before or caught a perch on a worm. It was one thing to pilfer wool blankets from Bostonians who used their second homes for a few weeks a year, if at all. But this was another matter.

Charley committed himself to capturing the hermit. He began by extensively reconnoitering the surrounding woods, figuring that the robber couldn't have gotten away with such a haul unless he'd made multiple trips to a nearby hideout. But when he found no prints in the mud except those of the resident moose, he began to consider the lake. A man could load a canoe with a lot of heavy bags and steel cans. If the hermit had come by water, then he could be living anywhere along the wide, marshy pond.

"I want you to go grocery shopping again," Charley told the camp director. "The hermit will be waiting for you to restock your pantry, and I want to lure him back here so I can spring a trap on him."

"I don't have the money to!"

"You're welcome to what I have in my passbook savings. Consider it a donation to the cause."

Lafontaine reluctantly agreed to Charley's offer. The warden even helped him load the shopping cart and pushed it down the warped wooden aisles of the A&P. They returned to the camp, restocked the shelves, locked up the mess with new padlocks they had purchased in Mott Stinson's store, and then drove off the grounds, making as much noise as possible and being sure to give the impression of vacating the property for the evening. Charley hoped the hermit would see their two sets of headlights disappear up the hill into the darkness.

When they reached the asphalt road, Charley told Lafontaine to drive home, to the farmhouse where he lived while the camp wasn't in session, and then the warden hid his truck in some alder bushes. He did his best to camouflage the vehicle and used a pine bough to swirl away the tracks the wheels had left in the mud. He zipped up his raincoat and buckled on his service revolver. Now that Nash was no longer perched on his shoulder, Charley usually kept the pistol locked in the glove compartment. He found the weight of the gun to be oppressive, and most of the time he only wore it for show. Then he took his flashlight and a pair of handcuffs and made his way cross-country back to the mess hall. He moved as quietly as he could, slipping from tree to tree as the Vietcong had done along the Ho Chi Minh Trail.

When he returned to the camp, he kept close to the buildings until he reached the bunkhouse across from the mess. He had noticed that there was a porch under which he could hide with a good view of the entrance. The windows were all boarded up, so the door was the only way inside. Charley wriggled into his place of ambush, and he waited.

It rained that night. Small ponds formed around Charley's knees, elbows, and bony hips. When dawn came, it was still raining, but the hermit had not appeared. Eventually, Lafontaine returned, and the two men—the camp director and the mud-soaked, shivering warden—inspected the mess hall, just to be certain the pantry remained untouched. The hermit had seemingly spent his evening out of the rain, feasting on hot fudge.

"He'll be back, though," Charley assured Lafontaine. "I'll bet you a penny he's here tonight."

The warden returned home to take a scalding shower and sleep in his solitary bed, but by nightfall, he was back at the camp. This time, he positioned himself on the rooftop of the infirmary. He spread himself flat on the asphalt shingles and peered down at the mess hall. He had come to the conclusion that the hermit might have anticipated an ambush from the ground. It didn't rain that night, but a cold wind stirred in the treetops, and he found himself wishing he had worn an extra pair of socks. In the morning, he climbed down off the roof with dead pine needles stuck to every part of him, as if glued there by an out-of-control arts and crafts class.

Every evening after that, Charley returned to the camp. He changed hiding places, returning to the damp hollow beneath the porch. He built himself a duck blind in the alders and crouched inside the woven rushes until the sun came up. He tried moving his vehicle a mile up the road in case the hermit had discovered its parking place and was waiting for the game warden to abandon his stakeout before raiding the camp again. Nothing he tried seemed to work. A strange notion began to form in his head of the hermit being some sort of cryptozoological creature, half-man and half-beast, with extraordinary powers of perception. He felt as if he were hunting for Bigfoot.

After a week of sleepless, freezing nights, a crazy idea occurred to him. "I want you to lock me inside the mess hall," he told Lafontaine.

"I've already tried that," the balding director said. "I had my wife padlock the door, and I put down a sleeping bag under one of the tables, but he never showed. Either that, or he sensed somehow that I was in there."

Charley pulled on his chin as he considered the problem from a new angle. "Can you pick me up at my house this afternoon?"

When Lafontaine arrived at the little ranch house the Warden Service had provided Charley, he found the young warden dressed for a blizzard. He was wearing a woolen parka, heavy leather boots, and a green hat with earflaps. He crouched down in the back seat with a blanket pulled over his head while the director drove back to camp. When they arrived at the mess hall, he had Lafontaine unlock the door, and then he quickly slipped inside the building, worried that even ten seconds in the open would alert the hermit to his presence.

"Now what?" asked Lafontaine.

"I want you to lock me inside the freezer."

"You'll freeze to death!"

"I might get a bit chilly, but it will be no worse than the nights I spent in the snow caves I built as a lad."

Charley explained that he thought the hermit had developed a means of determining whether a person was hiding inside the mess hall. Unless he had X-ray vision in addition to his other seemingly supernatural powers, he couldn't see through the stainless steel walls of the Master-Bilt freezer. It was Charley's intention to spring out at the burglar the moment he opened the door, taking him by complete surprise.

"This is the most insane idea I have ever heard," Lafontaine said.

"That is why it will work."

"You'd better hope I don't get in a car accident on my way home tonight," said the director, closing the steel door.

It was black inside the freezer, and Charley began wishing he had brought a blanket to sit on. The cold penetrated through his wool layers into the marrow of his bones. He tried standing up, then crouched on his heels for a while, but found no position that could be described as comfortable. None of them was worse, however, than the postures he had been forced to assume by his North Vietnamese captors.

Now that he was locked inside the box, various flaws in his reasoning began to sharpen into focus. He wasn't worried about Lafontaine failing to return in the morning; Charley Stevens had never been plagued by irrational fears. However, the hum of the machinery was loud enough that he was unlikely to hear the hermit approaching until the door opened, so he would have no advance warning to prepare himself. If his muscles tightened in the cold, he might be unable to leap out at the robber with requisite quickness. The success of the plan depended on the hermit not having the presence of mind to slam the door shut on his ambusher. The people who had seen the man in the flesh had described him as a husky gent, and while Charley normally considered himself a scrappy wrestler, his numb limbs would put him at a disadvantage in a scuffle. Fortunately, he had brought along his Smith & Wesson and realized it might come in handy, at least, as a prop.

He hunkered down to wait, figuring nothing was likely to happen until the wee hours of the morning, but after a while, his ass cheeks began to freeze solid again, and so he climbed once more to his feet and did a little French lumberman's jig to return blood to his toes. The timing was fortunate because things might have gone much worse if he had been seated when the door opened.

There was a crack, as of a seal being broken, and then a blast of cold air blew past Charley's ears toward a tiny light poking in through the darkness. Ahead of him, he heard a sharp intake of breath, and then Charley sprang forward, leaning with his raised shoulder at the spot he guessed the man's chest would be. What he encountered felt like blubber. The impact knocked both combatants to the floor, and the penlight skittered away beneath the sink.

Charley was the faster of the two to his feet. "Police!" he said through chattering teeth. "You are under arrest!"

The other man let loose with a series of asthmatic-sounding wheezes and slumped back to the floor. In the fuzzy light slotting in through the boarded-up windows, Charley couldn't make out many details, other than the fact that the hermit was the largest man he had ever seen.

Charley removed his own flashlight from his coat pocket and directed the beam at the outline of the man's head, hoping to blind him into submission. He saw, beneath him, a hugely fat man with an unruly salt-and-pepper beard and wire-rimmed eyeglasses that had been taped together after some previous mishap. The hermit raised his hands against the light, spreading gloved fingers that were as thick around as hot dogs.

Good lord, thought Charley. *It's the ghost of Ernest Hemingway.*

"Remain where you are, sir," the warden said. "I have no interest in fighting you. Stay there and catch your breath."

It took him a moment to locate the light switch on the wall. He understood that the hermit might be playacting submissiveness, in which case he should probably unholster his revolver, but when the fluorescent bulbs blinked to life, the big man was still sitting on his enormous posterior, blowing his cheeks in and out like two bellows. The hermit was wearing a pair of farmer's overalls that were too short at the ankles, a gray sweatshirt splattered with assorted stains, and a puffy blue parka that was spilling cotton batting through rips in the nylon. On any other man, the brogues he was wearing would have looked like clown shoes. Around his shoulders, he had strapped an overstuffed army backpack.

"I apologize for giving you a fright," Charley said. "But you forced me to resort to desperate measures to capture you."

The big man opened and closed his mouth a few times, but the sounds that came out didn't resemble words so much as throttled attempts at clearing his lungs of some pulmonary obstruction. One normally thought of hermits as scrawny creatures, but years of junk food had given this one a sizable gut and a mouth full of brown teeth.

"Why don't we sit down in the chow hall while you catch your breath," Charley said. In truth, the warden needed to warm up after his hour in the deep freeze, and he didn't want the hermit to notice him shivering. They sat across a picnic table from each other.

"What is your name, sir?" the warden asked.

Behind his eyeglasses, the hermit had large brown eyes that seemed like the adaptations of a nocturnal creature. A faint odor came off him of rotting leaves.

"How about showing me some identification?" Charley said.

The hermit held out both empty hands as if to indicate he possessed no such documentation, and there was no point in searching him.

Seeing that this line of inquiry was leading nowhere, Charley adopted a harder tone. "Well, what am I supposed to call you then? Sweet Tooth?"

"Sweet Tooth?" the hermit said hoarsely.

"Lo! He speaks." Charley leaned back on the bench. "You don't realize that the local populace has given you a nickname?"

The enormous man smoothed his beard with one gloved hand, but his eyes drifted toward the revolver peeking out from Charley's coat. "That's not my name."

"So what is it?"

The hermit folded his arms across his overinflated chest. "I've forgotten."

"You've forgotten your name?"

"It was of no use to me." The man spoke with a formal, almost professorial air, as if beneath the layer of sweat and grime he was a person of great accomplishment. "I have abandoned many things over the years."

"And taken a few other things that don't belong to you," said the young warden. "Why don't you show me what's in your backpack, and we'll start tallying the ledger."

Sweet Tooth removed the pack from his shoulders and set it on the table. It occurred to the warden that the man might have a concealed weapon hidden inside, but the burglar appeared content to remain seated. If anything, he seemed to radiate relaxation. Maybe it was a relief to him to have been captured.

Slowly, he began removing items and displaying each with a prideful smile: three cans of peaches, two bags of marshmallows, peanut butter and jelly, a box of crackers, matches, a coil of rope, a folded plastic tablecloth, wadded trash bags, an aluminum canteen, and a Tupperware container filled with mildewed bills of assorted denominations. He carried a hammer and a crowbar in a flour sack. Also, a screwdriver with electrical tape around the grip. The tools of a burglar's trade. "I was hoping to find some hamburger and steaks in the freezer," he said after he reached the end of his show-and-tell.

Just to be on the safe side, Charley gathered up the steel tools and set them on the bench beside him, out of reach of the hermit. "I am sorry for interrupting your shopping spree. You do realize that this is a camp for disadvantaged youngsters that you have been burglarizing?"

"Of course I do."

"And you have no remorse for your misdeeds?"

"I only took what I needed."

"People around here are generous. If you had asked for a handout, I am sure they would have been glad to help."

"I am not a beggar!"

No, Charley decided, he was more like a two-legged raccoon.

By this point, however, the warden was less interested in challenging the man than in plumbing the depths of his self-regard. "What are you, then?"

"A man in full, Warden. I am a man in full."

"From the weight you are carrying around your midsection, I can't dispute you on that point," Charley said. "But I suspect the district attorney will use a different term."

"There is only one who can judge me."

"He'll get his turn, too, but first, you'll have to face a man in a black robe down in Augusta."

The hermit moved his tongue around the inside of his cheeks as if it were a Ping-Pong ball. "So you're going to arrest me, I gather?"

"That was the general idea of me hiding inside that freezer," Charley said. "I went to great lengths to apprehend you."

Sweet Tooth folded his hands together across his belly with a certain satisfaction. "I saw you under the porch and on top of the roof. You're not very good at camouflaging yourself. Not very good at all."

"I guess you could say I'm learning on the job, though." He tugged an earlobe that was beginning to ache from frost nip. "So you're telling me that you've been hiding in these woods this past week, watching me run around the place like a fool?"

"This past week!" The big man smiled broadly. "I have been living in these woods for twenty-one years."

"Twenty-one years?"

"That is correct. I was eighteen when I left home."

"And no one ever went looking for you or reported you missing?"

"They never knew I was there to begin with."

Charley had suspected a bad family situation; it was a topic he knew something about himself. "Where exactly have you been hiding?"

"I'm sure you'd like me to show you."

"Yes, sir, I would. Because I have trouble believing that even a resourceful feller like yourself could camp out in the forest since 1956 without assistance."

The hermit's forehead drooped; he looked quite literally crestfallen. "You don't believe me?"

"Not without evidence."

Sweet Tooth pushed himself abruptly to his feet. The action was so sudden that Charley himself sprang backward and landed lightly like a startled cat.

"My camp is closer than you'd probably think," boomed the hermit. "You can almost see it from the counselors' quarters."

Now Charley was even more skeptical. Lafontaine had told him that the camp staff had beaten the bushes within a half mile of the property, looking for signs of the hermit. And the warden himself had done a thorough search of the surrounding woods, too. It scarcely seemed possible that this Sweet Tooth character had been hunkered down within earshot the whole time, with no one the wiser.

"Show me," said Charley.

It occurred to the young warden that the hermit might be contemplating some sort of breakneck escape into the darkened forest, so he decided to follow the big man closely. As they picked their way through the puckerbrush and damp leaves, Charley was struck by the hermit's style of walking. For such an enormous specimen of humanity, he moved lightly, almost seemed to dance. He hopped from one moss-covered rock to the next, always set his foot down on a tree root instead of a patch of mud, never seemed to snap so much as a twig. He left not a single footprint to mark his passage upon the earth.

Charley's disbelief began to melt a little. "So you say you've been out here for twenty-one years. What is the last thing you remember?"

"Elvis Presley," said Sweet Tooth. "I remember him singing on *The Ed Sullivan Show*."

"What drove you into the wilderness?"

The big man stopped so abruptly Charley almost collided with him, but he didn't turn his head to make eye contact. "Talking."

"I am not following you."

"I got sick of all the talking. Gab, gab, gab. I couldn't *hear* anything. Believe it or not, you are only the third person I have spoken to since I took to the woods. The other two were fishermen."

The hermit started moving again, forcing the warden to catch up. "You seem a talkative enough feller to me," Charley said. He was still dressed in his heavy winter clothes and boots and now found himself sweating profusely through his long johns. "Was there something in particular you were having trouble hearing?"

"Jesus."

The answer caused Charley to nod. "Oh, so you're a religious hermit, then?"

"The preacher at our church said, 'Pray and your prayers will be answered.' When I told him that wasn't the case, he said I wasn't listening hard enough. So I started going off into the woods by myself, but I kept hearing . . . nothing. So I went a little farther and stayed a little longer, and eventually, I was living out here by myself. That was nineteen years ago."

"Did you ever hear Jesus?"

"Not yet."

Beyond the bushy edges of the camp, the land took on a different aspect. Huge glacial erratic boulders appeared out of the darkness, forcing them to make a detour. Spring freshets cut ravines through the melting earth, too far to jump across and deep enough to make scrambling down one side and up the other a challenge. Before Charley had realized it, they had pushed through a dense green curtain of hemlocks, and the next thing he knew, he was standing in the middle of the most fantastic place he had ever seen.

The hermit's compound was completely hidden. Green tarps were stretched across the sky from tree to tree to form a waterproof ceiling. Metal trash cans were covered with dirt and moss so they would not shine in the sun. Brown blankets, draped over sagging ropes, formed curtains that separated a cooking area with a camp stove and an impressive store of empty propane tanks from the raised platform where the hermit had pitched his tent. There were buckets hanging from trees to collect rainwater and plastic tubs buried in the ground where the man could keep frozen meat cool well into the summer. Charley had seen the inside of Vietcong spider holes and tunnel mazes, but never had he seen an encampment so well camouflaged.

"Sir, I have to tell you, this is the most impressive camp I have ever seen."

"Thank you."

"And you've lived here for nineteen years—blizzards and all—without ever seeking shelter in a building?"

"I conserve my energy and hibernate."

"Incredible!"

Sweet Tooth seemed delighted to show off his home. He pointed out the mousetraps he had set near his food to protect it from vermin and the mattress he had sewn out of bedsheets and stuffed full of magazines.

"Let me guess," said Charley. "*National Geographics*."

The hermit smiled his rotten-toothed smile. "I am proudest of my commode. Building it was a problem it took me ten years to solve. My outhouse stands as my greatest achievement."

He gestured toward a leafy structure, a mass of sticks and vines and interwoven branches, downwind of the tent. This, Charley had to see.

The warden took four steps in the direction of the toilet when suddenly he heard a metallic snap and felt a crushing pain in his left leg that caused him to fall forward onto his elbows, howling. Just like that, the hermit was on him. Before Charley even realized that he had stepped carelessly into a hidden bear trap, he saw the huge man standing over him, holding his own service revolver. The trap had sharp steel teeth that bit into his boots. He was utterly helpless.

"If you had just believed me, none of this would be happening to you," Sweet Tooth said. "I told you my camp was here. I don't know why people just can't believe things."

Charley yowled, but he realized there was no one to hear his cries. He twisted his head, seemingly in pain, but really to look for a weapon. There was a fist-size rock within reach, but the hermit would shoot him before he had a chance to close his hand around it. "You don't have to do this."

"None of us has any choice in life." The hermit seemed genuinely sad as he said this.

"Can you do it clean, then? Right between the eyes?"

The big man squatted down on his heels and stretched out his arms, using both hands to grip the pistol. He closed one eye and squeezed the trigger.

There was a click as the hammer fell on an empty cylinder.

The sound seemed to confuse the hermit, who opened his other eye to look at the gun, then quickly pulled the trigger again.

Click, click, click, click, click.

Before Sweet Tooth understood that the revolver was unloaded, Charley had gotten hold of the rock and flung it squarely between the man's eyes, shattering the wire-rimmed glasses in the same spot they had been previously broken. The hermit fell like Goliath.

⁓

Charley drained the coffee dregs from his cup and screwed the plastic top back on the thermos. His expression remained deadpan.

"A bear trap, huh?" I said.

"One of the biggest bone crushers I ever saw. Must have weighed close to fifty pounds."

A school of fish dimpled the water thirty yards off the bow of the canoe. Something big and unseen was chasing the minnows to the surface. It might well be a pike. I remained still, holding the fly rod in my cold, cramped hand, studying my friend's weathered expression, waiting for it to crack.

Finally, he laughed. When he smiled, wrinkles radiated from the corners of his eyes. "You don't believe me. Do you?"

"I don't know. It's quite a story."

The old man bent down and rolled the left pant leg up, then turned the sock down over the bootlaces so I could see his pale calf. A crescent-shaped scar arced across the shinbone. Even now, decades later, it looked like it hurt.

"I was lucky I was wearing my winter boots in the freezer that night because the leather cushioned the bite of those trap teeth," Charley said. "We dug up two bodies from under the hermit's camp, and both of them had broken legs, the poor sons of bitches."

Backtrack

There were four doctors staying at the hunting camp. Two of them were brothers, and they owned all the land for a mile in every direction. I had tramped around those woods when I got assigned to the district, the year before, and I remember some nice stands of oak and beech and a couple of cedar swamps where the deer could yard up when the snow got heavy. It was a pretty sweet spot.

Then one of the doctors didn't show up after a day of hunting.

Ora was putting dinner on the table when the phone rang. Thanksgiving leftovers. There's nothing better.

"The man who's lost is Dr. Phillip Stoddard," the dispatcher told me. His friends had been searching for him since nightfall. They were worried he might be injured.

"How old is he, do you know?"

"Sixty-nine."

At the time, I was only twenty-nine, understand. Sixty-nine made the man a Methuselah in my eyes.

"One of them will meet you outside the Crossroads Variety Store," the dispatcher said. "His name is Dr. James Honig, the man I spoke with just now."

"And how will I be able to pick out Dr. Honig from the crowd?"

"Well, gee, I'm not sure."

The dispatcher never appreciated my cockeyed sense of humor. Crossroads was halfway up the backside of nowhere. I wondered how a business could stay open in such a God-forgotten place. And in fact, it closed soon after.

Ora gave me a hug, awkward on account of her pregnant belly. "You find that poor man, Charley. Don't you come home until you do."

"Whatever you say, Boss."

"I hate your calling me that. Just be careful, all right?"

"Ten-four, my love."

It hadn't started to snow yet, but I could smell snow on the air. There was already a foot of it on the ground from the last storm. Everything seemed beautifully reversed. The earth was pale and the sky was dark. Not so much as a glimmer of moon.

~

The variety had closed by the time I arrived forty minutes later. The lights were all extinguished, the gas pumps nonfunctional. I saw a sedan with Massachusetts plates parked at the edge of the plowed lot. Dr. Honig was inside, running the car to stay warm. I could tell from how the exhaust slunk away from the tailpipe that the air pressure was falling.

The hunter jumped out of that fancy automobile as soon as he saw me roll up. He was wearing one of those head-to-toe jumpsuits. Plus a blaze-orange cap. Only a blind man could have mistaken him for a deer, dressed as he was in all that fluorescence.

"Are you the game warden?" he asked.

"If not, I've got everyone fooled."

I don't know why I always had to be a cutup. The man was worried about his lost pal.

"You need to follow me! We have a man missing, my colleague, Dr. Phil Stoddard. We were supposed to meet back at the cabin after hunting, but he didn't return. He's the best woodsman among us, no question. We're terribly concerned he might have had an accident."

"Does Dr. Stoddard have any health problems you know about?"

"Health problems! I hope I'm in as good a shape as Phil is when I'm that age. We've been firing shots for him to hear, hoping he'd reply, but we haven't heard a thing. Please, there's no time to waste."

Some wardens would have resented the assignment. Locate some old doctor from Boston who didn't belong in the Maine woods in the first place. But my stomach told me I was going to find this Stoddard feller and deliver him to safety and maybe even get my name in the papers.

So I followed Dr. Honig's sedan back onto the Hornbeam Road with an excited optimism, I guess you could call it. We took a turn, then another, and then we were headed off into the williwags. The first flakes appeared in my headlights after we left the paved road.

It was coming down pretty hard by the time we reached the cabin. There was already an inch on the other Mercedes parked in the dooryard. The heavy air was pushing smoke from the chimney down among the trunks of the trees all the way to the snowpack.

The two other doctors came outside when they heard us drive up. One was the twin of Dr. James Honig, whip thin and balding. This was his brother Sam. The other was a bantam rooster named Dr. David Dinsmore. Dr. Stoddard seemed to have been some kind of mentor to the younger men. They threw a lot of information at me until finally I had to slow them down.

"Where and when was Dr. Stoddard last seen?"

"Here at lunch," said the first Dr. Honig. "We all came back from hunting, as was our practice. Afterwards, Phil and I decided to go back out and try our luck again while Sam and Dave played cribbage. That must have been around twelve thirty."

"Closer to one o'clock," Dinsmore said. The liquor on his breath nearly knocked me down.

"Did he say where he was going to hunt?"

"He was going to follow the stream to the cedar swamp," said James Honig. "He spooked a big buck there this morning."

"Is that the same brook we passed on the way in?"

"Yes."

"How familiar would you say he was with the country around here?"

"Very familiar. Phil's hunted with us the past three years, ever since he retired."

"Can you tell me what he was wearing?"

"What difference does it make what clothes he has on?" said Dinsmore. "He's the only one out there."

Dr. Sam Honig put his hand on his little friend's shoulder. "Dave, I think the warden means is Phil adequately dressed to survive the night outdoors."

"Why didn't he just say so?" The banty-legged man hugged himself against the chill. "Can't we have this conversation inside?"

"I'd rather not get warm and then have to go back into the cold again, Dr. Dinsmore."

Sam interjected himself. "Phil is dressed in a wool coat and a knit cap. His pants are also made of wool, I'm fairly certain. And he has on some pack boots from L.L.Bean he bought last night on the drive up here. Underneath everything, he's wearing one of those union suits with the buttons down the front and the flap behind. We were joking about it this morning."

"Does he have a compass? Does he know how to use one?"

Dinsmore raised his chin at me again. "Because we're professionals from Boston, we don't know anything about the woods. That's what you think. But Phil was a Marine in the South Pacific. He knows how to use a goddamned compass. Better than you, probably."

I was irked that Dinsmore had been able to peer inside my

skull and see my prejudices writhing around. But I was angrier at him for reading my mind than I was properly ashamed.

"What kind of rifle does he have with him?"

"An M1 Garand thirty-aught-six," James said. "The same rifle he used in the Philippines."

"What else might he have with him? Food? Water? A map? A flashlight?"

They looked around at one another's blank expressions.

"How would you describe his state of mind?" I asked. "Was anything troubling him?"

"Are you suggesting he was suicidal?" said Dinsmore. I could have warmed my hands off the glow from his face.

"That's not what the warden asked," said Sam the diplomat. "Phil seemed in good spirits, relaxed, laughing at lunch. He didn't have anything to drink, in case you were wondering. It's a rule here: no alcohol until you're done hunting for the day. How would you describe his state of mind, Jim?"

"He seemed a lot happier than last night when we arrived."

That caught my attention. "What happened last night?"

"He was just quiet in the car riding up. Phil rode with me, and Sam brought Dave."

"Dr. Honig, you said he is in excellent condition. How about his health history? Does he have any old war wounds?"

"None that I know of. Phil never talked about the war."

I understood that impulse well enough. Ora had stopped asking me about Vietnam after our third date. Not once had she prompted me to tell her how I got all my scars.

"Phil Stoddard is the strongest man I ever met," said Dinsmore. "The guy is as solid as the Cliffs of Dover."

I could guess from the glance that passed between the Brothers Honig that they weren't going to inform their friend that those English cliffs are made of crumbling chalk.

"One last question. Did you hear any gunshots this afternoon— even something faint in the distance?"

"No."

"No."

"No."

They wanted to help me with the search, of course. Dinsmore being the most ardent to do so. Drunk as he was, he realized his crack about taking shelter from the snow had made it sound like he cared more for his personal comfort than for his missing friend's welfare.

"Four of us searching is better than one man alone," he said. "We have a responsibility to Phil's family to do everything in our power."

The last thing I needed was to lose another of those city men in the snowbound woods.

Sam Honig rescued me from saying something impolite.

"The warden is a professional at finding lost persons, Dave. We all want to help, but the best thing is for us to stay behind and let him do his work. Maybe Phil will show up at the cabin on his own."

"I'll find your friend for you, Dr. Dinsmore. You sit tight and I'll be back with Dr. Stoddard in no time. You have my word on that."

I fetched my sled from the truck. It was an old toboggan I'd repurposed with ropes and tie-downs for hauling deer out of the woods. I got a lot of teasing from my colleagues about that kiddie sled, but it did the job and then some.

Pulling the sled behind me, I picked up Dr. Stoddard's tracks even before I reached the stream. The new snow was starting to fill up the boot-shaped indents. It wouldn't be long until they were vague depressions, nearly impossible to see.

Now a lost person, being confused and panicked, will often make errors in judgment.

Some walk in circles.

Others will climb a hill or even shimmy up a tree to gain perspective on their dire situation.

Most will follow a stream downhill, thinking there's civilization at the bottom when it's just as likely to be a cedar swamp or a beaver flowage.

Very few stay put and wait to be rescued. They keep on moving because they are embarrassed at being lost and overwhelmed by the need to do something to save themselves.

My suspicion was that Dr. Stoddard wasn't lost but had, more likely, twisted an ankle or even broken a leg. Worse case, he had hit his head on a rock when he fell. The doctor didn't sound like a candidate for a heart attack, but you can never tell about that enigmatic muscle.

I worried about his state of mind, though. Getting turned around in the dark can drive many a confident man to lose his nerve.

Dr. Stoddard's tracks showed a long, determined stride. Not what you'd expect from a hunter hoping to creep up on a buck. Could have been he was in a hurry to shoot a deer before the snow started and the darkness closed in.

Whenever I made a search for a missing person, I wore a whistle on a leather strip around my neck. I stuck the blowing part between my teeth and kept it clenched there. Every hundred yards or so, I would give it a sharp blast.

The only answer was the wind.

Then, about half a mile down the ice-crusted stream, I came to what looked like a deer bed. Took me a minute to realize the depression had been left by a man, sitting down and stretching out his long legs.

Now, no hunter I had ever met would plop his ass down in the snow. Not unless he wanted his cheeks to go numb.

Dr. Stoddard seemingly had sat there for a spell. Maybe he had felt dizzy or just needed a breather. But whatever he'd felt hadn't caused him to turn around for the cabin.

His tracks continued up the side of the little gully through which the stream flowed. The direction puzzled me. I couldn't figure out why he would move off the trail.

By this time, the snow was falling slantwise, and the tip of my nose was tingling. My flashlight beam bounced right off those fat flakes.

I decided to fire two shots from my revolver. The gun was a .357 Magnum and had quite the report. The sound carried for miles, even in branch-bending wind.

After I fired the last time, I cupped my hands around my ears and turned this way and that. I listened for five whole minutes.

No response.

I won't lie. I was getting anxious, mostly for Dr. Stoddard, but also because I couldn't stomach the thought of failing in my duty.

⁓

Once they were clear of the ravine, the pattern of the tracks underwent a change. Now they showed signs of stopping and pausing, as if the doctor really had lost his way. The prints zigzagged back and forth through the trees in a slalom-like fashion. They ranged off in an oxbow loop, then returned to the original path after a lazy detour.

The overall course might indicate a confused man wandering. Hypothermia can prompt a kind of delirium. Some sufferers even throw off their clothes and go naked through the woods.

As I rounded a cluster of balsams, pulling my toboggan on a rope over my shoulder, a buck exploded out of the powder at my feet. He was a big brute of a deer, let me tell you, a twelve-pointer, with a ridge of snow down his back like a white crest. He disappeared before I could get my flashlight on him. The gray ghost left behind a secret bed, the snow melted from the heat of his body, tufts of hair trembling in the wind before they got snatched away.

Being spooked by that buck got to me. I couldn't say why, but

I felt as if the missing man were toying with me. I spat out the whistle, reached for my pistol, and fired two more angry rounds into the blackness above.

After the echoes had been pushed aside on the wind, I did my ear-cupping trick. Again with no happy result. By now, the weather had erased all signs of the hunter's passage. I would have had an easier time following that trophy deer than locating Dr. Stoddard.

It was only the sharp crack of a branch breaking that saved me from turning tail. The sound came from a place to my left and slightly ahead.

"Dr. Stoddard!"

Another branch broke, this one not as loud. I set off into the thicker cover in pursuit. The trees were mostly pines of various widths and heights. And under one of the biggest, oldest pines was an impression like the one I'd found before: the outline of a man's bottom, legs, and bootheels. I bit off my mitten, passed my palm over the melted snow, and felt the same lingering warmth I had felt in the deer's bed.

Fresh tracks showed where the doctor had jumped up and fled into the forest.

What else could I do but chase down the poor delusional man before he injured himself or eluded me for good?

He'd tried to walk backward in his own prints, the way a child might hope to fool another child, but I recognized the gambit for what it was. I switched off my flashlight and let night vision take over.

I found him crouched behind a cabin-size boulder, one of those erratics the glaciers had left behind on their retreat north. He held his military rifle at waist height, pointed at where he thought his pursuer might appear, coming around the rock.

"You don't need that rifle, Doc," I said. "I'm one of the good guys."

"Who're you?"

His mouth had gone blue. And he was shivering so hard, the snow was dropping off him like it would from a wind-shaken pine. Hypothermia had addled his brain, I could tell.

"Warden Charley Stevens. Your friends were worried when you didn't return to the cabin. They asked me to come find you."

"I'm not lost!"

If you asked a child to draw an angry face, his would have been the result.

"There's no shame in a man losing his way. Hell! It happens to me at least once a month."

His dead lips couldn't spit out more than a few words at a time. "I know. What I'm doing. Please! Leave me alone."

"I can't do that, Doc. I can't abandon you out in this miserableness."

"How. Did you. Find me?"

"I am a Maine game warden. That's what we do."

I shouldn't have grinned.

"Cocksure! Son of a bitch. Someday you'll realize. The horrible mistake you made."

"Dr. Stoddard—"

"I'm dying. Damn you! Cancer. Pancreatic. I'll be dead. In months."

He might as well have slapped all that smugness off my face. My cheeks burned, but not from the wind or cold. It was from the brutal chastisement of his words.

"I am truly sorry to hear that." And I was.

"No one knows. My family. My friends. Only my doctors."

I was a young man. What did I know of delicate considerations? "Maybe if you shared the news—"

"My family can't know!"

I saw his plan now as if it were typed out on paper with

a spotlight shining on the page. He hadn't come to Maine to hunt. His secret intention had been to sit down in the snow, go to sleep, and let the cold carry away his soul. His family would believe that he had gotten lost in the woods and died of exposure. It would be hard, but they would be spared watching the cannibal cancer eat him from the inside out.

"Only way," he said. "If they suspect. Insurance company will. Screw my family."

I chewed that one over for a minute. I was scared but didn't know why. I'd done my job and found the lost man. Baffled by my fear, I grew short-tempered with him.

"You have hypothermia, sir. I can't be sure that you're thinking clearly."

His mouth seemed to be loosening up from the exertion. "Do you understand? In physical pain every minute. Every hour. You're not saving me. Condemning me to torture."

"I couldn't live with my conscience if I left you to die."

"Why is your conscience more important than my life?"

The cold went right through me then. I might as well have been a phantom.

"I'm not here to pass judgment on you, Dr. Stoddard. I am the last person to claim that right. If it were up to me, I would let everyone choose their own ending."

"You have that choice! It's one of the most important choices you'll ever make."

"Come back to the cabin with me, Doc. Things will look different in the morning."

He wobbled, seemed about to collapse. "So tired. Just want to sleep."

"I can help you."

"You could. But you won't."

"Things will look different."

I reached out my paw. He let me take his rifle and sling it

over my shoulder. He had no energy to fight me. He barely had enough to sit down on my sled, even with his self-anointed savior supporting his weight.

As I towed him out of that winter wonderland, I kept thinking how he was heavier than he should have been.

⁓

I kept my word and said nothing about his illness. When I left them all, the sick man was sitting silently beside the woodstove. There was a blanket draped over his slumped shoulders, and color was returning to his tearstained cheeks. The other doctors had decided to leave the next morning, before the next storm was forecast to hit.

Dinsmore sloppily offered him a glass of Irish whiskey. "You gave us a real fright there, Phil. I hope you're not getting too old to be left alone without adult supervision. Ha ha."

Dr. Stoddard gulped down the expensive alcohol. He thrust out the empty mug for a refill. The Honigs were sober enough to notice how the rescued man burned me with his glare.

"We were frightened for you, Phil," said Sam. He still sounded frightened. Maybe more than he'd been before.

"We're just relieved to have you back," said James. "Promise you'll never do that again."

Stoddard held out his empty cup.

⁓

About six weeks later, after the holidays had come and gone, I got word from the Marblehead Police Department in Massachusetts. Dr. Philip Stoddard had shot himself in his study. He'd called the cops before he took his life and told them what he was going to do and what to expect when they arrived. This time, he wouldn't let an officer argue him out of the decision. He apologized in advance for putting them through the traumatic experience. To the end, he was a conscientious man.

But it was his teenage granddaughter who found him. She'd come over to the house, after school, as a surprise.

You asked me about regrets.

I suppose I have as many as other men my age. Fewer than most, probably. I guess the Almighty gave me extra credit for effort.

But dragging that sick doctor back to the cabin is something I would reverse.

Now that I'm an old man myself, I understand what he was trying to tell me that night. The truth I was too young to hear.

I should have left him in the woods, is what I'm saying. Should have hiked back to the cabin and told his friends I had lost his tracks in the snow. We would begin the search at first light, I should have said.

Then in the morning, I could have pretended to find the lost doctor, and he would have been dead and all his earthly problems gone. Maybe his friends would have blamed me and leveled accusations of negligence. Maybe some of my cohorts in the Warden Service would have thought less of me as a tracker. But I would have had the comfort of my conscience over the past years.

Funny how the mind works. You'd think I would have a memory of Dr. Stoddard's face glaring at me. But that's not what I see. Instead, the image is of a man like myself sitting motionless in the morning sun. His back is propped against a big pine. He's got a rifle resting across his legs. And his entire body is wrapped in a cocoon of white snow.

It's a pretty picture. But a damned dangerous folly.

Rabid

I have a stop to make," said Charley Stevens.

It was one of those warm June evenings when you can feel the earth pivoting from spring to summer. The sun had just set behind the ridge, and now the sky was the color of purple lupines.

I kept my left hand on the steering wheel and reached down to lower the volume on the police radio. "Does it have something to do with that box?"

When the old man had loaded the big brown package in the bed of my patrol truck that morning, I had assumed it was something he'd intended to mail. But he hadn't mentioned the box again all day, and now the post offices were closed for the night.

Charley had a thick head of white hair that just about glowed in the dark. "The Boss asked me to drop it off for her."

"The Boss" was what he affectionately called his wife of thirty-odd years. Her real name was Ora, and she had the biggest heart of anyone I had ever met, even after an airplane crash had left her paralyzed below the waist. The situation couldn't have been any sadder: Her husband had been teaching her to fly his old Piper Cub, and she had lost control of the fragile plane. A life spent in the wilds of Maine had left Charley's face weathered, but I suspect guilt accounted for more than a few of the lines across his forehead.

"So where are we going?" I asked.

"You know that fire road off the Snake Lake Road—the one where we saw that sow bear and her two cubs? Drive all the way to the end."

Even for a man of his advanced age, Charley had an unusual way of speaking that was more than just a thick Maine accent. He had grown up in North Woods lumber camps and retained a peculiar dialect that had mostly died out with the last of the river drives. Sometimes I thought he hung on to it out of pure impishness.

He had been riding along with me on patrol all day. The retired game warden did that a lot back then, when I was stationed Down East. He seemed to miss the excitement of wearing a badge and gun and was living vicariously through his young protégé. He still yearned for the daily surprises that come with being a law enforcement officer—the what-the-heck occurrences that make you realize how endlessly inventive human beings are at screwing up their lives.

As directed, I made the turn Charley had indicated. I was unaware that there was even a house at the end of this particular dirt road. I was under the impression it just petered out at the edge of one of the vast wet peat bogs that soak up the rain and fog in easternmost Maine. It had gotten dark enough that I needed my headlights to avoid the lurking rocks and ruts.

Charley's uncharacteristic silence as we drove gave me a strange, almost sick feeling in my stomach. By nature, the man was a talker. He spun yarns like Rumpelstiltskin spun gold. Falling into any kind of reverie was unlike him.

"How's your love life these days?" he asked out of nowhere.

"Slow," I said.

My prior romantic entanglement had involved a beautiful recovering drug abuser who had slipped back into addiction before my eyes. I'd gone on a couple of dates afterward with a sultry Romanian waitress who had come to the US on a student work visa but had found we had nothing in common beyond the physical. I would never have confessed this to my friend, but the woman I was secretly infatuated with was his younger daughter, Stacey, a green-eyed wildlife biologist.

"Slow is good," said Charley, patting my knee. "It's best to take your time before you get hitched. People don't understand that a marriage is a living thing. It can grow and blossom, but it can wither, too—become diseased, even."

I wasn't remotely close to getting married, so I had no clue where this had come from.

We passed a small duck pond still swollen with spring rain. I knew it would shrink to half its size as summer made tinder out of the surrounding pine forest. Several small silhouettes flitted against the sky above the quicksilver water. They were bats chasing the insects that hatched at night.

My headlights struck a reflective, diamond-shaped sign that hung from a chain across the road. NO TRESPASSING. I slowed to a stop but kept the engine idling.

"Is this it?" I asked.

"'Tis."

Instead of opening his door, he remained buckled in with his big hands braced against the dash—almost as if he dreaded making the delivery.

"Is something wrong?" I asked.

"I need you to wait here. I know this sounds mysterious, Mike."

He almost never called me by my first name. It was always "young feller" or "son," although he was nothing like my own late father. I could see the strain in his tanned face. He wanted so much to confide in me about this mysterious errand.

"Look, Charley. You don't have to tell me anything you promised to keep secret."

He let out a defeated sigh. "Does the name Hussey mean anything to you?"

"Not unless you mean a fallen woman."

My quip didn't seem to sit well with him. "I'm talking about the Hussey family. I thought you might have heard the rumors or whatever you'd call them. The local kids dare each other to come out here, like it's a haunted house, only this one has a real person living inside it. Not yet a ghost."

I turned off the ignition and settled in for the tale. "What happened here, Charley?"

"Did you see the bats over that pond back there?"

"Yeah. Why?"

"Because it all started with a bat."

Later, I got Ora's version of the story, which was mostly the same, but different in key respects. If anything, it was even more horrifying. As is often the case when you hear two accounts of a tragedy—especially when those accounts come from a husband and wife—you should probably begin by assuming that the truth lies somewhere in between.

Back in the mid-1980s, Charley was the game warden for this very same district. The area around Machias then was much like it is now: a wild, underpopulated region of blueberry barrens and blasted heaths. Washington County was a land of evergreen forests webbed with shadows and of forgotten farms sinking back into the sandy soil: a place with many dark corners where you could hide from the world.

Charley enjoyed his four-wheeled patrols, but flying was his great love in life, and he had recently put in a request for a transfer to the aviation division. Every time the phone rang, he answered it eagerly, hoping it would be good news from Augusta, telling him he had been approved to become Maine's newest warden pilot.

That January night, however, it was a frantic woman on the other end of the line speaking in fractured English. "Is this game warden?"

"Yes, ma'am. Warden Charles Stevens."

"We have emergency here!" The woman had a distinctive accent that he identified, from his multiple tours of duty in South-
east Asia, as Vietnamese. "How quick you get over to Fire Road
Three?"

Charley caught the eye of Ora, who understood without being
told that work was taking him from the family again. She rose to
her feet and removed his bowl of venison stew from the table to
reheat later.

"What kind of emergency?" he asked.

"My husband been attacked," said the caller.

"By a human or an animal?"

"By a bat! He bleeding from face. We at end of Fire Road
Three. New house. Name Hussey."

Suddenly, Charley heard a man's voice raised in anger on the
other end of the line: "What are you doing? Who are you talking
to?"

Then came the slam of the receiver back into its cradle.

Ora returned from the kitchen with a worried expression.
She had high cheekbones and deeply set green eyes that often
made him wonder if her ancestors had been kings and queens in
the age of the Vikings.

"You need to go over there, Charley," she said after he'd recounted the full conversation.

"To catch a bat?"

"To check in on that woman to make sure she's OK."

He knew she was right. Ora was always right. And so the warden kissed his wife and his two little girls good night, put on his
red wool coat over his green uniform, and got the engine of his
Chevrolet C/K started.

The snow was deep, and he began to wonder if he might have
been better off taking the Ski-Doo, but when he finally reached
the fire road, he was startled to find it perfectly plowed, almost
obsessively so, nothing but straight edges and right angles all the

way down the hill. He noticed the POSTED signs tacked along the perimeter, too.

But there was no chain across the road back then. That came later.

At the bottom of the hill, he spotted security lights glowing intensely through the trees. Then he saw the house. Although it was clad with deeply stained clapboards, the rectangular home had all the charm of a barracks: corrugated metal roof, rows of square windows, and a concrete foundation painted fatigue green. A new Ford pickup, equipped with a professional-grade plow, was parked in the dooryard. Beside it was a cab-over Peterbilt tractor unit. So the man of the house drove a big rig, the warden deduced.

The door opened even before Charley had climbed out of his Chevy.

On the threshold stood a wiry man with a flushed face. He looked to be in his thirties but aged beyond his years. His hair was so blond it was almost white, while his skin was as red as a bullfighter's cape. The man had affixed a fairly large bandage under his left eye. He wore a sweatshirt with the sleeves scissored off and stonewashed jeans.

"You can turn around and go home!" said the man in a ragged voice. "We don't need any help here."

"Your wife said you had a bat problem."

"Not anymore."

Charley glanced at the windows, hoping to see signs of the wife. He walked purposefully toward the door with a disarming grin on his face. "You wouldn't mind if I came inside for a bit to warm up, Mr. Hussey? The heater in the old chariot is throwing out nothing but cold air. I think I've lost all feeling in my generative organ."

"Are you talking about your dick?"

The guy held a bottle of Molson beer in his hand, which bore a tattoo across the knuckles spelling out the word DEATH. The other hand had the word LIFE stretched out so the four letters could fill five knuckles.

The wife called from inside the house, "Let poor frozen man inside, John!" And then she rattled off something fast in Vietnamese that Charley—who understood the language from his time as a prisoner of war—didn't entirely catch. Maybe it was: "He came here to help you, and you're treating him like an intruder!"

John Hussey lurched free of the doorframe, barely allowing the warden to pass.

The inside of the house had a familiar smell that sent Charley spinning backward in time: aloeswood incense. He hadn't encountered the resinous perfume since he'd left Saigon on a stretcher.

The décor was Vietnamese as well—bamboo mats on the floor, mint-green walls, carved teak furniture, and a heavy crucifix in the hallway. The wife was small and pretty with heavy makeup that made her age indeterminate. She was dressed in a traditional ao dai: a silk tunic and pants.

Removing his cap out of politeness, he said to her, "Ngôi nhà của bạn là đẹp."

The woman smiled. Her teeth were crooked and had a grayish tint. "Cảm ơn bạn."

"You're welcome, ma'am," said the warden. "But my Vietnamese is rusty. Maybe we should stick with the vernacular. My name is Charley Stevens. And you are . . . ?"

"Giang," the woman said.

The husband stepped between them. "You were in 'Nam?"

"I was."

"What outfit?" Hussey's pupils were swollen, almost animal-like, not usually a side effect of alcohol.

"Two Hundred Twelfth Combat Aviation Battalion."

The drunken man seemed to consider offering a handshake but held on to his beer. "First Battalion, Ninth Marines."

Charley knew all about the 1/9s. "Khe Sanh?"

"Nah. I didn't join the Walking Dead until '71."

Charley had expected that having the war in common might soften the man's aggression, but the retired Marine still looked like he was one harsh word away from throwing a punch.

"Do you ever stop in to the VFW in Harrington?" the warden asked, already knowing that he had never seen John Hussey there—or at the American Legion in Machias, or anywhere else, for that matter. Charley knew most everyone in Washington County; he was a people person by disposition and had a near-photographic memory for faces.

"Why would I want to listen to a bunch of hairballs whining about how the war fucked them up?"

Charley had all sorts of questions. Most of them were for Giang, starting with how an elegant quý bà had ended up in this frozen wilderness. But he didn't feel welcome to pry into her personal life under the circumstances, with the husband looming.

"Your wife told me you were bitten by a bat?" the warden said.

John Hussey touched his blood-soaked bandage. "In my daughter's room. I don't know how the hell it got in there. Flying rat."

"It's probably been hibernating since the fall. Sometimes they find spaces behind curtains or even shelves. They'll come out if the room gets warm enough, thinking it's spring. How many children do you have?"

"One daughter," said Giang.

John Hussey rounded on his wife again. "I told her to keep the goddamn screens closed."

"Can I have a look at the bat?" Charley asked.

"Why? What for?"

"I should take it to be tested."

"I threw it into the woodstove."

Giang peeked around her husband's shoulder. "Tested for what?"

"Rabies," Charley said. "It's a serious disease. Fatal."

She clapped a hand to her mouth. She had long painted nails decorated with beautiful flowers. "You need get shot," she told her husband.

The man just about swatted her away. "The bat didn't have rabies!"

"We can't be sure," said Charley. "You're going to want to go to the hospital and get a vaccination."

"To hell with that."

Charley tried again, working hard to keep a smile. "The size of the needles are greatly exaggerated, as Sam Clemens might have said."

"You think I'm afraid of needles?" The drunk man seemed to interpret everything as an assault on his manhood.

"Maybe it would be best if I spoke about this with your missus."

Hussey's face grew redder. "You want me to leave you alone with my wife?"

Charley worked his knit cap back onto the top of his head. "Mr. Hussey, I can't make you do anything you don't want to do, but I'd highly encourage you to visit the hospital tomorrow morning and tell the doctor you were bitten by a potentially rabid bat." Then he turned his attention to the wife—so small behind her Marine husband. "Chúc ngủ ngo. Good night, ma'am."

"You speak Vietnamese language very well."

"I had a lot of teachers," he said, remembering the faces of his torturers.

⌐

What Ora recalled about that night was her husband's discomfiting silence when he returned home. It took a barrage of questions to get the story out of him. That had never occurred before in their marriage.

"Do you really think the bat was rabid?" she asked.

He stood with his back to the woodstove, warming himself. Steam rose in shimmers from his wet clothes as they dried. "Probably not."

"Then why did it bite him?"

"The poor critter was just scared. I'd be scared having a leatherneck chase me around the house."

"But it's possible the man might have gotten infected?"

"Possible enough that he should get a shot. But he won't, the fool."

Then Charley turned away from Ora to warm his thighs at the stove.

She watched him. As often happened when her husband became lost in thought, he started to feel with his fingers the injuries he had suffered during the war, the bone in his leg that had broken when he'd been shot down and then repeatedly re-broken by his captors; the shoulder they had dislocated that still ached on rainy days; the crooked fingers of his left hand; the smooth burns like baby's skin on his back; the pockmarks of cigarettes extinguished on his flesh.

Ora arose from the sofa and embraced him from behind, tucking her head against his damp collar.

"It's because he's a vet, isn't it?" she said. "Seeing him has really gotten under your skin."

"It wasn't seeing him. It was seeing her. If I'd come upon an orchid blooming out there in a snowbank, I couldn't have been more surprised."

Ora knew what a chivalrous man her husband was, always ready to rescue a damsel in distress. She also knew how some women affected distress to get would-be knights to do their bidding. From Charley's description of Giang Hussey, Ora didn't know what to think of the Vietnamese wife except that she didn't much sound like a delicate flower.

John Hussey, on the other hand, was a type she knew too well. So many of the veterans Charley had introduced her to seemed to have nitroglycerin running through their veins instead of blood. And not one of them had suffered the tortures her husband had endured in the Hỏa Lò Prison.

She could feel her forearms growing warm around him from the wood-fired stove. "I just don't understand it, Charley."

"Don't understand what, Boss?"

"How you went through hell on earth and came out a good man. So many others came back ruined."

Charley took a long time answering, as if the question had never even occurred to him. "I guess I was just lucky is all."

"Lucky? You were tortured. You spent years in a jail cell."

"I'm lucky I am the man that I am."

Blessing her own good fortune, she hugged him harder.

⌐

Two months later, Charley, Ora, and the girls were traveling home from Bangor on the old Airline Road. It was their monthly trip to the big city for a movie and Chinese food. The back of their Jeep Wagoneer was overstuffed with bags of new clothing from the Jordan Marsh department store. Each of the girls had a stuffed animal to play with: Anne, a duckling; Stacey, a saber-toothed tiger.

The twisting and turning road was clear of ice—which was unusual for March—and they were making good time when Charley saw flashing blue lights ahead. A state trooper, whose license plate he recognized, had pulled over an eastbound tractor unit just past the gate of the Call of the Wild Game Ranch. The truck was a red cab-over Peterbilt. The trooper had hauled the driver out on the salted shoulder for questioning. The headlights of the cruiser shined upon the two men as upon actors on a stage.

Charley said, "That trooper is Orson Bishop. And I believe that's the Hussey fellow I told you about."

"We should stop," said Ora from the passenger seat. The

Airline was a long, desolate road and police backup was almost always too far away to be of any good.

Charley slowed to a stop, then climbed out of the Wagoneer.

He called out before approaching the cruiser, not wanting to spook the patrolman. "Need any help here, Orson?"

Trooper Bishop turned without taking his eyes off the driver. He kept his hand on his holstered revolver. He was one of the older highway patrolmen in the state: long-nosed, wide-shouldered, and bald as a vulture's egg under his campaign hat. "Charley Stevens! Is that you?"

"In the flesh," said the warden. "And is that gentleman with you Mr. John Hussey of Fire Road Three in Whitney?"

"He won't submit to a field sobriety test, Charley."

"Because I'm not drunk!" Hussey had grown out his pale hair and started a beard since the warden had visited his house. But there were conspicuous scratches across one of his cheeks: deep gouges that looked as if they'd been made by fingernails. "Smell my breath!" the truck driver insisted.

"You were swerving all over the road, sir," said Trooper Bishop.

"I told you—a deer ran out in front of me."

"Then how come I didn't see it?" said the trooper. "I wasn't more than a hundred yards behind you."

The flashing blue lights didn't flatter either man's complexion, but Charley thought Hussey looked like he belonged in an open casket.

"Can I talk with you a moment, Orson?" Charley said.

"Keep your hands out of your pockets," Bishop commanded the trucker.

Hussey spread his fingers in the air.

The two law enforcement officers stepped back against the trooper's idling Crown Victoria.

Charley asked, "You were in Korea, weren't you, Orson?"

"Sure was. I was an MP."

"Did the docs over there hand out pep pills like they did in Vietnam?"

"You think he's on amphetamines?"

"I'm pretty sure he was hopped up on something the last time I saw him. His pupils were big as bullets."

"Well, hell," Bishop said. "I can't haul him back to Bangor and make him take a piss test. I've got no probable cause. It's not like he actually ran into a telephone pole."

"Do you mind if I talk to him alone?"

Bishop exhaled a cloud of coffee-scented breath. "If you think it'll calm him down, be my guest."

Charley ambled back into the lighted space between the cruiser and the back of the tractor where Hussey stood waiting.

"Wicked cold night, isn't it?" the warden said.

"What's that—small talk?"

Even with his head turned toward the lights, Hussey's pupils were enormous. As cold as it was, there was a film of sweat visible along his brow. And the cut on his face where the bat had bitten him still hadn't healed. It looked, in fact, as if the man had been picking at the mottled scab.

"How is Giang?" Charley asked.

"None of your business."

"Mr. Hussey, it wouldn't hurt you to be polite once a month. You might find it good practice."

"She's fine."

"How about your little girl? She and I didn't meet that night I visited you."

"Lisa's fine, too. OK? Are we done making nice?" Hussey leaned over the shorter warden. Can you just tell that asshole to let me go? I've been on the road for a week and need to get back to my family. Who knows what that crazy woman has done now?"

It wasn't the first time Hussey had referred to his wife as being unhinged. But Giang hadn't seemed unstable to Charley, not even remotely. If anything, the truck driver's insistence seemed to raise doubts about his own sanity.

"The trooper and I are concerned about you," the warden said. "We want you to make it home safe."

"I told you I'm not drunk!"

"You seem agitated. Have you been using stimulants to stay awake?"

The trucker seemed unable to relax a single muscle. "So it's against the law to drink coffee. Is caffeine a controlled substance now?"

Charley knew he'd reached a roadblock. "I don't suppose you ever got that rabies shot."

Hussey's mouth opened wide. He shook his head in disbelief. "You sound like my wife."

"She's worried about you and wants a doctor to check you out."

"That witch! She hopes I'm dying. She'll dance over my grave, that woman will."

Trooper Bishop returned. "How's it going here?"

Charley had a brainstorm. "Mr. Hussey just proposed a compromise. I told him it would put our minds at ease if he agreed to a police escort. He said he'd be happy to have you follow him home."

"You son of a bitch," the truck driver snarled.

"Well, Mr. Hussey?" asked Orson Bishop.

"Just as long as I can get on the road."

Charley slid back inside his warm vehicle. Both of the girls were animated from the excitement of the flashing lights, so he waited until they'd fallen asleep before he recounted the conversation to his always curious wife. Charley relied on Ora to help him get what he called a "round view" of a problem. The Husseys were the most problematic people he'd encountered in a long time.

"That man scares me," Ora said. "There's something not right about him."

"There's a poison in him, that's for sure."

It was the nature of the toxin that was a mystery.

⁓

Ora was working her usual evening shift at the library in Machias. Most nights, she had help, but the other librarian, Terri Sewall, had gone home early to attend to her sick daughter. That odd child was always ill. Besides, it wasn't as if crowds of people were venturing out into the torrential rain.

The only patron in the drafty old building was a widower whose last name was Huff and was only ever called Huff. Even his library card omitted his first name. He was a retired lobsterman, as leathery as a shoe, who enjoyed romance novels. He would read them sometimes in the library with his back to the room so that no one coming through the door could see the half-naked men and women on the covers.

It was because he missed his wife, Ora believed. The old lobsterman yearned so hard for love, and the only place he could find it now was in the pages of Harlequins.

She had re-shelved the last of the returned books, emptied all the trash cans into a green bag that she would bring the next morning to the town dump, changed out the pail that was catching the water leaking through the ceiling in the periodical section; had done everything but tell Huff it was closing time, turn off the lights, and lock the door when the Vietnamese woman and her little girl came in out of the night.

The first thing Ora noticed about Giang Hussey was how tiny she was, scarcely taller than her young daughter; the next thing she noticed was how absolutely soaked both of them were. As they paused, unsure, in the entry, water flowed outward from their boots as if they themselves were melting into puddles. Beneath their hoods, their hair was dripping, and their faces were as white as Ora's got after swimming in the ice water of Machias Bay.

"Let me help you with those wet things," Ora found herself saying, forgetting that the library was supposed to be closed.

"Thank you," said Giang. The rain had caused her makeup to run, and she seemed self-conscious about it, the way she hung her head. She had artificial lashes that were longer than any Ora had seen outside a fashion magazine.

"Let me bring you some paper towels," Ora said. "You can use as many as you want."

It turned into a fifteen-minute job, trying to dry them off, but their clothes were simply too soaked. Huff watched the whole show from his chair in the corner with an expression that seemed to alternate between amusement and suspicion. After a while, he returned to his bodice ripper.

"Did you have a breakdown?" Ora asked.

Giang seemed confused by the question. The mother looked at the daughter, who translated the question into Vietnamese.

"We have no car," Giang said. "We walk."

"You walked here from Whitney?" The township was more than ten miles from downtown Machias.

Giang turned again to her daughter and said something quickly in her native tongue. The tone of her voice sounded panicked.

"My mom wants to know how you know we live in Whitney," the girl said with a perfect American accent. She looked to be somewhere between eight and ten years old. The daughter had dark, almond-shaped eyes, but lacked her mother's ethereal beauty, as well as her birdlike bones.

"My husband is the game warden who came to your house when your husband was bitten by the bat. My name is Ora Stevens."

Afterward, Ora would doubt what she'd seen: a sudden and momentary intensity in the Vietnamese woman's gaze that seemed almost calculating in its intelligence, as if perhaps she were merely feigning not to understand English. Then it was gone, and she was back to being a wet and confused creature.

"I am Giang," said the woman. "This my daughter, Lisa."

"Hi," said the girl.

"Do you need any help over there?" Huff asked. The nature of the assistance he was offering made Ora blush with embarrassment, although neither the mother nor the daughter seemed offended.

"Shouldn't you be getting home, Huff?"

Ora waited for the old man to place the novel he had been reading on the counter (face down, of course) and to button himself up in his orange Grundéns raincoat. Only after he had stepped through the door, letting in a burst of windswept rain, did she turn back to the mother.

"You don't have to leave. You're not even dry yet. Take all the time you want. Is there something I can help you find?"

"You have book on rabies?"

The request took Ora aback. She thought they were there to find books for the daughter. "Let me check for you."

While she went searching in the card catalog, Giang excused herself to use the bathroom. Back then, the Machias library hadn't yet been computerized or connected to any database of titles—those years were long off in the poorest county in the northeastern United States. Ora couldn't find any books devoted to the subject of rabies, but there were medical texts in the reference section she thought might be of help.

Lisa followed her about the stacks like a kitten waiting to be fed. She seemed awestruck by the old building and fascinated by the shelves and shelves of books, as if she'd never been in a library before.

"I can't believe you walked all the way here on a night like this," Ora said, arms full of books.

"My dad won't let my mom drive."

Ora couldn't help herself from asking. "Couldn't he have driven her here?"

"He's on the road. He takes the truck keys with him while he's hauling logs. He doesn't even like her to leave the house, especially while he's away."

"Why not?"

Lisa chewed on her lower lip. When she answered, it was softly. "He's afraid she'll run off on him."

"Does he hit her?"

The girl glanced at the floor.

"Does he hit you?"

Lisa didn't respond or raise her eyes.

"You can tell me the truth, Lisa."

"My mom says he's sick."

Giang appeared before them, transformed. In the bathroom, she had wrung out her hair, used a comb to secure it, and reapplied her makeup. She looked not just younger but like an entirely different person. Ora's first response was to smile. Then she saw the darkness in the other woman's eyes and heard the angry tone she used with her daughter as she said something in Vietnamese.

Ora didn't understand Lisa's response, but she recognized it as an apology.

The line from Tolstoy about all unhappy families being unhappy in their own ways came into Ora's head. She set the medical books on one of the long wooden tables, explained to the daughter (who seemed more conversant with indexes and tables of contents) how to find the information they wanted, then left them alone.

Ora couldn't have eavesdropped if she'd tried, not being able to understand Vietnamese. But the daughter was clearly translating passages from the books, causing the mother to become more and more animated.

After a respectful interval, Ora returned to them. She had located a book about rabies in the state catalog and had written the title on a slip of paper, which she handed to Giang. "If you'd like, I can get it for you on interlibrary loan. You wouldn't even need to come back into town. I could have it mailed to your house."

"No!" Giang's face blanched again. "No mail."

"Or I could drop it off."

"Thank you, no." Giang rose from the table, and her daughter did the same. They exchanged words again in their shared language.

"My mom says you're very kind," said Lisa. "She says she found the information she was looking for. She thanks you for your help."

They began to put on their wet jackets again.

"Can't I at least offer you a ride home?" said Ora. "I wouldn't mind at all."

"No, thank you, Ora."

Giang pulled her hood over her head. She helped her daughter get zipped up. Ora watched the two of them step out into the storm. She watched them as they hurried beneath the rain-swirled streetlamp. She kept watching long after they'd disappeared into the darkness.

$$\sim$$

"I don't know, Boss," Charley said when she arrived home.

The girls were asleep upstairs, and he had been reading in his leather armchair with their springer spaniel, Baskerville, at his feet. He'd been working his way through Shelby Foote's history of the Civil War. You wouldn't know it to look at Charley Stevens, but the man was a constant reader.

She unwound the wet scarf from her neck. "What don't you know?" she asked.

"I don't know if you should be getting in the middle of this."

"Charley Stevens, I am ashamed of you. The encyclopedia says that one to three people die of rabies in the US each year. And tens of thousands die around the world. What if he really does have it? The symptoms it describes—"

"Like what?"

"Insomnia, agitation, sweating, hallucinations."

"I've met plenty of vets like him before who were still dealing with shell shock years after they came home—"

"It's called post-traumatic stress disorder now, Charley."

"That man has problems with drugs and alcohol, Ora. It doesn't mean he's about to start chomping on people or foaming at the mouth."

"That isn't funny!"

"The rabid critters I've dealt with have been clearly deranged, not just aggressive but berserk-seeming. And some do get white around the teeth."

"The encyclopedia said it's always fatal when symptoms begin to show."

"But if he won't agree to see a doctor, and if he hasn't hit her or the child, I'm not sure what—"

"Of course he's hit them," Ora said. "He's hit them both for years."

"Did she tell you that?"

"She didn't have to."

"Ora."

"That man is obviously sick, and whatever's wrong with him, he's getting sicker, and how many times have you seen this play out in your career? Rabid or not—"

She let the sentence hang unfinished between them as she left the room.

Charley remained alone in the parlor for a while.

Ora had said that Hussey was off on the road again and away from home. He considered paying the wife and daughter a visit to interrogate them himself, but he knew there were risks to his doing so. If the husband, upon his return, were to hear that the law had made inquiries, who knows what new violence it might bring forth?

The next morning, however, Charley began asking around about John Hussey and his Vietnamese wife. And what he discovered was that no one—or next to no one—seemed to know anything about them.

The woman in the deeds office said that Hussey had inherited the land a year or so before from an uncle who had spent the past two decades wasting away in a nursing home: long enough for most people to have forgotten he had ever existed. Hussey had built the home himself (Charley had suspected as much). He had even drilled his own well. Hence there were no builders or electricians or plumbers with stories to tell about the new residents.

At Helen's Diner, Charley struck up a conversation with the superintendent of schools and verified that the family had obtained a waiver to homeschool their daughter.

They didn't shop for groceries at the IGA in Machias, which meant they must have driven the extra miles to Calais for some reason. Occasionally, the husband would stop in at Bill Day's store out on the Airline Road for milk, eggs or, usually, beer, but Bill (who was a taciturn man himself) never engaged him in conversation.

The warden asked around the Legion post and got the name of someone with a nephew in California who had served in the same unit as the mystery man: First Battalion, Ninth Marines.

"This feller's name is John Hussey," Charley said when he reached the retired Marine by phone. "He told me he was there in 1971. Might have had tattoos on his knuckles, LIFE and DEATH."

"Oh, that guy! I know who you mean. He married a nun."

Giang had been a nun? Charley knew grunts who had fallen in love with Vietnamese women, sometimes favorite prostitutes, and had even managed to get them home to the States. But he'd never heard of anyone who'd persuaded a vestal virgin to abandon her vows. "That's a new one."

"Well, she wasn't really a nun. She was just a girl at a convent school. Came from a wealthy family who thought Hussey was the devil. She must have loved him, though. Christ only knows why."

In bed that night, Charley told Ora about the conversation. He wondered what she thought it said about the couple.

"Assuming it's true?" she said, leaning her head against his strong shoulder. "I don't know, Charley. But can you imagine what a strange life's journey it's been for that woman—from a cloister in Saigon to a house in the Maine woods? This must seem like an alien world to her."

"Or hell itself," he said.

⌐

Charley was on patrol when the book arrived. Like all interlibrary loan parcels then, it came in the mail wrapped in brown paper. Ora had ordered it without telling him, and the act had felt like such a betrayal she'd felt obliged to confess it to him. She opened the mailbox and felt a sense of panic not unlike having received a ticking bomb.

It was a sunny day in April, and the girls were playing in the dooryard. Anne was picking snowdrops from the flower beds and placing the white blossoms in her hair, pretending to be a fairy princess. Stacey seemed spellbound by an anthill, watching the tiny insects go about their endless, unfathomable labors.

Ora smoothed her pants, sat down on the porch, and unwrapped the package. Like any librarian, she turned first to the pocket in back and removed the card showing how often the book had been checked out. This hardbound copy had come all the way from the stacks in Portland—the largest city in the state—and yet only a handful of readers had borrowed it over the previous few years.

She started at the index and found a section that seemed devoted to the history of rabies in human beings. Then she flipped forward and began to read.

Fevers spike high during this final phase of the disease. The mouth salivates profusely. Tears stream from the eyes. Goose bumps break out on the skin. Cries of agony, as expressed through a spasming throat, can produce the impression of an almost animal bark. In the throes of their convulsions patients have even been known to bite.

Ora shut the book so loudly both girls looked up in alarm.

She made her best attempt at smiling, but Stacey sensed something was wrong. "Mommy?"

"Go on playing," Ora said. "Mommy just needs to go inside for a minute."

She bothered the operator, a friend from the League of Women Voters, for Giang's phone number. If John answered, she would hang up. That was her plan.

The phone rang and kept ringing. The Husseys didn't seem to own an answering machine. Charley was always going on about Ora's supposed powers of precognition—which she herself discounted—but now she felt a tingle go through her nerves that spoke of some dire event having occurred.

She opened the phone book to the pages devoted to state agencies. She ran her index finger down the list of numbers, not sure what term she should be looking for. Family services?

Just then, the phone rang, and without thinking, she picked up.

"Stevens residence," she said. "Maine game warden's residence."

Charley often got work-related calls at home.

"You just called me," a man said. It was John Hussey. He must have dialed *69.

"I apologize for disturbing you." Ora was an unpracticed liar. "I dialed the wrong number."

He made a strange, lip-smacking sound when he spoke. "You said game warden."

"My husband is a warden."

"The one who came to my house that time?"

"Yes."

"Did my wife call him again? Is that how you got this number? Why were you calling?"

"I apologize for the intrusion," Ora said.

Through the receiver, she heard him yell one last word: "Giang!"

What have I done?

Through pure thoughtlessness, she had put that woman and girl in even greater danger. She could call the sheriff's office and ask them to send an officer to the Husseys' home, but she knew how her request would sound to the deputies once she explained the reason for her concern. She knew these men and how reluctant they were—even the few who weren't chauvinists—to interfere in domestic dramas.

She needed to talk to her husband—she needed to talk to Charley.

In the 1980s, Maine game wardens didn't have cell phones. When they were away from the radios in their trucks, they were just about unreachable. Very often their own police dispatchers had no idea where in the woods they might be.

Charley had mentioned something about helping the tribal warden do a boat patrol of fishermen on Big Lake. There were other, prejudiced wardens in the division who refused to work with the Passamaquoddy wardens, and it disgusted Ora to overhear the derogatory jokes these so-called peace officers made about Native Americans living on the nearby reservations in the worst poverty she had ever seen.

She had no way to reach her husband, she thought again.

Or maybe she did. There was a new warden working the district around Grand Lake Stream. She found his home number on Charley's list posted above the desk. The odds of catching him were slim, it being salmon season, but many wardens came home for lunch. She held her breath, waiting for an answer.

"Game warden," said Mack McQuarrie.

"Mack, this is Ora Stevens," she said with relief.

"Why, hello, Mrs. Stevens."

"Call me Ora, please. I was wondering if you could get a message to Charley?"

"Is something wrong at home?"

Suddenly, she felt foolish for having called McQuarrie, a man she barely knew. She felt unprepared and unwilling to disclose sensitive information about the Hussey family to the young warden. If he was like most law enforcement officers, he would have a knee-jerk reaction against anything that smacked of interfering between a husband and wife. Even her beloved Charley, who was more progressive in his thinking than his colleagues, seemed to feel reluctance.

"I just need to get a message to him," Ora said. "Charley told me he was patrolling Big Lake today with Nick Francis. If you happen to run into my husband, or catch him on the radio, please tell him I got that book about rabies from the library."

"Ma'am?"

"He'll know what I mean. It's important that he get the message as soon as possible."

"You're sure there's nothing wrong there?"

It wasn't her house she was worried about.

Now what? she thought. It might be hours before Charley got the message or had a chance to call back. Ora Stevens was not prone to panic, but when she looked at her hands, she saw that they were shaking.

She called Judy Beal down the road and asked if she could watch the girls for an hour, and Judy being Judy, she agreed without needing an explanation.

Ora put on a heavy sweater that she'd just put away for the summer but which already smelled of mothballs. Then she went into the mudroom and collected the girls' coats, boots, and hats.

"Mommy needs to go see a friend," she told them as she buckled their seat belts.

Stacey, always the inquisitive one, asked, "Who?"

Ora set the library book on the seat beside her and glanced at her younger daughter's expectant face in the rearview mirror. "You haven't met her yet."

Judy was waiting at the end of her long driveway when Ora arrived. The bosomy, pink-cheeked woman had twelve grandchildren and loved each as much as the next (though they didn't deserve it equally, in Ora's opinion). She was exactly the sort of person Ora hoped to become someday when her daughters had children of their own.

"I'll be back as soon as I can," she said.

"Take as long as you need, de-ah," Judy said. "A mother needs her alone time."

As Ora set off again, the sun slid behind strangely colored clouds that reminded her of the strips of linen used to bind a mummy. The pale light gave the budding woods a softened, almost dreamlike quality devoid of shadows. Minutes earlier, it had been warm enough to drive with the windows open. Now she felt a coldness that penetrated all the way to the marrow.

Ora had no idea what she was going to do. She couldn't very well knock on the door and wait for a potentially ill and definitely violent man to answer. And yet if she were being honest with herself, she very much wanted to see John Hussey again with her own eyes. The extent of his deterioration would tell her what she must do.

She parked the Wagoneer at the top of the drive. Now that she had arrived, she felt the house pulling on her like gravity. She glanced around the vehicle for something that might offer protection. Unlike most wardens, her husband had no particular interest in firearms and only grudgingly wore his service weapon. There was no pistol in the glove compartment. There was, however, a tire iron. She concealed the long metal rod up her sleeve and started down the hill.

As soon as she came within view of the house, she saw that the front door was open.

The black flies hadn't yet begun hatching from the brooks,

but there were other bugs about. No one in Down East Maine left their door ajar this time of year. She clutched the hidden tire iron for reassurance and continued on across the dooryard, trying to approach from an angle that allowed her to see as deeply as possible into the interior. It seemed to her that the birds had gone silent, but in truth, she'd stopped hearing them.

Twenty feet from the door, Ora was brought up short. She thought she heard a moan. Then a small shadow detached itself from the others within. She shook the tire iron loose from her sweater sleeve and into her hand. Then she took a step forward, onto the stoop. Despite her better instincts, she whispered, "Giang?"

It took Ora a moment to realize her mistake.

The figure wasn't Giang.

It was Lisa.

The child staggered toward her covered in blood.

~⌐

Out on Big Lake, a chop had picked up with the wind, and now the bow of the Grand Laker was throwing so much spray in his face, Charley wished he'd worn a raincoat.

Aside from being drenched, he'd had a pleasant morning patrolling Big Lake with Nick Francis, the tribal warden for Indian Township. They hadn't witnessed any gross violations or written any tickets, but they'd enjoyed a wide-ranging conversation that covered everything from the ineptitude of the Bureau of Indian Affairs to the proper way to prepare fried clams: battered versus breaded. Nick had given Charley a brief tutorial in the Passamaquoddy language, and then they'd debated the chances of the Red Sox finally winning the World Series. Charley was certain this would be the year. Nick was doubtful.

"I'm an Indian," the handsome young man had said. "Pessimism is self-preservation for my people."

Charley threw back his head and laughed with characteristic abandon. But his good humor evaporated the moment he saw

Mack McQuarrie's truck waiting at the boat launch. If another warden had personally come to fetch him, it could only mean bad news.

McQuarrie climbed out of his pickup and waved as Nick killed the outboard motor. He was a barrel-shaped young man with hair thicker than an otter skin and a perpetual bulge in his cheek from chewing tobacco.

Holding the painter, Charley leaped into the water as the boat glided toward the shallows.

"What's wrong?" he shouted.

"Just thought I'd see how you made out," McQuarrie said. "How many salmon poachers did the Lone Ranger and Tonto pinch today?"

Francis busied himself bringing the boat to shore as if he hadn't heard the insult.

Charley scowled. "Don't be a jackass, Mack. What's going on?"

The younger warden spat a nicotine stream onto the slanted boat ramp before he spoke. "Your wife called to say your library book was in."

"What?"

"She said you'd know what it meant."

Charley stood in the water, holding the rope, while Nick Francis went for his trailer. "That's all she said?"

"I figured it was some sort of secret man-and-wife code you two used."

Charley was no expert on females—far from it, he would admit—but Mack McQuarrie's ignorance was a bottomless pit. Library book? He stroked his chin and stared across the windswept lake. Ora had admitted to having ordered a book about rabies for Giang Hussey. But why would she need her husband to know that it had arrived?

Unless she was planning some mischief.

"Hey there, Mack," Charley said, splashing onto dry land. "What are you doing this afternoon?"

"I thought I'd scope out the Hatchery Pool. I know there's at least one bastard there using worms."

"Change of plans. I need you to come with me."

"To fetch a frigging book?"

Charley didn't bother replying. He climbed behind the wheel of his truck, started the engine, and radioed the dispatcher, asking her to try calling his wife at home. As he'd expected, she came back on the air a few minutes later and told him there'd been no answer at the house.

Charley knew his wife well enough to guess where she was headed.

It was a solid half-hour drive from Indian Township to Whitney, where the Husseys lived, and McQuarrie badgered him nonstop on the radio, asking where they were going and what the hell was really happening.

"There's a lady in danger," Charley finally admitted.

He hated being so blunt on the public airwaves, knowing what proportion of the citizenry in Down East Maine owned police scanners.

By the time the two wardens reached the Snake Lake Road, the muscles in Charley's neck and forearms ached from the tension of driving so far at high speed.

He hit his blinker a quarter mile before the fire road to give McQuarrie advance warning that they would be making a sharp turn. Even so, Charley hit the corner so hard he nearly whacked the side of his pickup against a pine tree standing sentinel at the intersection. He overcorrected and scraped evergreen boughs on the far side of the road. The drive twisted again almost immediately, and he hit the brakes. A good thing, too, or he would have slammed into the back of Ora's parked Wagoneer.

She had left it at the top of the hill, near the first of the POSTED signs.

Charley blew out his breath as if he'd just dived to the bottom of a deep quarry. He was the reckless one in the family. Ora was supposed to be sensible. What could possibly have compelled her to venture alone and unarmed down to that cursed house?

Then he saw the little girl sitting in the front passenger seat of the Wagoneer.

He circled around to the side of the vehicle. The window was rolled down, but if Lisa Hussey heard his footsteps on the gravel, she didn't show it. She was as motionless as a department-store mannequin.

"Honey?" Charley whispered.

Her face was the shape and profile of her mother's, oval and flat, but her hair had some of her father's curls. Her eyes seemed unnaturally heavy and unfocused.

He heard McQuarrie's heavy step behind him. Out of the corner of his eye, he noticed that the younger warden had drawn his .357 Smith & Wesson revolver.

Charley tried again. "Honey? Are you all right?"

The girl finally moved. She blinked and lifted her fingers to her mouth absently. Only then did he notice that her hands were covered in blood. The words came out slurred: "She said to stay here."

Now he understood what had made Ora take such an uncharacteristically dangerous risk.

He turned to McQuarrie, wishing he had been more forthcoming about the situation. He pulled the other man out of hearing range of the girl. "My wife is down there. I think this little girl's father just killed her mother."

"Jay-sus," the young warden said.

Now that he had an idea of what he might be facing, Charley had grown calm. It was his natural reaction to stress: the same genetic good fortune that had saved his life during the war and many times after.

"Get on the horn with Dispatch," Charley said. "Tell Nora to send the nearest trooper and an ambulance."

"You don't want me to go with you?"

"It's important you stay with this child, Mack. Keep her safe. I'll be back directly."

He didn't run. He walked at a deliberate pace. He removed his own revolver from its creaking holster and raised his arm at the elbow, pointing the barrel ahead of him. The gun felt as if it weighed twenty pounds. Charley's grip was strong, and his heartbeat was steady, but he was aware of the adrenaline flooding his bloodstream. The trick, he had learned long ago, was to acknowledge the hormone but not be overcome by it: to focus the mind on one's surroundings.

Even before he saw the house, he saw the red of the Peterbilt tractor through the stricken forest.

No need for stealth, he told himself. Only caution. And clearness of mind.

When he came around the truck rig, he noticed that the front door of the house was standing open. No light issued from inside. It was just a rectangle of emptiness.

He took a breath, let it out, breathed in again, and stepped forward.

At that moment, Ora emerged from the darkness as if she'd sensed him coming. She couldn't possibly have seen or heard his approach. The look on her face was not one he had ever witnessed before. He wouldn't see it again for years, until the day she awoke in the hospital, broken beyond repair from the plane crash, and learned that she would never walk again.

She mouthed two words: "Charley. Help."

He rushed forward and leaped up the stairs, taking them two at a time, as Ora turned sideways to let him pass. Shades covered the windows. One of the electrical lights in the living room had been knocked over during the fight, but amazingly, the bulb continued to glow from the floor. It was the only light in the room.

The man and the woman were both stretched out in unnatural positions, arms crooked, with their legs tangled together. Neither of them moved. Their mingled blood continued to spread slowly across the hardwood, finding the cracks between the boards the way streams find the low places between hills. The husband, shirtless, was crisscrossed with many cuts—some shallow, others deep—but there was no doubt that the kitchen knife sticking from his neck was what had finally killed him.

Just one side of the wife's face was visible, but Charley could see the mark where her husband's strong fist had shattered her cheekbone. Her mangled left hand was pressed to her breast and had stained red the silk of her tunic.

He crouched down, extended his arm toward her jawline to feel for a pulse.

At the touch of his fingers, Giang's whole body gave a jerk. She moaned, and her head lolled on its thin neck toward Charley and Ora. Only then did he see the bloody socket where the crazed man had gouged out her eye.

⌒

"So you can understand why she doesn't welcome visitors," Charley said to me. It was fully dark now in my truck. The frogs had started up in the pond behind us. "The way that poor beautiful woman was mutilated . . ."

"What exactly happened?"

"He attacked her in a rage after the call from Ora. He was raving, out of his head. Would have killed her without a doubt if she hadn't gotten hold of that knife. By then, he'd already bitten off the little finger of her left hand. We found it in the kitchen sink, where he must have spit it out. You could see they'd fought through the whole downstairs. He must have gotten his thumb in her eye before he bled out. With that blow to the head, it was no wonder she lost consciousness.

"After she came to, she started screaming. We had to hold her down to keep her from scrabbling around looking for her missing eye. Ora found some rags to bandage her poor hand. And the ambulance arrived soon after I did. She kept telling the paramedics she wanted a rabies shot."

I listened to the chorus of mink frogs singing from the vernal pool. "Why does she stay there?"

"She has no friends or family in the country. But mostly, I think, it's because of her face. She was very proud of her beauty, Ora thinks."

"But how can she live in that house after what happened?"

"She gets checks from the government, and Hussey must have had some life insurance. Her daughter married a lobsterman down in Jonesport and brings her most of what she needs. Ora and I deliver her things now and again. But as far as I know, Giang hasn't been seen in public in years."

In other words, she was still a prisoner in that godforsaken place. She'd slain the devil but was trapped in her own private hell.

Just then, the question that had been on my mind while I listened to his story finally burst out. "So did Hussey have rabies or not?"

"Of course he didn't," my friend said.

"So why did he—?"

"Not every disease is carried by bats. I've met plenty of vets like him who brought the war back home. Even now, they walk around with it pinned to their backs like Peter Pan's shadow. John Hussey was a violent son of a gun who drank too much and took pills that ate away his brain tissue. Hell, maybe he even came to believe what his wife kept telling him. Maybe he thought he was rabid. Whatever the truth was, it was such a bloody, confused mess the attorney general decided to leave it alone. He never brought a charge against her."

Charley opened his door, and I opened mine.

"You can't come with me, son," he said. "I can't violate her privacy like that."

"I'll stay back in the shadows. She'll never see me."

"I gave my word, you understand."

I nodded. But as he lifted the brown-wrapped package from the truck, I said, "So what's in there, anyway?"

"New clothes. Ora orders outfits for her from a shop in California. Silk tunics and pants and shoes. Gifts to help her feel less . . ."

And with that, he turned his back and began making his way down the dark road, carrying a load far heavier than the contents of the box.

I stood in the cooling night beside the truck, listening to the sounds of the forest. In those days, curiosity affected me like a physical sensation: an actual itch. I waited a few minutes and then began to walk softly, heel to toe, until I saw a glimmer of light shining through the boughs of the pines.

I pressed my body against a tree trunk and waited until the door finally opened.

I saw Charley emerge. He put on the cap he had taken off for the sake of politeness and wished Giang Hussey a good night. In the doorway, the figure of a woman held up her hand to wave goodbye.

My breath caught in my throat.

Charley always walked at a good clip. I barely made it back to the truck before he did.

My friend came from the old school where men never wept. But I heard the catch in his throat when he said, "Let's get out of this cussed bog. Coming here always makes me want to rush home to Ora."

⁓

"Did Charley happen to mention what the paramedic told him?" Ora Stevens asked me later that night.

"Do you mean the paramedic who arrived at the Husseys' house that night?"

We were sitting together beside the woodstove, drinking

dandelion tea. Ora was in her wheelchair, as always, with a plaid blanket drawn up across her lap. Charley was out walking his hunting dog, Nimrod. His temporary absence from their cabin had given me a chance to ask Ora about her memories of that horrible afternoon.

Decades had passed, and yet Ora Stevens was still a beauty. People in Hollywood would have assumed that she'd had plastic surgery, but I have come to agree with the sentiment that as we age, we all get the faces we deserve.

"The paramedic who treated Giang said he'd been to the house six months earlier to bring John Hussey to the hospital. He'd said the homeowner had received a puncture wound he got from tripping on a sharp log in the forest. But it sure looked like a stab wound."

I leaned forward in my rocking chair. "You think Giang had previously stabbed her husband?"

Ora folded her hands on her lap blanket. "And I bet Charley didn't mention the book on rabies the police found under Lisa's bed. The edges of the pages were folded at the list of symptoms."

"She was really worried."

Ora raised an eyebrow. "Maybe."

"I don't understand."

"You're too young to remember," the old woman said. "But it was a different time back then in Down East Maine. There were still police officers who thought domestic violence was just a normal part of marriage. An abused woman—especially one from another country, surrounded by strangers—had no recourse if her husband threatened to kill her. Judges tended to look hard on females who came into their courts claiming self-defense. I've never blamed Giang for doing what she had to do. And the punishment she ended up suffering was worse than anything the law could have done to her."

"Ora, what are you saying?"

"Giang was terrified what would happen to her if she killed him in self-defense. But she was desperate for a way out and thought she'd found it. She didn't realize that John's dead body would be tested for rabies."

I leaned back in my rocking chair until I nearly tipped over. "You think she used the disease as an excuse to kill him."

Ora smoothed the blanket on her lap. "I don't think she reckoned on him fighting so hard to the end—what he did to her eye. Her face."

"Have you shared your suspicions with Charley?"

"There's no point in it. It's better that he believes what he believes. He's a wily fox when it comes to catching bad men. But when it comes to women, he doesn't want to suspect the worst."

We heard the door on the screen porch creak open and then slam shut on its spring.

"Nimrod has done his duty!" Charley announced.

"We're in here, dear." Then Ora beckoned me in close to whisper one last thing. "The crime scene investigators found no skin or bone fragments in John's mouth to indicate he'd bitten down on a human hand. Those hapless men didn't even think to wonder why."

My father had been a trapper, and he would often tell stories of finding the gnawed-off paws of raccoons and coyotes in his sprung traps, so desperate had the animals been to escape.

I thought back to what I had seen myself at the Hussey house when I'd been lurking at the edge of the light. I remembered the shrouded figure in the doorway waving goodbye to Charley with her maimed hand. How far would a desperate woman have gone to escape the trap that was her life? Far enough to bite off her own finger?

Just then, Charley entered the room with the dog at his heels. "Did I miss anything?" he asked with an innocent smile.

The Imposter

Twelve-Gauge Gaynor had been rowing his skiff from the town landing out to his lobster boat, the *Dragon Lady*, when he'd spotted a metallic glimmer coming through the blue-green water. Gaynor had been fishing out of Roque Harbor for fifty years, and this wasn't the first vehicle he'd seen take a bath. On most but not all occasions, the driver had managed to escape from the drowning machine and swim to shore. Gaynor told the dispatcher he had a spooky feeling there was at least one dead person at the bottom of the harbor.

I'd heard the report come over the radio and had decided to drive down in my patrol truck to watch the recovery efforts. Most of the town seemed to be present. Anticipation hung in the air as unmistakably as the smell of the sea. Everyone was waiting to see whose body the divers would find. In a community as tightly woven as Roque Harbor, the deceased was sure to be related to someone or other.

"Bet it's Merrill's boy," Gaynor said to the lobsterman beside him.

"Luke or John?"

"They're both wild as tomcats. Hell, it might be both of them."

Cigarette smoke wafted from the crowd behind me. Gulls,

drawn by the prospect of thrown food, chattered overhead. It was a beautiful midsummer morning.

I stood on the dock beside Gaynor, who was glorifying in his central role in the day's drama. His first name was Thomas, but everyone called him "Twelve-Gauge" for reasons no one had yet explained to me. I was the new game warden in Down East Maine, and the locals—who tended to be suspicious and close-mouthed even with one another—hadn't decided whether they approved of me or not.

The sheriff had come out to oversee the recovery. Her name was Roberta Rhine. Because of her black braids and fondness for turquoise jewelry, some people thought she was part Indian. She wasn't, though; she just had a flair for the theatrical. Her deputies had cleared the landing and set up a cordon so the divers could go about their bone-chilling work. It might have been the middle of July, but the temperature in the Gulf of Maine was still in the low fifties.

After a while, the state police divers emerged from the deep with what looked, from a distance, like a department store mannequin. The sheriff and two of her deputies leaned over the edge and, with gloved hands, pulled the corpse onto the dock.

Murmurs started behind me. The same question over and over. "Who is it?" Gaynor's friend asked. "Do you recognize him?"

The lobsterman grunted, "No."

Rhine and her officers stooped over the body. Then they all glanced in my direction. The sheriff beckoned me forward.

"Hey, Bowditch!"

The dead man lay exposed to the sun. He looked like he was wearing a mask of wet papier-mâché that might slough off if handled roughly. He was dressed in army fatigues, but one of his combat boots had come off, along with his sock. His toenails badly needed cutting.

The sheriff held out a wet wallet flipped open to the driver's license. I couldn't read the name, but the picture showed a young

guy with a buzz cut and a lazy eye. I looked from the photograph
to the thing at my feet, then back again.

"Who is he?"

"He's you," she said.

I peered closer. The name on the license was Mike Bowditch.

Two months earlier, I'd gotten a disturbing phone call from my
supervisor.

"What are you doing?" Sergeant Marc Rivard had asked.

"Just rolling and patrolling."

"I have a question for you." Rivard had a faint French accent,
common among older Mainers, but almost unheard of among
people under forty. "Did you stop a station wagon full of teenagers out on Route 9 on Saturday night?"

"No. Why?"

"You're sure you didn't?"

"I think I'd know if I did! What's this about?"

"The lieutenant got a call from a guy who says his teenage
daughter and her friends were stopped for speeding by a game
warden. She says he was driving a green truck with a flashing
blue light. They thought he was a police officer, so they pulled
over. There were four girls in the station wagon. They'd just come
from a party at a gravel pit."

"What happened?"

"So this 'warden' comes up to the driver's window, and evi-
dently, there's something strange about him. He asks for all of
their licenses, not just the driver's, and sorts through them, looking at the photos. The prettiest girl is in the back seat, and she's
the one he tells to step out of the vehicle."

"Oh, Jesus."

"He orders her to open her mouth and stick out her tongue so
he can smell her breath. Then he asks if she knows how serious
the punishment is for underage drinking. He says he's going to

have to pat her down before he gives her a field sobriety test. The other girls are all freaking out now, and the driver—she's the bold one—jumps out of the vehicle. The warden pulls his handgun and yells at her to get back inside."

"What happened next?"

"They were lucky another car drove up," he said. "It came to a stop behind the warden's truck and just idled there. The guy turned white and told the girls that they were free to leave with just a warning. The last they saw of him, he was screaming west on Route 9 with this bright yellow sports car in pursuit."

Somehow a blackfly had found its way inside the patrol truck. I could feel it creeping into the notch behind one of my ears. "You honestly thought that was me, Marc?"

"I had to ask."

Like hell he did. "Did the girls give you a description of the guy?"

"Early twenties," he said. "Tall like you. On the thin side. Hair buzzed down to the scalp. They said there was something funny about one of his eyes."

"Funny how?"

"Just funny. What I'm telling you came secondhand through the father of the girl driving the car."

"Did this imposter give a name? Or show some kind of identification?"

"They were just kids. Plus they'd been drinking wine coolers."

"What about a license plate?"

"You don't seem to be listening."

I had been waiting for Rivard to get to the plan of action, but he seemed in no hurry. "So what do we do about this?"

"Put it out quietly among law enforcement to be on the lookout for some jackass pretending to be a game warden."

"Shouldn't we warn the public?"

"And give the crazies an excuse not to stop for blue lights?" He pitched his voice high with mockery. "'But, Your Honor, I thought it was that police impersonator behind me. I was afraid he might kill me if I pulled over!'"

"What about the yellow car?" I asked.

"What about it?"

"Shouldn't we try to locate the driver? Find out who he is and what he saw? How many yellow sports cars are speeding around Washington County?"

"Bowditch, do you realize how limited my resources are at the moment?"

"It seems like catching this phony warden should be a priority."

"I am making it a priority."

Two weeks passed without the warden impersonator making another appearance. Then came the home invasion.

I remember it being a particularly dark night, overcast, with a new moon afraid to show itself. I was working the smelt run on a skinny little brook that spilled out of the hills above Sixth Machias Lake. I had just issued a summons to a chucklehead who'd netted about ten gallons of smelt, the bag limit being one quart, and made him dump the shimmering fish back into the brook.

My phone rang as I was marching the smelt poacher to his truck. The dispatcher told me there was a man in the next township claiming he'd been terrorized at gunpoint by a game warden gone rogue. The location of the alleged "home invasion" was a trailer parked illegally at the mushy edge of a beaver bog.

By the time I arrived, half the law enforcement officers in the county seemed to be on the scene. Among them was Rivard.

My sergeant had black hair and what people, behind his back, called a "porn 'stache." He had been married three times and fancied himself a debonair playboy. By the standards of backwoods Maine, he probably fit the definition.

He grinned wide enough to expose his bicuspids. "The criminal always returns to the scene of the crime!"

I was baffled by the joke, but it brought smiles to the faces of the assembled deputies and troopers.

"Is the victim still here?" I asked.

"The sheriff's taking his statement. She told me to send you in."

"Why me?"

"You'll see."

The camper was a suppository-shaped silver Airstream. The inside smelled of weed. There were, no doubt, other odors, but they were entirely overridden by the marijuana smoke baked into the rugs and upholstery.

Every drawer had been pulled out and overturned, and every door was ajar. Clothing, canned goods, and assorted crap littered the room. From the damage, you might have thought an extremely localized tornado had passed through.

Sheriff Rhine, wearing her black polo with an embroidered star on the breast, chinos, and cowboy boots, sat at the kitchen table. Across from her was a gaunt, bearded man with strips of duct tape dangling from his body and a loose pile of discarded adhesive around his bare feet. He looked like he'd just escaped being mummified alive in shiny silver ribbons.

The sheriff raised her chin as I entered the room. "Is this the warden who tied you up, Alvin?"

The scrawny man spun around in his chair. He had greasy brown hair tucked behind ears that were almost elfin in their pointedness. His eyes were so heavy-lidded it seemed he might be dozing off.

"Who? Him?"

"Is this the game warden who tore up your home and held a gun to your head?"

"The warden who ripped me off was all bruised and shit— like he'd been stomped pretty good in a fight. And he had one of those crazy eyes."

"You mean lazy eyes?"

"Crazy, lazy—what's the difference?"

Rhine took a calming breath. "And what did you say this 'warden's' name was, Alvin?"

"Bowditch," he said, fiddling with a strip of tape clinging stubbornly to his thigh.

"This is Warden Bowditch."

"Are they related?"

"No," I said.

"You need to find the other one and ask him what he did with my toilet."

The sheriff rose to her feet. She was a tall woman. "Stay here, Alvin. I'll send in Deputy Corbett to help you get the last of that tape off."

Neither Rhine nor I spoke until we were clear of the trailer. Flashlights flickered between the trees as the deputies searched the property. The piping of spring peepers in the bog was so shrill it just about pierced my eardrums.

"The impersonator is using my name now?"

"Apparently so."

"Why me?"

"That's a good question. Maybe it's because you're new around here and not everyone knows what you look like. Or maybe you issued him a citation, and it's his way of getting back at you."

I was certain I would have remembered writing a ticket to a jittery young man with a crazy, lazy eye.

"What the hell happened here, Sheriff?"

The man inside the trailer was named Alvin Payne, Rhine said, and he was well known to the Washington County Sheriff's Department, having been a guest in their hospitality suites on several occasions.

Earlier that evening, Mr. Payne was treating a herniated cervical disc with medical marijuana and listening to some Zeppelin when a man claiming to be a Maine game warden started pounding on the door. Alvin, being a good citizen with nothing to hide, had let him in.

The warden said he had proof that there was a cache of illegal deer meat inside Payne's freezer and commanded him to take a seat. The next thing Alvin knew, his hands were being bound behind him with duct tape.

Even more puzzling: The officer didn't bother looking inside the freezer at all. Instead, he ransacked the closets and kitchen cupboards. The first thing he confiscated was Alvin's supply of prescription cannabis.

It was dawning on Payne that the situation might not be what it seemed.

"What's your name and badge number!" he demanded.

"My name is Mike Bowditch," the warden answered in a tough-guy voice. "And my badge number is zero-zero-fuck-you."

He then applied a strip of tape across Alvin's mouth to curtail further conversation.

Payne claimed he had nearly suffocated watching his trailer be turned inside out and upside down. It was obvious this Warden Bowditch was growing agitated that he couldn't find whatever he'd been looking for. Finally, he returned to his prisoner and ripped the tape from his lips.

"Where's the pills?"

"What pills?"

"The pills your cousin gave you." Then he pressed the barrel of his gun to Payne's temple.

Alvin just about wet himself. "All he gave me was a honey bucket because my toilet don't work."

I held up my hand to interrupt Rhine. "What's a honey bucket?"

It was a primitive commode, she explained, made from a prefab toilet seat that attached to a five-gallon plastic pail. The generic name was bucket latrine.

While I had never heard of a honey bucket, the name had meant something significant to the guy pretending to be me. As soon as he heard it, he disappeared out the door, leaving Alvin Payne bound to the chair.

I followed the sheriff behind a flowering shadbush that functioned, more or less, as a privacy screen. A roll of tissue still hung from a nearby branch, but there was no sign of the portable shitter itself.

"Wasn't it risky hiding pills in the bottom of a toilet?" I said, trying not to inhale. "What if Payne dumped them out?"

"Maybe they were attached to the bottom somehow. Or buried in the ground underneath. It was actually a clever place to hide pharmaceuticals from any drug-sniffing dogs that might have searched the property."

"I assume the pills were oxycodone."

"Probably, but it could've been a mix of prescription painkillers. Codeine, hydrocodone, et cetera."

"Who is Payne's cousin?"

"A Canadian smuggler by the name of Dylan LeBlanc. The DEA and ICE have no clue how he's been getting his drugs across the border from New Brunswick."

"So LeBlanc gives cousin Alvin a honey bucket as some kind of secret drug stash. But if he's such a wily smuggler, how did our warden impersonator know he was caching his drugs out here?"

"That's another good question. Alvin claims to be ignorant of his cousin's profession, and I believe him."

"Why's that?"

"Because after he gnawed himself free, he called 911 to report the home invasion."

The sheriff's phone rang. It was the Maine Drug Enforcement Agency.

I stood alone in the darkness, listening to the earsplitting frogs and feeling myself growing angrier and angrier at the thought of a two-bit robber using my name to commit his crimes.

Maybe pulling over those girls had just been a trial run to see if he could fool people into believing he was a warden. Maybe this heist had been his master plan all along. The pretender simply hadn't reckoned with the extent of Alvin Payne's potheaded stupidity.

I made my way through the trees to Rivard, who was still holding court to a slightly smaller audience of cops. "So what did you do with the honey bucket, Mike?" he said. "Come on, tell the truth."

"I don't find this situation particularly amusing."

"A stoner gets duct-taped to a chair by a fake warden who then runs off with a portable toilet full of narcotics. Yeah, you're right. There's nothing funny about this at all."

Blood warmed my cheeks. "It's a crime to impersonate a law enforcement officer."

"You take yourself too seriously, Bowditch."

Several nights later, an unidentified vehicle dumped Alvin Payne in the parking lot outside the hospital in Calais, a five-minute drive from the international bridge that crosses the river into New Brunswick. Multiple bones in his arms and legs had been broken, most likely with a two-by-four. When he emerged from hours of surgery and finally awoke from anesthesia, the luckless stoner told Sheriff Rhine he'd injured himself falling from the roof of his trailer.

The next time I saw Marc Rivard, he refused to meet my eyes.

⌒

Now it was summer and a man was dead.

The driver's license was fake, of course. I stood on the wet planks with my doppelgänger at my feet while the sheriff circulated the plastic card among her officers first and then, when no one recognized him, among the good people of Roque Harbor.

Who was he?

Not a single person could say.

The man who'd discovered the submerged truck decided he could remain the center of attention by turning to comedy. "How does it feel to be dead, Warden?" Twelve-Gauge Gaynor asked in a loud voice. "Did you see a white light before you swallowed the sea?"

The sun was growing unbearably hot, as if its rays were being focused through a giant magnifying glass. I could almost feel it burning a hole through my black ball cap.

The divers, meanwhile, continued their underwater investigation.

Their first significant find was an empty fifth of Fireball Cinnamon Whisky, the slogan for which is "Tastes Like Heaven, Burns Like Hell." There was a good chance that my namesake had consumed the bottle prior to his daredevil jump into the harbor. As a rule, most vehicles that end up going off wharves are driven by individuals with blood alcohol levels in the double digits.

The divers were unable to locate any papers in the vehicle, not even an automobile registration. Even the license plate, it turned out, had been stolen a month earlier off a security van parked outside the Bangor Mall.

"The law of the sea says I should get salvage rights to that truck for finding it," Twelve-Gauge Gaynor said to his dwindling audience. "Unless our dead warden here wants to stake a claim."

Finding the gun took a while. The impact and influx of seawater had knocked it around the inside of the truck cab. One of the divers finally located the weapon—an old Smith & Wesson .357 Magnum revolver—wedged in a crack under the glove compartment. It was almost certainly the one the imposter had been wearing the night he stopped the girls.

Finally, Sheriff Rhine pulled me aside. "So you don't recognize this guy at all? You and he never crossed paths?"

"I wish I could help you."

"I do, too."

"What about your deputies, Sheriff? I can't believe no one in your department recognizes him."

"Don't take that tone with me, Warden."

"It was my name this man stole to commit his crimes. I think I am entitled to be pissed about it."

"Not with me, you're not," she said.

"Any indication whether this was a homicide or a suicide?"

"His skull was cracked, but that might have been from the impact. The medical examiner should be able to make a determination. If his lungs are full of water, it means he drowned. If there's no water, it means he was already dead when he went under."

"But you're positive this is our imposter?"

"We sent a picture to the girl driving the car he stopped. Reese Brogan made a positive ID."

"Is Reese Brogan the daughter of Joe Brogan, who owns Call of the Wild Guide Service and Game Ranch?"

"Yes, she is. Why?"

"Just trying to make a connection."

Joe Brogan leased miles of fenced timberland that he populated with all manner of exotic animals: bison, red deer, mouflon sheep, boars, even an ill-fated zebra once. Hunters from across the country rented his cabins and paid sizable sums to shoot these essentially tame creatures. Brogan knew what I thought of his vile business. It would not be inaccurate to say we hated each other's guts.

I could only imagine what a violent son of a bitch like Joe Brogan might do to a half-witted punk who had terrorized his little girl.

A bronze GMC pickup pulled up at the end of the line of police vehicles. It was Rivard's unmarked truck. He came toward us without any of his usual strutting.

"Sorry I'm late," he said. "My ex-wife and I really got into it, and—"

Rhine pointed at the body bag. "We need you to take a look at the deceased, Marc."

Rivard stuck his hand in his pocket and removed a tin of

moist snuff. He dug his fingers into the soil-colored tobacco. He wedged some of it between his cheek and gums.

The sheriff must have sensed he was stalling. "Ready when you are, Sergeant."

She lifted the edge of the plastic. Rivard didn't even need to study the face. One glance and his Adam's apple began bobbing in his throat.

"You know him, then?" she said.

"His name is Tommy Winters."

"Where do you know him from?"

"The Narraguagus Sporting Club. His dad, Tim, is the range master there part-time. The Winterses live over in Aurora, I'm pretty sure."

It was a hamlet in the next county and therefore out of Rhine's jurisdiction, which partially explained why neither she nor her deputies had recognized the dead man.

"Does this make any sense to you, Marc?" the sheriff asked.

"Does what make any sense?"

"Tommy Winters impersonating a game warden? Did he have a reputation for breaking the law or pulling dumb stunts? Was he an opioid addict looking for the score of a lifetime?"

Rivard hung his head over the wharf and spat tobacco juice into the water. "I barely remember meeting him."

"So this is all a big surprise to you?" said the sheriff doubtfully.

"I honestly had no idea. All I know is this is going to break Tim's heart. That man has had the worst run of luck of anyone I know."

"How so?"

"He was a lifer at the mill in Bucksport until he took a tumble from the top of a machine to the shop floor. Then his wife, Karen, was diagnosed with a brain tumor. I'm pretty sure Tommy was their only child, too. If this isn't the last nail in Tim's coffin, I don't know what will be."

I sometimes forgot that my sergeant, for all his failings, was a father himself. It was always easier for me to view him as a cartoonish villain. We never want to see the people who annoy and infuriate us as three-dimensional human beings.

⁓

Half an hour later, I found myself bringing up the rear of a three-vehicle caravan led by Rhine in her Crown Vic cruiser, followed by Rivard in his unmarked GMC pickup, and then me in my battered patrol truck. The sheriff had requested I accompany them to the Narraguagus Sporting Club to notify the next of kin. She hoped Mr. Winters might be able to shine some light on his son's decision to use my name to commit crimes.

The route took us along logging roads down which eighteen-wheelers stacked high with timber would come barreling, forcing us off into the lupines that grew with such exuberance along the gravel shoulders. By the time we turned off the main road, my recently washed pickup was coated with a quarter-inch layer of dust.

I heard the gunshots—the pops of small-caliber pistols and the rapid bursts of AR-15s—even before we pulled into the parking lot. Like most fish and game associations, the Narraguagus Sporting Club included an outdoor shooting range. As range master, Tim Winters was the man charged with keeping trigger-happy members from carelessly shooting one another.

The clubhouse was one story and constructed of varnished logs. Its roof was orange with fallen pine needles.

I counted four vehicles in the lot: two blue pickups, both beat to hell; a black SUV of the kind I associated with Mafia dons; and a vintage red Mustang that someone had recently restored and repainted.

"I made some calls on the drive over," said Rhine. "Tommy Winters was twenty-one. He had five speeding violations, but no history of violence or substance abuse. He was expelled from Brewer High for an incident involving a failed attempt to conceal himself in the girls' locker room. The consensus, among the teachers who remembered him, was that he was on the autism spectrum. His last job was at a hardware store in Ellsworth. He lasted two weeks."

Rivard began fiddling with his tin of Red Man snuff again.

"Do you want me to do this, Marc?" Rhine asked.

"Tim knows me," he said. "I'd feel like shit if I let anyone else break the news to him."

We made our way around the outside of the low-slung building. There were five stalls set up along a roofed concrete breezeway. Each station had a bench where a shooter could sit and steady a gun. Each wooden table faced an open field with targets staggered at intervals. Four hundred yards in the distance, a berm of bulldozed earth served as a backstop for the bullets.

Standing in the last stall were two hairy, potbellied guys, both of whom were wearing ripped T-shirts and jeans. They were the ones firing the AR-15s. Shells jumped crazily from their semiautomatic rifles.

A third man—dapper, clean-shaven, hair going silver—was the one shooting the pistol. It was a long-barreled .22 Walther GSP, the kind used for serious competitions. I followed the muzzle to the bull's-eye fifty yards away. The marksman hadn't once missed the center circles.

The fourth man sat on a folding chair with his back to us, keeping watch on the shooters. Like the others, he wore ear protectors clamped over his head. This was the range master, Tim Winters.

The dapper pistolero spotted us from his stall. He paused to stare at us through yellow-lensed shooting glasses. Then he cleared the chamber of his gun and ejected the magazine.

Winters, alerted to our presence, turned his head. He was in his fifties, wearing a too-tight polo to show off pectorals that, despite his best efforts, were beginning to sag. He studied us without expression, then raised an air horn from beside his chair and let off a blast.

"Cease firing!" Winters shouted in the silence that followed.

"What's going on, Marc?" Winters's hair was dyed that reddish-brown color that never fools anyone. He carried a holstered .45 on his hip. "What's with the retinue?"

"Hey, Tim. Any chance you can shut down the range for the rest of the day?"

"They all paid for the hour."

"It's important we speak with you alone, Mr. Winters," said Sheriff Rhine.

"Let me talk to the guys, make sure they're good with this. You all can go inside. Help yourself to soft drinks."

I didn't know what to make of the fact that he hadn't asked us why we'd come. It would have been my first question.

Rivard led the way into the darkened interior. The room resembled an empty restaurant, a cheap one, with plastic tables and chairs. There was a shellacked counter with a cash register and a display rack of chips and pretzels. Behind it were shelves of ammunition for sale and assorted guns to rent. The log walls were decorated with posters from the National Rifle Association and framed targets, some human-shaped (one resembled Hillary Clinton), riddled with tightly clustered bullet holes.

A question had been nagging at me, and I took the opportunity to confront Rivard about it. "Marc, how come you didn't tell me that one of the girls Tommy stopped that night was Joe Brogan's daughter?"

"Because I knew you and Joe had history," he said sharply. "I knew it would just get you worked up."

The sheriff said, "Are you suggesting, Mike, that we should be looking at Brogan as a suspect?"

"Joe's no murderer!" Rivard said.

"What about that crazy Viking who works for him?" I said. "Billy Cronk?"

The sheriff cleared her throat with great and sudden force.

Winters had appeared in the doorway. His broad shoulders

were backlit by the bright July afternoon. It was only as he stepped inside that I noticed how he lurched when he walked.

"I'm going to sit down, if you don't mind," he said. "God-damn back acts up when I stand too long."

There was absolutely no physical resemblance between father and son. Tommy was the stereotypical ninety-pound weakling. Tim looked like a former powerlifter whose muscles had turned to fat.

"Let's hear it," he said. "What did the kid do now?"

As police, we had been taught how to deliver a proper death notification: which words to use, which words not to use. Never resort to euphemisms, we'd been told. Always emphasize to the recipient that their loved one is dead, deceased, expired so there is zero confusion. People have difficulty accepting the worst.

Rivard removed his hat. "I've got bad news, Tim. I'm afraid Tommy is dead."

The clock on the wall was one of those battery-powered models that loudly ticks off every second.

Winters's voice was flat when he finally spoke. "How'd he do it? How'd he kill himself?"

I did my best to hide my shock at the cold-bloodedness of his reply.

"The medical examiner hasn't yet determined the cause of death," Rhine said, "so we can't say with confidence."

The clock ticked off another twelve seconds.

Winters fidgeted, seemingly bothered by the pain in his back. "You're the Washington County sheriff, correct?"

"Roberta Rhine. I wish we were meeting under better circumstances."

The range master turned his craggy face in my direction next. "And who are you?"

Rivard interjected before I could introduce myself, "This is Warden Bowditch."

I watched for an indication that my name meant something

to Tim Winters, but he didn't so much as blink. He returned his attention to the sheriff. "So where did he do it? Where did he kill himself?"

"His truck went off the dock in Roque Harbor."

"So he drowned, you're saying?"

"It's too soon to tell," said Rhine. "Tommy's on his way to Augusta for an autopsy."

"Is that absolutely necessary?"

"An autopsy is legally required when the cause of death isn't immediately apparent."

"I suppose I have to go down there to identify him."

"That won't be necessary. I can show you a photograph." She produced her cell phone, brought up the pictures she'd taken on the wharf, but hesitated before she handed the device to Winters.

"Yeah, that's him."

"Was your son depressed recently?"

"Depressed? Of course he was depressed. His life was shit."

Once more, I bit my tongue. Amazingly, I felt offended on behalf of the young man who'd stolen my identity.

"In what way was his life shit?" Rhine asked.

Winters counted the reasons on his fingers. "He got kicked out of high school for being a Peeping Tom. He couldn't keep a job. He was still a virgin, as far as I know. He wanted to join the army but failed the GED three times. Do you know how severely stupid you have to be to do that?"

I tried to remind myself that anger was a fairly common reaction to news of a suicide. Of all human emotions, grief is the most protean. It can take a thousand different forms.

The sheriff said, "Do you remember Tommy acting differently recently?"

"The kid was always different. 'Special,' his mother said. She always made excuses for his failures."

"Did Tommy use drugs, Mr. Winters?" Rhine asked.

"I wouldn't know. Probably. Half the kids his age are druggies. More than half."

"Did he own a gun?" the sheriff said.

"Smith & Wesson .357 Mag. Couldn't shoot with it for shit. He was scared of the recoil."

"Did he ever dress in army fatigues?" Rhine asked. "Or own any police gear?"

Beads of perspiration popped from the pores on the man's forehead. "You're welcome to search his bedroom. I left him to himself. I have enough problems of my own."

The sheriff leaned forward. "What kind of vehicle did your son drive, Mr. Winters?"

"Silverado. Green."

"What about money? Did you notice him making any big purchases recently? Items he shouldn't have been able to afford?"

A wet splotch had appeared on the front of Winters's shirt, over his sternum. "I told you the kid couldn't keep a job. What does any of this have to do with him killing himself?"

Rhine drew herself up to full height. "We have reason to believe your son was impersonating a law enforcement officer."

"Is this some kind of joke?"

"Your son was identified by a girl whose car he pulled over, allegedly for speeding. He identified himself to them as a game warden. He did the same to a man whose trailer he robbed."

The range master rubbed his big forearm along his wet brow and shook off the moisture. He slid from the stool. "I need to use the facilities."

None of us spoke as he limped into the next room. We heard a door close and a muffled fan start up.

"He's really lost weight since I last saw him," said Rivard. "Twenty, thirty pounds."

"You're kidding." To my eyes, Tim Winters was borderline obese. I leaned close to the sheriff. "He's really perspiring. More than normal. Have you noticed?"

"I have."

"It's a hot day, for Christ's sake," said Rivard. "And his son just died."

We heard the toilet flush and then water running from a tap.

When Winters reappeared, his forehead and forearms were dry. He seemed to have composed himself in the bathroom. And he had changed his shirt to a polo with the club logo on the front.

An idea must have come into his head while he was cleaning himself up, because he glared at Rivard.

"You're the one who planted the idea in his head. The last time you were here, he grilled you about becoming a game warden, wouldn't stop asking questions."

The sergeant moved the tobacco in his mouth around with his tongue. "I don't remember that."

Rhine reached into her pocket and removed a folded piece of paper. She opened it to reveal a mug shot of a man with eyes like a dog's and a chin bristling with black stubble. The only features Dylan LeBlanc had in common with his cousin Alvin Payne were pointed ears—except that they looked more demonic than elfin on the drug dealer.

"Do you recognize this man?" she said.

Winters accepted the picture from her. "Yeah, I recognize him." "You do?"

"He's come out here to shoot a few times with a couple of guys. Who is he?"

"His name is Dylan LeBlanc, and we believe he's a drug smuggler. You wouldn't happen to know when he was here? Presumably, you had them show identification and sign in."

"April, maybe? I can check my files."

"Do that, please."

Winters disappeared into his office for five minutes. When he returned, he had sign-in sheets with three names from April 24, 26, and 28, none of which belonged to Dylan LeBlanc. "I'm pretty sure this was them. They gave me fake IDs, I'm guessing."

The fact that the men had used aliases didn't seem to surprise Sheriff Rhine. "Do you remember if your son was ever here the same time Mr. LeBlanc was?"

He paused so long it seemed he'd forgotten the question. "Maybe."

"Would Tommy have had an opportunity to talk with Mr. LeBlanc or overhear one of his conversations?"

"I suppose. Tommy worked the register for me a couple of times. And he was always eavesdropping on other people's private discussions. What's this about?"

"Your son stole a significant stash of drugs from an Airstream trailer belonging to a man named Alvin Payne."

Winters laughed. "Tommy didn't have the balls to do something like that!"

Rhine flared her nostrils. "Do you mind my asking you a personal question?"

"Isn't that what you've been doing?"

"Would you like to continue this later after you've had a chance to process what happened to your son? It's not uncommon for people to feel shame when there's a suicide in the family."

"You can stop trying to get in my head, lady."

"Sheriff," I corrected him.

But Winters chose not to acknowledge me. "Yeah, I was ashamed of the kid. Who wouldn't be?"

"But he was your son," I said, unable to hold back.

Winters responded with a harsh laugh that shocked us all into silence.

"How is that funny?" Rhine asked.

"Because he wasn't my son! Biologically, I mean. Karen couldn't have kids, so she convinced me to adopt him. Worst mistake of my life. You adopt a baby, they should tell you whether he's defective. You should be able to return him. Not that Karen would've done it. She made me swear never to tell Tommy he wasn't really ours."

"But you did tell him," I said. "After she died."

Winters gazed at me, his expression searching, his pupils over-large in the unlit room. "How the hell did you know that?"

Because my own father had also been a cruel man, I thought.

⁓

The sheriff and I waited for Winters to finish closing up the shooting range, but Rivard had to leave for a meeting with the Warden Service colonel in Augusta. Marc clearly relished the excuse to sneak off. By leaving, he could forestall an awkward conversation with Rhine about how Tommy Winters had never entered his head as a suspect when we were hunting for the imposter.

The sheriff and I stood in the blistering parking lot. Dog-day cicadas whined in the treetops. The air smelled of pine bark drying to tinder in the sun.

"No wonder the kid killed himself," she said. "With a father like that."

"You're thinking now it was suicide?"

"I didn't before we came here. Now, though?"

Winters emerged from the door with a trash bag full of discarded bullet casings he'd brushed up from the range. He dumped the shells into a steel bin and then padlocked it shut. I wondered how much money the club made from recycling the thousands of cartridges left behind by shooters. The last I'd seen, spent casings were going for a dollar fifty a pound.

The Mustang belonged to Winters. We followed it out to the main road. We had to wait for the range master to close the heavy gate behind our vehicles. The elaborate process involved a bolt, a chain, and a padlock.

It took us half an hour to drive to the village of Aurora, where Winters lived.

I could easily identify the Winters residence by the state police and sheriff's cruisers waiting for us. It was a big clapboard farmhouse with a yawning barn that no longer sheltered livestock. I recognized a K9 team from the Maine Drug Enforcement Agency. The German shepherd had been trained to sniff out narcotics.

Winters pulled the Mustang into the shadows of the barn and came out to meet us, still wearing the .45 on his hip.

Rhine said, "We appreciate your opening your home to us, Mr. Winters."

"I've got nothing to hide."

"All of us want an answer to what happened to Tommy."

"Like I said."

Without Rivard to keep tabs on me, I took the liberty of following the others inside the moldering, old house. The curtains were drawn, and the darkened rooms stank of cigars and uncleaned dishes. Winters led us down to the basement, which smelled even mustier.

Tommy's bed was unmade, the sheets ripe with body odor. There were empty pizza boxes and soda bottles, magazines that weren't pornographic per se but featured female bodybuilders on their covers or babes in leather chaps straddling Harley-Davidsons.

The only noteworthy aspect of the room was the abundance of personal photographs. There were framed pictures on the walls. Others in stands on shelves. All the photos were of the same person: a middle-aged woman with a blond perm, a prominent underbite, and the sunken eyes of someone who rarely enjoyed a full night's rest.

"That's Karen," Winters explained. "My late wife."

Rhine rested her hands on her gun belt. "Would you mind waiting upstairs for us, Mr. Winters? It's difficult to work when there are people crowded around. Why don't you keep him company, Mike?"

I expected Winters to put up a fight. Even though he had expressed a willingness to cooperate, few homeowners are comfortable letting cops poke around their residences. If anything, the man seemed too compliant.

I followed him into the kitchen, where he grabbed a can of Coors from the refrigerator and then went out onto a porch overlooking the woods that had sprung up where the farm fields had once been. He cracked his beer and removed a cigar stub from an ashtray on a table and lit it.

"Did Tommy know anyone who drove a yellow sports car?" I asked.

His reaction was to cough out some smoke. "What kind of question is that?"

"A yellow car seemed to be following him the night he pulled over those girls on Route 9. Did your son have a friend who—"

"Tommy didn't have any friends." He narrowed his eyes. "You sure this yellow car was following him?"

"According to witnesses, it was."

"What witnesses?"

"I'm not allowed to say."

"So he was pretending to be you, huh?"

"It seems that way."

"You ex-military?"

"No."

"I served in Desert Storm. You have the look of a vet."

I'd heard the comment before and had come to the conclusion that killing people in the line of duty had left me with scars visible only to those who had themselves taken the lives of other human beings.

"My father was a Ranger in Vietnam," I said.

He studied me with pupils that had constricted down to mere pinpoints. "And you didn't want to follow in his footsteps?"

"That was the last thing I wanted. But you know how it is—I never asked to be his son."

Winters, I was fairly sure, recognized the jab for what it was. He took a long pull from his beer can. His gaze drifted to the tree line.

"The man your son ripped off," I said. "He's going to want his drugs back. Or he'll want the money Tommy might have made selling them."

"And?"

"He might come out here. Now that he knows your son's real identity. He might expect you to make good on what Tommy stole."

Winters patted the holstered firearm. "Let him come."

"Dylan LeBlanc put his own cousin in the hospital because of the stunt your son pulled."

A trooper appeared on the porch. "Mr. Winters, the sheriff would like to see you."

Back inside we went.

Rhine stood waiting at the top of the stairs. She held a sheet of paper pinched between her gloved fingers. "Is this your son's handwriting?"

The letters were large, blocky, and scrawled in pencil. Even from a distance, I could read the words of the suicide note:

BURY ME NEXT TO MOM.

Standing behind him, I couldn't see Winters's face. But I heard his voice crack when he spoke.

"I need to use the facilities."

~⌐

There was still the open question of what Tommy Winters had done with the opiates he had stolen, but the drug-sniffing dog detected nothing in its search of the house and the property.

I roamed around a bit, made small talk with some of the troopers, tried to stay out of the sun. I peeked in the barn and saw that Winters was in the process of restoring a Trans Am that was scarcely more than a steel shell. The concrete floor was dappled with red paint.

I crossed paths with Rhine again in the driveway. She was

watching the afternoon breeze ruffle the leaves of an ancient elm standing solemnly on the property: the sole survivor of a scourge that had wiped out nearly all of its species.

"So now what happens?" I asked.

"I go back to Machias to type up my report in air-conditioned comfort. And I presume the Warden Service would appreciate you returning to your official duties. On a scorcher like today, you could probably write up a dozen drunk boaters on Gardner Lake—not that I'm telling you what to do."

Instead of following her advice, I made my way back down to Mopang Plantation and drove in on the jeep trail to see if luckless Alvin Payne had returned to live in his Airstream.

I shouldn't have been surprised to find the trailer gone. Payne had been squatting on the land. Following the home invasion, the sheriff's office would have informed the property owner, who, in turn, would have evicted his unwanted tenant and dragged the silvery camper off to an impound lot. The cinnamon ferns and bracken had sprung back so quickly that the impression left by the heavy Airstream was scarcely visible.

I stooped to collect a discarded beer bottle, and that was when I noticed something gold glinting from between the grass blades. The mystery object hadn't been there the night of the home invasion or the searchers would have found it. Someone must have just dropped it in the days since.

It was a pin-on badge. Not even made of metal. Just a cheap piece of plastic I myself had given away on school visits. Imprinted on the front were the words JUNIOR MAINE GAME WARDEN.

⌐

The next morning, just after sunup, I drove out to the Call of the Wild Guide Service and Game Ranch.

Brogan's guides all used the same white monster trucks, but the vehicles owned by the lodge guests tended toward expensive

SUVs that had never been driven off road, plus a handful of sedans representing the pinnacle of Teutonic engineering.

I made my way up the board stairs to the porch. The lobby was "decorated" with the heads of trophies taken at the ranch. There was a red deer, a bison, and a perplexed-looking zebra that should never have been transported to the woods of Maine.

I could hear loud conversation and plates rattling in the adjacent dining room, but there was no receptionist behind the check-in desk. My hand hovered above a bell guests and visitors were expected to ring if they found the lobby empty. I brought my palm down three times in quick secession.

A teenage girl appeared from an adjoining room. She had thick, brown hair that grew low on her forehead, heavy eyebrows, and a mouth that was disconcertingly sensuous in a person so young. She wore a camouflage-print shirt and the annoyed, slightly bored expression that is the default among so many adolescents.

I flashed my best smile. "You must be Reese. I'm Mike Bowditch. I'd like to talk with you about that incident with the fake game warden."

"Everyone's saying he's dead."

"We're still trying to answer some questions about why he did what he did."

"How do I know you're really a game warden?"

"I can show you my badge."

"The freak who stopped us had a badge."

"Mine's not made of plastic." I smiled again, and this time, she smiled back. "I just want to ask you a few questions. There are still a few loose ends we need to wrap up."

"I heard you haven't found those drugs he stole."

"You seem to hear a lot."

"I've got ears." She glanced toward the dining room, then back. "You're the one he was impersonating."

"Yes."

"You don't look like him at all!"

My God, she was flirting with me now.

"The first question I have is about the yellow car you saw the night he stopped you and your friends. Was it your sense that the impersonator—his real name was Tommy Winters—recognized the driver?"

"All I can say is he was scared shitless."

A voice boomed from the staircase leading to the second-floor rooms. "What the hell are you doing here?"

Joe Brogan was not a big man, but he was burly with the calloused hands of a former logger. He had a heavy, brown beard and hair so thick it reminded me of a beaver pelt. He smelled heavily of bug repellent.

"I was just talking to your daughter about Tommy Winters, the man we found dead in Roque Harbor yesterday."

He lowered his bushy eyebrows over his dark eyes. "Does Rivard know you're here? I told him I didn't want to see you around my place."

"I apologize if I've caught you at a bad time," I said.

"There's no good time where you're concerned," Brogan said, closing the distance between us. "Honey, get Sergeant Rivard on the phone."

"Do I have to?" Reese Brogan said. "That guy creeps me out."

Brogan's face turned a deeper shade of red. "What's that?"

"He's always looking at my tits."

"You never told me that!" Joe Brogan glared at me as if I were to blame for my sergeant's lewd behavior. "You game wardens. You call that guy an imposter, but in my book, you're all a bunch of fake cops."

"Just answer me something, Brogan, and then I'll leave you in peace. What would you have done if you'd found out it was Tommy Winters who terrorized Reese?"

"I would've gone over to his house with a baseball bat. Next question?"

⁓

The phone rang before I had driven a mile clear of the game ranch. It was Rivard.

"The autopsy came back," he said. "Tommy Winters had seawater in his lungs. He also had scratches on his abdomen and blood under his nails where he tried to get the lap belt off. He must have had second thoughts at the end."

"Survival is an animal impulse," I said.

"Has anyone ever told you that you have an odd way of putting things?"

I'd set the toy badge on my center console. Was that why Tommy had chosen to impersonate a game warden and not a deputy or some other kind of cop? That silly piece of plastic?

"Have you told Tim Winters yet?"

"Rhine tried but couldn't get him on his landline or cell. He's probably still sleeping off a drunk. Not that I blame the SOB."

I cruised along. "Marc, there's been something bothering me. I'm still puzzled why Tommy Winters chose me of all people to impersonate when we had no connection. You wouldn't have happened to mention my name when you were at the Narraguagus Sporting Club?"

"Why would I have mentioned your name?" he said at last.

"I have no idea."

In fact, I could easily imagine my sergeant bitching about the troublesome new warden he'd been assigned.

"It's a mistake trying to get in the minds of nutcases. Listen, I've got another call coming in." He paused to check the number. "Christ, it's Joe Brogan. What does he want?"

I could only imagine.

Without really making a decision, I started west toward Aurora.

I made a pass by the Winters house, but the Mustang wasn't in the driveway or parked inside the shadow-webbed barn. Maybe Tim had run off to the corner store for another case of Coors and another box of Montecristo cigars.

My phone rang again as I was driving home to Washington County. I feared it was Rivard calling to lambaste me for visiting the Call of the Wild. Instead, it was Reese Brogan.

"I wasn't completely honest about everything before," she said. "I kind of know who the driver of the yellow car was. I didn't recognize him, but later I found out it was this guy named Luke Merrill."

"From Roque Harbor?"

"I don't know where he lives. I heard he was passing by and saw there was something fishy going on. I heard he chased the fake warden and forced his truck off the road and beat the shit out of him."

"What about the yellow car?"

"He was just test-driving it. He was gonna buy it off some dude selling it on Craigslist, I heard. If you talk to Luke, please don't tell him it was me who gave you his name. My friends say he's got a wicked temper."

I promised her I wouldn't. "What made you decide to call me, Reese?"

"I was wondering if you had a girlfriend."

⁓

My next stop was Roque Harbor. I had a few questions about Luke Merrill.

As I passed the boat launch, I saw a trio of kayakers floating in the approximate area where Tommy Winters's truck had settled. The paddlers were peering into the turquoise water, trying to catch a glimpse of the still submerged vehicle.

I pulled up outside the low, weathered building where the lobstermen bought their fuel and hung out before and after their long days on the water. I parked beside a line of rust-pitted pickups and entered through the bay doors of the fishermen's co-op.

The room was unlit except for the sun shining in at the edges, and it smelled of salt water and the seaweed used to pack live lobsters into crates for shipment to exotic destinations.

From the dark, a voice exclaimed, "Well, if it isn't the dead man!"

I squinted and saw Twelve-Gauge Gaynor sitting at a card table with several other men.

"Hello again," I said.

"Heard you identified the Great Pretender?"

"Word travels fast," I said.

Gaynor smiled, showing off coffee-stained teeth. "We've got our sources. Also heard it was a suicide."

I pretended not to register the last part. "Is Luke Merrill around?"

"He's still out hauling. Should be back before dark. Whatcha looking for him for?"

"Which boat is his?" I said.

"The *Sweet Caroline*," Gaynor answered, his smile gone now, his tone flat.

There was another silence, this one even longer.

"Which boat is really Luke's?" I said.

From behind me a voice said, "*Miss Conduct.*"

It was Merrill. He'd been eavesdropping from the kitchenette. Now the tall young man came striding across the wet floor. He had blond scruff, a deep tan that probably ended above his short sleeves, and hair pressed down from wearing a baseball cap all day.

"How about we step outside?" I said.

"We can talk here," he said. "These guys are just going to gossip about us, anyway."

I shrugged. "You were the driver of the yellow car, the one who chased down Tommy Winters on Route 9."

"I never knew his name before today. But yeah, that was me. I knew he wasn't no warden, and I was worried he might try to molest those girls. I caught up with him and set him straight."

"With your fists?"

"No, I persuaded him with my silver tongue. You just said the guy offed himself. What's this really about?"

"The drugs he stole are still missing."

"And you think I know where they are?" He let out a rasping laugh. "Look, man, as far as I'm concerned, I performed a heroic act, beating the shit out of that gimp."

"You wouldn't happen to know Dylan LeBlanc, would you?"

"I might've heard the name."

"You don't know him personally?"

He studied me, then raised a finger to one nostril and expelled a snot rocket onto the floor. "If that's all you've got for questions, I've got shit to do."

He stepped through the bay doors into the sunlight. I watched him climb into a black Camaro. He revved the engine long enough for the noise to echo through the co-op. Then he peeled out.

"Well, that went well," Gaynor said.

I turned to the old man and found him grinning at me with ocher teeth.

Somehow, by having been the unwitting victim of Tommy Winters's criminal prank and therefore a part of local lore, I had gained admission into Roque Harbor's exclusive community.

"You understand why I'm taking a personal interest in this thing."

"Luke and his brother don't have half a brain between them."

Another old salt piped up from the shadows. "I know Tim Winters. Never met that son, though. Heard about him enough."

"What did you hear?"

"How he couldn't keep a job and wouldn't move out. Every week, Tim had a new complaint about the boy. The day my son received a Bronze Star—everyone was buying me drinks at the range—Winters was so sour, I asked him what his problem was. He said he envied me, having a son who was a hero."

"Sounds like my old man, may he rot in peace," said one of the others. "Where did you say this Winters works again?"

"The Narraguagus Sporting Club over on Route 9," said the old salt.

"Never saw the point in paying to shoot a gun when I can practice on gulls all day," said the other lobsterman. "What about you, Twelve-Gauge? You ever shot at that range? Oh, that's right. You and firearms don't get along so good."

The other men broke into rough laughter.

"Come on, Twelve-Gauge," one of them said, "show the warden."

Gaynor reached down the length of his pants to his knee. "The only reason I'm doing this, you understand, is to shut up these sons of whores."

The lobsterman removed his rubber boot, revealing a stockinged foot that seemed somehow wrong in shape. He rolled down the sock to show the prosthetic that helped him to walk in lieu of his missing toes.

"My old man always said I ought to have taken a hunter safety course before I went chasing deer with a twelve-gauge shotgun," he said with a stained smile.

⁓

I ate my bag lunch on the raised causeway outside downtown Machias. Locals called it "the Dike." During the summer, antiques vendors, basket weavers, even a doughnut maker set up a little market there along Route 1. Tourists drifted from booth to booth. The festivity of the scene reminded me, strangely enough, of the events the prior morning in Roque Harbor, when the entire town came out to watch the recovery of a drowned body.

My cell phone rang as I was inspecting my teeth in the rearview mirror.

I didn't recognize the voice. "You don't know me, but I was shooting at the Narraguagus Sporting Club yesterday afternoon. My name is Pete Rawson."

The dapper pistolero.

"What can I do for you, Mr. Rawson?"

"I'm outside the gate now. I decided to drive over here because I thought there was a chance that Tim might have come back to work. He hangs out at the club constantly and, well, I wanted to give him my condolences."

"So what's wrong?"

"When I got here, I found the gate locked. The thing is, Tim has a particular way of wrapping the chain and locking the padlock to keep someone from driving through the gate. We had a break-in a couple of years ago, and some guns were stolen. The thieves dragged away an entire gun safe."

Now that Rawson mentioned it, I remembered the care Winters had taken securing the gate behind us.

"Doesn't anyone else have a key?"

"Just Bill Day, but he's off in Yellowstone. I'm worried about Tim."

He didn't need to say more than that.

"Just stay outside the gate until I get there."

I didn't really believe that an anguished Tim Winters had returned to the shooting range to take his own life. More likely, he had driven there—possibly drunk—because he had nowhere else to go. In his impaired state, he had probably failed to lock the gate behind him in his usual meticulous fashion. And yet, I couldn't be certain about any of these suppositions.

I started the engine, flipped on my blue lights, and sped off in the direction of the Narraguagus Sporting Club.

Twenty minutes later, I found Peter Rawson standing along the road outside the shooting range: a trim, silver-coiffed man wearing a black polo and black slacks. I skidded to a dusty halt behind his SUV.

"Show me the lock and chain," I said.

Even from a distance, I could see how lazily the gate had been secured.

Rawson kept up a running monologue while I made my examination. "I was sad to hear about Tommy. He worked for me for a while—it was a favor to Tim—but I couldn't keep him on. His registers never added up at shift's end. And he was inappropriate with some of my female customers."

I glanced up. "Where did he work for you?"

"I own some hardware stores. Tommy worked in my Ellsworth location."

"You don't happen to sell honey buckets?"

"Yes. Why?"

Because Rawson's store was another possible point of connection between Tommy and Dylan LeBlanc. It offered an explanation why the warden imposter had known to look for the drugs under Alvin Payne's bucket latrine when he learned of its existence. Tommy might very well have sold the portable toilet to the smuggler himself.

I returned to my truck, removed my tactical shotgun from behind the seat, and locked the doors.

"What's with the firepower?" Rawson asked.

"Suicidal people can be unpredictable."

"The sad thing is Tim seemed to be happier lately, almost giddy at times. After all the bad luck he's had in his life. The fall he took at the mill really did a job on his spine and pelvis. He was in traction for months. When he came to work here, you could see the pain it caused him to take even a few steps. Then Karen died, of course."

"What do you mean 'giddy'?"

"He's always been so intense. Never cracked a smile. Lately, though, he's been so mellow. I swear I heard him giggle the other day."

Sudden weight loss, constricted pupils, violent mood swings.

I vaulted the gate. "Wait here!"

The driveway down to the shooting range was lined with trees. I kept stepping from patches of light into shadow and back again. I was hot, then cold, then hot until finally the sun disappeared once and for all behind the towering pines. The sweat beneath my duty vest turned icy. I started shivering as if I'd just crawled up from the frigid waters of Roque Harbor.

There were two new sets of tire prints on the road, overlapping the marks we'd made leaving the range earlier.

I recognized one set of tracks. The vehicle was rear-wheel drive and had made frequent trips onto and off the property. They had to have been left by Winters's Mustang.

The muscle car had driven down this road recently. But it hadn't yet returned.

It was the other set of tracks that worried me.

They had been made by a larger, heavier vehicle: a half-ton pickup or SUV built on a truck platform. These prints clearly showed that someone had entered the club and then exited. My working theory was that it was the driver of this unknown vehicle who had carelessly locked the gate after he'd left.

Adrenaline made the blood tingle in my arteries. I pumped a shell filled with buckshot into the action of my shotgun.

Winters's Mustang was parked oddly. It was neither in a designated spot nor parallel to the front of the building. The haphazard position of the car suggested the range master had been in a rush.

I approached the screen door and saw that the heavier door behind it was standing open.

"Mr. Winters?" I called.

There was no answer.

I stepped into the darkened interior. "Tim?"

I padded softly into the big room with the humming soft drink cooler and the list of guns for rent and the framed targets. The clock ticked off the seconds.

A soft breeze sighed through the screen door that led to the shooting range. The air smelled of sunburned grass and resinous pine cones.

I stepped outside and came to a halt at the first stall. I stared over the shooting bench before me, past the first set of bull's-eyes, to the distant rifle targets. There, bent over the wooden rack used to secure the paper targets, lay the bloody body of Tim Winters.

Someone had used him for shooting practice.

Winters had been duct-taped to the wooden trestle, facing the club building so he could see the man or men aiming at him. There were nonfatal gunshot wounds to his arms and shoulders. And one to the pelvis he had shattered at the paper mill.

The fatal shot was a red hole the size of a dime in the center of his forehead.

I backed away from the dead man, called the dispatcher on my cell, and told him what I had found.

Afterward, I made a circle around the outside of the club-house. From this angle, I realized why Winters had parked his Mustang where he had. He'd hoped to keep the locked bin of gun cartridges from being noticed by whomever had forced him to drive here: presumably Dylan LeBlanc and his cronies, searching for their missing narcotics.

But Winters's willpower had given out under the pain of being shot and shot again.

The doors of the bin stood open. Thousands of brass cartridges had spilled onto the dirt. It was here he must have hidden the drugs Tommy Winters had stolen for the man he'd called his father.

Skin and Bones

I

It had snowed the night before, just a trace, but now the sky was a deep blue, and a faint breeze was blowing powder off the boughs of the pines. Spellbound by the glitter in the air, I slowed my patrol truck and thought how it might have seemed to someone more innocent than myself—a small girl, perhaps—as if I had happened upon a piece of fairyland in the North Maine Woods. Then the moment passed, and my real-world anger returned.

I had come on a mission to the house of my friend.

Before he'd retired from the Warden Service as chief warden pilot, Charley Stevens had patrolled districts all over the state, including the same western mountains where I had grown up. The crafty geezer was still the best woodsman I knew, which is why I had brought my problem to him.

His old hunting dog Nimrod, having recognized the sound of my truck, came limping down the shoveled steps, wagging his tail.

Charley was nearing seventy now, but he shared none of the elderly animal's stiffness. He was just as wiry and vigorous as he'd been as a young game warden, people said. He still had a full head of hair (white where it had once been brown), a handsomely weathered face that culminated in an oversize chin, and a perpetual squint—as if he couldn't help but view this broken world of ours with skeptical amusement. His hands were huge and rough from splitting firewood, and he just about crushed mine in a welcoming grip.

"To what do I owe the pleasure?" he asked in a thick Maine accent.

I gestured with my thumb toward the back of my battered GMC pickup. "I need your professional opinion."

I was wearing my winter uniform: black knit cap, green parka over black snow pants, and insulated boots made by L.L.Bean especially for game wardens. The hem of the coat had a zip to allow quick access to my service weapon. Keep in mind I was only three years on the job—"greener than a sprout" in Charley's words—and expected every license check to end in a shoot-out.

Charley peered into the truck bed, and his grin vanished so fast he seemed to become someone else entirely: a strange and dangerous man.

Snow from the evergreens had fallen upon the dead eagle as I'd driven through the forest, and it had coated its feathers. The bird was powdered sugary white, except for the rust-red crystals where the bullet had shattered the bones in its wing.

"Where did you get him, Mike?" Charley asked without unlocking his gaze from the frozen raptor.

My hot breath showed in the air. "In a cedar swamp on the north end of Third Machias Lake."

"Where the stream comes in?"

"That's the place. I got an anonymous call that an ice fisherman had shot him at dusk for no reason at all."

"Boredom, I expect," said Charley. "Boredom and meanness. The bird was hanging around the ice shacks because the fishermen were feeding him chubs and such. And then one of the anglers decided drinking beer and watching trip flags wasn't enough of a thrill for him. But the son of a biscuit only winged the eagle, and he wouldn't go chasing after it in that dense puckerbrush."

He was correct in every detail. I didn't ask how he'd deduced this sequence of events. His mind could always find a path to the truth, whatever tangle of questions he faced.

"My informant was offended enough to call me but not so offended that he would share his buddy's name. He said it bothered him, as a veteran, to see our national symbol treated so disrespectfully."

"I wouldn't judge the man too harshly. The sight of an eagle always moves me, too, and not just on account of its magnificence."

My friend had been a pilot and a POW in Vietnam, I had to remember.

"The bald eagle also happens to be a federally endangered species," I said (which at the time it was). "I looked up the punishment for killing one—a maximum five years in prison and a two-hundred-fifty-thousand-dollar fine."

A pileated woodpecker passed overhead, rising and falling as they do on the wing. Charley followed the red-crested bird with his eyes. "What's your game plan, Warden Bowditch?"

"After I pass the eagle off to a biologist, I'm going to tear apart the ice-fishing camp on Third Machias. Want to join me, kicking down doors?"

He gave me a look of fatherly forbearance. "Your shooter won't be there, you know."

"What should I do, then, Charley?"

"Stoking that anger inside you won't help catch the bastard. Take it from me, young feller." He pulled thoughtfully on his chin. "What sort of man shoots an eagle for sport, would you say?"

"An evil one."

"What sort of man shoots an eagle for sport but won't claim his trophy if it means getting scratched up and wet in a beaver bog?"

For once, I wished he wouldn't play Socrates with me.

"A lazy and cowardly one. He was probably drunk, as you said, and got out his rifle on impulse. But after he shot the bird, he had second thoughts. Maybe his buddies laid into him for being an idiot. I bet he didn't stay long at the camp."

Charley nodded his approval of my reasoning. "Do you really think he'll be there tonight?"

"No."

"Which means what?"

"I identify the regulars at Third Machias, and then I spy on the shacks to find out which of them is missing."

(This was, in fact, how I later apprehended the shooter.)

My gaze returned to the dead bird. Beneath its crystalline shroud, it looked less like a formerly living creature than a macabre sculpture. My gloved hand moved of its own volition to brush the powder off its hooked yellow beak.

"In all your years as a warden, did you ever see something this awful?"

The old pilot tensed beside me, enough that his dog noticed and drew close to his leg for a reassuring pat on the head.

"Charley?"

"I've seen something . . . similar."

"What happened?"

He took a step back and tucked his bare hands inside his snowmobile bibs. "I don't know as it would be wise to tell you the story."

"Why not?"

He considered my question a long time. A fresh gust filled the dooryard with shimmering snow particles that no longer seemed magical.

"Because it involved a man by the name of Jack Bowditch," he said finally.

"My father? He shot an eagle?"

"You know your dad was a poacher, the most cunning and elusive poacher I ever chased. But Jack never killed a critter that he didn't eat or give away to someone hungry. He wasn't Robin Hood—we both know that—but he followed his own code, I guess you'd say. Jack was like a lot of combat vets I've known; he thought the system was rotten, and laws were just excuses fat cats made up to keep poor people down. I don't know as he believed in God, but he believed in justice, however queerly he defined it. And he felt almost a compulsion to deliver it himself."

This preamble could only mean my father had done something despicable. I had spent most of my life in childish denial about my dad's capacity for violence. Then, several years earlier, Jack Bowditch had led the Maine State Police on the biggest manhunt in its history, and I had been forced to let go of my innocence—or so I'd thought.

"What did he do, Charley? I deserve to know the truth."

"It's not what he did. It's what I did, too."

These words, coming from the mouth of my trusted mentor, sent a chill through me. "I don't understand."

He glanced at the house in the pines. The face of his wife, Ora, showed in the front window. She was a woman of high morals whose conscience Charley relied on when his own failed him.

"Let's go inside for this," he said. "It's a story better told in its entirety and by the fire. But I should warn you first."

"Warn me of what?"

"You might not like how it ends."

2

Twenty-three years earlier, Charley was driving home after a long day checking ice-fishing licenses on Spencer Lake when a pickup came roaring up behind him, as if the driver were intent on ramming his tailgate and forcing him off the frozen road.

Such an attack was not unthinkable. The game warden, being good at his job, had collected more than his share of enemies, and this stretch of the Lower Enchanted Road, lined with old-growth pines, was a prime spot for an ambush, especially after dark. But panic was an alien emotion to Charley Stevens, who had flown O-1 Bird Dogs through fusillades of AK-47 rounds.

He had his snowmobile in the bed of his truck, the weight of which limited his maneuverability. He downshifted, pressed his brake pedal gently, and turned on his hazards for good measure, coming to a smooth, slow stop.

The truck behind him braked too fast, slid, and swerved on the ice. It only came to rest when its front bumper kissed Charley's tow hitch. The proximity of the two pickups prevented the high beams of the pursuer from shining into the warden's cab; hazy light merely leaked from between the vehicles. Even so, Charley was taking no chances. He slid across the bench seat and popped quietly out the passenger door between the truck and the snowbank.

He crouched alongside his bed and listened to his pursuer exit his own pickup and advance, crunching on the snow. He was headed toward the driver's window of the patrol truck.

Charley snuck around both vehicles (he recognized the battered Ford F-150 at once) and emerged onto the road with his revolver drawn, while the man who had been chasing him stared in confusion into the empty cab. The tall, broad-shouldered silhouette matched the owner of the Ford.

"Something I can do for you, Jack?"

The response was the last thing the warden expected from the man, a known poacher and bar brawler. Instead of spinning around with a drawn handgun, Jack Bowditch broke into laughter.

"That's one hell of a trick, Charley. You mind if I borrow it?"

"Just as long as you don't try it on me."

The lightness in his voice disguised his wariness. Like himself, Bowditch had seen combat in Vietnam—assigned to the 101st Airborne, then two tours with the Rangers doing long-range reconnaissance—before a grenade explosion sent him home with a Purple Heart. Charley Stevens knew better than to assume anything around a man who'd done and seen that much killing.

"While you're back there," Jack said, shaking a cigarette out of a pack of Marlboros, "have a look in my truck bed."

Charley shifted his eyes to see an oblong object swaddled in a blanket. His first, errant impression was of a mummified tomcat.

Bowditch was close enough now that Charley could see him clearly in the vehicular light. Ora claimed Jack was the handsomest man in three counties. Blue eyes blazed out of a deeply tanned face, and even his beard, which started just below his cheekbones, couldn't hide the strength of his jaw. He stood half a foot taller than Charley and was dressed in oil-stained canvas and denim work clothes that smelled now of the glandular lures he concocted to bait his bobcat, mink, and fox traps.

"Unwrap it," he said.

Charley holstered his pistol. "I've never cared about opening presents—to the deep disappointment of my girls."

"How are Anne and Stacey?"

The fact that Jack knew the names of his young daughters put Charley back on his guard. It was a power play. The warden knew Bowditch had a wife and son but was frustrated he couldn't recall their names.

He tilted his chin at the bundle. "What do you have for me that's so important you nearly killed us both in a collision?"

Bowditch reached into the Flareside bed, drew out the mystery object, and, kneeling, set it on the frozen road. Carefully, he peeled away the layers until he had uncovered the largest bald eagle Charley had ever seen. With raptors, the females are almost always larger than the males, both men knew.

"I measured her before she froze up," said Jack, speaking with the cigarette in his mouth. There was bourbon on his breath as well as tobacco, just a hint of alcoholic sweetness. "Three feet tall. Wingspan of seven feet and change. I'd estimate the weight at sixteen pounds. That bird's what you might call an impressive physical specimen."

The cause of death was evident: The eagle had been shot through one eye.

Small-caliber bullet, judging by the entry hole. Probably a .22 Long Rifle. Poachers preferred the caliber.

"I didn't shoot it, in case you wondered."

"I didn't figure you did, being as you were so eager to show it to me."

Unless someone saw him do it, Charley thought. And he wanted to get ahead of the gossip.

"I'm not spinning you, Stevens," Bowditch said, as if he had sensed the accusation.

"I believe you, Jack."

The admission seemed to catch the man by surprise. "You do?"

"I also expect you have a notion of who committed the crime."

"Why's that?"

"For one, you ended up with the carcass. For another, there's not much people do in these woods that you don't hear about. What I can't square is why you came to me with the evidence."

Bowditch flicked away the still-burning cigarette. It seemed to explode on the road. "What do you mean?"

"Instead of confronting the man yourself."

"Because it's a public crime!" Working himself into a state of anger was never a problem for Jack Bowditch. "Yeah, I take it personally. But you're an officer of the law, Stevens. If you can't deal with this, then what fucking good are you?"

Charley stood with his feet apart and rested his hands on his gun belt. "So who shot her?"

"A scrawny, no-good piece of shit named Tim Grindle. You must know the kid and his asshole brother?"

Charley did indeed.

Tim Grindle was sixteen or seventeen and had lived with his much older brother, Ed, since their parents had died in a motorcycle crash. Charley knew the Grindle brothers professionally, in that he'd had cause to arrest them both for separate yet equally reprehensible crimes.

Tim, the younger brother, was a poaching prodigy who refused to purchase a hunting or fishing license. He had never taken a deer in season or during the day, used a makeshift trident to illegally spear redhorse suckers on their spring spawning runs, set a wire snare for a coyote that had instead strangled a beagle before her owner could loosen the bloody garrote from around his pet's throat.

Ed, the older brother, was a big blob of a man whose pastimes were model trains, drinking beers by the case, and terrorizing his scrawny sibling. If he received a sunburn from float-tubing shirtless down the Dead River, Ed took it out on Tim. If his truck got a flat tire, Ed took it out on Tim. If it rained on his day off, Ed made Tim pay for the uncooperative weather.

3

The boy would show up at school—back when he bothered showing up at school—and claim his cuts and bruises, sprains, and breaks were from rock climbing.

No one had ever seen Tim Grindle climb so much as a chain-link fence.

Having visited Ed's house on several occasions and stopped him once when he was weaving all over Route 16, Charley had come to believe the older brother had no personal animus against the younger one. He was just a violent SOB, and Tim was unlucky to be close at hand. The warden even harbored a controversial and unprovable belief that the brothers secretly cared for each other.

A few light flakes of snow began to fall, gray as ash against the darkening sky.

"Tell me why you suspect Grindle shot this eagle," he said to Jack Bowditch.

"Aside from his history of doing shit like this?"

"I need concrete proof."

"How about this, then?" he said. "Two weeks ago, I was snow-shoeing over Bates Ridge when I came upon a set of lynx tracks. I'd seen plenty of bobcat prints down in the valley, but you know how rare lynx are, and so I decided to follow them, and I came upon that Grindle kid setting a leghold trap. I crept closer and closer while he went about his business until I was near enough to jab him with the butt of my rifle. He just about jumped out of his skin when I said, 'Boo!'"

"What did he say he was doing?" Charley asked. "Trapping bobcat?"

Bowditch removed a flask from the pocket of his jacket, unconcerned the warden might question his sobriety to drive a motor vehicle. "That's where you're wrong. He knows my reputation, and he wasn't going to lie to me. He said, 'I got a buyer for rare critters. The harder to get, the better. He paid me two hundred bucks for a frigging spruce grouse. You want to partner up to catch a lynx and split the bounty?'"

Charley said, "I take it you declined."

"If you mean I told him to go to hell—then, yeah."

"So you think an eagle was on his shopping list, too?"

"Both are endangered."

"But did you see Grindle actually shoot the bird?"

Jack took a pull from his flask. "Didn't need to. I know it was him."

"How?"

"I was over at Grand Falls this morning when I heard a gunshot downstream. When I found that eagle, it was still warm. The kid must've spotted the bird across the river. Only problem was, the water's open, and he couldn't cross without going miles around."

"Like I said before, I'm surprised you didn't confront the boy yourself."

"This is our fucking national bird. I figured that the serious nature of the offense warranted arrest by the Warden Service."

And you probably feared you'd hurt the kid, Charley thought.

More than one cop had described Tim Grindle to him as having a "punchable" face. Some teenage boys thought a smug expression made them look tough when all it ever brought was trouble. Tim was one of those perpetual truants that the school stops chasing because the administration doesn't want him around.

"You think I'm lying to you," said Bowditch. "You don't think I'm capable of being a responsible citizen."

Charley was at pains not to reveal his honest response. *No, I don't.*

Again, Bowditch seemed to sniff out the warden's disdain. "Well, maybe this will convince you."

He yanked off his canvas jacket and flung it to the snow. He rolled up the sleeve of his flannel shirt and pushed up the thermal beneath to expose a tattoo on his forearm. It was the Screaming Eagle insignia of the 101st Airborne Division. A white scar of the same vintage ran across the beak. Charley recalled that his fellow veteran had the Ranger insignia inked on his other arm.

"This is a sacred animal to me," said Bowditch. "I'd no more shoot one of these birds than I would a guy in my platoon."

The snow was now swirling all around them.

"You were right to bring this to me, Jack," said the warden. "Consider yourself relieved of your burden."

But Bowditch would not be relieved. "Well, what are you going to do?"

The snow showers would obscure the prints of whoever shot the eagle, if they hadn't already. And Tim Grindle knew to retrieve his spent rifle casings while poaching. The shot through the eye was a through-and-through, meaning there was no slug to match to a rifle barrel. There would be, in other words, no hard evidence to connect young Tim with the crime. The kid certainly wasn't going to confess. But Charley had ways of teasing the truth out of overconfident criminals.

"The Grindles live across Flagstaff Pond from me," he said. "I'll make a pit stop on my way home."

Bowditch squatted down and snatched up his coat. He shook the snow off it. "I'm coming with you."

"That wouldn't be advisable, Jack."

"I need to hear him admit what he did."

"The boy won't admit anything if he's being threatened."

Bowditch shrugged his coat on, still clutching the flask. "Maybe that's because you don't know how to properly threaten someone."

Charley felt his own anger rising. "If you follow me, I'll be obliged to radio Sheriff Hatch and say I need one of his deputies to help with a potential drunk driving arrest."

Again, Bowditch went silent. There was something wolfish about the intensity of his stare. The man was a natural-born killer, bound only loosely by the fetters of conscience, Charley told himself.

"Maybe you do know how to threaten someone after all," Jack said, grinning. "All right, I won't follow you. I want to know what he says, though."

Charley nodded.

He let Bowditch drive out of the woods ahead of him. When they reached the hardtop of Route 201, a snow squall was blowing, and they both turned south toward civilization. Charley kept Jack's brake lights in sight until the other man pulled into the parking lot of the Solon Hotel. The bar there was infamous for its brawls. He pitied the luckless, unsuspecting saloon-goer upon whom Jack Bowditch might take out his rage tonight.

4

It pained Charley to pass the camp road leading to his home on Flagstaff Pond. He'd hoped to kiss his daughters good night before Ora tucked them in. Having been married to a game warden for more than half a dozen years, she rarely, if ever, waited up for her husband. Most of their breakfast conversations consisted of Charley recounting his adventures and misadventures of the night prior.

The snow squalls had left the Flagstaff Road as pale and greasy as lard.

His destination was a place called Pickle Hill. He'd read that it had been named for its shape, but he'd never seen the resemblance to a gherkin, and in the darkness and blowing snow, he had no view of it.

The Grindles lived halfway up the north slope. Whoever had constructed their house had managed to find a property that spent the entire year in shadow. Even during the spring solstice, the home remained untouched and unblessed by the sun. Patches of ice lingered in the dooryard through the summer like the harbinger of some new glacial age.

Security lights flicked on as Charley crept up the hill. The bulbs cast a bluish-white light across the scene, making it seem even colder. He thought of the autopsy room in the state medical examiner's building. A wall of cordwood ran along the driveway, and woodsmoke hung in the air.

The house was one of those drive-under designs, built into the hillside with the living quarters up top, and the elder Grindle parked his truck inside the first-floor garage. There were no tire prints to suggest he had driven out that night. Ed's and Tim's sleds were both parked in the dooryard beneath fresh sheets of snow.

A dog began to bark ferociously inside the house. Charley touched the canister of pepper spray on his belt for reassurance. He had a way with watchdogs, but some animals could not be sweet-talked.

As he took a tentative step out of his vehicle, a door opened on the second floor, and a Doberman came flying down the external stairs as if unbound by gravity. It had nearly reached him when it crumpled in midair and fell, whimpering, to the ground. Only then did Charley breathe, and only then did he notice the shock collar around the dog's throat.

Ed Grindle emerged onto the second-story deck holding the remote control in one hand and a can of Bud Light in the other. He wore a train engineer's cap and a camo-colored vest over his usual sweat clothes. For all his bulk, the man possessed the deceptive strength that can come by way of compensation to heavyset people whose every movement is equivalent to lifting hundred-pound weights. Ed hadn't yet reached the age of thirty, but his stubble was all gray, in stark contrast to his wavy black hair.

"What do you want?" he asked in a voice made hoarse by beer and cigarettes.

"You've got a new pet, I see. What happened to your Akita?"

"Ran off. Got hit by the plow truck. What do you want?"

"I was hoping to speak with your brother."

"What did he do now?"

"Nothing!" said a voice.

Tim Grindle peeked out of the garage's side door. Charley recollected a rumor that the boy chose to sleep down in that unheated, subterranean space so he could sneak in and out of the house. He wondered now if the purpose of the watchdog wasn't to frighten off intruders but to alert Ed to his brother's attempted escapes.

The young poacher looked even worse than Jack had described him: nothing but skin and bones. His unwashed hair, as black as his brother's, was so slick and stiff it might have been sculpted with axle grease.

"Where were you today, Tim?" Charley asked.

"Why?"

"Answer the warden's question!" Ed said.

The younger brother crept outside in his buckskin moccasins to soothe the anxious Doberman. He wore only loose jeans and a flannel shirt that accentuated his scarecrow physique. "Where I was today ain't none of his business."

"Yeah, but it's my business as long as you live under my roof. The man is here for a reason, dipstick. What did you kill today? Another beagle?"

"Not a goddamn thing!" Tim unfastened the shock collar from around the Doberman's throat.

Ed waited until his brother had the device in hand before he hit the button.

Tim's arm spasmed, and he flung the collar reflexively into the air. "Fuck!"

Just then, Charley heard a truck creeping up behind him. He didn't need to turn to know it was Jack Bowditch.

"Shit," Ed rumbled from above. "What does *he* want?"

Charley stepped away from his truck so that he could keep all the parties in view. His mind was plotting out half a dozen scenarios he could see unfolding, most of which would end in violence.

He made what he knew was a vain appeal. "Get back in your truck, Jack. You left this to me, remember?"

But Bowditch had turned his predator's stare on Tim Grindle. "I found the eagle, kid! I took it before you could cross the river. I bet you wondered where it went."

Tim looked blank.

Charley noted the boy's lack of expression.

"Hey there, Jack," said Ed in a voice that was intended to sound friendly but instead communicated fear.

Grindle outweighed Bowditch by a hundred and fifty pounds, if not more. And unlike most men his size who relied on body mass and brute strength to subdue opponents, Ed knew how to throw a punch. Even so, Jack had beaten the giant into bloody unconsciousness not once but twice at the Red Stallion.

"Your brother shot a bald eagle."

"I didn't!" said Tim with convincing astonishment. "I was with my girl all day. She'll swear I was. She don't lie."

Jack had advanced as far as the snarling Doberman, which he ignored with such reckless self-confidence it left Charley feeling almost envious.

"The bird's in the warden's truck if you want to come down and have a look, Ed."

"Damn right I do!"

Meanwhile, Tim Grindle had backed toward the fir trees at the edge of the lighted yard. His hollow eyes were wide enough to see the whites around the irises. His Adam's apple was pulsing up and down as if he were trying in vain to swallow an actual apple.

The dog whined as Ed's massive shadow fell across its flanks.

Charley knew that whatever hopes he had of tricking Tim Grindle into admitting his crime were gone. Now he had an explosive situation to defuse.

"Let's take this down a notch, gents."

But he might as well have been a ghost, unseeable and unhearable.

Jack reached brazenly into Charley's passenger seat and produced the swaddled bird. He cradled it with the care he might have shown his own young son. He peeled back the edge of the blanket to reveal the golden beak.

"Damn, that's a big one," said Ed. "And my brother shot it, you say?"

"I saw him do it," lied Jack Bowditch.

A thin voice cried from across the yard, "Ed! Ed! I swear he's lying."

The big man stepped back, bumping the woodpile the Grindles had stacked against the coming winter. Too late, Charley saw him snatch up a length of birch and whip it, with astonishing accuracy, thirty feet across the dooryard.

The log caught Tim Grindle in the chest. There was a loud crack, and the boy fell limply to the ground.

When Charley saw Ed grab two more pieces of hardwood, he hurled himself onto the man. He knew pressure points in the wrist and elsewhere that would cause a person debilitating pain. But Ed Grindle was so layered with fat that none of the warden's disarming holds succeeded in causing him to drop his improvised weapons.

"Help me, Bowditch! Get ahold of his legs!"

But even the considerable strength of Jack Bowditch was insufficient to stop Ed from advancing toward his gasping brother. The warden and the poacher found themselves being dragged along helplessly, like very small children clinging playfully to their father's legs.

Ed sent another log flying, but his aim was off, due to Charley's hands around his wrist.

The writhing mass of men had reached Tim's snowmobile. It was on the unfortunate sled that Ed Grindle now unleashed his full fury. He brought the remaining log down hard, shattering the dials on the dash. Then took off one of the handlebars with a swipe. Smashed the headlights with the next blow. And crumpled a strut with another.

All while his brother, still unable to rise from the snow, pleaded for him to stop.

Having thoroughly wrecked the snowmobile, Ed hurled the log at Tim.

This time, he missed because Tim knew what was coming and had rolled clear. As Charley and Jack succeeded at last in wrestling his brother to the ground, the younger Grindle fled in his shirtsleeves and moccasins into the forest.

Ed Grindle's wrists were too thick for handcuffs. It was minutes before the warden could get zip ties around them. Bowditch had decided to vamoose before other cops appeared on the scene. By then, Charley knew Tim was long gone. Even injured, the boy was too fleet of foot for him to catch.

5

Three days later, Charley was having lunch at the Dead River Inn with his wife and daughters when he discovered a note under his plate of liver and onions. The message had been scrawled on the back of a meal ticket, and Charley concluded that it had been delivered by their waitress: a wan, bespectacled girl of fifteen named Ricki Tripp.

He leaned back in his chair and opened the folded note on his lap to read it without attracting the attention of his family. The girls were engaged in a guessing game: What was Anne's favorite food?

"Chicken fingers!" said Stacey correctly.

"No, it ain't."

"*Isn't*, Anne," said Ora. "No, it *isn't*."

"What are you reading, Daddy?" Stacey asked.

Charley could never sneak a thing past his younger child, she was so unnervingly observant.

"My presence is requested in the kitchen," he said, rising from the table. "The cook doesn't know how to properly butcher a porcupine. It seems he's now stuck all over with quills like a pincushion."

"Ouch!" said Anne.

Stacey slid off her chair. "I want to see!"

Ora looked at him quizzically but trusted he had a good reason for not disclosing a secret in front of the girls. She focused her energy instead on returning the rambunctious Stacey to her seat at the table.

Charley passed into the hotel lobby, where the waitress, Ricki, was waiting for him in the alcove behind the old-fashioned telephone booth. Guests sat down behind a closed door to make their calls on the rotary dial.

"Oh, thank you, Warden Stevens!" she said. "I didn't know if you'd come."

He raised the note. "You underlined the word *please* three times, so I had no choice."

She looked at him vacantly through her photochromatic glasses. In the dimness, the self-tinting lenses had become as clear as spring water. She had lovely but sad eyes, he realized for the first time.

"How can I help you, Ricki?"

"It's about my boyfriend."

"Relationship advice is not my forte, I'm afraid."

"He's vanished without a trace!"

It was not unheard of, in Charley's experience, for teenage boys to treat their girlfriends in this manner. "Would I know the young man's name?"

"Tim Grindle. I'm worried his brother, Ed, might have hurt him bad. When Tim called me Tuesday night, he said Ed had thrown a log at him and broke his wishbone."

At once, he regretted his patronizing treatment of the girl. Tuesday was the night the boy had run off into the woods.

Charley had called in a favor with a state trooper to take Ed down to the jail in Skowhegan while he searched the logging roads for signs of Tim. But he'd been exhausted and pessimistic; the young poacher was hardly going to reveal himself to the warden who had just accused him of committing a felony.

"You said Tim phoned you, Ricki. What time would that have been, and where was he calling from? Do you know?"

"Just after eight, I'd say. My dad was watching that cable news show he likes to yell at. Tim said he was calling from outside the Bear's Den in Bigelow. He said his toes were frostbitten from walking in the snow! His voice sounded weird—all raspy and huffing."

Charley visualized the hurled birch log striking the boy in his narrow chest.

"Did he mention having chest pains?"

"You know how boys are. He tried to pretend he was OK, but I could hear the pain he was in. Like I said, his voice sounded weird."

"What else did Tim say?"

"He said I should pack my stuff, and we'd run away in the morning after he scraped some money together. He figured we could take Ed's sled and ride up Trail 115 to 89 to 84 and across to New Hampshire. He said there were trails all the way to Burlington, Vermont, and we could sell the sled there and catch a Greyhound bus south. With enough money, we could ride all the way to Florida or Texas. He told me to meet him at Langstrom's Gas & Go at ten the next morning, but he wasn't there."

Charley doubted Tim Grindle had a bank account. Whatever cash he might possess would likely have been hidden back at his brother's house.

"Did Tim say where he was getting his money?"

"He said he had some stashed where no one could find it, and there was also a man he could squeeze for cash."

"Do you have any idea who this unknown moneyman might be?"

"He never mentioned a name. But while we were still on the phone, he said, 'Speak of the devil.' Then he told me he needed to go and hung up."

"So it sounded like Tim might've spotted the man he'd intended to 'squeeze'?"

"I guess so."

"Did Tim say anything about returning to his brother's house?"

"No."

In fact, Charley had waited in the woods outside the Grindle residence the next morning while Ed was still in lockup. He'd hoped Tim would return, knowing his brother was in custody. But he had been forced to abandon his stakeout when he was called away to deal with a deer-car crash on the Rangeley Road.

The warden had figured he would catch up with Tim Grindle eventually. Working in rural law enforcement, he'd come to understand the cyclical nature of domestic disputes. Until one party escaped or tragedy struck, the patterns of abuse repeated. There was bound to be another blowup at the Grindle house.

"Will you look for him?" Ricki asked.

He gave her his most reassuring smile. "You have my word on it."

The woman who owned the inn walked past and barked at the waitress to return to the dining room where she belonged.

After Ricki left, Charley took a seat inside the wooden phone booth—it reminded him of a confessional, minus the kneeler—and pumped some change into the coin slot.

"Yeah?" Ed Grindle said thickly.

"Ed, this is Warden Charley Stevens. May I speak with your brother, please?"

"He ain't here."

"When do you expect him back?"

"Tonight, tomorrow, next week. I don't know, and I don't give a shit."

"Do you know where he is?"

"What's this about? Did he shoot another eagle? What's going on?"

"I'm merely checking up on the boy."

"Because I don't look out for him?" Ed asked. "Because the state of Maine wants to take him away from me again? I told that bitch from the Department of Human Services—anyone who tries to break up my family will enter a world of pain. Don't call here again."

Charley listened to the dial tone, then returned to the dining room and picked at his liver while Ora sent him questioning looks across the table. He had promised his daughters ice cream if they finished their dinner, and he would keep his promise because he always did. On the day he'd married Ora, he'd sworn to his new bride that he would never sacrifice his family for the job. He'd never imagined how hard that oath would be to keep.

6

Back home, he pulled Ora aside while the girls were out checking the chicken coop and told her about Ricki and the note. His wife was a teacher and librarian by education and temperament; she understood, appreciated, and didn't look down upon the inner lives of children. She didn't know Tim Grindle, except by reputation, but she had taught boys like him, and she also had ideas about young Ricki Tripp.

"She isn't a fantasist," Ora said. "She's young and in love, but she's not a fool, or less of a fool than girls her age. Something happened to this boy, Charley."

"His brother doesn't seem overly worried."

"Why should you trust a brute like Ed Grindle to tell the truth?"

"I don't, but there are limits to how much I can interfere. Legally, he still has custody of his brother. Human Services is opening a case file based on what happened the other night, but until they—"

"But what are *you* going to do?"

Ora had a way of cutting through his excuses like a butcher with a cleaver.

"I swore to Ricki that I'd investigate Tim's disappearance. The least I can do is call around to see if anyone's seen him."

"That's good because this burden has fallen on you, my love, whether you like it or not. The Roman emperor Marcus Aurelius once wrote, 'Fate is at your elbow; make yourself good while life and power are still yours.'"

Charley took hold of Ora by the shoulders. He gazed directly into her deeply set, jade-colored eyes. She was the most beautiful woman he had ever known. And more importantly, she was the best.

Because this was an official inquiry, he put on his uniform before going into his home office. (Charley was particular that way.) He made a dozen calls, not just to cops but to anyone who might know Grindle or have seen him Tuesday evening or afterward. When he came out of the office, the sky was lavender with approaching twilight. Ora had packed a sandwich and an apple in a bag and filled his thermos with coffee.

"You're right about it being my elbow, or whatever old Marcus meant about fate," he said. "The local constabulary has no knowledge of Tim's whereabouts. There's no trace of him after he got off the phone with Ricki."

"Where will you start looking?"

"At the place he was last heard from—the den of iniquity."

It was their (admittedly obvious) nickname for the Bear's Den: a combination bar and motel in the nearby village of Bigelow. The place was a waystation on one of the snowmobiling highways that extended from Upstate New York across northern New England and into Canada. The locals mostly avoided it as an unsanitary dive, safe for a bottle of beer or a shot of tequila, at best. It had seemed impossible for the Bear Den's reputation to decline, but over the past year, the establishment had been closed by the health department on several occasions. The first time was after a party of sledders fell ill with food poisoning. Subsequent violations involved dead rodents.

Charley was therefore not surprised to find fewer than ten snowmobiles parked in the unlighted lot. The owners of two vehicles with ski racks and out-of-state plates hadn't gotten the warning about the Den. The only car the warden recognized, a

Saab 9000, belonged to a well-off man who seemed to enjoy wallowing in the dive's sleaziness.

Inside, Dwight Yoakam was twanging his heart out through the sound system in praise of guitars and Cadillacs. The owner-bartender was a gray-faced shell named Levasseur. He was prematurely stoop-shouldered, as if the state fines, attorney's fees, and insurance premiums had taken a toll on his body and spirit, as well as his pocketbook.

Charley took a seat at the bar beside the motel's hooker in residence. The woman was on the payroll as a housekeeper but made her real money (which she split with Levasseur) off hours. She was forty but looked sixty, an age the warden doubted she'd ever reach.

"Good evening, Patty-Ann."

"How're you, Warden?"

"Upright and taking nourishment."

Because Levasseur knew exactly what Charley thought of him, he moved to the far end of the bar and stared up at a wall-mounted TV. The Bruins were losing again. A cardboard sign over the service window said KITCHEN CLOSED!!!

Charley took that as a bit of good luck for the hapless skiers who might otherwise have ordered hamburgers.

The customer on the far side of Patty-Ann, the man who was buying her Sea Breezes tonight, peeked over her fleshy shoulders and said, "Haven't seen you in here before, Charley. Can I buy you a beverage?"

The man's name was Warren Whittaker, and he reminded Charley of a toad. Not the drab Maine species but a bright poisonous version from the Central American rainforest. He was bald and pop-eyed but dressed in colors most local men avoided: yellows, purples, and emerald greens. Tonight, he was wearing a pink puffer vest over a teal button-down and lavender jeans. He was one of Patty-Ann's regulars—and an enthusiastic one, she said.

Whittaker was the sole survivor of a wealthy family down in Kingfield, and like many people who had grown up with a trust fund, he'd always had the freedom to pursue his obscure interests. Among these were collecting vintage posters, selling grandfather clocks, playing jazz clarinet, and, most recently, taxidermy. (The bear's head snarling above the bar was Whittaker's work, and Charley had seen worse mounts in his time.) Even though Warren had had jobs with companies and organizations affiliated with his family—he currently "directed" the Dead River Nature Center, bankrolled by his late father—he was conceptually unable to understand what it meant to work for a living.

"Thank you, but no," Charley said to the offer of a drink. "I dropped in to speak with the lady."

"Me?"

Patty-Ann's bloodshot eyes gave him a look of confusion that turned to gratitude. It must have been years since someone had used that term about her without irony.

Whittaker snorted his drink out his nose. He was notorious for ordering a single Tom Collins and nursing it over the course of three hours. He hid his mocking smile behind a bar napkin.

"You wouldn't happen to have seen Tim Grindle around the past few days?" Charley said, ignoring the rude man.

"What day is it? Monday?"

"It's Friday."

"Why are you looking for young Grindle?" asked Whittaker, leaning forward.

"Poor kid's run away again," said Patty-Ann. "Ed nearly beat him to death with a log."

"I've always said that fat slob is going to kill someone someday," said Warren Whittaker. "When did this happen?"

"Tim was last reported making a call on the pay phone outside on Tuesday evening," Charley said. "Do you remember seeing him around that night, Patty-Ann?"

"Maybe," she said, then amended herself. "I don't know. I don't remember."

"What about you, Warren?"

"Tuesday was that presentation on damselflies and dragonflies at the nature center," said Whittaker. "It's depressing when you spend months promoting an event and only seven people show up—including the director. I'd thought about stopping in for a consolation drink, but I didn't."

Charley scanned the barroom. "Anyone else here that night I could speak with?"

"Besides the saloonkeeper, you mean?" said Whittaker. "Where did he go?"

Charley had watched Levasseur slip away to the kitchen. "Mr. Levasseur has other concerns. What about the cook and dishwasher?"

"Kitchen's closed," said Patty-Ann.

"But was it open on Tuesday night?"

The phone behind the bar rang.

"That's annoying." Whittaker slid off his stool and called into the kitchen, "Hey, Levasseur!"

The phone went silent.

Five seconds later, it began ringing again.

Patty-Ann nearly knocked over her Sea Breeze, reaching across the bar to pluck the cordless phone from its cradle. Because she was an employee of the Bear's Den, she must have felt obligated to answer in her boss's absence.

"Yeah?" She thrust the handset at Charley. "It's for you."

Charley accepted the phone—it was sticky with aerated oil from the deep fryer—and held it as close to his face as he dared.

"This is Charley," he said.

"It's Bowditch."

"Now, how did you happen to know where I was, Jack?"

True to form, Bowditch ignored the question as not worth his time. "I was wrong about the Grindle kid. He didn't shoot that eagle. But I know the piece of shit who did. Meet me at Mountainside Estates in fifteen minutes."

"How about you tell me who we're visiting first."

"Penobscot Indian by the name of Tomer Elmut."

Charley had been ready to reject Jack's demand—his priority was finding Tim Grindle—but the name took him aback.

When the kitchen was open at the Bear's Den, Tomer Elmut was the supper and late-night cook. He was, in fact, one of the men they'd just been discussing.

Speak of the devil.

"The trailers aren't numbered, but it's first on the left," Jack said. "Be there in fifteen minutes or don't blame me for what happens."

7

Mountainside Estates was misnamed twice over. The mobile home park was located in the floodplain of the Dead River, and the mostly vintage trailers that made up the community could not be defined as estates under even the loosest definition of the word.

The neighborhood was, however, quiet and clean. Unlike many mobile home parks Charley had known, Mountainside was not regularly illuminated at night by flashing blue or red lights. He had it on good authority that several of the longtime residents—millworkers and their families who belonged to the same Baptist church—took it upon themselves to run off renters who tried to deal heroin, meth, or even pot out their front doors.

By the time he arrived, the God-fearing, rifle-toting neighborhood watch was already on the scene.

Outside the first trailer, a familiar Ford pickup was blocking a Subaru Baja from backing out of its driveway. But the real action was fifty feet down the road, under the single streetlight, where a dozen heavily bundled people had formed a semicircle around Jack Bowditch and Tomer Elmut, holding both men at gunpoint.

"Am I late to the firing squad?" Charley asked.

A grizzled man in insulated Carhartt winter coveralls said, "No need for you to trouble yourself with this, Warden. We've got it in hand."

"I can see that. But maybe you can elucidate the situation for me."

Despite the firepower aimed in his direction, Bowditch seemed less angry or afraid than bored. The grip of a Colt .45 protruded from the waistband of his jeans in a phallic display. No doubt he had resisted all orders to throw down the pistol. Knowing the size of the man's balls, Charley thought he might even have been taunting the vigilantes, daring them to shoot him.

Elmut, on the other hand, was bug-eyed, shivering, and bleeding from the mouth. "He came here to kill me!"

Tomer Elmut was a member of the Penobscot Nation of Native Americans, which owned much of the Carrabassett Valley but had its tribal offices on distant Indian Island, north of Bangor.

It wasn't just that he was a proud Penobscot, though; Tomer Elmut was openly, even outrageously, *not* a white man. He defined himself entirely in opposition to the culture and values of his Caucasian neighbors. He might have been wearing a sleeveless T-shirt, for instance, but his leggings were handmade of buckskin, with fringes along the seams, and the patterned blanket wrapped around his shoulders was genuine Navajo, a souvenir of a pilgrimage he'd made to Canyon de Chelly. His hair was more brown than black, but he wore it long and had tied an eagle feather to his forelock so that it dangled beside his oblong face.

"If I wanted to kill you—" said Jack.

Charley addressed the residents of Mountainside Estates. "Folks, I'll take it from here. I guarantee you there will be no further disturbances tonight."

"But are you arresting them?"

"That decision depends upon the outcome of my investigation."

"Investigation?" the Carhartt man said, breathing steam. "What's there to investigate? They were fighting in the street!"

"He only means he wants us to disperse," said someone else.

"You've got two days to get your stuff out of here, Elmut!" a rosy-cheeked woman with a Remington called from the back of the scrum.

"I'm on a lease!"

"I thought you weren't bound by 'white laws,'" said someone else. "Or do our laws only apply when they protect you?"

"Mr. Elmut, go back inside before you freeze your feet off," said Charley. "Jack, I need a word in private."

Elmut didn't need to be told twice. The residents were less obliging. Crowds have minds of their own, and if there's one thing a crowd doesn't like, it's dispersing. The warden had to offer additional assurances before the residents shouldered their firearms and returned, grumbling, to their homes.

By then, Jack was leaning against the hood of his pickup, taking the last pulls from a pint of Jägermeister between puffs from his ever-present cigarette. He wore only blue jeans, a thermal crew, and calf-high LaCrosse hunting boots. Cold never seemed to touch the man.

"You care to explain what this is about?" the warden asked.

"You saw the damned feather in his hair."

"The laws are different for Native Americans, I suspect you know. They're allowed to possess eagle feathers under certain limited circumstances, but they can no more legally shoot an eagle than you or I."

"I heard from Elmut's cousin that he's making himself an eagle headdress," said Bowditch. "No way is he going to do that picking up stray feathers. His cousin Truman told me for a fact Tomer's been poaching eagles."

"And this cousin—?"

"Is too scared of me to lie."

"Where does this leave Tim Grindle?"

"What do you mean?"

"The boy hasn't been seen or heard from since the night he ran away from Ed's house. I feel responsible for his well-being.

The only reason we were there was because you accused Tim of killing that bird."

Bowditch tilted his head back to blow smoke at the sky. "Look, I was wrong about the Grindle kid. But he brought suspicion on himself for not giving a shit about the law."

"Who does that sound like?"

"Fuck you, Stevens. I'm not going to weep for poor Tim Grindle. And if the kid ran away, I can't say I blame him, given what a mountain of moose shit his brother is."

"So you haven't seen him?"

"Why would I have seen him? He's not my poaching apprentice." He tossed his empty bottle against Elmut's Subaru so that it shattered against a door panel. "Give me five minutes with the Indian—or hell, just tear the place apart—and we'll get the truth out of him. I bet he's got a pillow stuffed with eagle feathers."

"I'm not giving you five seconds with him. The man already needs stitches. You just about detached his lower lip."

"He fell while I was chasing him."

Charley refused to dignify the lie with a response. "I can't legally rifle through the man's possessions. I seem to recall you telling me to get a search warrant when I came looking for that eight-point buck you jacklighted."

Bowditch felt no need to disguise his guilt for the now-unprovable violation.

"You heard what those people said. Elmut tries to have it both ways. He goes on and on about not paying taxes to the same government that nearly wiped out his kind. He says he's not obliged to obey the law. He won't even claim to be an American citizen!"

Charley was in no mood to debate; he lowered his voice and stared straight into the taller man's eyes. "You're going to leave this alone now. You gave that eagle to me, and I won't have you threatening people over it. I made a mistake allowing you onto the Grindles' property—should have known you'd follow me—and because of my negligence, I've got a missing and possibly injured boy to find. You and I aren't partners."

Jack's smile was wolfish. "And I was just beginning to like you, Warden."

"Interfere again or get in my way, and I promise you'll regret it."

The insolent expression was gone, and now Jack Bowditch's free hand was creeping toward the butt of his pistol. In his rage, arrogance, and almost drunkenness, he had forgotten what a dangerous enemy Warden Charley Stevens could be. After a tense moment, he pretended to hitch up his jeans.

"Don't try to scare me, little man," he nearly snarled. "That badge won't protect you. Lots of bad accidents happen in the woods, especially to a man alone."

"Go home, Bowditch. Marie and Michael are waiting for you."

Since their last meeting, Charley had remembered the names of the other man's wife and son.

As intended, Jack bristled at the mention of his family. "I'll be seeing you around, Stevens. And make no mistake, it'll be before you see me."

8

Charley wondered whether Elmut would welcome him inside the trailer—the Penobscot really could be a self-righteous prick—but he must have received enough of a scare from Bowditch that he put aside his principles and permitted the agent of the white man's state to enter his sanctuary.

The injured man met him at the door, holding a bag of Green Giant frozen corn to his mouth.

"Is he gone?"

"I watched him drive off, but that's no guarantee he's not lurking nearby or won't come back. That seems to be his modus operandi."

Elmut's face was shaped like a stretched oval, but the overall largeness was offset by the enormity of his pitch-dark eyes. He was still wearing the woven blanket like a cloak around his shoulders, but he'd put on a pair of ankle-high moccasins made of silky gray fur to warm his feet.

"Fuck, man!" he said. "I still don't know what I did to provoke the guy. And now my neighbors have gotten out the torches and pitchforks. Those racist fucks have been looking for a way to push me out of this place. If I don't move, they're going to burn me or string me up—or both."

Charley scanned the room with a deadpan expression.

The mobile home was a single-wide with boxboard walls and

so little insulation around the doors and windows that the cross-wind drafts caused Elmut's eagle feather to flutter. The place was a mess: not dirty so much as cluttered. There wasn't three inches of cleared space on any of the surfaces.

A bookcase was overflowing with books, all of which bore stickers on the spines identifying them as the property of public libraries. Charley couldn't imagine Tomer Elmut going to the trouble of obtaining a library card for the purpose of borrowing Martin Yan's *A Wok for All Seasons*. His stealing these titles was another peaceful protest against the white man's system.

Stray antlers and moose sheds lay scattered about. Some impressive taxidermy mounts, including two monster brook trout, an Atlantic salmon, a pair of wood ducks in flight, and the head of a piebald doe, hung from the walls. Charley remembered a pale deer being reported in Highland Plantation that summer; the doe had come every day at dusk to a field planted for hunting with alfalfa and clover. The last time anyone had seen the delicate creature was a week before deer season had begun.

Circumstantial, Charley thought. *But not necessarily irrelevant*.

"You do all these mounts yourself, Mr. Elmut?"

"You can't prove any of them are in violation of your so-called laws."

"Jack Bowditch claims you shot a bald eagle. Did you?"

"Eagles are sacred to my people. That's why I wear this." He fingered the feather.

It was not, Charley thought, *a denial*.

"How about lynx?"

"What are you talking about, man?"

Charley identified what he guessed must be the visitor's chair, as it didn't face the big-screen TV. He removed a stack of pilfered library books and set them on the floor.

"Would you mind if I had a seat?"

Elmut moved the bag of frozen food away from his jaw. The plastic was smeared with blood.

"Depends if you came here to accuse me of a criminal offense. Because I don't answer to you or your laws, white man."

"What about Levasseur? Do you answer to him?"

Elmut rolled his eyes. "He signs my paycheck. That's all."

"That's a handsome pair of sealskin moccasins you're wearing, Mr. Elmut. They look new. Import of seal pelts into the US has been prohibited under the Marine Mammal Protection Act since 1972. But I suspect that you don't believe that federal law binds the *Wôbanaki*."

Elmut cracked a painful-looking smile. "Listen to you, trying to speak skeejin. Where'd you learn that one, Kemosabe?"

"Friend of mine is a Passamaquoddy warden."

"'Some of my best friends are redskins,' right? You gonna confiscate my moccasins?"

"No, but I'm going to ask you again. Did you shoot a bald eagle on Tuesday at Grand Falls on the Dead River?"

His hesitation was so brief another person might not have noticed. "Tuesday I was working at the Den."

"From what time to what time?"

"I don't have to answer your questions."

"Levasseur can tell me," Charley said. "But I'm assuming it was your usual shift. So you went in early afternoon?"

Elmut loomed over his chair. He had recently showered and smelled of Old Spice deodorant. "You can leave now."

Charley crossed one knee over the other and clasped his right kneecap casually. "How late were you there?"

"Midnight, same as always. I like to get going before closing time and the drunks hit the road. What's that got to do with this eagle?"

"I never said it had anything to do with the eagle. I was wondering if you happened to notice Tim Grindle hanging around the Den on Tuesday night. You know Tim, I take it?"

Elmut drew the blanket closer around his shoulders. "Yeah, he wanted me to teach him taxidermy because I was Native. What is it with you people that you keep asking me to teach you taxi-dermy? Stuffing dead animals is a white thing."

"Why do you do it, then?"

"Because you people pay good money for it."

"Taxidermy is messy business. Where do you do your work? Not in this cramped trailer."

Again, a hesitation. "Friend has a barn in Kingfield he lets me use."

Charley couldn't deny the quality of the mounts on display. But he also knew that, for all his big talk, Tomer Elmut wasn't as remotely woods-wise as his ancestors, which was probably why he'd resorted to poaching that piebald doe.

"You didn't buy a spruce grouse from Tim Grindle?"

"If I wanted a fool hen, I could get one on my own. I don't need some wannabe Davy Crockett to do my hunting."

"Tuesday night, did you see Tim Grindle?"

Elmut covered his bruised and swelling mouth with the frozen bag. His eyes gave nothing away. But Charley's intuition told him that thoughts were scratching and scurrying around the man's mind.

"I was cooking," he said from behind the ice pack. "When I'm in the kitchen, I don't know who comes in. Let alone who's hanging around outside."

Charley grinned. "I never said the boy was outside."

"Kids aren't allowed inside the bar unaccompanied. Don't try to trip me up with your double-talk. I didn't see him. Is that all you've got for me? Are we done?"

The desperation in his voice was as good as an admission for Charley: Tomer Elmut *had* seen Tim Grindle on Tuesday night.

"How long have you been cooking at the Bear's Den, Mr. Elmut?"

"Fourteen months. Why?"

"Do you like it?"

"No, but I need specie to function in your capitalist system."

"I'm unfamiliar with that term. Does it mean 'money'? 'Legal tender'?"

"Nothing tender about capitalism," Elmut said, smirking at his own joke.

"I have been pondering all the problems you've had in your kitchen."

Elmut let the bag of corn sag from his face. "It ain't my kitchen. It's Levasseur's kitchen. I guess you could say he's had a run of bad luck."

"I noticed the kitchen was closed when I was there earlier. Given the Bear Den's recent history, I deduced there'd been another health and safety violation. Because Friday wouldn't be a normal night off for a bar cook."

"Inspector found a slab of expired bacon in the back of the fridge. Levasseur swears he just looked at the date on the package, and it was good for a month. Almost like someone substituted the fresh bacon for an old, rank slab."

"*Mocelomogewinuwiw*," said Charley.

"Is that something else your Passamaquoddy buddy taught you? Is it supposed to impress me?"

"No, sir. I don't think that at all."

Elmut was clearly less fluent than he let on, and he didn't want to ask the question, but he was unable to stop himself. "What is it supposed to mean? Your pronunciation sucks."

"It means your boss is an unlucky person."

It must have hurt Tomer Elmut to grin because his split lip began to bleed again.

9

Ora awakened when Charley returned home. She sat up in bed. Her hair was mussed in the way he found attractive. She listened to him narrate the events of the past hours as he undressed.

"Where are you with this?" she asked.

"Nowhere."

"That's not true, and you know it."

He appreciated his wife's willingness to serve as both a sounding board and a spur to action.

"Tim hasn't been seen since Tuesday night when he made that call to Ricki Tripp outside the den of iniquity. My gut tells me Tomer Elmut saw him there. The odds are good that Elmut is the man who was buying Tim's illegal game."

"Do you think he might have hurt the boy?"

"Elmut talks like a revolutionary, but I don't know if he's ever spent a night in jail for his hijinks. I doubt he would've hurt Tim if it meant risking Ed Grindle's wrath. But if he knows what became of the young man, he isn't telling."

"So where might Tim have gone?"

Charley drew his service revolver from its holster and slid the gun into the nightstand drawer. Then he unbuckled his heavy duty belt and hung it in the closet beside his uniform.

"Well, he would have known that his brother was in lockup

and the house was empty. So he might have walked home through the woods for his things and whatever money he had in his squirrel cache. He'd mentioned stealing his brother's snowmobile to Ricki. I should have asked Ed if his sled was missing."

"So call him again."

"Ed won't talk to me, assuming he's even conscious. I'll have to go over myself in the morning to see firsthand. If the sled's gone, I'm not sure what it means. If the sled's there, then I'd better start searching the woods between Bigelow and Pickle Hill for Tim's frozen corpse."

"You reported his disappearance to the state. Why isn't Human Services making him a priority?"

He unbuttoned and unzipped his wool pants and stepped out of them. "You've had students like Tim, Boss."

"Don't call me that, Charley," she said, trying to hide a smile because she secretly enjoyed the nickname. "Tell me more about this Tomer Elmut."

He turned from the closet in his boxer shorts, his welterweight's physique crisscrossed and pockmarked with scars he'd received in the war. "Tomer thinks of himself as a political activist, but he's more like one of those yippies who went around throwing pies in people's faces in the sixties. I'd bet a penny he's behind all those health and safety violations at the Den. He's trying to sabotage his employer's business. How Levasseur hasn't cottoned to the truth is a mystery."

"Tomer Elmut would do those things even if it means losing his job?"

"He doesn't care two cents about that. The man is what a buddy of mine from Wyoming used to call a *professional saddle spur*."

"And you're certain that he and Tim were acquainted?"

"He admitted that the boy had asked him for taxidermy lessons."

"In exchange for supplying illegal pelts as some sort of protest against federal protections?"

Charley shrugged. "The Penobscots would disown the man if they knew what an embarrassment he is in the woods. Hitting a roosting eagle would be pushing the limits of his skill as a marksman. I could see him enlisting Tim's help in obtaining pelts and skins for mounting."

He had almost convinced himself of his own hypothesis. But as he sat down in his boxers on the side of the bed, Ora said, "Does Tomer Elmut strike you as someone who could afford to pay Tim Grindle two hundred dollars for a spruce grouse?"

They'd never slept together on anything but a full-size mattress. The springs creaked as he leaned over her. "Damn it, Boss, just when I think I have a watertight theory, you pull out a pin to prick it."

She put a hand against his face. "I wouldn't be any good to you if I didn't push you to be your best."

He crawled under the covers, reached across her bed-warmed body to turn off the lamp, and growled in her ear until she couldn't stop herself from laughing.

10

S unrise the next morning found Charley heading north on his Ski-Doo across frozen Flagstaff Pond. The wind had turned southerly in the night, bringing forty-degree temperatures to the North Maine Woods. The top layer of ice was already melting, there were puddles between the pressure ridges, and the sled's tracks sent spray into the balmy air. The unseasonable warmth was transmuting the ice and snow into vapor. Pickle Hill was hidden behind a wet white sheet of fog.

Charley had always been a daredevil at heart. Instead of checking his speed, he used the limited visibility to test his reflexes, jumping ridges, swerving around ponds. If he kept up this recklessness, Ora warned him, he was destined for a nasty crash.

The trees along the north side of the pond came up on him fast. Charley made a sharp turn as he braked. He followed the icy shoreline until he found the marked trail leading into the woods.

In the forest, where the cold lingered in the shadows, the mist was thinner. Coming around a bend, he was surprised by the vivid greenness of a patch of Christmas ferns that seemed not to know it was midwinter.

The warden was so enjoying the ride that he took a wrong turn where the trail forked. He recognized his mistake immediately, but instead of backing up or turning around, he continued forward. This trail also would get him where he wanted to go; it intersected the Flagstaff Road up ahead. From there, he could follow it east to Pickle Hill.

In his mind, he began to recite Robert Frost's "The Road Not Taken" (he had grown up during a time that valued memorization). Ora had told him the poem didn't mean what most people assumed. Charley didn't care; he enjoyed the plainspoken beauty of the language.

By the time he'd reached the last line, he found himself nearing the end of the path, as well. He decelerated as he crested a plowed snowbank; the weight of the engine dropped his skis onto the sand-strewn logging road.

It was a rough ride after that. The skis and track of his snowmobile made a hell of a racket, louder than a wheeled motor vehicle. And he felt every jolt in his joints and ligaments.

As slow as he was going, he was surprised to catch up to a pair of hazy taillights. A pickup was idling in the fog. Grouse hunters often crept along in this manner, edging quietly in their vehicles to blast the chicken-size birds out their open windows. But Charley's instinct told him this was no "heater hunter."

The driver of the truck seemed to be searching for something in the snowbanks.

He saw now that it was a blue Silverado with a dimly lit vanity plate:

GRNDL

What the hell was Ed Grindle doing? Charley remembered the man saying that his last dog, an Akita, had gotten loose and been run over by a snowplow. Had the same fate befallen the Doberman?

He considered hanging back to watch.

But patience had never been one of Charley Stevens's virtues.

He opened the throttle and shot forward, coming up beside the idling Chevy before Ed knew what was happening. Damned if Grindle wasn't sobbing inside the cab.

As the truck rolled to a stop, Charley left the engine of his Ski-Doo running. The warden removed his helmet, set it on the seat, and ran a hand through his buzzed hair. Then he approached the driver's door.

Tears streamed down Grindle's hairy face. His nose was red enough to light a sleigh.

It's not a dog he's looking for. It's his brother.

Words rarely failed Charley, but he was having trouble forming the question he needed to ask. He was still struggling when Ed produced a handgun from the passenger seat, pressed the muzzle to his own temple, and fired.

11

W hat happened?" murmured Ed Grindle.

"You flinched," Charley said. "Lots of people do. The next time you shoot yourself, put the barrel in your mouth with the front sight against the palate. You're more likely to have success."

Grindle was stretched across the bench of his pickup with his shins and boots hanging out the driver's door. Charley stood outside the passenger's door so he could wrap his patient's enormous head with gauze secured by an ACE bandage. Fortunately, the bleeding was slight.

"As it is, you barely grazed yourself," the warden said, not unkindly.

Ed groaned and tried to sit up, but he lacked the energy.

The floor mats were littered with crushed beer cans. The grainy, alcoholic funk coming off the man turned Charley's stomach. But Grindle's appearance—the crumbs in his stubble, the lemony tinge to the sclera of his eyes—and his raw emotional state awakened a feeling of pathos in him.

He tucked a rolled blanket under the man's melon-size head. It would slow the bleeding and keep him from passing out. "While you're regaining your strength, why don't you tell me what you were doing?"

The question prompted Ed to begin leaking tears again.

"I killed him."

"You killed your brother?"

"You saw me do it. He was the only family I've got left!"

"But how can you be certain, I mean?"

"When I came home from lockup, Tim had left a message saying he was feeling worse. He said he was going to make me pay. But he sounded like he was dying. And he never called back."

"What did you do with this voice message?"

"Erased it."

"So you've been cruising the logging roads because you think he collapsed walking back to your house."

"I know he's dead." Ed gazed up with wet, pleading eyes.

"How do you know?"

"His ghost told me last night."

Charley ran a hand through his hair and considered the situation from several angles. He rarely concerned himself with the protocols surrounding an arrest. Some officers worried that if they didn't get the confession recorded and signed in triplicate, it would be tossed out at trial. But he was certain that Grindle's admission would qualify as "a spontaneous utterance."

On the other hand, the confessed killer was beyond plastered. And he'd just sustained a gunshot wound, however glancing, to the head. Ed Grindle's certainty that he had committed homicide was based upon an irrecoverable voice message and a statement made by a phantasm.

Charley decided to take his time before he got the state police on the horn.

"Let's take another run at getting you upright," the warden said. "I'm going to drive you home."

Charley moved his sled into the woods, then took hold of Grindle by the shoulders. The warden pushed with all his strength, but his boots slid on the icy road. He returned to his Ski-Doo to fetch his cleats. With the added grip, he made headway. In all, the process of rearranging Ed Grindle took ten minutes.

He confiscated the Glock pistol Ed had used to attempt suicide and tucked the gun into the waist of his trousers. He adjusted the seat for his short, slim stature. As he drove, he was forced to lean forward because there was blood on the headrest.

The heat from the rising sun was melting the snowbanks, but the water had nowhere to go on account of the ice below, and it seemed to him like he was driving down a placid stream instead of a road.

When he arrived at the house on Pickle Hill, he heard barking and realized he had the Doberman to deal with, too. But the watchdog, chained in the yard, was so terrified of his master that he slunk away while Charley helped Ed through the garage door. It took all his strength to keep the big man upright.

Tim Grindle's "bedroom" was even sadder than he'd imagined. The boy's bed was a folding cot that just about collapsed under Ed's weight when he fell across it. A comically large hunting knife, like something used by Tarzan of the Apes, was tucked beneath the lone pillow, presumably for self-defense. A cheesecake poster of Pamela Anderson in a red swimsuit was duct-taped to the cinder block wall.

Charley didn't bother asking the homeowner for permission to search. Ed wouldn't remember giving it when he sobered up. If push came to shove, it would be the warden's word against the self-confessed killer's.

Beneath the cot, he found dusty, wadded socks, a dog-eared issue of *Penthouse*, and a paperback titled the *Home Book of Taxidermy and Tanning*. Most of Tim's other possessions were stowed in a cheap footlocker or stuffed into a trash bag of unwashed clothes. A tool cabinet contained the boy's rifle, a poacher's special Savage Model 64, as well as assorted wire snares, leghold traps, and bottled lures. Nothing unexpected or out of the ordinary.

Charley zip-tied Ed to the cot and took the poaching rifle to be on the safe side. Then he went upstairs to use the phone.

He couldn't rule out the possibility that the boy might still be found alive. Young Grindle was sneaky enough to let the world think he was at death's door as part of some scheme. But was he cruel enough to play games with Ricki Tripp's emotions? Charley thought not.

The time had come to accept the awful truth. The Grindle boy had almost certainly died of his injuries.

So where was his body? Enough time had passed that if Tim had collapsed on a snowmobile trail, a sledder would have found him. The same went double for the local roads. Even the remotest logging roads around Flagstaff Pond saw occasional truck and ATV traffic.

The dying boy might have sought shelter in the dumpster behind the Bear's Den. The motel basement was another possibility; it was always steamy from the commercial washer and dryer Patty-Ann used to clean the sheets and towels. Charley doubted the door to the laundry was even locked.

In his head now, he could hear Ora telling him to call in the cavalry.

He telephoned the sheriff's office in Skowhegan and told the deputy who answered that Ed Grindle had just confessed to killing his missing brother. He said there was good reason to believe the boy was indeed dead. The deputy went quiet, then asked if he could have Sheriff Hatch call Charley back.

The phone rang a moment later.

"What trouble are you going to cause me now, Stevens?" said Joe Hatch.

"You must know that a boy by the name of Tim Grindle is missing. I reported it several days ago."

"My guys tell me the kid's a budding criminal and regular runaway."

Charley chose to ignore the implication that the boy wasn't worth the police exerting themselves. "His brother, Ed, is convinced that Tim is dead. The two had an altercation on Tuesday night. Ed Grindle hurled a log at his little brother. I believe the blow caused internal injuries."

"This Grindle is that whale we had in lockup?"

"If you mean the violent man you released on his own recognizance—"

"It's a good thing you don't work for me. I don't tolerate smart-mouths."

Charley was saved from saying something he would regret.

"Where's the whale now?" the sheriff asked.

"Passed out downstairs on a cot in his garage. I'm calling you from his house."

"So bring him to the jail!"

"I came here on my sled, and while Ski-Doo makes a quality product, I believe Mr. Grindle alone exceeds the recommended weight limit."

"What did I say about smart-mouths?" said Hatch. "So what's your evidence that Ed Grindle killed his brother? The last I heard, the kid was still missing, and we haven't found a body."

"Ed Grindle just confessed."

"This was before he passed out?" Hatch didn't pause for an answer to his rhetorical question. "Why should we believe anything that drunk says?"

"Because he tried to shoot himself out of grief. Fortunately, he flinched but—"

"Is the man in need of an ambulance?"

"No, the bullet just grazed him, and I was able to patch him up. You should be able to transport Ed directly to the jail. The infirmary nurse can clean up the wound. With all due respect, Sheriff, it seems like you're coming up with excuses not to take action here."

"And it seems like you're determined to ruin my day, Warden. In my experience, any time someone uses the words *with all due respect*, it means the opposite. If I send a deputy to the house, I assume you'll be there when he arrives?"

Charley murmured his assent.

He assumed the conversation was done until Hatch came back with one last jab.

"You've been a busy beaver, Stevens. I heard you made an appearance last night at Mountainside Estates. Tomer Elmut might be a horse's ass, but how is it OK with you that Jack Bowditch broke his jaw?"

Charley didn't understand. "Sheriff?"

"A few hours ago, someone dumped that Indian outside the ER in Farmington with his mandible hanging down around his nut sack. Did you not notice the extent of his injury when you left the trailer park last night?"

Of course Bowditch had returned to Mountainside, Charley thought.

"How is Mr. Elmut?"

"Uncooperative. He won't even write down the name of the man who attacked him. The only reason we know it was Bowditch was because a nurse, on her smoke break, recognized his truck in the lot. I don't give a hoot about the Indian refusing to press charges. I've told my men to bring your buddy Bowditch in for questioning."

Charley hung up the phone. He checked briefly on Grindle to be sure the man was in no danger of choking on his own vomit. He left the garage door open so that the responding deputy would know to enter. Then he ran as fast as he could back to his sled.

I2

Ora had gone grocery shopping and the girls were at school when he arrived home to grab the keys to his truck. The hospital in Farmington was an hour's drive from Flagstaff. Out of habit, he cast a glance at the answering machine in his office before he left.

The red light was blinking. It was probably Hatch raging about being hung up on.

Charley hated to be delayed, but the past few days had taught him the folly of making assumptions.

It might be Ricki Tripp with news.

It was unlikely, but it might even be Tim Grindle himself.

The last voice he expected to hear was that of Jack Bowditch.

"It was Elmut who shot the eagle," the poacher said. "I got the truth out of him just now. He thinks he knows where Tim Grindle is, too. I owe it to the little shit to go make things right. Some things can't be left to the law."

Bowditch sounded sober, steady, and dangerous.

He said he owed it to Tim to "make things right." Where else could he be going but to murder Ed Grindle?

Charley had just left Ed cuffed, alone, and helpless. According to the time stamp on the answering machine, the call had come two hours earlier, more than enough time for Jack to speed up

Route 16 from the Farmington hospital to the house on Pickle Hill. He sprinted out to his truck.

What kind of man viciously breaks a person's jaw, then drops him outside the hospital?

A man who didn't just believe in frontier justice but embodied it.

He turned the key in the ignition and reached for the radio. The sheriff had already informed his officers to be on the lookout for Jack Bowditch. But that was before the armed and dangerous man had set out to avenge Tim Grindle.

Charley's hand paused as it closed around the radio handset.

In his haste, he had skipped over something else Bowditch had said: Tomer Elmut "thinks he knows where Tim Grindle is, too."

How was he to interpret that sentence?

Did it mean Tim was alive somewhere? Or was Elmut referring to the location of the body?

In either case, wouldn't Bowditch seek out the missing boy before he exacted vengeance on his brother?

Only one person could tell Charley where Bowditch was going, and that person was lying in a hospital bed many miles to the south.

13

He'd nearly sped past the Bear's Den before an insight caused him to hit the brakes.

How does Tomer Elmut know where Tim Grindle is?

Charley swung his patrol truck into the vast expanse of muddy slush and standing water. Vestigial snowbanks steamed along the edge of the near-empty lot. He left the engine running as he tried to work through the problem.

Elmut and the boy were acquainted. Tim had asked the Penobscot to teach him taxidermy. And the cook had all but admitted he'd seen the boy outside the Den on the night he disappeared.

Had Elmut given Tim a ride after his shift ended?

Had Elmut seen Tim catch a ride with someone else?

The pay phone, from which Tim had made his calls to Ricki and his brother's answering machine, was at the foot of an exterior staircase that led to the guest rooms above the restaurant. One of the motel doors was open with a maid's cart outside.

As Charley watched, Patty-Ann emerged from the room for a restorative cigarette. She removed a pack of Virginia Slims and a lighter from her uniform smock. He waved, and she smiled back, raising her hand with the unlit smoke. He remembered overhearing Levasseur tell a customer how he'd stopped putting bottles of complimentary mouthwash in the bathrooms because Patty-Ann would knock them back to ward off the shakes.

His gaze drifted away from the maid and back to the pay phone.

Ricki had said Tim had spotted a man who owed him money, or could be persuaded to part with some, and used the phrase, "Speak of the devil."

Tomer Elmut wouldn't be in a hospital bed if Jack had thought him a child killer. He would be lying dead at the bottom of a ravine where coyotes would already be making short work of his carcass.

Charley splashed across the lot until he was standing beneath the railed balcony where Patty-Ann was taking her smoke break: Romeo to her Juliet.

"Heya, Charley," she said. "What's going on?"

"I'm a confused man, Patty-Ann."

"Confused how?"

"My thoughts are dark and far-ranging—like a murder of carrion crows."

The smile vanished, then tried without success to reignite itself, but she had no clue what he meant, and he couldn't blame her.

"Last night, I asked you who was at the bar on Tuesday evening," he said. "It would help me a great deal if you could try again to remember who you saw."

She tapped her cigarette so that the ash dropped fifteen feet to the ground.

"There was Levasseur and Tomer, of course. And the new dishwasher, Santiago. A. J. Langstrom came in for a Seven and Seven. A group of sledders were here, speaking French. I think there were five of them. They laughed when I smiled over at their table. I don't speak the language, but I know what *putain* means. Is there someone in particular . . . ?"

"Warren Whittaker."

"Warren had some event at the nature center that night. Something to do with bugs, I think."

"He didn't stop by afterwards?"

"I expected him to, but he never showed."

Whittaker had volunteered as much; gone out of his way to answer a question the warden hadn't even asked him.

Why would he have felt obliged to do that?

"Patty-Ann, I'm going to start calling you Mnemosyne. She was the Greek goddess of memory."

"Gee! That's so romantic."

Because he didn't want her to get the wrong idea, he stepped quickly to the pay phone without saying anything more.

He dialed the operator and put in an additional quarter to have her connect him.

A woman with a quavering voice answered. "This is the Dead River Nature Center."

"May I speak with Mr. Whittaker, please?"

"Warren isn't here this morning. May I ask who is calling?"

He knew the woman on the end of the line—a chattering busybody—and as much as he hated being rude, he chose not to identify himself. "Do you expect him soon?"

"Honestly, I am not sure. It isn't like him not to call. I am sorry, I didn't catch your name."

But the phone was already halfway back to its cradle.

The nature center was located north of the village, near the confluence of the east and west branches of the Dead River. Whittaker would have had to pass the Bear's Den on his drive home to Kingfield, twenty-odd miles to the south. Maybe he'd planned to stop for a drink but had been waylaid in the parking lot by Tim Grindle.

Like the boy, Warren Whittaker was a budding taxidermist.

Hadn't Tomer Elmut complained about "everyone" asking him for lessons in the morbid art? Elmut had also mentioned having a barn in Kingfield where he did his own taxidermy work. It was the same town where Whittaker lived.

Was the eccentric Warren Whittaker the person Tim had mentioned: his buyer for "rare critters, the harder to get, the better"?

The toad-like man seemed harmless, delicate, even comical in his affectations, but how might he have reacted if young Grindle had attempted to extort money from him?

As Charley sped south now along the Carrabassett River, he felt the surge of adrenaline through his heart. Time was again his enemy, as it had so often been in his dangerous life.

He had no idea what he would find when he arrived at the home of Warren Whittaker. He only knew he would be too late.

14

The Whittaker house was located at the edge of the village of Kingfield. Listed in the National Register of Historic Places and built in the Georgian style, it turned a square and solemn face to the road. Its rigid symmetry befitted a family of politicians, jurists, and merchants. Marble steps ascended to a capped pediment; four white columns flanked double doors through which generations of Maine's most prominent citizens had passed. Over its long life, the house had been a landmark in every sense of the word.

The first thing Charley noticed about the place, however, was that the front walkway was unshoveled. The yard was so perfectly white and flat, it was hard to believe the wind alone had sculpted such smoothness. Clearly, the last surviving Whittaker received no visitors through those storied doors.

Instead, Warren must have entered and exited the house through the back. Many Mainers followed the same pattern of behavior, especially during the winter months.

As Charley turned into the drive, he saw confirmation of his worst fear. A single set of fresh tire tracks led through the slush around the building.

Jack Bowditch had beaten him there.

He found the blue Ford pickup blocking the carriage house that Warren had converted into a garage for his winter and summer rides: a vintage Land Rover Defender and a classic Cadillac

Coupe DeVille. Nearby was a barnlike structure with footprints in and out. None of the tracks looked recent to Charley's trained eye, however.

Was that barn the space Tomer Elmut borrowed to create his perfect taxidermy mounts? Did Whittaker allow him to use it in exchange for lessons?

Charley considered calling for backup but was restrained by his ignorance of the situation.

Jack's presence didn't positively prove a crime was in progress or had been committed.

Nevertheless, he undid the snap holding his revolver securely in its holster.

He opened the truck door as quietly as he could, knowing anyone inside would have heard him come around the building, and immediately smelled tobacco on the air.

Jack was sitting in the mudroom door with his unkempt head bowed and a Marlboro burning down to the fingers with which he pinched it.

Without raising his eyes, he said, "Hello, Stevens."

"Bowditch."

"I figured you'd be along eventually. I wasn't sure how you'd put it together, but I knew you would solve it after you heard my message."

"It was good of you to drop Elmut at the hospital after busting his jaw."

Jack kept his head bowed, almost as if he were afraid to show his face. "Who said I did? Not Tomer."

"A nurse recognized your truck."

"I was just giving the poor man a ride. You can put away the six-shooter. You won't have need of it."

"You understand why I might not be inclined to take your word on that score. Where's Whittaker?"

"Inside."

"Dead?"

"I didn't check." At last, Jack raised his head, and even though he was entirely in shadow in the doorway, his eyes seemed filled with a blue light. "What's the worst thing you saw in 'Nam?"

"You'll pardon me if I focus on present concerns rather than swapping war stories with you."

Charley took a step toward the door, but the other refused to budge.

"I used to think it was the burnt bodies," Jack said as he brought his cigarette up to his mouth for one last draw before flicking the filter away. "Not a worse way to go, in my opinion, than napalm frying you to a crisp."

Charley found himself pushing away nightmare visions.

"I don't know why," continued Jack, "but mass casualties never made the same impact on me as the solitary deaths. Like once, after we'd bombed the shit out of this ville near Quảng Trị, I saw this ARVN lieutenant feeding scraps to a stray dog. Took me a minute to realize he was cutting meat off a dead VC. I said, 'You shouldn't do that.' He looked up, all glassy-eyed, and nodded. And then he shot the fucking dog."

"Step aside, Bowditch. I'm going inside."

The larger man used the doorframe to gain his footing as if he'd been overcome with weakness.

Inside, Charley recognized Warren Whittaker's pink vest hanging in the hall. The house had an odd odor: not just the mustiness of an old building with dusty furniture and rusting radiators. It was a sharp, acidic smell.

Ants, he thought.

And in the same moment, a memory came to him of being a boy and reading in *National Geographic* that the natives of the Amazon made a kind of lemonade out of crushed ants.

Formic acid.

Behind him, Jack called from the mudroom, "Whittaker ran into the kid outside the Bear's Den on Tuesday night. Tomer was having a cigar and saw them talking. I got Warren to confirm it before . . . He said the Grindle kid was coughing and massaging his chest. Made the boy get into his Rover. Said he was taking him to the hospital in Farmington for X-rays when the kid just . . . died."

It was a plausible story, but he could tell that Jack didn't believe it, and he realized he didn't, either.

"So where is Tim?"

Jack seemed to be one of those storytellers who would not be hurried.

"Whittaker told me he panicked. He didn't know what had happened to the kid. He admitted that he and Grindle were engaged in certain enterprises, and he thought the police might draw the wrong conclusion if they pried into the nature of their relationship. He told me he dropped the body in a cedar swamp in Freeman Township. Said he could take me there. But I knew he was lying."

"How?"

"Because I know what a man will say when he knows he's about to die."

"Does it change anything for you that Ed Grindle confessed to the crime?" Charley asked angrily. "You and I both know it was that log he threw that really killed Tim. An X-ray will show broken bones in his chest and determine conclusively that death was caused by trauma to his heart and lungs."

Jack grinned. "That's funny."

Charley had let the hand with the revolver drop to his side. He resisted the urge to raise it. "I don't think so."

"It's funny because you still haven't figured this thing out."

"Where's Whittaker?"

"Basement. He was showing me around. He fell down the stairs on his way back up. Hit his head."

"People have a habit of falling around you."

"You have no idea."

Charley wondered how the medical examiner could determine whether someone had been thrown down a flight of steps.

"Why don't you lead the way, Bowditch."

"No, thanks."

"Then turn around and kneel so I can put on the bracelets."

"Maybe you should have a look downstairs before you read me my rights."

Ever since he'd arrived, Charley had wondered why Jack Bowditch seemed different. The man he knew from the bars and the woods was cunning, arrogant: a scrapper with a hair trigger. But the man who'd told the Vietnam horror story appeared intro-spective, shaken, even afraid.

Charley found the door to the basement ajar and an incandes-cent glow rising from the stairs into the wood-paneled hallway—almost as if the odor was carried not by air but by light.

"You go first," Charley said, raising the pistol. "'No' isn't an answer."

"You won't shoot me, Stevens. I've known a lot of game war-dens in my time, and they've all been cowards. I thought you might be the exception, but—"

Charley calmly fired a bullet past Jack's ear. The sound of the explosion was magnified by the tightness of the hall. The slug wedged itself in the hardwood lintel at which Charley had aimed. Jack clutched a hand to his ringing ear.

"Damn it, Stevens!"

"You don't know the first thing about me," the game warden said. "Now: downstairs."

Jack descended.

Charley followed.

Warren Whittaker lay on his back on the concrete floor, blood haloed around his bald head. His dead eyes were seemingly fo-cused on the naked bulb hanging from the webbed ceiling. For some reason, he'd rolled up his shirt cuffs and was wearing a pair of yellow dishwashing gloves.

Bowditch remained silent, but his gaze was focused over Char-ley's shoulder.

Slowly, the warden turned. The basement was cavernous, divided by concrete pillars that held up the ceiling and the floor above. A roll of chicken wire leaned against the nearest support. A headless mannequin stood beside it. Beyond was a capped steel drum. A pry bar lay on the concrete floor as if it had been suddenly dropped.

Charley felt drawn to the barrel. The force pulling him seemed to be coming from inside the drum. He slid his Smith & Wesson back into its holster. He was no longer worried about Bowditch. The locus of his fear had shifted.

"I'll admit he had a talent for it," said Jack. "He could have learned a lot from Elmut if they'd kept up their private classes. There's a room full of mounts upstairs. Warren did a pretty good goshawk. And that spruce grouse he got from the Grindle kid came out real nice."

Charley reached for the crowbar.

The lid came off without any effort, although the harsh citrus odor caused him to gasp. He peered over the brim and saw that the barrel was full of a liquid that he deduced was a mixture of water and formic acid. Submerged below the surface was a pallid bobbing sheet. He stared at it for a long time before his mind would accept he was looking at Tim Grindle's flayed skin.

15

Charley Stevens, white-haired now and weathered, fell silent. He reached down from his rocking chair to pat the old dog sleeping beside the woodstove. Nimrod was prone to bad dreams.

"How have I never heard this story?" I asked after I'd caught my breath.

"I could say it was a different time, and there's truth in that," he said. "Back then, papers mostly reported what they were told, especially when it concerned folks like the Grindles. Even today, how much do journalists poke around when a poor feller goes missing? A pretty white girl, it's different. But Ora was right about Tim Grindle: No one in Flagstaff or Bigelow wanted him back except his brother and his girlfriend."

"What did you tell Ed, though?"

"I didn't."

I came close to rising from my chair. "What?"

"The deputy who arrived at Ed Grindle's house didn't arrest him. Sheriff Hatch was peeved I had left the scene, and he told his officer to let Ed sleep it off. As soon as Grindle sobered up, he found another pistol and took my ill-considered advice about sticking the barrel in his mouth. I feel bad about that, but I would've felt worse if he ever learned the truth about Tim. Same with Ricki Tripp. Her living with being jilted seemed preferable to her knowing about that drum full of acid."

"So she never found out, either?"

"No."

Charley was answering my questions truthfully, I knew that much. And yet there remained a void at the center of the story that terrified me. There was a reason that I had never heard the names of these people before, a reason that went beyond lazy reporters and a convenient suicide.

"Did Tomer Elmut know what Whittaker was doing in that basement?"

"If he had, he would have told your dad. Jack went to see him again after he got out of the hospital. Tomer fled the area soon after."

I glanced out the frosted window. A flock of redpolls had taken over a chokecherry bush near the porch. From its safety, the song-birds made quick forays to the thistle feeder in case a Cooper's hawk was waiting in ambush.

I realized I had forgotten all about the eagle in my truck while Charley had been talking.

"What you're telling me is there was a cover-up," I said. "Some-one decided the story of Warren Whittaker skinning a boy was too horrific—that if it ever got out, it would doom Maine tourism."

"Not exactly." He cleared his throat. "How many times have you driven through Kingfield? What did the Whittaker house look like the last time you saw it?"

I paused to ransack my memory. "When you were telling me the story, I realized I couldn't remember ever having seen it."

"The next owner cleared away all the debris after the fire. It gutted the building even before the first pumper truck arrived. The state fire marshal spent days poking through the wreckage before he found what was left of Warren Whittaker. Apparently, the taxidermist was trapped in the basement when the electric panel shorted out. Setting a fire like that is nothing to a former Ranger."

I felt like Tim Grindle being stuck in the chest by a fatal object. "Charley, no."

"When I saw what Whittaker had done," he said wearily, "I realized I wasn't going to arrest your old man for pushing him down the stairs. Not that the detectives would've found clear evidence of murder. You know how your father was. The more grievous the crime, the more careful he was to protect himself. I went outside to call the state police on my radio, but for the longest time, I just couldn't bring myself to do anything but sit there. I should have known better than to leave your old man alone in the house. I figure my subconscious understood perfectly well what he would do."

A piece of wood sizzled in the stove between our chairs.

"My father burned it all down," I said.

"I don't think I've ever seen a place go up faster. I remember watching your dad come flying through the smoke like the proverbial bat out of hell. He had this look on his face. Like he knew I wouldn't stop him from driving off—and he was right."

"None of the neighbors saw you there?"

"The Whittaker house was at the edge of the village, as I said, and we were parked behind the building, out of sight. I told the firefighters who answered the call that I was driving past and happened to see the smoke, but that I wasn't quick enough to save Warren Whittaker."

"The fire marshal found no trace of Tim Grindle inside?"

"Warren had only kept the skin. That's all he needed for his little project. Maybe he really did dispose of the rest up in Freeman, like he told your dad. Technology wasn't as advanced then, you need to remember."

I found myself parched and took a sip of coffee from the mug I'd barely touched. It was cold as ice water.

"You had a duty to report what happened," I said.

"A legal duty, sure. But when I heard about Ed Grindle's suicide, I couldn't think who would be better off hearing the truth. This is the first time I ever told the story from start to finish. Even Ora doesn't know every detail, but that's because it's her choice." His eyes had misted up, but he was unembarrassed by the tears. "If you're judging me harshly, it's no worse than I've judged myself—both for what I did and what I failed to do. Will you forgive me, Mike?"

"Me? I'm not in a place to judge you, Charley."

"I just need to hear the words spoken."

I reached for his hand. "I forgive you."

He allowed me to squeeze it briefly, then withdrew. He was a man of his generation in that regard. "I'm grateful for that."

"I'm surprised my father never tried to blackmail you somehow."

"Your dad had his own code of justice, as I said. And in his mind, he alone was responsible for Tim's death. We never would've gone to the Grindle house if he hadn't brought me that eagle. He rationalized everything he did afterward as making things right. Your father was a self-involved, self-justifying man, and I don't think it occurred to him to think about how I was affected. Jack Bowditch saw himself as a punishing fury. I have no doubt he would have flayed Whittaker alive if he'd searched the basement before he pushed him down the stairs."

"Why do you say that?"

"Because it was just the skin from Tim's body in that drum. Whittaker must have been afraid the boy's hair would fall out during the pickling process. I found the face and scalp in a Tupperware container over the laundry sink."

The Caretaker

I was seated on the porch of my old friend Charley Stevens, the two of us enjoying the quiet calm of Little Wabassus Pond and the flutter of southbound warblers in the pines overhead, when we heard a car approaching down the dirt track that led to his house deep in the Maine woods. A visitor of any kind was surprising enough here, ten miles from the nearest logging road and twenty from the nearest village. Even more surprising was that the car was a brand-new Tesla with Massachusetts plates.

"Whoever they are, they must be lost," I said.

"Not at all," said Charley, rising from his rocking chair. "I figure these folks are exactly where they want to be."

"You know them, then?"

"Not yet."

The retired game warden could be insufferable in this way. Charley was a born performer who enjoyed playing with people's assumptions the way a cat does with a spider. More than once, I had heard him amplify his natural Down East accent to bait an out-of-stater who was treating him like some ignorant hick. Even I, his self-appointed apprentice, was not spared his occasional teasing. The only reason I let Charley get away with it was because he had the sharpest mind I'd met in my young career in law enforcement, and I was eager to learn everything I could from the wiry old woodsman.

The man and woman who emerged from the dusty Tesla (she was the driver) were as surprising as their vehicle. They were so mismatched I had trouble imagining the nature of their relationship. She was a tawny-skinned blonde, very thin, about my age. He was graying, florid-faced, grossly overweight, and wearing a leg brace that suggested recent knee surgery. Both were dressed in sun-faded sailing shirts with the collars popped, pastel shorts, and boat shoes, as if they'd come directly from some distant yacht.

"Hello! Are you Warden Stevens?" asked the woman as we came forward to meet them. Her sunglasses were so enormous they hid half her face.

"I used to be."

"Excuse me?"

"I have been retired a few years. But this young feller is Mike Bowditch, and he's still in the employ of the Maine Warden Service, though he's not wearing his uniform today, being on vacation."

"Thank Christ!" said the man, whose jowls had begun sweating the moment he left the air-conditioned car. He had a plummy British accent I associated with costume dramas on public television. "I thought we'd taken a wrong turn. According to the GPS, we've driven right off the map and into the netherworld."

"This far out in the woods, telemetric signals get a little sketchy," said Charley. "But you've arrived at your appointed destination."

"How did you know that?" the woman said, her voice sharpening with suspicion.

"You asked for me by name," Charley said. "And since you called me 'Warden,' you were under the assumption I was still on active duty. Not many people know the way here, and those that do generally grant me and my wife privacy, so you would had to have been persistent about asking directions, which means you're desperate. I guess you've come to report a crime that you can't get the authorities to take seriously."

"How did you know the police had blown us off?" the man asked. "Someone must have called you."

"No, sir," said Charley, smiling one of his wry smiles and running a hand through his shock of white hair. "I see that you're from the South Shore, and most people visiting Maine from your neck of the woods would go to the police with a problem. The cops would've referred you to the district warden—young Bard—who gave you my name rather than assisting you himself."

I had watched the woman flash a white smile as Charley laid out his reasoning.

The man, meanwhile, only grew redder. "How can you possibly know we live on the South Shore?"

But the woman had already figured it out. "Our license plate, Josiah. The Tesla dealership in Dedham stamps its name on the frame so people will know where we bought it. It was hardly a difficult deduction."

That was easy for her to say. I hadn't guessed how Charley had done it, and I prided myself on being quick on my feet.

"Now that I've shown off for you," said my friend, "I have to confess that your names are beyond the limits of even my prodigious mental powers."

"Violet and Josiah Baker," she said.

She had removed her sunglasses, and I saw that she had a delicate face under her bleached hair. Her brown eyes were big and heavily lashed. To my unsophisticated mind, her features suggested West Asian ancestry; her family might have had its origins anywhere from Lebanon to Pakistan. Her accent, however, was generically American, as lacking in regional cues as a TV newscaster's.

"Come up on the porch, Mr. and Mrs. Baker, and tell us about your troubles over glasses of sun tea."

Five minutes later, Charley had poured us all drinks. His ancient German short-haired pointer, Nimrod, had wagged his tail in greeting when the Bakers had appeared but had settled at his master's feet when it became clear that neither visitor cared to pet him. Only then did Josiah Baker begin their story.

"Over the winter, we purchased a cottage—I guess you Mainers would call it a *camp*—on Purlington Pond."

"I didn't realize old Brunton was selling that place," he said.

"He wasn't." Josiah Baker turned to his wife. "Perhaps you can explain how he knows which cottage is ours."

"There are only two camps on the pond," said Violet. "Warden Stevens had a fifty-fifty chance."

Charley toasted her with his glass. The tea was freshened with wild mint he'd foraged from the wetlands along the Machias River, and it was delicious.

"You two are making me feel a dunce, I must say," Josiah Baker said.

I restrained myself from nodding in agreement.

Violet decided to take over the story from her husband, who was perspiring heavily from both the unseasonal September heat and his growing embarrassment.

"You need to understand first that Josiah and I both have high-stress jobs. He is a partner with one of Boston's top advertising firms, and I am an architect, just starting my own practice. Last fall, we took a trip to Nova Scotia and, passing this way, happened upon Grand Lake Stream. It's such a magical village, like someplace in a fairy tale. We'd been talking about finding a remote retreat off the grid. We wanted to be able to tell our colleagues, 'Sorry, we don't have cell or internet at the cottage.' Poking around, we happened on Purlington Pond, and I knew at once it was absolutely perfect."

Perfect was not a word I would have used to describe that mosquito hatchery, but remote it certainly was.

"We made Mr. Brunton a cash offer, and he accepted the same day," she continued. "This spring, we began renovating the building. Josiah's job kept him in the city, but I have been up in Maine most weekends, working with our contractor. I haven't camped out since I was a child, but even alone at night, so far from civilization, I never felt unsafe. Not until the first incident."

Charley sat forward in his rocker, his blue eyes shining from his craggy face. "Now we're getting to the meat of the matter."

"I know you'll find this impossible to believe, Warden Stevens, but two weeks ago, I returned to the cottage for the weekend and found the house . . . rearranged. The furniture had been moved entirely around. The kitchen table was upside down. The wine fridge was on its side. Every chair was stacked on top of each other in a leaning tower on the porch. It was as if we'd been visited by mischievous elves."

"Was anything missing?" I asked.

She responded to Charley as if he'd been the one to ask the question. "No! That's just it. We hadn't brought anything up here of real value, but still, I would've expected the vandals to have stolen something."

"So what did you do?" Charley asked.

"Called the police, of course," interjected Josiah Baker. "The sheriff's deputy who took my call seemed to think it was comical, or maybe he assumed I was some mad Brit. He said it was probably just local kids, riding around on all-terrain vehicles and getting into trouble. I had told Violet we needed a high-tech security system."

She put her small hand on her husband's thick-fingered one. "I keep reminding him that connecting our cottage to satellites and the internet defeats the purpose of our being here."

The way Josiah Baker flicked his eyes as she spoke hinted he'd never been entirely on board with his wife's plan. "The deputy suggested we invest in better locks for the doors and new shutters for the windows. And, most importantly, that we hire a caretaker. He said the best ones have reputations among the locals that their properties be left alone—or else."

"Did you hire a caretaker?" asked Charley.

"We tried, but it was the damnedest thing—"

"I'm getting to that, Josiah," Violet Baker interjected. She seemed intensely concerned about laying out the facts in a proper order. "Last week, I had my builder fortify some of the doors and windows with shutters like those used in hurricane country."

"But it didn't prevent a second incident," said Charley.

"If anything, the threats have only escalated. Yesterday afternoon, we drove up from Norwell—the trip takes six hours, in traffic—and arrived after dark. Josiah found these at the foot of the back porch."

She produced her cell phone and presented an image on the lighted screen to Charley. First, he smiled, then he furrowed his brow, then he grew grim as he handed the phone to me. The picture showed two enormous footprints in the mud.

"Sasquatch?" I said. "Or maybe a malevolent circus clown?"

"I'm glad you think it's funny," said Violet Baker with surprising fierceness. "Deputy Corbett and the other warden did, too. What is it about police that they're so quick to discount everyone's testimony? Does the oath you took to uphold the law mean nothing to any of you?"

I felt stung by these words until it entered my mind that her anger seemed disproportionate to the lame joke I'd made. Sometimes a person will have a bad experience with one cop, and it colors their attitude forever after.

"I'd judge the boots that made those prints to be size sixteens," said Charley. "It hasn't rained since the evening of September 10. The mud was still soft when your trespasser left these tracks. But I'm guessing those prints weren't what brought you to see me. You said, 'The threats have only escalated,' Mrs. Baker."

"Tell him, Josiah."

Her husband seemed unprepared to take over the narrative.

"This morning, we went for a walk," he stammered. "My orthopedist wants me to move this new cobalt-chromium knee every day. But it was all I could do to make it a quarter mile before we had to turn around."

"And when you got home?" said Charley.

"We found this in our bed!" said Violet, showing us a new image.

This picture showed a female sex doll, naked, made of silicone, and anatomically correct, lying with its head on a pillow and its dead turquoise eyes seeming to stare at the ceiling. A piece of duct tape covered its mouth, and more tape bound its wrists together. A pink slash ran from ear to ear along the throat.

"You sent this to the police, I hope," I said.

"Of course we did!" said Josiah. "But by now, that Chief Deputy Corbett—he's the man we've been dealing with—thinks we're a couple of loons."

"You're all missing the most important point!" said Violet. "Josiah and I were walking on the road. It's the only way in. No one could possibly have driven past us. So whoever did this horrible thing was watching the cottage and waiting for us to leave. We had locked the door, and there were no signs of forced entry, so how did he get in?"

Charley stroked his lantern jaw as he often did when he was working through a problem.

"What's the name of your builder, Mrs. Baker?"

"What are you suggesting? That Jack Small constructed a secret entrance—or a hidden chamber?"

"Preposterous!" said Josiah.

"I was thinking of a second set of keys," said Charley. "But if you have no reason to distrust the man, I think it's time you told us about your failed attempts at finding a caretaker."

"We approached several around Grand Lake Stream," said Josiah. "Or Violet did, I should say. I was back in Boston recovering from surgery."

"I gathered some names in town," she said. "Unfortunately,

the first two I approached—Mr. Brunton's son being one—had too many commitments to take on a new property, especially one so far from their others. It was the third man who gave me the creeps."

"Who was he?" I said.

She had prepared for this moment. From a leather case, she produced a business card, which she handed to Charley, who handed it to me. The stock was cheap, like something done on a home printer, with blocky letters.

KEVIN MORAN

PROPERTY MGMT · HANDYMAN · PORTRAIT PHOTOGRAPHY

"Do you know him?" demanded Josiah Baker.

"I do," said Charley.

"Well?"

"He does possess very large feet."

"That's all you have to say?"

"Kevin Moran is an odd duck, to be sure," said Charley. "But there are flocks of those living in the woods."

Josiah Baker struggled to rise on his bad knee but had to give up. "This was a mistake, expecting help from a game warden."

"Take a breath, Mr. Baker," said Charley, and as he spoke, I noticed his accent growing thicker, a sure sign he'd felt demeaned. "Mr. Moran lives alone and always has since he moved here, twenty-odd years back. Comes from somewhere in the Middle West, I believe. He hasn't earned the negative attention of the local constabulary, as best I know. But Warden Bowditch here can speak to that point better than yours truly, as he used to be the district warden in these parts."

I was grateful to be given a platform to establish myself as more than just my friend's youthful flunky.

I tried to keep my tone professional. "Everything Charley has said, I can vouch for. Moran keeps to himself. He doesn't hunt or fish, but he has a motorboat he takes out onto Big Lake at night. He was always compliant when I checked his registration and safety devices, although not particularly friendly. His hobby is nighttime photography. He has a strange sense of humor, too. Inappropriate."

"It's more than that," said Violet Baker. "There's something predatory about this Kevin Moran, and I think you both know it."

"Just what did he say or do to give you the creeps?" Charley asked.

"He asked if I'd been spending much time alone at the cottage. And when I'd be there."

It occurred to me that a potential caretaker, who happened to be a socially awkward man, could ask those questions with no malicious intent, but I was hardly going to suggest to Violet Baker she might have drawn the wrong impression.

Now it was Charley's turn to rise to his feet. He was past seventy and had suffered many injuries over his long life, but I am not exaggerating when I say he had the energy and athleticism of a man half his age. "I take it you left the doll on the bed."

"Of course!"

"Well, then, let's go have a look at it." He offered his strong forearm to Josiah, who grudgingly accepted the assistance escaping the rocking chair. "Mike and I will follow you there. Come on, Nimrod. We're going for a ride."

And just like that, the ancient pointer was on his feet and thwacking his tail against Josiah Baker's bad leg.

"There's something about their story that doesn't ring true to me," I said, driving with care through the dust cloud kicked up by the Tesla.

"Such as?"

"She's an architect starting up a new practice, and she wants to cut herself off from the rest of the world? I haven't known many architects, but I get the sense that making yourself unavailable to your clients while a project is in the works is a bad career decision."

"Maybe she's got a partner? But I share your skepticism about the Bakers, I have to admit. Even if they're telling the truth about wanting to build a retreat in the woods, it's queer they would choose a piss-poor excuse for a pond like Purlington when there are so many beautiful lakes hereabouts. God knows they seem to have the money for finer accommodations."

After fifteen minutes, we turned onto the Stud Mill Road, heading east. It was a dirt-and-gravel superhighway that led, more or less, from the mills north of Bangor to the Canadian border through alternating expanses of industrial timberland and wooded nature preserves. Logging trucks had the right of way on the Stud Mill and other commercial roads, and I wondered if we might witness the Tesla getting flattened against the grille of an oncoming eighteen-wheeler.

"She's not wrong about Moran being a creep," I said. "An interest in nocturnal photography seems like a good excuse to roam around after dark, peeping into houses. How did you know he's from the Midwest?"

"I asked him once!" Charley was utterly unafraid of being blunt with strangers. "Said I couldn't place his accent."

"What did he say?"

"That he was from Indiana originally."

"How did he end up in Down East Maine?"

"He said there were too many people where he used to live, and this was one of the last uncrowded places on the map."

"Nothing suspicious about a loner who likes to skulk around after nightfall."

My friend was one of the few people whose laughs could rightly be described as guffaws. "A wise man once said, 'Just because a man is a hermit doesn't mean he's hiding from something. But it doesn't mean he's *not* hiding, either.'"

"Who's the wise man?"

"Me, of course."

We made a few more turns, first south, then west, before we reached a rutted road with grass growing in the middle, the blades of which brushed the underside of my truck. Multiple heavy vehicles had recently been in and out of the property. I could tell from the dried tire marks, crushed vegetation, and dusty puckerbrush along the road.

A brand-new NO TRESPASSING sign had been nailed to an ancient cedar. Someone had wrapped barbed wire around the trunk ages ago, probably as part of a jerry-built gate system, giving the tree a pinched look where it had expanded around the wire.

I had gotten it into my head that the Bakers had merely rehabilitated Brunton's old hunting and fishing camp, but the new building that appeared out of the trees was as striking as it was out of place. It was all flat surfaces and sharp angles—as if Frank Lloyd Wright had set out to thumb his nose at New England's

architectural heritage. The building had southward-pointing solar panels, which must have provided a small amount of electric-
ity to power their lights and appliances.

"They built this place since the spring?" I asked in awe.

"I guess these folks don't wait around after they make a
plan."

"The roof is flat," I said. "There's no place for the snow to slide
off. It's going to cave in under the weight. They're going to need a
caretaker just to shovel it off after every storm. Didn't their contractor tell them?"

I pulled up behind the Tesla, and we got out. As I did, I caught
a glimpse of the land behind the house. Someone had cut down
the trees and cleared the bushes between the back porch and the
pond in violation of state wetland protection laws.

Josiah was leaning against the porch rail. "What do you think?
Isn't Violet a genius?"

"It's certainly unique," I said.

"We noticed that the cottages around here all have corny
names," said Josiah, "so we've decided to call this place Sequoia."

"There are no sequoias in Maine," I said.

"Yes, I know."

Violet Baker was tapping a combination into a keypad beside
the door. "My husband thinks he's so clever at times."

"What's the point of those electronic locks?" Charley asked.

"They're wired to an alarm," she said, "but all it does is make
a shrill noise to frighten away an intruder, theoretically speaking.
I expect the serious housebreakers learn that they're nothing to
take seriously."

"The alarm didn't go off this morning?"

"Whoever broke in must have known how to bypass it."

"You're sure about your contractor?" I said.

"Jack is the best builder I've ever worked with," said Violet,
showing another flash of temper. "I told you, neither he nor his

crew had anything to do with the crimes committed against us. Now would you please come have a look at the bedroom?"

The scene was mostly as it had appeared in the photos. The naked doll was made of silicone but smaller than I'd guessed— barely four feet in "height"—although it boasted ridiculously outsize breasts. The knife cut across its throat looked clean and careful, as opposed to a violent slash. The doll was such an art-less representation of the human form that I was surprised to find myself so horrified by what had been done to it.

"Are you going to dust it for fingerprints?" the husband asked me.

I was tempted to make a quip about how I kept my container of dusting compound in my other pair of jeans.

Charley saved me from the ill-considered wisecrack. "Anyone smart enough to get past your electronic lock would've worn gloves, I would think. And, as you know, neither Warden Bowditch nor I are forensic evidence technicians. Could we have a look at the footprints now?"

"That's it?" said Violet. "You don't want to take pictures of this mutilated thing yourself?"

"Yours will be sufficient if this incident prompts a criminal prosecution," said Charley.

"If?" said Josiah Baker.

But Charley was already headed to the back porch.

There were two boot prints in the dried mud at the foot of the stairs leading to the pond. In person, they looked even more gar-gantuan than they had in the picture. The tracks were positioned in such a way as to suggest a man had stood gazing up at the building without daring to climb the steps.

Charley crouched down beside the tracks and nodded. Then he looked up at me.

"Could you take over here, Mike? I realized that old Nimrod is going to irrigate the back seat of your vehicle unless I take him out."

I had no idea what he meant by "taking over," but I agreed. He left me with the Bakers, both of whom were looking increasingly frustrated.

"He couldn't have walked the dog before?" said Josiah.

Violet, meanwhile, edged toward the corner of the building as if to watch Charley walk to my truck.

"These are size sixteens, all right," I said, using the length of my hand—eight inches from the heel of the palm to the tip of my index finger—as a measuring stick. "Vibram soles, which narrows things down significantly. But I'm not expert enough to identify the brand or anything. I will say, there's something strange about them, though."

"Strange?" asked Violet, edging back in our direction.

"I would have expected them to be deeper. A man with boots this big should weigh a fair amount. And the tracks he made entering and leaving your property are so faint, you'd miss them if you weren't looking closely."

I discreetly glanced at Josiah Baker's scuffed boat shoes. They couldn't have been larger than size eights.

The sound of a truck door opening, then closing, told me that Charley had liberated Nimrod from my vehicle. I was grateful not to have to clean up one of the elderly dog's accidents. I'd just detailed the Scout before setting off to visit Charley while his wife, Ora, was away.

Josiah went inside to pour himself a single malt that almost certainly didn't agree with whatever pain medication he might be taking for the knee. The rest of us had declined his offer of a midday tipple. His family apparently had some ancestral connection to the Hebridean island from which this whiskey hailed.

Violet, meanwhile, had gone quiet. The intensity of her attention affected me like a spotlight shined in my eyes.

"I guess I could take a few photos of that doll while we wait for Charley to return."

I was surprised not to see him as we circled back to the front of the cottage (whatever else the place was, it was no camp). All I could figure was that he had walked Nimrod back down the road.

"Where is he?" asked Violet, echoing my thought.

"I hope he has a plastic bag with him to pick up after that animal," said Josiah. "I don't want to be out for a walk and step in shit."

I was tempted to say that Nimrod wasn't the only animal in these woods and if he didn't want to tread on scat, he should learn to watch where he put his feet.

Back inside the house, I took a handful of photographs of the tortured doll, including one of a serial number on its foot.

"You'll take it with you, I hope," said Josiah Baker.

"No, sir, but I'll help you get it into a trash bag. I can give you the number of the Grand Lake Stream transfer station attendant unless you'd rather take it to Baileyville to avoid being associated with a sex toy."

Josiah huffed. "That's all we need, getting the reputation of being perverts in addition to out-of-staters. Isn't it, Violet?"

But when we both turned, we found she had left the bedroom.

We located her on the front porch, watching Charley return from his dog walk. He had just put Nimrod back inside the Scout and wore a big grin on his weathered, almost handsome face.

"Is everything all right?" Violet Baker asked him.

"When you get that dog started, he doesn't want to stop. This is a mighty impressive house—not just the design but the craftsmanship. What did you say the name was of the contractor who built it?"

"Small and Son. Jack is the son. But I told you, he had nothing to do with this."

"Are they a Maine-based firm?"

"They're out of Boston," she said.

"That explains why I've never heard of them."

"I've worked closely with Jack on several projects. I knew he'd execute the design to my standards."

In college, the most brilliant woman I knew—a literal genius who graduated with the school's highest honors and a Rhodes Scholarship—had suffered from anorexia nervosa. Violet's ferocious drive for perfection and almost emaciated appearance made me wonder if she didn't suffer from the same condition.

"And you settled your accounts with this Small feller?"

The diminutive connotation of the man's name didn't please her. "What are you suggesting, Warden?"

I heard ice rattle in a glass as Josiah approached from behind us. "That we haven't paid our bill, lamb."

"Even if that were the case, Jack Small is not capable of these gross, offensive acts—as I keep telling you. And he lives hours from here in Milton, Massachusetts. Are you honestly suggesting he drove all this way to gaslight us for no conceivable reason?"

"No, ma'am."

But it was clear she didn't believe my friend. Worse, she seemed to have decided we were two small-time, small-minded lawmen.

The skeptical smile returned to her full lips. "You're just going to drive off and maybe head into town to gossip about us and have a few laughs at our expense."

"You have the wrong idea about us, Mrs. Baker," said Charley.

"Is that so!"

"From here, Warden Bowditch and I are headed over to Wood land to have a conversation with that caretaker, Kevin Moran."

Her eyes narrowed. "You are?"

"Indeed."

"It simply has to be that Moran character who's stalking us," said Josiah. "I can't think of a single person locally who might wish us ill."

His use of the word *locally* caught my notice.

"You should watch yourself around him," said Violet. "Moran strikes me as the type of man who might react violently to being confronted. The last thing we need is for you to stir him up and then leave us here unprotected."

"I don't think you're in any personal danger, Mrs. Baker," said Charley.

"Of course we are!" she said. "After everything you've seen here, how can you say that?"

It was unlike Charley Stevens to offer empty assurances, so I was as surprised as she was by the certainty in his tone. Usually I had some window, however small, into the old warden's mind. But for the moment, that window was closed.

"We'll let you know what Mr. Moran has to say for himself," said Charley in his thickest Down East drawl.

I don't know why you told the Bakers they weren't in danger."

"Is that what I said?" He seemed to be fighting back a smile.

"Crimes have been committed, Charley. At the very least, breaking and entering."

"More than we know about, I would say. But I think we're in time to prevent a worse one."

He was being insufferable again. I knew enough to shut up and focus on my driving, and soon we had reached the paved road that crossed the bridge above Grand Lake Stream. I caught a glimpse of anglers wading in the Dam Pool. It was too early in the fall for big salmon. But one of the pleasures of fishing is never knowing what you might catch.

The road took us through the reservation of the Passamaquoddy Tribe along the shores of Big Lake, and then across yet another bridge into the predominantly white town of Princeton, which was, perhaps, less poor than its neighbor but dwelt beneath a similar cloud of despair.

We continued east, stopping only for convenience store coffee before we reached the outskirts of Woodland, sometimes called Baileyville, where Kevin Moran lived. Several towns in Maine had two names, and I always wondered how and when they had acquired their aliases.

As it happened, Moran was engaged in a carpentry project

in his open garage as we pulled up to the house. The home was modest, a simple ranch that was neither the shabbiest residence along this country road nor the grandest. It didn't look like a hermit's retreat, in any case.

Moran emerged from the garage as we stepped out of the Scout. He wasn't as tall as I remembered, not much above six feet, but he had put on weight since I'd last seen him. He was wearing a short-sleeved work shirt over a tee, canvas pants, and a pair of enormous Timberland boots. The front of his clothes was covered with sawdust. Some of the beige powder had also adhered to the perspiration on his face, giving him the look of a man wearing a mask. There were flecks of it, too, on his horn-rimmed eyeglasses.

As usual, my genial friend took the lead in approaching the man. "Howdy there. I don't suppose you remember us."

"Hmmm. Let me think." Suddenly, the caretaker's face broke into a smile. "How is a game warden like a laxative?"

"How?" said Charley, playing along.

"They both irritate the shit out of you. I'm just joking. You're Stevens. You and your wife have that place down on Little Wabassus Pond. Beautiful spot, out on the point."

If I had been in my friend's position, I might have asked how he had come to know the specific details of my property, as isolated and hard to access as it was.

But Charley just gave him one of his signature jack-o'-lantern grins and said, "And you're Kevin Moran."

"That's what my license says. It's sad because when I was a kid, my mother told me I could be anyone I wanted to be. Turns out, identity theft is a crime."

Charley laughed like he'd never heard anything so funny. "What are you building?"

"Teeter-totter for the church playground."

"Which church?" I said, feeling the need to insert myself into the conversation.

Moran, having found me unreceptive to his jokes, directed

himself at my companion. "I know you guys didn't come here for my stand-up routine. So what can I do for you?"

His voice was deep and monotone and, now that I was listening for the accent, I perceived a faintly Southern drawl. I had no clue how people from Indiana spoke, but I wouldn't have identified the state as his birthplace from his way of speaking.

"You were recently approached by a couple from Massachusetts by the name of Baker?" said Charley.

The smile disappeared as suddenly as it had appeared. "That's right."

"They interviewed you about taking on their cottage?"

"I only spoke with the wife. She made me drive all the way down to the camp in person and then asked me two questions before saying I was unfit for the job—whatever that meant."

"Do you remember the questions?" Charley asked.

"She wanted to know the services I offered. I made a joke she didn't appreciate."

"What was the joke?" I asked.

"I don't remember."

Like hell he didn't.

"What was the second question?" I asked.

"The second question?"

He paused, then removed his dusty glasses and cleaned them with a handkerchief that had been hanging from his back pocket. The lenses had magnified his eyes. Without them, they seemed very small, rimmed with fat and almost piggish.

"She wanted to know where I was based out of," he concluded. "How far away I lived from their cottage. I gave her a straight answer. She seemed to mull it over. Then she told me I was unfit for the job, like I said."

"Do you have any idea why she might have come to that conclusion?"

Moran was one of those people whose appearance changes so utterly when they stop smiling that they become someone else.

"Maybe she didn't like the smell of my deodorant. Granted, I'm no daisy. But the twat looked at me like I reeked."

At the moment, there was nothing objectionable about how he smelled. His Old Spice was up to the demands of the day. His rude term for Violet Baker, however, was another matter.

"You must have been angry," I said, "being asked to drive all the way out there for a two-question interview."

"I didn't appreciate it, no. But after meeting the woman, I didn't want the job, anyway. Life is too short to work for assholes. Maybe you've heard the joke: Why did the Invisible Man refuse the job offer? Because he couldn't see himself in it."

"And you're the Invisible Man?"

Again Moran spoke to Charley. "What's this about, Wardens? You still haven't told me."

"We'd like to show you some photographs," I said, pulling out my phone.

Charley said, "I don't think there's any cause for that, young feller."

But I hadn't liked what I'd heard out of Moran—neither the comic version nor the new, sullen one—and was not to be deterred. I pulled up the pictures of the boot prints and held the screen six inches from the tip of his dusty nose. "What size boots do you wear, Mr. Moran? Sixteen, are they?"

"Where was that taken?" Moran asked. "Are those supposed to be mine?"

"That's enough, Mike."

But I had switched photos. An image of the violated sex doll shined on the screen.

Perspiration popped through the pores of Moran's forehead as I swiped to the next close-up. "What the heck is that thing?" he asked.

"Don't pretend you haven't seen one before."

"Of course I've seen *pictures* of one, but why are you showing it to me?"

"I think you know."

"Is she accusing me of doing that?" Moran said. The sweat running down his cheeks was making rivulets through the sawdust. "Because I've never seen that doll before in my life."

"There's a serial number on the foot that we can trace to the person who bought it."

Suddenly, Charley took hold of my wrist with a steely grip and pulled my arm down. "Mr. Moran, we apologize for interrupting your work."

But the caretaker didn't seem to hear him. "That lying bitch sent you here to accuse me of doing that. Didn't she?"

"Watch your tone, Kevin."

"I think I have a right to be angry. This is harassment."

"Harassment is planting a mutilated sex doll in someone's bed. Stay away from the Bakers."

Charley leaned in close and whispered in my ear, "It's time for us to leave, Mike."

Inside the Scout, Charley was silent for the first few minutes as I pulled a U-turn and headed back toward the forests and lakes west of Grand Lake Stream.

"I hadn't expected you to get so aggressive with him," he said at last. "That was my mistake."

"He's obviously lying. You heard his stupid jokes. Everything that happened at the Baker place reflects his sick sense of humor. You don't think he's seen that sex doll before? He probably kept it under his bed, dressed in lingerie."

"We don't know that."

"Maybe not for a certainty, but my gut tells me it was him. And now we've put him on notice to leave the Bakers alone. I have no regrets about what I said or did."

Charley didn't answer. He only gazed out the window.

I was barreling past the turnoff to the Bakers' modern cottage—what a ridiculous name, Sequoia!—when Charley said, "We need to pay them another visit."

I didn't brake, but I eased up on the gas. "What for?"

I had hoped to do a little fishing.

"To tell them about our conversation with Mr. Moran. And they don't have cell service, remember? Besides, there's something I need to see down there with my own eyes."

Mr. Moran!

I hated that Charley insisted on using a courtesy title for the jerk, but I wasn't going to refuse his request.

The rattling, dusty drive back to Purlington Pond seemed faster the second time, now that I knew where I was going, but on the last stretch, Charley leaned forward, searching with his eyes through the windshield.

"Stop here!"

Both sides of the road were unremarkable at first glance. I saw mixed woods growing out of a substratum of hobblebush and cinnamon ferns that had already begun to shrivel before the inevitable autumn. But as I was idling, Charley hopped out—prompting a whine from Nimrod in the back—and approached a tree stump at the edge of the road. It was almost perfectly flat, as if it had been cut for the purposes of making a place to sit. He crouched down to inspect the dirt at its base.

Then, rising with a smile, he wiped his hands against his pants. "Keep an eye on the odometer from here back to the camp."

I knew better than to ask why. Charley Stevens would explain all, and with a flourish, when he was ready.

As we approached the building, I was surprised to find the Tesla gone.

"I guessed we missed them."

"There's a window open. See? I doubt they would leave it that way after what's been happening lately."

And as we came to a stop, the door opened, and Josiah Baker hauled himself onto the porch. He had changed into a horizontally striped shirt of the kind worn by French sailors and was moving even more gingerly than he had been that morning. His tin knee must have run out of oil.

"Howdy there!" Charley said. "Where's the missus?"

"Violet took the Tesla into Baileyville to use the Supercharger and to pick up a few supplies. It's a good thing she isn't around to hear you use that word. Violet doesn't forgive those kinds of labels, even from a man your age. I was shocked she took my last name when we married. It seemed so out of character."

"What was her maiden name?" my friend said.

Based on Josiah's grimace, I concluded that *maiden name* was also on his wife's list of unacceptable terms.

"Dawson."

"I don't mean to be intrusive," said Charley, which was a signal he was about to start prying. "But how long have you and your bride been wed?"

Now I winced along with Josiah.

"Three years. Pardon me for sitting, but the meds aren't doing anything for my pain, and if I have another scotch, I'm finished for the day."

"You're from England, obviously," said Charley. "But your little woman, she wasn't born in the USA, either."

To my ear, Charley was going out of his way to use archaic, impolitic language. His own wife, Ora, would have clobbered him if he dared to refer to *her* as his "little woman."

What's his game?

"She came here as an orphan from Afghanistan, if you must know," said an exasperated Josiah Baker. "She was part of a program for war refugees run by some nonprofit or other. She was placed with a series of foster families until she was finally adopted by the Dawsons of Lexington, Kentucky. If you knew half of what that woman went through to become who she is . . ." Once more, he caught himself. "How did you deduce she's an immigrant? I didn't know myself until she told me."

"I detected a faint accent earlier that I couldn't place, and she possesses a rare strength of character I've seen in other new Americans. It was more of a guess than anything, but I had the conviction she's overcome great obstacles in life."

"She has indeed. Now can we get off the topic of my absent wife?"

"My apologies."

"So what did that Moran character have to say for himself?"

"He won't be bothering you again," I said, trying to sound tough.

"How can you be sure?"

"He knows we're onto him."

"Mr. Moran said something interesting, though," said Charley. "He claims that Mrs. Baker invited him here for an interview that lasted all of a few minutes. Is that typical of her?"

"Violet has always been decisive. Are you implying that conversation is what stirred up the man—that he felt mistreated by her?"

"Some people are quick to anger," I said, speaking from intimate experience.

"Some, but not all," Charley said.

"You're not exactly reassuring me that this Moran isn't going to show up tonight with an axe in his hands. Violet says we should get a gun."

Charley and I both spoke at once, "No."

"Why ever not?"

"Have you shot a gun before, Mr. Baker?" I asked.

"Not one that fires bullets. In my thirties, I played paintball with some of my fellow associates. I wasn't a marksman, but I was hardly the worst shot among us. Violet read somewhere that a shotgun is ideal for home defense."

"I would strongly advise against that," Charley said. "For your own safety, Mr. Baker."

"But if we loaded it with rock salt—"

"It's still a bad idea," I chimed in, reciting a speech I had memorized for these occasions. "Researchers have consistently found that having a firearm in the house increases one's likelihood of being killed with it by huge margins, whether from accidents, suicides, or having the gun taken away by your assailant and used against you."

"The young feller is right."

I was relieved that Charley and I were of one mind on this point, at least.

"Mr. Baker," he continued, "I can't impress on you with sufficient seriousness the personal danger you will be in if you permit your wife to bring a firearm into this house."

"Violet is going to do what she's going to do, as you've already seen."

"It's imperative for your sake that you persuade her against the idea," said Charley, and from his pocket he produced a small device resembling a miniature handheld GPS unit. "This is a satellite communicator that allows you to send emergency text messages. I'm going to loan it to you until you can buy one of your own. I've set it to text me directly. I wasn't in the cavalry when

I was in the army, but I've been known to ride to the rescue on occasion."

Josiah Baker accepted the gift with a darkening expression. "I am not sure whether this makes me feel rather better or worse about our situation."

For my part, I knew my friend well enough to understand he never would have loaned the communicator to the Bakers if he wasn't genuinely worried about their safety.

We said our goodbyes and were halfway to my vehicle when Charley turned and called out, "One last thing, just to satisfy my curiosity."

Josiah looked up from his new toy. "Yes?"

"Your wife said you went for a walk down the road this morning. How far did you get?"

"A quarter mile, more or less."

"And then you had to sit down and rest?"

"Not exactly. Violet had to run back to the house to use the bathroom. We had planned to go all the way out to the road, but once I sat down, my knee locked up. She had to drive out in the Tesla to get me."

"And after that was when you discovered the doll on your bed?"

Baker flushed. "You're not implying that Violet— Why would she do something like that?"

"I'm sure she wouldn't," said Charley. "Forget I asked."

Of course, that would be impossible, I knew. If his intention had been to prompt Josiah Baker into suspecting his wife, my friend had succeeded. He had certainly made me doubt her accounts of the threatening incidents she had supposedly experienced.

"Are you going to share your suspicions with me?" I asked once we were back on the road.

"I don't have suspicions."

"Like hell you don't."

"What I have, young feller, are questions."

And that was the end of the discussion for the remainder of the drive.

When we got back to Charley's house, the sun was out, and I noticed rings like scattered raindrops forming on the flat surface of the pond. It was a caddis fly hatch. I asked my friend if he wanted to grab his rod and join me on the water, but he said he had some calls to make, and so I took the canoe out and caught a dozen or so brook trout, two of which I brought back for dinner.

When I returned an hour later, I was surprised to find Charley still on the phone. He had his big feet propped on the desk in his office. As I entered the room, he switched to speaker mode.

"Thank you for calling me back, Mr. Small. As I said in my message, I'm helping Violet Baker with a problem."

"What kind of problem?" The tone of the contractor's deep voice sounded suspicious.

"She's having an issue with one of the locals trespassing on her property here in Maine."

"Who are you again?"

"Charley Stevens, Maine Warden Service, retired."

There was a significant pause on the other end.

"I need to call her before talking with you. I need to hear that she's given permission for this conversation."

"I can assure you her husband, Mr. Baker, has done so."

"I need to talk with Violet. I don't know the husband."

"Really? Isn't it strange for you to take on a residential construction without meeting both of the owners?"

"Whoever you are, you can stop talking," Small said. "I don't violate the confidences of *any* of my clients. I'm going to call Sam—"

"Sam?"

After a long pause, Small said, "If Violet gives her permission for us to talk, then I will call you back."

The line went dead, and Charley turned off the speaker.

"We won't be hearing from Mr. Small again," he said, stroking his long chin. "Why did he call her 'Sam,' do you think?"

"I have no idea."

"It's curious. So tell me, what did you catch out there?"

"A dozen brookies, and I kept two for dinner. How did you even locate the Bakers' contractor?"

"Just because I'm an old fart doesn't mean I don't know how to use Google."

On his computer, he tapped a key that caused the screen saver to stop gyrating. The browser was open to the website of the construction firm of Small and Son. A photo showed a dashing older man standing beside a dashing younger man, both dressed in blue denim.

Nimrod had gotten up from one of his naps, and I let him smell my hand, still pungent from fish slime. His tail began to thump expectantly. When his wife wasn't around, Charley always let the dog lick the bacon grease from the cast-iron pan we used to fry the trout.

"You think she's having an affair with him?" I said. "Or was having an affair with him, and he's behind this weird vandalism?"

Charley laughed. "Imagination is a gift. But one to be used in moderation in your line of work."

"If you don't suspect Jack Small, why did you call him?"

"You're about to get your answer."

He smiled opaquely and swung his boots off the desk. Then he reached down to scratch the haunch of his aging pointer.

Sure enough, the phone rang again.

This time, Charley let the call go to his old-school answering machine.

"Warden, this is Violet Baker. I'm in Calais running some errands, and I just got a disturbing call from my builder. He said you contacted him with personal questions about my husband and myself. While I appreciate your helping us with the caretaker situation—assuming you and your sidekick haven't provoked Moran into doing something rash—I resent your prying into our private lives. Clearly, it was a mistake to involve you in our predicament. You can leave us alone from this point forward."

"Sidekick?"

"There are worse things to be called. If she's mad now, wait till she gets home and Josiah tells her about our conversation with him. Did you catch her accent change, by the way? It was ever so slight. I heard it before when she got all exercised about how the police don't uphold their sacred oaths."

In fact, I had. "Maybe it comes out when she's upset."

"That's often the case. Some people won't show you who they really are unless you poke them with a sharp stick."

"Charley, what mischief have you been up to?"

"I thought I would have a look at Mrs. Violet Dawson Baker's professional résumé after our chat with her husband. She's an accomplished architect for such a young woman! But nowhere on her website or in the articles written about her is there any mention of her having been born in Afghanistan, which is her prerogative. But I was curious to read about the refugee resettlement program that brought her to the US as a young girl. And even more interested when I'd heard she'd been adopted by a family from northern Kentucky."

"Because Moran is from Indiana, just across the Ohio River?"

His smile told me he was pleased with the quickness of my thoughts. "What would you say if I told you Kevin Moran didn't exist before nineteen years ago? There's no record of him before he moved from Indiana—if that's where he is actually from—to Maine. I called up a favor with a federal agent to check the national databases, and he came up blank."

"Maybe Moran changed his name?"

"That would've shown up in the records."

"He's living under an assumed name, then."

"Why would he be doing that? Who was he beforehand? And

is any of this connected with his harassment of the Bakers? Do you see what I meant about having questions rather than suspicions?"

A loon began to call out on the lake. Outside, the shadows were stretching their limbs as the sun descended into the treetops.

"So what do you want to do?" I said.

"Eat! I'm as hungry as a bear in April."

Just before midnight, I was awakened by Charley opening the door to the guest cabin.

I sat up with a start. "What is it?"

"Get dressed. We need to haul ass back to the Bakers' cottage. And be sure to bring your sidearm."

"What's happened?"

"Hopefully, nothing yet. All I know is I've been a smug fool, and now a man's life is in danger."

An image flashed into my mind of the rotund Josiah Baker struggling with his bad knee to get out of the Adirondack chair.

Charley had spent hours after dinner silently pursuing trails of information about the mysterious Bakers, their contractor, and their rejected caretaker, and I'd had the sense he'd only run into dead ends. Eventually, he gave up and retreated with a cup of coffee to his darkened porch to listen to the loons while he pondered the mysteries of the man calling himself Kevin Moran.

I'd done a bit of online searching myself—with even less success—before giving up and picking up the book Charley had inexplicably left on my bedside table while I'd been fishing, *The Count of Monte Cristo*.

A light rain had begun to fall, turning the road dust to a sort of khaki paste that splattered and stuck to the withering ferns. It was a rough ride. My Scout had a suspension built for serious off-roading, but the ruts and bumps kept jouncing us into the air as I raced toward Purlington Pond.

"What do you think is happening, Charley?"

"A plan is about to come to fruition with violent consequences."

"Whose plan?"

He refused to answer.

We'd just turned onto the Stud Mill Road, spooking a ten-point buck I wished to meet again come hunting season, when Charley's cell phone buzzed.

It was a text from one of the Bakers using the handheld satellite communicator he had loaned Josiah. He read the message to me, as well as his responses as he typed them.

Help! This is Violet Baker. He tried to get in here!

Moran?

Yes!

What did you do?

Not me. Josiah! It's horrible.

My friend looked wounded. I could sense the thought going through his head.

Josiah is dead?

No, Moran!

"Where did the Bakers get a gun so fast?" I wondered aloud. "There's no chance they got one away from Moran."

But Charley wasn't listening to me.

Don't touch a thing now, Violet. The scene must remain undisturbed. We'll be there in 15 minutes. I'll call the police.

I cast a glance at my friend sitting in the passenger seat with the glowing screen in his lap. He was readying himself to call the dispatcher.

"You knew this was going to happen," I said, marveling at his steadiness.

"I feared it."

"You knew Moran would come after them tonight. And it's all my fault for goading him."

"If it was anyone's fault, it was mine for not seeing the chessboard under our feet. The game was skillfully played. But I'm not willing to concede the contest quite yet."

Before I could ask him to explain, he was on the line with the dispatcher, who said she'd send all units. By the time the call was over, I was pulling up to Sequoia, parking beside Moran's rust-eaten pickup and the Bakers' rain-washed Tesla.

The caretaker lay on his back in the mud as if he'd been blown off the porch. Bloody shards of bone protruded from his hollowed-out rib cage. His eyes were open, unblinking and insensate to the raindrops falling on their membranes. A small hatchet lay near his hand.

In his wound, I recognized the signature of a shotgun blast: double-aught buck.

The weapon itself lay on the porch, where it had been dropped. It was a new Stoeger Condor. The popular double-barrel was for sale at the Walmart in Calais or any one of the sporting goods shops between Grand Lake Stream and the New Brunswick border. The gun had almost no moving parts. All you had to do was load a shell into each of the chambers, close the action, and make sure the safety was off before you squeezed the trigger. As self-defense guns went, the Stoeger was as idiotproof as you could find.

The door to the cottage stood open. As we rushed inside, I noticed a shallow notch in the wood near the doorknob, as if from a hatchet blow.

Inside, we found the Bakers sitting side by side on the couch.

Josiah looked queasy and so uncharacteristically pale he scarcely resembled himself. He seemed not to know that his wife was holding his fat hand and didn't respond to our entrance until Violet let it drop and sprang to her feet.

"Thank God you're here," she said, her body shaking with agitation. "I didn't expect you so soon."

"Not soon enough, it would seem," said Charley coldly. "If we'd arrived thirty minutes ago, we might have been in time to stop this from happening."

"I wish you had!"

"Do you?"

"That man came here to kill us. If I hadn't thought to buy that shotgun today, we'd both be dead. But I don't understand why you were already on the way here when I texted you."

Charley became deadly serious. His whole body went still. "What happened here, Mrs. Baker?"

"Moran showed up and tried to break in with a hatchet. He was enraged that we'd sent you to threaten him. He was shouting all kinds of obscenities about how we were trying to destroy his reputation. Then he attacked the door."

"Weakly," said Charley, "judging by that notch in it."

"I've never been so terrified in my life," said the refugee from a war-torn nation.

"Mike, maybe you should take Mr. Baker into the bathroom and see if he suffered any injuries."

"He didn't," said Violet Baker, intercepting me. "He's fine where he is."

"Then maybe you and I can step outside to talk," said Charley.

"I know what you're doing, Warden Stevens. You're trying to separate us. I'll stay right here with my husband until the real police arrive. Josiah just killed a man in self-defense. You can see the shape he's in. I'm not going to leave his side."

"I can see that you have no intention of doing that, Mrs. Violet Dawson Baker."

Suddenly, her shaking hands went still. "Why did you call me that?"

"My apologies. You haven't been Violet Dawson for some time. Just as you haven't been Samira Ghulam since you left Afghanistan as a child."

"How dare you pry into my life!"

Josiah Baker robotically raised a glass of whiskey to his mouth and drained it. He gave no sign he was following any of this. His young wife, however, had come so close to Charley she was inches from his chin.

"I have no idea what this is about, but I want you out of my house. Neither my husband nor I are saying another word until the real police arrive."

"That's your prerogative, ma'am."

She thrust out her arm toward the open door. "Get out!"

I looked at Charley, and he nodded. But on the threshold, he turned.

"Mr. Baker, you might find it of interest that your wife isn't the only one here who changed her name. Nineteen years ago, Moran was someone else, too. Back in Rickenbaugh, Indiana, he went by the name Kevin Crowley."

"Get out!"

But her husband seemed to be recovering himself somewhat, and his puzzled expression was all the permission Charley needed to continue speaking.

"His last job there was as the caretaker at a camp on Tipsaw Lake in Hoosier National Forest. It ran programs for refugee children—kids from war-torn places who were having difficulty adapting to safe and peaceful America. It's not there anymore. But your wife can tell you about it."

For the first time since we'd met, I saw a wave of vulnerability pass through Violet Baker. I was a poor judge of such things, but if I had to guess, it was some combination of astonishment and fear.

"How did you track down the man who molested you, Mrs.

Baker?" Charley asked, his voice now calm and empty of all provocation.

"I have no idea what you're talking about."

"You never attended that camp on Tipsaw Lake?"

"Hundreds of kids did. But no one was ever charged with molesting any of us!"

"Was it because you were war refugees, afraid to talk with the authorities?" Charley asked. "And the man who abused you only took naked photographs no one ever found."

"Violet? What is he talking about?" Josiah Baker's words were slurred. He was drunk and probably had been before Moran showed up.

Charley said, "From what I could find in my search, Crowley was never even arrested. He wasn't even fired. He was permitted to quit."

"Violet?"

"Don't listen to him, Josiah."

"Is it just a coincidence that you chose to buy land on this marshy pond and build a cottage here? That you approached the former Kevin Crowley to be your caretaker, having no memory of him from Tipsaw Lake?"

Josiah seemed to be coming around. "Are you saying Violet already knew the man?"

"Knew him and tracked him down."

"And set him up," I said, finally seeing the pattern Charley had perceived hours earlier. "Moran wasn't the one who rearranged the furniture or left the boot prints in the mud. It was Violet! She put that sex toy on the bed, too. She must have done it when she ran back to the house to use the bathroom!"

Josiah Baker tried, but failed to stand. "That's not what happened. Is it, Violet?"

"Of course not!"

"How did you lure him out here tonight?" Charley asked her. "How could you be so sure there wouldn't be a record of calls between you? If the police check his phone logs, will they find a number from a prepaid burner? Maybe a disposable phone purchased this afternoon at the Walmart in Calais?"

"Walmarts have cameras," said Violet Baker with a casual display of her cunning. "I was never there."

I became aware of an approaching siren. The "real police" were arriving to take over the investigation. Those were the last words she ever spoke to us directly, and if it wasn't a kind of confession, it would have to do.

Charley waited outside while the police detectives separated the Bakers and got them to tell their stories. They were looking for inconsistencies or any details that sounded suspiciously coordinated. Predictably, they found nothing. Josiah Baker had all the characteristics of the perfect dupe. A brilliant wife would have had no difficulty keeping him in the dark about her vengeful scheme.

Their story held together, too.

Violet had arrived back at the cottage, livid from her phone calls with Charley and her contractor, but also in possession of a new shotgun she'd purchased from a gun shop in Baileyville (without even handling it, according to the owner). She had also bought a carton of man-killing double-aught buckshot shells, which she had her half-drunk, half-drugged husband load into the firearm.

The only fingerprints the evidence technicians found on either the gun or the shells belonged to Josiah Baker. Just as the only prints they located on the hatchet handle were those of Kevin Crowley a.k.a. Kevin Moran, although the techs noted that the grip seemed wrong. But the edge matched the unconvincing gouge in the front door.

Josiah's memory of the fateful moments were fuzzy. He recalled his wife screaming in fear that Moran had driven up to the house and that he should fetch the shotgun. He *thought* he recalled hearing the blow of the hatchet against the door. But when he returned with the gun, he was positive he saw Moran looming above his cowering wife in the open doorway. He'd pulled the trigger in self-defense.

Charley and I both gave statements to the detectives, as well. The primary on the case was one of those investigators who held game wardens in low esteem, and it was clear he blamed us for instigating the whole bloody business. Predictably, he found the connection between the former Samira Ghulam and the former Kevin Crowley impossible to accept as anything but a coincidence.

"You honestly think this tiny woman plotted and executed an elaborate revenge?" he lectured us. "It sounds more like you're covering for yourselves, if you ask me."

Even before he dismissed us from the crime scene, just before dawn, we knew that the state would not be bringing homicide charges against Josiah Baker, let alone his accomplished, wealthy (and "tiny") wife.

On the drive home, I was, perhaps predictably, in high dudgeon.

"She came to us because she'd heard game wardens are rubes."

"Your word, not mine."

"She needed to establish a pattern of harassment and a history of complaints so it would look like her husband killed Moran in self-defense. But she couldn't risk having 'real police' take an early interest in her molester or take action that might stop her from executing her plan. So she concocted these weird 'incidents' she knew the cops won't take seriously. And then she came knocking on your door because she'd heard around town that you're the Down East version of Inspector Clouseau."

"That sounds about right."

"You don't feel insulted?"

"What happened tonight isn't about *me*, son. Although I am sure she's worried now that she *came to* underestimaate my intellect—and yours."

"How do you think she managed to persuade Moran to drive out to Purlington in the middle of the night?"

"With an apology, I reckon. She called him on her burner to say she was sorry about us threatening him. Maybe she offered to hire him as compensation for the insults he'd endured. Maybe she dangled a retainer. If it were a big enough check, he would have rushed over there in no time flat."

"Meanwhile, she found a hatchet at some yard sale to plant."

"And gotten her lesser half juiced enough to believe whatever she told him was happening."

"And if something went wrong, Josiah would have been the fall guy."

"It does make you wonder about the future of their union as man and wife."

Three weeks passed.

The attorney general was quoted in the news saying that he didn't intend to bring charges against the Bakers. An examination of Kevin Crowley's computers by police discovered a stash of child pornography, although no pictures of refugee children taken decades earlier. After great deliberation, the prosecutor had decided that whatever took place or didn't take place at Tipsaw Lake, Indiana, two decades before was immaterial to the homicide at Purlington Pond, Maine.

A month later when I went to visit the Stevenses, I noticed a FOR SALE sign at the intersection of the Stud Mill Road and the dirt lane leading down to the Bakers' place. Upon my arrival, Charley told me that Sequoia had gone on the market for half a million dollars and was already under contract to a couple from Brooklyn. The sophistication of the cottage's design had been the selling point, as had the lurid story already attached to the place by the tabloids. Violet Baker was one of the nation's up-and-coming architects, and the residences she'd designed were apparently slated for an article in *Dwell*.

Once more, Charley and I sat on the porch and listened to the loon.

I scratched Nimrod behind the ears. "To go to all that trouble to commit a murder," I said. "And to think she's going to make a profit on it, too."

"A good architect takes as much pleasure in the planning as the building, I've heard."

"I don't like to think of her getting away with it."

"The way Kevin Crowley got away with traumatizing her and those other children, you mean?"

I looked out at Little Wabassus Pond, now edged with red along the shore where the leaves of the swamp maples had begun to turn.

"*All* criminals should be brought to justice, Charley."

"A wise man once said, 'Justice is revenge dressed up in a three-piece suit.'"

"Was that wise man you?" I asked.

But he only winked at me.

Snakebit

I

The woman on the phone refused to give her name, but she swore she'd just seen a rattlesnake on her hike up Black Cat Mountain.

"I almost stepped on the frigging thing!"

The man on the other end of the call was a Maine game warden named Mike Bowditch. "Did you get a picture of it?"

"No, I didn't get a picture of it. I was running for my life in terror. For real."

Bowditch had taken the call in his patrol truck, the air conditioner of which was busted again. Sweat slithered down his temples. He had rolled up the windows thinking it might be cooler without the radiant heat from the asphalt wafting in. He couldn't decide if it was better or worse.

"Can you describe the snake for me?"

"You don't believe me about it being a rattlesnake. I can hear it in your voice."

"That's not it," he lied awkwardly. "But you have to understand that timber rattlers aren't native to Maine, so it would be highly unlikely—"

"Why is there a Rattlesnake Mountain in Casco? And a Rattlesnake Island in Kezar Lake?" Her throaty voice cracked. She sounded gleeful and triumphant, like a litigator who had caught a hostile witness in a lie. "Don't tell me I didn't see what I saw."

"There used to be rattlers here, don't get me wrong," he said as traffic whipped past his stopped GMC. "But people wiped them out in the nineteenth century. The snakes would gather underground in the winter in what are called *hibernacula*, where they could be doused with kerosene—"

The woman hadn't come to him for a lecture in herpetology, but Bowditch was prone to over-explanation, a character defect in himself he seemed incapable of correcting.

"I called you as a public service! I don't want some dog getting snakebitten up there. Or a little kid, even."

Bowditch couldn't help but note that, for his unknown caller, child safety took second place to canine safety. On this scant evidence, he deduced she was a childless dog owner. Making quick and dirty deductions about people was another of his self-admitted flaws.

"I appreciate that," he told the woman. "But sometimes we get calls from hikers who think they've seen rattlesnakes when they've stumbled across native milk snakes. They have this defense mechanism—milk snakes—they vibrate the tips of their tails against the ground to simulate a rattle and scare off predators."

"Dude, it wasn't a frigging milk snake," she said, her deep voice breaking high again. "You'd better head over to that trailhead and catch that rattlesnake before someone gets bitten and dies. For real! And FYI: Mansplaining is bad enough without throwing in gaslighting."

She hung up. Bowditch decided the air trapped inside the truck was hotter than the steaming day outside. He rolled the window down.

2

The warden had no intention of rushing up Black Cat Mountain in search of a spurious rattlesnake, but later that afternoon, after he'd spent hours in the sun at the Range Ponds public landing, checking the hulls of sport-fishing boats for an invasive weed called milfoil, he found himself passing the trailhead on his drive home and felt obliged to stop.

His thoughts were still mired in milfoil as he climbed the short path up the hill. His department's program to arrest the spread of the lake-choking weed was worse than futile—it was an utter waste of his time. Mere shreds of the plant, caught in an outboard's propeller or stuck to a hull, were enough to spread the pestilence from one pond to the next, rendering the water unboatable, unswimmable, and ultimately uninhabitable to certain aquatic life. The warming climate was bringing many new species into the state of Maine: red-bellied woodpeckers, emerald ash-borer beetles, maybe even timber rattlesnakes if his caller was to be believed. The milfoil scourge seemed less like an invasion "from away" than from an alien galaxy.

The Black Cat Mountain trail was overspread by native white pines and white oaks, the sheltering leaves of which did little to break the late-June heat. When he reached the top, he emerged onto an east-facing ledge with a vista of Lower Range Pond. He'd hoped for a cooling breeze at the summit, but the air was as breathless as at the base. He had hoped, also, to meet hikers whom he could ask about the reported snake, but the only people he encountered were a surprised, half-dressed teenage couple who had the smell of cannabis and coitus on them and ran behind bushes at his approach.

"No, man, we haven't seen any snakes," the boy said, enunciating slowly, taking pains not to sound stoned. He had rock star hair and a trace of scruff that made his face look more dirty than rugged.

"No snakes," the girl giggled, clutching her bra to her sizable chest because it was unfastened beneath her blouse.

Bowditch was twenty-seven.

He guessed the lovers were a decade younger than he was, but as he was dressed in his field uniform, with its heavy bulletproof vest and heavier gun belt, he couldn't help but feel grizzled and world-weary in their adolescent presence. His colleagues in the Warden Service had rightly warned him that the cares of the job would age him. But he was only now beginning to mourn what he had traded away to wear the badge.

He would have thought the prospect of rolling around on the same hilltop where a rattler had been reported might prompt the lovers to leave. But they remained crouched behind the bushes, waiting for him to depart.

"There ain't any dangerous snakes in Maine," the sweaty boy offered.

"I know that."

"So why're you saying there are?"

"I'm just telling you what someone reported." He handed the kids business cards with his name and number and told them to call him if they spotted a snake of any kind.

Then he left Adam and Eve to begin again their innocent gropings amid the serpentless trees.

3

That night, he was awakened by another phone call, this one from the warden who patrolled the adjacent district, a twice-divorced cynic named Tommy Volk, who embodied everything Bowditch feared becoming.

"You're not going to believe this," Volk said. "I just got a call from a buddy of mine who drives an ambulance for Sebago EMS. He and his partner are transporting a kid to Maine Med who was bitten by a rattlesnake."

Bowditch kicked off his top sheet. "Don't tell me it happened on Black Cat Mountain."

"No, it was at a keg party in a gravel pit in Casco. The kid had been passed out in some weeds when his friends heard a scream. Some girl found the poor guy with a timber rattler attached to his leg."

The hair follicles on Bowditch's arms tightened into welts. "How do they know it was a rattlesnake?"

"Because the kid who rushed to the rescue beat it to death with a two-by-four. He sent me a picture he took of the carcass. I'm headed out to the pit now to fetch the thing. I thought you might want to tag along. You studied natural history at Colby, right?"

In fact, Bowditch had majored in human history, but he saw no reason to correct Volk, who was not alone in the Warden Service in considering him to be overeducated and therefore suspect.

"What's the kid's name? The one who was bitten?"

Volk needed to look at his notes. "Jax Stevenson."

The name meant nothing to Bowditch. "Do the EMTs think he'll survive?"

"Given that Maine ambulances don't carry antivenin for supposedly nonexistent venomous snakes, it ain't fucking likely." Volk cleared something thick from his throat. "Why'd you ask if it happened on Black Cat Mountain?"

"I don't know," Bowditch lied. He was lying more and more with every year on the job, he realized. He was getting good at it. "Where do *you* think the snake came from?"

"Where else? It escaped from some idiot's menagerie."

"You don't think it could be wild? There are rattlers in New Hampshire."

Volk hacked again as he laughed. "When I was a kid, my grandfather told me they were still in Oxford County, too. He swore to Christ he saw a rattlesnake back in the fifties. Gave a very detailed description of it crawling across a ledge."

"Really? Where?"

"Nowhere! He made it all up. The old man didn't own a pair of pants that weren't scorched in the ass from lying."

4

Somehow Bowditch beat Volk to the scene.

He had expected to find the gravel pit deserted. Backwoods parties tended to attract people who had cause to be furtive: illegal drug users, underage drinkers, and the older men who lurked at the edges of bonfires, eyeing the teenage girls until they were too impaired to give consent. Instead, he was surprised to find a half dozen cars and trucks parked in a semicircle with their headlights making a luminous space for a scrawny teenager to show off the snake.

The speaker had an oversize head, heavy black bangs, and quick eyes that acknowledged the warden before returning to the rapt and wasted members of his audience. He wore a Mossy Oak tee, nylon gym shorts that exposed his twig legs, white socks, and flip-flops. Bowditch had never seen a person possessed of such natural self-confidence as the adolescent oddity named Ricky Elwell.

Ricky seemed to be giving an oration to his young audience by the light of the remaining vehicles. He held the rattler aloft with its body hanging limp and sinuous while, at the same time, he used a lighted cigarette in his free hand to direct their attention to aspects of the creature's anatomy.

"Now, timber rattlesnakes have what you might call a sixth sense," he was saying, his voice echoing off the walls of the pit.

"See these holes between the eyes and nostrils? Down inside them are these nerve bundles that 'see' infrared radiation that is invisible to the genus *Homo*. That's why they're called pit vipers. It's just a coincidence this bastard was lurking in an actual gravel pit."

Bowditch should have known it was Ricky Elwell who'd leaped into the breach and beaten the hapless reptile to death. The kid had taken over his late dad's deer-cutting and taxidermy business before he'd finished his freshman year in high school. The young butcher had carved up every huntable species in the Maine woods, and a few that were forbidden, and he knew these critters inside and out.

"We're going to have to leave things there on account of the law having arrived. I need to consult with Warden Bowditch about the disposition of this serpent, but I'll post on my social if he allows me to perform a dissection."

Bowditch paused for the kids to disperse, leaving a single vehicle to light the rocky amphitheater, an ancient pickup that was presumably Ricky's. Bullet holes pockmarked the sides of the rusted bed.

"Isn't he a beauty?" Ricky presented the snake for Bowditch's inspection. "I measured him as four feet two from nose to rattle tip."

The rattler was lighter than Bowditch had expected and stiffening as rigor mortis took hold of its muscles. The scales were dry and roughly abrasive when he ran his hand against the grain.

"Any idea how it got here?"

"Don't you want to hear the blow-by-blow first?"

"By all means."

Ricky explained that he'd been a late arrival to the party, as he'd been working on a turkey mount for a taxidermy client. No sooner had he arrived than he heard a girl scream. She'd been sneaking into the bushes to pee and had tripped over a heavily intoxicated but not insensate young man thrashing on the ground with a snake attached to his calf.

"I figured it was a water snake—some of them get pretty big," he said, gesticulating with his cigarette. Ricky chain-smoked Old Golds, and the tips of his nine fingers (he'd cut one off in a butchering mishap) were stained ocher. "I reached for the first weapon I saw, which happened to be a piece of lumber. But that bastard had his fangs deep, and it took me two swings, the second being the death stroke. Generally, a rattler won't hold on like that when it bites, but critters can be unpredictable in my experience."

When he'd realized that the serpent was, in fact, a timber rattlesnake, he said that partygoers had encouraged him to suck out the poison like they did in Westerns, but Ricky Elwell, with his encyclopedic knowledge of wildlife biology, knew that particular treatment was an old wives' tale.

"I don't know the dude well—Stevenson—but I could tell he was royally fucked, so I held his hand until the ambulance showed. His leg was swelling up from his ankle to his wiener. I knew he was in trouble when his breath got all ragged and he started twitching spastically. But the EMTs didn't want to hear my professional opinion on the dude's prognosis."

These details weighed on Bowditch, who had been feeling intimations of guilt as soon as he'd gotten the call from Volk. Maybe if he hadn't dismissed that young woman's story about seeing a snake—?

But no, this can't be the same rattler. Black Cat Mountain is miles from here.

"So you mentioned having some ideas about how a rattlesnake got here," the warden said.

"It might have slithered over into Maine from New *Hamster*, but it's my clinical opinion this viper was deliberately released into the wild."

"And why do you think that?"

"Because the Goreckis live over that hill."

"Who are the Goreckis?"

"I forget you're new around here. Ted and Fay Gorecki, the

weirdos who want to bring timber rattlers back to the state of Maine. They used to run a snake lab in Windham, milking venom to make antivenin."

He took a deliberately long draw on his smoke.

"The lab burned down when I was just a kid," added the seventeen-year-old. "Arson, you'll hear some folks say."

Bowditch had been patrolling the district for months; he'd poked around every woodlot and marsh, sucked up local gossip like a sponge, and yet somehow, he had never heard of these husband-and-wife snake handlers before. This affected him as a grievous failure.

He heard an engine growl and tires crunch behind him and then saw the sweep of headlights across the curvature of the pit. Volk, as was his obnoxious habit, let out a blurt from his truck's siren, announcing his arrival.

"This piece of shit," groaned Ricky.

"Why didn't you call me instead of Volk if you don't like him?"

"Because I've known Tommyknocker my whole life, and that counts for a lot around here. No offense, but I've been burned by new wardens who were all smiles and bullshit until they wrote me up for some made-up violation."

Volk's shadow preceded him as he approached, diminishing in size until it was smaller than Bowditch's own.

"Hey, Ricky!" the older warden said. "Lost any new fingers?"

The teenage butcher flashed a maimed hand. "Just the one I was diddling your mother with last week."

Tommy Volk just about shoved Bowditch aside to grab Ricky's shirt. "What did you say, mouth?"

The veteran warden had a hard jaw and big fists he enjoyed using. For a moment, Bowditch felt he might need to restrain his fellow officer for the boy's safety.

"Relax, man," said Ricky, utterly unafraid. "I was just telling Warden B. here that this snake probably belonged to the Goreckis. Can you believe he'd never heard of those freaks before?"

Volk released the shirt and smoothed it against the boy's negligible chest. Then he turned to Bowditch with a raised eyebrow.

"Seriously? I guess Ted and Fay have been out of the news for a while. But you must know their run-down farm on the Rolfe Brook Road. It's the one with the razor-wire fence and the KEEP OUT signs and general air of decrepitude. So you think the Goreckis have decided to reintroduce rattlesnakes to Maine on their own, Ricky?"

"I'm just extrapolating based on the geography and Ted's reputation as a herpetologist, not that I've ever met the man."

"He's disabled, a recluse," explained Volk as he seized the snake from Bowditch.

The sudden motion caused the rattle to signal its now purposeless warning.

Ricky spoke with the cigarette held loosely in the corner of his mouth. "Supposedly, old Ted knows more about venomous vertebrates than anyone in New England. The man is, like, off-his-rocker crazy on the subject of *Crotalus horridus*. That's Latin for—"

"Timber rattlesnake, I get it," said Volk. "Ricky here talks like he has a Ph.D. in biology but everything he knows he's learned watching *Animal Planet* on his mom's big-screen TV."

Ricky grinned at them from under his bangs. "Now about this specimen . . ."

"Forget it!" said Volk.

Bowditch forcibly retrieved the snake from his colleague's grasp. "I need to have it tested first, Rick. The department's chief reptile biologist will want to inspect this snake for anything that might indicate whether it was born in the wild or in captivity."

"Tell your guy to call me if there's anything he can't understand," Ricky said. "I'm always glad to offer the department my expertise."

Volk punched the kid playfully in his bony shoulder and nearly knocked him to the ground.

5

The Mallard Mart in Bridgton was the only store that stayed open twenty-four hours a day. Having two warden trucks in the lot didn't seem to hurt its late-night business, which was based upon the four staples of rural life: gasoline, beer, cigarettes, and scratch tickets.

Bowditch and Volk leaned over the bed of the younger officer's GMC, looking at the big cooler into which they'd folded the increasingly rigid snake and half buried it in bagged ice. Both men drank hot coffees, and Volk had a wad of Skoal tucked between his teeth and gums. The imagined flavor combination of black coffee and wintergreen dip made Bowditch want to retch.

"Why were you late, by the way?" he asked. "What happened to you?"

"I found another rattler squashed on Route 11. It had been pretty well flattened, but when I saw it was a dead snake, I thought it was worth pulling over for a look, and sure enough, there was a broken rattle on the tail. I cut it off for testing." He reached into his pocket to display his prize. "Seriously, Bowditch, what the hell is going on here?"

"It's like the eleventh plague of Egypt. Someone must've seriously pissed off the Big Guy."

The biblical allusion seemed to befuddle Volk, who, normally, would have had a quick rejoinder. Instead, he dribbled some tobacco juice onto the blacktop.

Rather than explain the Book of Exodus, Bowditch changed the subject. "Any news about Jax?"

"Who?"

"Jax Stevenson, the kid who was bitten?"

"The docs think he's going to pull through. But he will lose the leg. It was swollen up like a balloon animal, I heard."

The novelty of the injury would once have energized Bowditch, but he was now more likely to imagine the boy's future as an amputee. On his patrols, he found himself confronted daily with the lingering human toll—the horizonless aftermath—of the crimes and crashes he'd attended.

"So tell me about the Goreckis."

"Husband-and-wife lunatics. He was a big-time professor at some university in Massachusetts before he got fired for having a fling with his student, Fay. They moved up here—this must've been nineteen, twenty years ago—and opened a weird little lab in Windham milking venomous snakes to make antivenin. They did tours of the facility and everything. Then, about ten years ago, it all burned down."

"Ricky suggested it was arson. Did they have enemies?"

The older man expelled a tobacco stream into his now-empty coffee cup. "Ted, the husband, was a zealot. He was trying to force the state to reintroduce timber rattlers into Maine—as if that wasn't the dumbest idea ever. The media loved those two because Ted made for good stories and Fay was a looker. Swiss Weems, the department snake expert back then, nicknamed them 'Nut and Honey.'"

In Bowditch's experience, there was always some group pushing to reintroduce a species that had been long extirpated from Maine. Caribou, wolves, mountain lions—the kinds of animals to which his girlfriend, Stacey, referred as "charismatic megafauna."

Publicly pushing for the state to bring back rattlesnakes struck him as likely to succeed as a campaign to establish breeding populations of murder hornets and black widow spiders.

"I can't say I'm surprised nothing came of it."

"All the towns around here started passing ordinances prohibiting people from owning venomous snakes. Everyone was freaked out the Goreckis might secretly breed and release them into the woods. So yeah, you could say they had a few enemies who might've wanted to torch their business. I don't remember what the fire marshal determined about the cause."

"Why I've never heard of these people if they were so infamous?"

"Because, after the fire, they gave it all up."

"What do you mean 'gave it all up'?"

"Honestly, I was under the impression they moved away or . . . something. The last time I heard Ted's name was when he cosigned a letter of support when Massachusetts wanted to turn an island in the Quabbin Reservoir into a rattlesnake sanctuary. I remember reading the letter online and seeing his attached name and thinking it was like hearing the voice of the dead."

Bowditch followed a moth with his eyes as it ascended into the false moon of the arc light above. He'd been feeling bored and stuck in his job, but this bizarre incident had shaken him out of his mild depression. He felt his mind fully engaged by the problem of determining where the snakes were coming from. He needed to know if Jax Stevenson had been the victim of a crime or simply gross misfortune.

"I got a call from a woman yesterday who reported seeing another rattler on Black Cat Mountain."

"So that's why you mentioned it! Who was she?"

"A hiker. She didn't give me her name. I had a look along the trail but didn't come across so much as a garter snake."

Volk crumpled the coffee cup in his strong hand. "I don't trust anyone who won't give me their name. Anonymous people are always playing an angle. What have they got to hide?"

"Everyone has something," said Bowditch.

"Now you've got me wondering about you," the older man said without a trace of irony.

6

Bowditch couldn't sleep. His girlfriend, Stacey, was away with college roommates on a canoe trip down the wild St. John River, and he missed not just her presence but also her counsel. She worked as a state wildlife biologist, and even though her area of expertise was moose, she could have helped him make sense of this sudden reptilian invasion.

He grabbed his laptop and propped it against his knees in bed and began searching the web for information about the Goreckis.

They made quite a couple. In photographs and several old video clips, Ted appeared every bit the severe and humorless ex-academic: a bespectacled man of late middle age with a jutting chin, a butting forehead, and a wide, lipless mouth. Volk had mentioned him being disabled, but at the time, Ted showed no signs of physical limitations. If anything, he seemed robust.

Fay, the wife, was indeed a honey with honey-colored hair cut in a Joan of Arc style and eyes as hot as coals still smoldering in the first light of dawn following an auto-da-fé.

Ted was undeniably quotable. In an interview with the defunct *Maine Times*, he'd remarked, "Of course rattlesnakes are dangerous! They're dangerous in what they reveal about our prejudices. These shy animals threaten any claim humans have to being morally and intellectually evolved. No wonder people fear and hate them."

Fay Gorecki came across as more measured. "All we're suggesting is speeding along the inevitable," she was quoted as saying. "Timber rattlesnakes are already repopulating their native range across the Northeast. They're in Massachusetts and New Hampshire and will be here in Maine eventually. We should welcome these wonderful creatures home from their banishment."

Before sunrise, Bowditch dashed off an email to the retired head of the wildlife division. Swiss Weems had been the Goreckis' favorite punching bag during their quixotic campaign.

The warden was surprised to receive an answer from the man—a fellow insomniac, seemingly—almost at once.

Those two were the banes of my existence for a few years, I don't mind saying. They walked right up to the legal line of defamation and criminal threatening. There were times, after a contentious public meeting, I thought I might find a rattlesnake under the seat of my vehicle. I worried about their sanity and the well-being of their kids. They have two daughters, I believe. What I've never understood is why they disappeared so utterly. The Goreckis didn't go out with a bang or a whimper. They just vanished one day. I would've thought they'd moved away if I didn't hear people say they saw Fay occasionally at the supermarket in Webbs Mills.

Leaving his bed, Bowditch decided he would detour past the Gorecki farm on his way to Augusta to deliver the snake to the current state herpetologist for dissection.

As he set out on his journey, he could see the planet Venus, a burning ball in a sky from which all the darkness was draining.

He circled the north shore of Sebago Lake, looking for but not finding any road-killed snakes, although he counted two dead snapping turtles and greasy spots that had recently been frogs. From Webbs Mills, he turned off the paved road onto a rattling gravel track named Rolfe Brook Road. He was beginning to recall the place now from his early patrols, when he'd been exploring his new district, its pine barrens and leatherleaf bogs, trying to commit the land to memory with the focus of a straight-A student trying to memorize an epic poem.

The property abutted the south side of Rattlesnake Mountain where the cliffs tumbled down to a particularly forbidding wetland. The woods had been heavily and repeatedly cut at the base, leaving the trees stunted as if they were in no hurry to grow tall enough to attract the interest of greedy men with saws and axes.

Even before the Goreckis' fields came into view, he encountered the first warnings. In addition to the razor wire, the owners had properly posted their acreage with signs spaced one hundred feet apart so that no trespasser could seriously claim to have wandered in without seeing one.

The Goreckis had also allowed bushes to grow up as a partial screen: a dusty partition of sumacs, dogwoods, and viburnums hiding their land from prying eyes. But the shrubs made for an imperfect wall. Between the insect-attracting blossoms, he could see a weathered farmhouse that should have been larger—an original wing had seemingly been torn down—leaving the structure unbalanced as if some essential part of it had been amputated. A panel of glass was missing from an upstairs window; one door had come off its hinges and was awaiting repair. Nearby was a barn in even worse shape. If not for the Subaru parked in the dooryard, he might have assumed the property had been abandoned years earlier.

Bowditch lifted his foot from the brake and idled forward to the driveway where a cable gate blocked him from proceeding up to the farmhouse.

He had just climbed out of the truck when he glimpsed a female figure leave the house and cross to the barn.

"Hello!"

The woman paused but did not move her head to look at him.

She wore denim overalls. Her short hair might have been prematurely gray. But Bowditch had no doubt she was Fay Gorecki.

The woman refused to answer or move. The air rippled with heat rising from the baked earth. In her motionlessness, she seemed to be steadily losing definition behind the distorting haze.

"Mrs. Gorecki? Can I have a word with you?"

He stepped up to the taut cable to signal he wouldn't be leaving without a conversation.

Still she remained motionless.

"I only want to ask you a few questions," he said, trying to project his voice without shouting. "I want to talk with you about rattlesnakes."

The Goreckis raised vegetables—he spotted a field already tangled with squash, an acre of young corn behind it—but he saw no livestock, not even chickens. And yet a familiar yet unexplained odor hung on the air. He smelled what he was half-sure were rabbit hutches, but no cages were visible.

She put down a galvanized bucket she'd been carrying. Even from this distance, he could feel the dark intensity of her gaze boring into him.

Finally, she spoke. "I can't help you."

He glimpsed someone in the upstairs window of the house now. He had the impression, from the posture and the narrow silhouette, that it might be an adolescent girl. The younger of the two daughters?

Bowditch tried to put a little lightness into his tone. "Would you mind coming closer so I could explain without yelling?"

"I'm not going to help you," Fay Gorecki said.

The firmness of her refusal didn't give him reason to think he could cajole or sweet-talk her.

He raised his voice. "In the past few days, three timber rattlesnakes have been reported in the vicinity. People are saying the snakes escaped from your farm."

"We don't breed snakes." She declined to approach any closer. "Not anymore. Not for a long time."

"But you did."

"I'm not going to help you. You're only wasting your time. I have work to do. Don't come back here."

And with that, she turned on her heels, picked up her pail, and, deaf to his entreaties, disappeared into the maw of the ancient barn. The girl in the window had also vanished, he realized.

7

At the department headquarters in Augusta, it wasn't just the state biologists who were eager to see the rattler but everyone from the senior wardens to the license clerks in their cubicles. Many took snapshots with their phones of the snake stretched across Bowditch's tailgate until the commissioner learned about the commotion in the building and came out of her office to warn them that any employee caught posting a picture online would be strung up by their toes.

"I won't have a panic about poisonous snakes in Casco," she said.

"*Venomous* snakes," Bowditch corrected her.

The commissioner—a small, sharp-nosed woman with a boy's haircut—had been a major donor to the governor's election and knew little about the outdoors aside from the ski slopes at Sugarloaf and the posh golf club in Belgrade where she was a member.

"Excuse me?" she said.

It was generally known in the building that no one talked back to the commissioner, least of all a junior warden.

"*Poisonous* means that they're dangerous to eat. *Venomous* means that they secrete toxins to paralyze or kill their prey."

The staff who hadn't already scattered fell silent. No one corrected the commissioner.

She pulled at an earlobe in which was set a fourteen-karat gold hoop. "You know what I meant. Now why don't you stop acting like a teenager and get back to the work the state pays you to do."

Instead of leaving, however, Bowditch made his way to the office of the woman who kept the archives of permits issued by the department to individuals and organizations to own "restricted species." Reptiles belonging to the family Viperidae were Category 1 Restricted Species—along with exotic animals ranging from tigers to kookaburras—meaning the state of Maine made prospective owners fill out copious forms to prove they had legitimate reasons to import these luckless creatures and hold them in captivity.

The clerk found the folder of documents—actual hard copies, because the materials were so old—pertaining to the Goreckis when they ran their lab providing venom to biotech firms to make CroFab antivenin. Ted and Fay hadn't just farmed timber rattlesnakes, he learned, but also diamondbacks, coral snakes, copperheads, and cottonmouths. The file included import forms and annual reports from wildlife inspectors who had visited the Goreckis' facility.

"There's nothing here about the fire," Bowditch said to the clerk.

"There wouldn't be, Mike," she told him. "If the snakes all died, the owners would have just stopped renewing their permit applications since there were no critters left."

This assumption bothered Bowditch.

Had state inspectors simply taken the Goreckis' word that no serpents had survived the blaze?

"There's nothing in here about them continuing as private individuals to own pit vipers," he said.

"If they are, they are violating the law."

This, too, struck Bowditch as suspicious. Fire or no, surely a noted herpetologist like Theodore Gorecki wouldn't have adopted a snakeless existence. People don't surrender their passions without a knock-down, drag-out fight.

He paused at the door of the Warden Service's second-highest-ranking officer, Major Patrick Shorey, but was stopped before he could enter the room, let alone take a seat.

"I have a meeting in five, Bowditch."

"This will just take a minute."

The major had let it be known in the bureau that he considered Bowditch to be an arrogant, insubordinate asshole and the worst hiring mistake he'd made.

"The answer is no," Shorey said, rising from behind his desk.

"I haven't asked the question."

"The answer is still—"

"There's circumstantial evidence that the rattlesnake that bit Jax Stevenson came from a farm owned by a couple named Ted and Fay Gorecki."

The major held up his hand before the warden could speak again. "And you'd like my help securing a warrant to search their property for other contraband rattlers? The answer is no."

"At least let me lay out my case—"

"I have an important meeting."

"And three rattlesnakes being reported within a ten-mile radius of their farm is unimportant? What happened to Jax Stevenson is already in the news. The media is going to be all over us to find out where these animals are coming from."

"I'm not saying the situation is unimportant," Shorey said, approaching the doorway in which Bowditch stubbornly hovered. "I'm saying it's too important to be handled by an immature officer who can't obey a simple order to get the hell out of my office. I'm giving this one to Volk."

Shorey's insistence on rewarding stupidity made Bowditch understand, finally, the crux of his career crisis. The young warden was derided by the brass as a troublesome know-it-all—which he certainly could be—but these same officers refused to give him opportunities to prove himself. And by so doing, they stood in the way of his advancement to a position where he could put his intelligence and grit to better use. Endless shifts spent inspecting motorboats for milfoil was penance for the sins of his ambition.

Bowditch was done playing coy. "Tommy isn't up to the job."

"I'll let him know you said that."

"This can go wrong all kinds of ways, Major. You know I'm the right person to manage this case."

"If you're so sure of yourself, why don't you apply for that opening we have for a warden investigator?"

Bowditch coveted the job, which was a detective-level position within the bureau. He had daydreamed about putting in an application but figured he didn't stand a chance at winning the promotion, given his history of insubordination.

"Would the hiring committee give me a fair hearing?" he asked.

"We'd absolutely give you a fair hearing, Bowditch," the major said. "We'd give you a fair hearing before unanimously rejecting you."

Shorey slammed the door so hard, the glass in the adjoining window rattled its frame.

8

Driving back to Casco, Bowditch devised his unapproved plan.

He phoned the manager of the A&P supermarket in Webbs Mills, where Fay Gorecki was known to shop, and asked him to call the next time the reclusive woman visited the store.

"Has she done something wrong?"

"No."

The manager seemed mildly disappointed by this, judging from his long pause. Then he purred, "But you suspect her of being up to something? She's an odd woman, that one. I've rung up her groceries myself and tried more than once to strike up a conversation. I'm lucky to get three words out of her. She has dead eyes, one of my clerks says. She gives us all the creeps."

"Do you know why her husband never comes with her?"

"He doesn't go out in public is all I've heard."

Bowditch had second thoughts about enlisting the manager in a scheme that was already making him feel slimy. It wasn't simply that he'd made the call without first contacting Volk. It was the man's almost gleeful reaction to being enlisted as a clandestine operative. When the manager started listing the items Fay Gorecki regularly purchased, Bowditch cut the call short.

Next, he tried to divert himself by checking in on Jax Stevenson at the hospital with a phone call. The nurse who oversaw the ICU told him the young man was sedated.

"Did you save his leg?"

"The doctors did everything in their power but were forced to amputate it."

"Can I speak to one of his physicians, please?"

"You understand that these are busy people dealing with life-and-death emergencies? I can take your name and number and ask one of them to get back to you."

"Tell me this at least. When do you think Jax might be alert enough to give a statement?"

"I can take your name and number and ask one of the doctors to get back to you," the nurse repeated. "There's no need to call again is what I'm saying."

The hot air inside his vehicle seemed to be running short of oxygen. He rolled the window down and got a face full of exhaust from a passing logging truck. Choking, he cranked the window up again.

His work phone buzzed with an incoming text before he could put the transmission into drive. It was from Tommy Volk.

> Fuck you

Shorey hadn't wasted any time sharing Bowditch's intemperate remark with his fellow warden.

> I didn't mean you're not a fine officer, Tommy.

The response came at once.

> When you're explaining you're losing

Bowditch wrote:

> I've learned some things about the
> Goreckis you should know. They never
> renewed their permissions to keep re-
> stricted species after the fire at the lab.

He had planned to share with Volk his deal with the supermarket manager to be alerted the next time Fay paid a visit to
the store.

> I don't need your help on
> this. UNDERSTOOD?

Bowditch knew Volk had a right to be angry. It wasn't Tommy's
fault that Shorey and his kind resented any display of initiative
for which they could not claim credit. But he couldn't explain his
predicament to his frustrated fellow officer—namely, that he had
no choice but think his way out of the box in which they were
determined to keep him confined for the rest of his career.

He turned on his signal and peered into the dusty side mirror,
waiting for an opening in the stream of cars.

The phone buzzed again. This time it was a call, not a text. The
number was unknown to him but was ostensibly from someone in
Portland. He experienced a moment of hope that it might be Jax
Stevenson's doctor.

"Mike Bowditch, Maine Warden Service."

"I understand you're asking questions about my mother," said
a female voice, creaky in the manner of many young celebrities.

"Who is this?"

"Mel Gorecki. Ted and Fay are my parents. A friend of mine
from Webbs Mills texted to say you've asked the clerks at the
A&P to trap Fay the next time she comes in."

The truth of the accusation caused him to wince. But as he
was preparing to apologize, he realized that there was no anger
in Mel Gorecki's voice. Her tone might even have been described
as *amused*.

"Yes, I did. Sort of."

"It won't work. She won't speak with you. Take it from me. I know that woman better than anyone."

"Were you the daughter I saw at the farm?"

She paused. "No. I'm the one who escaped by the skin of her teeth. I heard about Jax Stevenson being bitten by a rattlesnake no one can explain. I can guess why you want to speak with Fay. I'm prepared to help you."

"Really? Why?"

"Did you miss what I said about my barely getting out of that house alive? I don't mind driving up from Portland to meet you after work. I've got the lunch shift at the Old Port Tavern this week. I tend bar."

He said he could meet her for supper that evening.

She suggested a hamburger takeout on the Naples Causeway between Long Lake and the Songo River. "That place makes the sickest burgers ever."

It didn't sound like much of a recommendation. "How will I recognize you?"

"You won't." Mel Gorecki laughed creakily again. "But if you're in uniform, I won't have any trouble recognizing *you*."

9

Bowditch arrived early, as he always did when meeting strangers. He preferred to have the advantage of sizing up people before they could do the same to him.

He backed into a parking space along the causeway where the truck would be conspicuous. He wanted it visible. Then he drifted across the two-lane road and sat down on a bench, out of the setting sun. Ring-billed gulls and herring gulls, many miles from the sea, wheeled above the steady, slow-moving traffic, waiting for dropped fries from tourists at the takeout stand.

He checked his phone, waited five minutes, then checked it again.

He'd done a quick web search for a Mel Gorecki and come up with nothing at all. He tried every social media platform, too, with no more success. The woman on the phone might as well have been a wraith.

After a quarter of an hour, he concluded that Mel Gorecki—if such a person existed—had stood him up. Maybe she'd had second thoughts. Or maybe she'd been toying with him earlier, perversely wasting his time.

Then, through the gaps that opened and closed between moving vehicles, he noticed a woman across the road, checking out his truck. She was whip thin with limp blond hair dyed radioactive green at the tips. She wore dark shades, a faded T-shirt for a rock band whose members were all geriatrics, and jeans that were as tight as a second skin. The way she furtively approached his pickup, she might have been a snatch-and-grab artist searching for a way inside.

Between the flow of traffic and the shadows in which he'd taken cover, she hadn't yet seen him.

He watched Mel Gorecki pull out her smartphone and begin typing.

His own buzzed with her text message.

I am here.

Instead of responding in kind, he arose and darted through the momentarily stopped cars along the bridge.

"Mel?"

Her face was narrow and concave beneath the cheeks, but she possessed her father's wide mouth. "How did you recognize me?"

"You looked like someone who was looking for someone."

She flared her nostrils when she smiled. The self-satisfied expression might almost have been described as a smirk.

"Sorry I'm late. The rush-hour traffic headed out of the city was brutal. Are we getting food? I haven't eaten here in, like, ten years. It used to be good."

He pegged her age as twenty-one or -two. She'd mentioned working bar in the Old Port Tavern, which would have meant she was of legal drinking age. But he might easily have mistaken her for a teenager.

She was wearing a pair of the darkest shades he'd ever seen. It bothered him that he couldn't look into her eyes; it put him at a disadvantage. Bowditch removed his own sunglasses, hoping to prompt her to do likewise, but she didn't take the hint. He wondered if she feared being recognized.

At the window, she ordered like it was her last meal: a double cheeseburger deluxe, a large fries, a small onion rings, and a chocolate shake. It was obvious she expected him to pay, which he did.

Because the takeout didn't serve coffee, he contented himself with a Pepsi from the fountain; the drink came in a waxed cup the size of a small wastebasket.

"You mentioned that you knew Jax Stevenson," he began.

"I knew lots of Stevensons. But not Jax. What happened to him, do you know?"

"Only that a girl found him behind a boulder with the snake already attached to his leg."

"He must've stepped on it. You have to go to some trouble to get a rattler to bite you. I know *a lot* about snakes. For real."

After Mel's number was called, they found a bench that wasn't too gull-spattered with a view up Long Lake. She'd drenched her fries in ketchup. She licked her fingers clean after consuming every bloody one.

"You're working from the assumption that the rattlesnake escaped from my parents' farm," she said. "Or that they released it deliberately."

"According to state records, your folks no longer possess any venomous snakes."

This statement caused Mel to choke on a french fry. "And people in your department seriously believe that?"

"Shouldn't they?"

"Let me tell you about Ted and Fay Gorecki. People describe them as *eccentric*. But they're not eccentric. My parents belong in an asylum for the criminally insane."

"That's quite an indictment, coming from their own daughter."

She sucked hard on the straw, causing her hollow cheeks to become caverns. "You don't know anything about me. Do you?"

Bowditch shrugged deliberately.

"When I was twelve, the state took me away from them."

"Your parents were abusive?"

"If you call being injected with snake venom *abusive*. You

know that they ran a serpentarium in Windham. My first job, I shit you not, was milking copperheads at the lab. Ted and Fay thought it was safest to start me on *Agkistrodon contortrix* since their venom is less lethal. How fucked up is that?"

She spoke with such knowing matter-of-factness that he was willing to reserve judgment about the truth of her account.

"Ted had this idea that anyone could build up a natural tolerance to snake venoms if they were exposed to the toxins in small, daily doses. So they started injecting me as soon as I began working with the animals. They both took the shots, too."

"What happened?"

"They made me swear not to tell anyone, but one day, I had a bad reaction. I broke out in hives and my windpipe started to close, and they had no choice but to rush me to the hospital. They lied about what they'd been doing, claimed they had no idea what was causing me to go into anaphylactic shock, but there was no hiding the injection marks. The docs called the Department of Health and Human Services, and I haven't seen the inside of their home since. For real."

"That's a hell of a story, Mel."

"It's not a story. It's the truth."

"Were your parents prosecuted?"

"The district attorney tried to bring a case. But Ted Gorecki was, like, a renowned pioneer in developing a polyclonal that would act as a universal broad-spectrum antivenin in humans. I told you I know a lot about snakes. And since significant discoveries were being made by researchers using the antibodies that came from his and Fay's blood . . ."

When she used the medical terms, her youth dropped away, and she seemed even older than her biological age.

She wiped her face with a paper napkin but missed a spot of ketchup at the corner of her mouth. She looked like she'd bitten her thin lip.

"Amazingly, what they did to me wasn't enough to land them

in jail. Someone convinced the DA that the most important thing was my being removed from their custody. Ted and Fay hired a lawyer to fight the court order. But after someone set fire to the lab, they retreated behind their fence. I haven't seen them in years. It's a shame I missed Ted's comeuppance. I wish I'd been there for that."

"His comeuppance?"

"He continued to juice himself with venom after I was taken to foster care. He thought he was a genius and the rules didn't apply to him, and he pushed the limits. It cost him his arm. And he had a stroke in the process."

That more than explained why the man had become a recluse, Bowditch thought.

"You haven't mentioned your sister."

"Naja's seventeen now. She's still their prisoner."

"If the state removed you from the house because your parents were so dangerous and unhinged, why didn't they remove Naja?"

"Because they hadn't started in on her yet with the inoculations. Maybe they never did. Naja's immunocompromised. Juvenile idiopathic arthritis."

Again, her casual use of medical jargon made her sound like another, older person.

"Are you in touch with her?" he asked.

"No."

"Really?"

"One hundred percent. It sucks because Naja and I were super close as kids. She was like my mini me, you know? Followed me around. Wanted to dress in my clothes. Cut her hair like mine. After the state took me away, we texted for a while, but she ended up blaming me and getting all mad and weird. She's still trapped there with those nutjobs. She thinks I abandoned her. But I worry about her every day, for real."

"Naja is the same age as Jax Stevenson."

"She wouldn't know him. My parents homeschool her. She's

very sheltered. The girl's still a virgin, I guarantee." Mel wadded her greasy take-out bag into a ball and hurled it at a nearby garbage can. She missed, and the trash bounced to the next bench, where a sharp-eyed gull was waiting to pounce. "I'm in the process of legally changing my name, first and last. In a few months, I'm going to be Melanie Angell with two Ls."

"I assumed Mel was short for *Melanie*."

She laughed a little too hard. Laughed until she started tearing up and was forced to remove her sunglasses. Her eyes were as beady black as those of her mother. But they were anything but dead.

"Mel is short for *Melusine*. It's a name from French folklore. Melusine was this creature like a mermaid, but instead of being a fish from the waist down, she was a serpent. That was the name Ted and Fay gave their first daughter. What more do you need to know about them than that they named me after a monster?"

Bowditch set his enormous cup of ice cubes down on the bench. "Do you believe your parents are raising and releasing rattlesnakes into the wild?"

"Hell yeah, I do. Get yourself a search warrant and I guarantee you'll find the barn filled with heat lamps and freezers full of dead mice and everything else you'd see at a serpentarium. There will be neonates and breeding stock with DNA that matches the other rattlesnakes you've recovered."

"You sound pretty sure of that."

"I have a brain—I can make connections."

Of everything they'd discussed, one topic kept pressing itself to the forefront of Bowditch's mind. "Getting back to your sister, Naja—"

"We're not in touch, OK?"

"The fact that she's the same age as Jax—"

"It's just a coincidence. Naja is innocent of whatever my frigging parents are doing. They're the ones you should be after. Ted and Fay spent years saying that rattlesnakes should be reintroduced into the wild. And suddenly, rattlesnakes are showing up in the wild. I'm not trying to gaslight you. What's happening is no big mystery, dude."

She put her sunglasses back on. He could feel the intensity of her scorn through the lenses.

10

The next morning, Bowditch was parked outside the A&P in Webbs Mills waiting for Fay Gorecki to roll through the doors behind a cart of groceries. Shortly after the store had opened, he'd gotten a call from the manager, who'd whispered that Mel's mother had just arrived on her weekly milk run. The warden had wasted no time rushing to the scene.

After his meeting with the future Melanie Angell, he'd reached out to Volk to share the news with him, but the other warden declined to take his call. Tommy's stubborn refusal to hear new information proved what Bowditch had said about him being the wrong officer to run this investigation.

Worse, as the case manager, Volk was the only one who could apply to the district attorney to secure a search warrant of the Goreckis' farm. Unless Bowditch could convince him to expedite a request, he would be forced to find some other way to access the property. He had enough evidence, based on his conversation with Mel, to exercise his power as a game warden to disregard the NO TRESPASSING signs and explore the outsides of the buildings, the area prosecutors termed *the curtilage*. But to do this would be to bring the wrath of Major Shorey down upon his head. And what if they were breeding the snakes somewhere other than the barn? He wasn't ready yet to take a desperate chance.

Now, while he waited for Fay, he typed a text message he expected Volk might delete without even reading:

> I spoke with the older of the Gorecki daughters, and she's certain we need to search their farm for contraband snakes. Screw your pride, Tommy. You need to get a warrant ASAP.

As soon as he'd hit Send, he regretted writing "screw your pride," knowing it would only increase Volk's mulishness.

A string of shoppers emerged from the supermarket. At the end was a short-haired woman pushing an overloaded cart. She wore the same outfit—denim overalls over a man's T-shirt—as the day before.

Bowditch was out of his truck in seconds.

Fay Gorecki froze again—it seemed her natural response to danger—as soon as she saw the imposing warden striding across the asphalt.

Up close, Bowditch had a better sense of her faded beauty. He wouldn't have described her eyes as "dead," but her irises were as smoothly black as obsidian, and he understood why others might have used that word to describe their unsettling darkness.

"I won't talk with you," she said. Her speaking voice was rough and husky.

"I think you need to."

"How did you know I was here?" Then she cast a glance back to the building, where the manager and several clerks and shoppers had stepped out to watch the drama. "This is harassment."

"No, ma'am. It's just me trying to initiate a conversation."

"Will you let me pass, please?" She raised her key fob and pushed a button that caused an old Subaru Outback to beep.

"You'll want to hear what I have to tell you. I met with your daughter Melusine last evening. She told me the story of her life."

She swallowed hard. "Mel? Where?"

A Jeep had rolled up on them and was waiting for the woman to push her cart out of the lane.

"Why don't we get out of the way of these vehicles?"

He followed her to her Outback and waited while she loaded her bags. She seemed like she had her emotions under control until she slammed the hatch with surprising violence. Her expression became at once furious and pitiable.

"She told you her snake venom story, didn't she?"

"She said you and your husband injected her as a minor to build up an immunity to bites."

"It's not true. Not a word of it. My daughter is deeply disturbed."

"You never injected her or yourself with venom?"

"My husband, Ted, did. It was a misguided experiment that cost him dearly. But I refused to participate, and we would never have done that to either of our daughters. They were just children!"

"Mel claims it was why the state took her into foster care."

"Foster care? Mel was sentenced to the Long Creek Youth Development Center."

It was the custodial facility for underage criminals. "Excuse me?"

"I don't suppose she happened to tell you about the copperhead she 'borrowed' from its tank? She brought it to school and put it in the locker of a girl who'd been mean to her. And then Mel scratched the face of the cop who was called to kill the thing."

The accusation threw him off-balance. He'd been under the impression the Gorecki girls had been homeschooled, for one thing. Nor had Mel mentioned the incident or her subsequent confinement by the state. This was a twist he had never seen coming.

"Your daughter was a juvenile offender?"

"My daughter *is* a pathological liar."

"Mel stated to me that you and your husband continue to possess venomous snakes without permits from the Maine Department of Inland Fisheries and Wildlife. She believes you are releasing timber rattlesnakes, including one that maimed a local boy two nights ago, because the state shot down your proposed reintroduction plan."

Fay Gorecki blinked. It was the first indication that he might have hit a vein of truth.

"I told you she lies."

"Which is why I'd like your permission to search your property. We can clear this up in half an hour if you let me onto your land. I promise to leave you alone if I don't find anything."

"Ted and I have dealt with wardens before," she said, showing the same smirk Mel had given him at the causeway. "Years ago, when we were causing problems for your department, they sent armed officers to tear apart our house. They hoped to find proof that we were members of the Monkey Wrench Gang. Do you know what they found? Not a single frigging thing."

Bowditch felt off-balance again. The files he'd been shown about the Goreckis hadn't included information about a warranted search of their property. There had to be another, secret folder, he realized: an action plan prepared by the brass to discredit the husband-and-wife gadflies.

"I'd like to speak with your younger daughter, too," Bowditch managed to say. "I understand Naja still lives with you."

Fay seemed on the verge of spitting out a reply, but she caught herself in time. Once more, she answered him with silence.

"Will you grant me permission to search your property, Mrs. Gorecki?"

Without a word, she opened the driver's door and climbed in. He approached the window and saw her let out a sigh. Then she rolled her eyes. He interpreted the gesture as a grudging invitation that he should follow her.

But when he returned to his vehicle and was strapping himself in, he saw that the Subaru was already on the move.

By the time he escaped the bumper-car parking lot, Fay Gorecki had disappeared down the road.

11

She must have hit the gas as soon as she turned the corner, because when he arrived at the Goreckis' farm, he found the gate already padlocked in place. He could see her Subaru parked abruptly between the barn and the house. No sign of its driver.

"Shit."

Bowditch halted at the bottom of the drive and laid on his horn.

He suspected he could blare away all morning and the Goreckis would simply wait him out.

Stopped behind a cable he could have easily stepped over, he felt frustrated and impotent. These were dangerous emotions, he had learned, more so for a person in his line of work. They awakened in him a desire to exert power. He'd witnessed how similar feelings had brought Volk, for instance, to the point of brutality. Cops taking their licks at defiant, foul-mouthed suspects no longer mystified him. There was no greater virtue than restraint.

Use your brain, Bowditch.

He had yet to locate a current phone number for the Goreckis, not even in the documents he'd reviewed in Augusta. Their permits had included an out-of-service line in the town where they'd had their lab.

Then a figure manifested again in the upstairs window. This

time, the sun was shining from the right direction, and he could see her through the glass: a sylphlike girl in cotton pajamas, long hair hanging limply along a narrow face.

Naja.

Climbing down from the pickup, he raised his arm to hail her.

There was no doubt the girl was watching him, but she didn't respond at all, didn't wave or shrink back into the shadows.

He cupped his hands around his mouth and shouted the girl's name as loudly as he could.

She might or might not have smiled. Bowditch had better-than-average vision, but the old glass distorted her expression.

He remembered what Mel had said about her estranged sister. That girl hated her parents as much as she herself did.

Then he thought about what Fay had just told him about her eldest daughter. Certain words the mother had used to describe Melusine:

Deeply disturbed.

Pathological liar.

Mel's juvenile record would be sealed, he knew. But if she had indeed brought a copperhead to school to frighten another girl and then attacked the hapless cop called in to deal with the bizarre situation, surely the incident lived on in local memory. It might take a few calls, but he should be able to get confirmation of Fay's accusation in minutes.

Best to start with the accused, though. *Let's hear what Melusine has to say for herself.*

He removed his phone from its charging cable and brought up recent numbers.

The call landed in a voicemail box.

"Mel, this is Warden Bowditch. I just spoke with your mother, and I need to confirm something she told me. Please call me back when you get this."

As soon as he'd hung up, he began second-guessing his choice of words. Mel Gorecki possessed a keen, analytical mind. He'd barely shared any details in his message, but what he'd said was more than enough to put the young woman on her guard. She would undoubtedly have answers prepared when she contacted him again. And odds were her excuses would be exculpatory.

I brought that copperhead to school because that girl wanted to see a real viper . . .

He removed his cap and wiped the sweat from his forehead with the back of his forearm.

In his first years on the job, he'd been manipulated more often than he cared to admit: by lifelong scofflaws who knew the tricks cops used to secure confessions, by lying eyewitnesses hungry for attention, by the political climbers in his own department.

At age twenty-seven, Mike Bowditch refused to be anyone's fool.

He was under no obligation to continue pursuing the case. Maybe the better part of valor here would be to surrender the investigation to Volk.

And yet he understood himself well enough to know it wasn't in his character to fold his tents and steal away into the desert under the cover of night.

He would persist because it was who he was and all he knew how to do.

12

When he got home, he washed his truck, which was befouled with pollen from the red and white pines that shadowed every back road. The water from the hose ran like yellow slime to the ground. The puddles were thick with scum until he squeezed his finger against the nozzle's trigger and the force of the jet broke the pools apart.

Afterward, he sat in his home office, making calls, trying to track down someone from Lake Region Middle School who could confirm or deny Fay's story about her daughter bringing a copperhead to class.

Unfortunately, school was out for the summer. The one teacher he knew was too young to have worked Lake Region at the time and said that the current principal was a bear when it came to protecting the privacy of his students, past and present.

"What about the janitor? They usually stick around for years. Custodians are the institutional memory of any school."

The teacher gave him the man's name, which he'd found in a public listing, along with a landline phone number.

"Oh yeah," said a man's slurred voice when he called the number. "I remember it well. Little Mel put a dangerous snake in the Nason girl's locker. Then she nearly blinded that poor officer with her nails. There was a furor, let me tell you."

With the story now confirmed, Bowditch put in another call, unanswered, to Melusine Gorecki, followed by a text:

It's important you call me ASAP, Mel.

Less than a minute later, a message arrived from her.

Did you get a search warrant?

Not yet. It is VITAL we talk, Melusine.

But there was no further reply from her, and when he tried calling, it went straight to voicemail.

For supper, he microwaved one of the burritos that stocked his freezer and which Stacey implored him to stop eating for the sake of his arteries. He routinely checked the phone for a reply from Mel, knowing he would have heard it buzz if a text had come through. Eventually, he retreated to the armchair in his living room with a bottle of beer. He fell asleep to the droning play-by-play of the Red Sox; the game bored him even before it went into extra innings.

He awoke from a dream in which he'd been thrown by unknown hands into a pit of vipers. He lay at the bottom, looking up at a grave-shaped rectangle of sky while he heard the serpents hiss and felt them slither over his exposed flesh. Strangely, the snakes refused to bite. Even stranger, he felt no fear of them.

Bowditch opened his eyes and realized that the game was over, and the local news had come on the television. A reporter stood outside Maine Medical Center recounting the horrific injury sustained by Jax Stevenson, age seventeen. His parents must have given permission for the media to reveal his name. The station had scraped a picture of the teen off social media and broadcast it now for everyone to see.

Bowditch jerked upright, dislodging the cell phone that had been resting on his chest.

Jax Stevenson was a delicately handsome young man with long hair, studded ears, and a pointed chin darkened by facial scruff. He was the kid who'd been smoking dope with a half-naked girl on Black Cat Mountain.

The warden scrambled for the phone.

Despite the hour, a reedy voice answered at once: "Elwell's Deer Cutting. You shot it, we gut it."

"Ricky, this is Mike Bowditch. I have an important question for you."

"One condition. Will you give me that dead rattler if I play ball? I've never dissected a venomous critter before."

"My question is: Are you positive Naja Gorecki wasn't at the party in the gravel pit?"

Ricky clucked his tongue. "I told you that viper must have come from the Goreckis. If that girl had been hanging around, don't you think I would have mentioned her? But I'm happy to put out a call to my associates to ask if anyone saw her in the vicinity of the kegger."

"I don't need to tell you anything twice, do I, Ricky?"

"Indeed you do not."

Just then, as the news on the TV shifted to the weather (a heat wave was forecast for the last week of June and the first week of July), Bowditch noticed that one of his outside lights was illuminated. It was a motion-sensitive unit he'd installed around the rental property when he'd moved in. Game wardens made enemies in their work, most of whom were practiced at sneaking around the woods in the dark. This light was focused on his driveway with a sensor aimed at his patrol truck.

Grabbing his sidearm from the gun belt slung over a chair, he rushed outside. He made a quick circuit of his pickup, then walked the length of the asphalt to the mailbox. At the bottom of the drive, he squinted into the shadows up and down the road.

A car's taillights snapped on eighty yards away. The distance was too great for him to get more than a quick glimpse before it rocketed off. The vehicle was white, almost certainly Fay Gorecki's Subaru.

It's like she was waiting for me, he thought. *But why would she give herself away like that?*

When he turned back to the house, he spotted nothing to suggest vandalism. Perhaps his trespasser had been scared off by the motion sensors. He used the decocking lever to make his gun safer.

Only as he neared his newly washed GMC did he notice a footprint in the congealing mud. It had been made, unmistakably, by a woman's shoe: a hiking sneaker with a Vibram sole. A size six or seven. As a warden, he'd found the study of human tracks to be as useful to his work, if not more useful, than the study of animal prints.

Bowditch hadn't made a note of the feet of either Fay Gorecki or her daughter Mel.

He hadn't seen any reason to do so.

As he was straightening up, he put a hand against the wheel arch panel of the truck. A heavy sound came from the bed.

There was something alive inside.

Even before he peered over the edge, he knew what he would see, but the sudden hiss of the snake and the rattle as it beat its tail hard against the polyethylene liner caused him to jump back. Reflexively, he brought the pistol up before realizing it would be unwise to put a bullet hole in his government vehicle. The rattler was half the size of the one that had bitten Jax Stevenson. He doubted the young serpent possessed the venom to kill him. But he wasn't taking any chances.

Bowditch went to the mudroom of the house, grabbed his keys, and returned stealthily. The snake continued to make its warning sounds, but at a lower volume now that its enemy had seemingly retreated.

Crouching so as not to be seen, he reached for the latch. The heavy gate fell open, and the surprised rattlesnake lashed out at the place where it expected to find its attacker. But Bowditch had backed away even as the door was falling.

Having failed to sink its fangs into flesh, the snake now realized it had been presented with an escape route across the open tailgate. It was as thick around as the warden's wrist, and it dropped heavily to the mud.

Bowditch had anticipated this move. Despite never having dealt with a live rattlesnake before, he knew how creatures generally reacted when in danger—they sought cover in darkness—and so he had put himself into position. Before the snake could disappear under the chassis, a .357 bullet from Bowditch's SIG Sauer blew off its triangular head.

13

As he turned onto the darkened road leading to Casco, Bowditch hit a preprogrammed number on his phone.

Volk answered sleepily. In the background, a woman moaned her displeasure upon being disturbed. Tommy's second divorce wasn't even final, and he'd already scrounged up a replacement. The man lacked intelligence, humor, charm, riches, and good looks, but he was oversupplied with self-confidence and never lacked for female companionship.

"What do you want, Bowditch?"

"I'm on my way to the Gorecki place and need you to meet me there."

"What?"

"I confronted Fay earlier, outside the A&P. I thought I convinced her to let me have a look around the farm. But she sped away, and when I got there, the gate was up."

Volk was fully awake now. "Shorey told you to stay away from this. It's my fucking case."

"I haven't finished. One of the Goreckis snuck onto my property just now and put a live rattlesnake in the back of my truck."

"No shit?" Volk sounded almost envious. "What did you do?"

"I shot it."

"Was it bigger than the one at the pit?"

"The snake isn't important. What matters is why she put it there—I'm assuming it was Fay, but I can't be sure. Whoever it was tripped the motion sensors on my outdoor lights and then was waiting for me in a Subaru down on the road. She took off as soon as I stepped out of the driveway."

"Maybe she wanted to see you get bit."

"Maybe."

Except the rattler was too small to have killed a man his size, he thought. The Goreckis were intelligent people, smart enough to anticipate he would do exactly what he was doing—dash out in a rage. Putting the snake in his truck wasn't some nefarious attempt to hurt him. It was intended as a provocation. For some reason, Fay wanted him to chase her back to Casco.

Bowditch lifted his foot from the gas pedal. "I've changed my mind. I'm turning around and going home."

"Like hell you are."

"Now isn't the time for us to bust down their door. We need to come up with a plan, Tommy. I'm pretty sure this is a setup."

"I don't believe you."

"What?"

"I don't believe you're turning around. I know you're going to the farm alone. You want to prove to Shorey that he was wrong handing me the case. You want to show how smart you are again, because you're an arrogant prick."

Bowditch pulled over, braking so hard his tires slid on the sand shoulder. "I swear that's not it. Tommy—?"

But Volk had disconnected.

Bowditch tried calling back.

No answer.

Now he had no choice but to continue to the Gorecki farm if only to keep Volk from going in first with his gun drawn.

Ricky Elwell had called him back while he'd been on the line with Tommy.

"Nobody remembers seeing Naja," the young butcher reported.

"But the gravel pit wasn't, like, super well lighted. It wouldn't be a real party if you couldn't sneak off into the shadows to hook up."

"Is it strange she wasn't there? Wouldn't Naja Gorecki have been at a party just over the ridge from her house?"

"She's not real social."

Bowditch drummed his fingers against the steering wheel. "What about a boyfriend? You don't know if she has one?"

"You mean like Jax Stevenson? I can see where you're going with this. The guy is a well-known player. It's possible he hooked up with her, but if so . . ."

"What?"

Ricky paused to take a drag from his perennial cigarette. "There's been something bothering me about how Jax got bit."

"Go on."

"Rattlesnakes are, like, shy and reclusive critters. They might be 'deaf,' but they can pick up vibrations through the ground."

"Like the idling of pickup trucks and the bass line of loud music blasting from a speaker?"

"That party would have been torture for that serpent's nerves. We're talking a mega-seismic disturbance. With all those people dancing and what have you, it should have slithered off."

"Ricky, you are a zoological prodigy."

"Tell me something I don't know, man."

"For all the help you've given me, I have a reward you're going to appreciate. I managed to find another rattlesnake for you—if you don't mind this one missing most of its head."

Ricky laughed hoarsely. "You know what, Warden B.? I have a feeling you and I are going to be good friends."

In the silence that followed the end of the call, Bowditch stared at the still-lighted phone screen.

After a moment, he tapped to open the web browser. He typed "Naja Gorecki" into the search box, but there were no matches. He tried again, using only her first name.

Naja is a genus of venomous elapid snakes commonly known as cobras.

The photo that illustrated the entry showed a rearing serpent with its doll eyes focused, its hood spread, ready to strike.

14

Rounding the last turn before the farm, he spotted, through the trees, pulsing blue lights as if multiple UFOs had set down in the cornfield. He couldn't understand how other police vehicles had arrived at the scene before him.

Two of the cruisers were black-and-gold SUVs belonging to the Cumberland County Sheriff's Office. The third was an unmarked Ford Interceptor: a make and model driven by state police detectives. All three had their high beams blazing and their take-down lights focused on the gate. Silhouettes of men with drawn guns threw long shadows down the road and against the bushes.

The cable was hanging limply from a post, and the Subaru was parked with the left front door ajar and its interior lights on as if the driver had fled the scene on foot.

Bowditch heard the first gunshot before he could even skid to a stop. He missed seeing the muzzle flash. He had no idea whether it was a police officer who had discharged a weapon.

Then one of the blue strobes caught the detective with his shotgun aimed at the ground, almost at his own feet.

What the hell is he doing?

Flame leaped from the muzzle, explosive gasses combusting into light, and the roar of the big twelve gauge was loud enough that Bowditch could feel the noise in the chambers of his heart.

The deputies began shooting, also at the ground. They fired up the long eerily lit driveway. They fired into the weeds beyond.

Someone had set loose the snakes, Bowditch realized.

The scene had become a carnival shooting gallery. Somehow it was even more absurd and grotesque than a sideshow.

He sprinted toward the three men, shouting, "Cease fire! Cease fire!"

But adrenaline and gun blasts had rendered them temporarily deaf.

Fay Gorecki appeared now in the barn door. Hard light etched her silhouette. She shrieked as she ran toward the armed officers, holding a long, hooked tool above her head. "Leave them alone! You fucking bastards!"

Bowditch called again, "Cease fire!"

But still the unhearing cops continued the slaughter.

Fay was halfway down the drive when she stumbled, crumpling at the waist as if she'd received a sucker punch to the solar plexus. She fell hard, dropping the snake hook.

Afterward, the technicians from the state police Evidence Response Team would determine that a bullet had clipped her femoral artery. One of the deputies had missed the rattler at which he'd been aiming. The slug had ricocheted off a rock and struck Fay Gorecki in the leg. A red geyser erupted from the wound, and the mother of two was dead from catastrophic blood loss in minutes.

What Bowditch remembered vividly—the image that would stay with him—was that one of the escaped rattlesnakes chose to tuck itself against the dying woman's body, almost protectively.

At first, its presence prevented the warden from administering first aid. Then he caught sight of the dropped snake hook. He snatched up the tool and lifted the viper clear, at which point, against Bowditch's wishes, the detective blew the rattler into smithereens with a blast of buckshot.

Still holding the hook, Bowditch glanced up at the lighted barn, where two people stood in the open doorway: one an old, disfigured man in tears, the other a slender girl, standing apart.

15

This was how the police had come to be there before he had. One of the deputies had been parked along a darkened roadside near the Naples Causeway when a white Subaru went speeding past. The driver had refused to stop after the officer hit his lights and siren. She had increased her speed, in fact, he later testified.

The pursuing deputy was joined first by another patrol officer from his department, then by Detective Roger Finch of the Maine State Police, who had been returning to his residence in Bridgton. None of the policemen got a good look at the female driver as she'd sprinted from the car into the barn, not a good-enough look to make a positive identification. By the time they'd conferred at the base of the drive, snakes had begun slithering out into the light coming from the open door of the barn.

In the minutes following Fay Gorecki's death, Finch took command. He dispatched the deputies to control access to the scene. They waved through Warden Volk, then a reserve officer from the Fryeburg PD who was passing—a sweating, overweight man who offered no help and embraced the role of spectator—then finally the ambulance. The emergency medical technicians spent all of thirty seconds determining that the victim was "pulseless, apneic, and lacked organized cardiac activity." She was, in other words, dead.

After he'd cleaned Fay's blood off himself, Bowditch went up to the house, where Detective Finch had taken Ted Gorecki so that the scientist could sit down while he was being interrogated. This was the warden's first look at the infamous provocateur and environmental extremist, but what he saw wasn't so much a wild-eyed zealot as a ruin of a man.

Gorecki's shoulders were lopsided, and one half of his face was palsied. The stroke had left his mouth so slack he had to clamp a handkerchief to one corner to contain the saliva. The amputated stub of his left arm, purple and white, protruded from the sleeve of the T-shirt he wore with pajama bottoms.

"I don't understand," he kept repeating. "I don't understand what's happened."

"You didn't know your wife had left?" Finch demanded.

"I was asleep. I woke up when I heard the sirens. Fay and Naja were in the barn."

Protocol required that the officers interview the surviving witnesses, father and daughter, separately.

Detective Finch insisted on interviewing Ted, believing the husband to be the most important person in the household. He was content to leave the girl with the wardens. Bowditch was not unhappy with this arrangement. At the detective's direction, he joined Tommy Volk in the barn to get a statement from Naja.

He found the older warden with his pad out and a pen raised but not a single note taken after what must have been minutes of conversation.

"So you had no idea what set your mom off?"

"I think she just went crazy."

Naja was dressed in an olive sweatsuit that appeared black unless she stood directly under one of the moth-beaten lights. She had her father's stony jaw, her mother's dark eyes, and her sister's lifeless hair minus the green dye.

"But your mother was definitely the one who planted the rattlesnake in Warden Bowditch's truck?"

"I don't know anything about that. I just know she was away somewhere, and when she came back, the police were behind her, and she went into the barn and began knocking over the tanks."

Bowditch inspected the barn. Heat lamps hung from the ceiling over the glass cages that comprised the family's illegal serpentarium. Several of the big tanks had been knocked over, shattering as they fell, and bright shards glimmered amid the straw like so many discarded jewels. Occasional hisses and rattles sounded at intervals from the remaining terrariums.

The rear of the old building housed the rodents the Goreckis bred as food for their vipers. The strong odor of hundreds of mice and rats was what Bowditch had mistaken for rabbit hutches, he now understood.

Naja hung her head and sputtered, "Why did you have to shoot her?"

"We don't know that she *was* shot," Volk said with characteristic petulance. "We don't have all the facts yet. But you can be assured the attorney general will do a thorough review of what happened here tonight."

"I have a question," said Bowditch, crossing his arms.

Volk frowned at him.

"I'd like to back up a bit. Naja, were your parents releasing rattlesnakes from captivity?"

She raised her unlined face; her skin showed no hint of color, and her eyes were dry. "Yes."

"Can you say why?"

Her chin lifted. "Is that a frigging joke, dude? Ted and Fay have been preparing for this from before I was born."

"Can you describe how they were executing this plan?"

"They'd researched the historical hibernacula in the area and did GIS mapping to place the animals in the most promising locations—away from built environments, roadways, et cetera."

Naja, it seemed, shared her estranged sister's esoteric vocabulary.

"Did you assist them?"

"I'm in charge of feeding the ophids—the snakes. But I never went out with them at night to assist with the releases."

Volk had lapsed into silence, unsure where his fellow warden was headed, and seemed resigned to listen as Bowditch forged ahead.

"So you were nowhere near that party in the gravel pit when Jax Stevenson was bitten?"

"I don't go to parties."

"That's not what I asked. Do you know Jax?"

"No."

"This is for the record, Naja. Your statement is that you have never met Jax Stevenson?"

"Yeah, I mean, I've met him and seen him around and stuff. But you asked if I *knew* him."

In the narrowness of this answer, Bowditch saw a future for the young woman as an attorney.

"I'm going to be interviewing every person at that party, and if you're lying to me about not being there, I'm going to find out."

"Why are you being so mean? My mom was just killed in front of me!"

Her voice rose and cracked, but her deportment belied her words. She wasn't shaking or even breathing hard. Bowditch understood that teenagers processed and expressed emotions differently from adults. But the vibe coming off Naja Gorecki wasn't anger or disbelief. She possessed instead the inconvenienced and impatient air of someone who had places to go and things to do.

Volk stepped between Bowditch and the girl. "Warden, can I have a word with you outside?"

"I almost called you!" Naja snapped, directing her attention at Bowditch alone now. "I almost called a game warden to inform on what my parents were doing. I was worried someone might get hurt."

"Someone did get hurt," he said. "Jax Stevenson."

"I meant someone innocent. Jax deserved to lose his leg. It's too bad he didn't lose his dick, too."

"I thought you didn't know him."

"Mike," whispered Volk, grabbing him by the arm.

But Naja had gone from bored frustration to high dudgeon. "If this is, like, an interrogation, then you're breaking the law. I'm a minor. You can't interrogate me without Ted giving consent or an authorized adult being present."

"That only applies if we're interviewing you as a suspect in a crime," said Bowditch. "But you're right. Maybe we should ask your dad how one of his snakes ended up biting a boy you have a grudge against."

"Maybe we should!" And she smiled without showing her teeth.

16

On their way to the house with Naja in tow, Volk pulled Bowditch aside.

"What the hell's wrong with you, Mike?"

"The girl's playing you, Tommy."

The older warden bristled at the insult. "She's just a kid who's been manipulated by her parents her whole life. It's obvious those two freaks controlled her. The girl's a victim. I don't get why you're treating her like some sort of criminal mastermind."

Naja, meanwhile, had stopped between the barn and the house. She had her head cocked, seemingly to eavesdrop on the two men.

"Did you not hear what she just said about Jax?"

"I heard it," Volk claimed, but it was obvious to Bowditch that the import of the admission had eluded him.

"Can we hurry this up?" Naja called. "I want to see my dad. I have a right to be with him."

"We're coming," said Volk.

Inside the house, Detective Finch had moved from gentle questioning to harsh interrogation. He glared at Naja and the two wardens as they entered the kitchen. For a moment, it seemed he might order them all out again; then he reconsidered, maybe thinking that he could use the "grieving" daughter to force a full confession out of an uncooperative Gorecki.

"With Fay gone, I don't care what happens to me," the old man was saying.

"What about Naja? Do you care what happens to her?"

"Are you threatening—?"

"I'm merely stating the reality here, Ted. You and your wife have been knowingly releasing dangerous animals into the wild in violation of state law. Isn't that correct, Warden Volk?"

"It's a violation of Title Twelve."

"Which would normally add up to a half dozen misdemeanors, except one of your snakes happened to attack a kid a mile from here. Now he's lost a leg. It's a miracle he didn't lose his life. So we're looking at reckless endangerment—at the minimum. I guarantee you that will just be the beginning of the felony charges the DA will be presenting at your indictment. If you don't want to lose your daughter, too . . ."

"Dad, he's trying to trick you," Naja said, surprising everyone except Bowditch with this perceptive observation. "The state is going to take me away no matter what you say. It already happened with Mel. These men want you to deny everything you and Mom have stood for. Don't let them do that to you—for her sake."

Bowditch started to slowly clap.

"What are you doing?" Volk growled.

But Naja's words had already had their intended effect on Ted Gorecki. "Yes, I admit it. Fay and I acted because the bureaucrats were too small-minded and cowardly to do what needed to be done. Nor will I apologize for anything. Those animals resided here before the first European ever set foot on this land. They have an absolute right to reclaim their habitat. They have a greater right to this place than any of us do."

It took everything the broken, grieving activist had to summon the old fire and brimstone, and when he had finished, he was breathing heavily and had to mop his slack mouth with his handkerchief.

Finch seemed momentarily distracted by his victory. He focused instead on the phone he was using to record the interview, wanting to be sure he'd captured every word.

"Detective," Bowditch said, "would you mind my asking Dr. Gorecki a question?"

"Go ahead."

"Do you know why your wife would've come to my house tonight to place a rattlesnake in my truck, Dr. Gorecki?"

He gazed up. "What?"

"Her vehicle was seen speeding from my home, which is why the deputies gave chase. That's why we're all here. That's why Fay is dead."

Finch snapped back to attention. "Warden, where are you going with this?"

Bowditch pointedly avoided looking at Naja standing in the doorway beside Volk with her arms wrapped protectively around her torso. "Or is it possible someone else was driving your wife's Subaru?"

Despite his inner tumult, Gorecki grasped what would happen if he faltered now. He stared into his daughter's face, which had grown masklike and unreadable. He swallowed, dabbed his lip, and let his head fall so that he seemed to be inspecting the floorboards beneath his chair. "No, it was Fay. I suppose she—I don't know why she went to your house. I don't know what she was thinking."

Bowditch was ready with his next question. "And you claim your wife was the one who smashed the glass tanks in the barn when the police arrived, allowing the snakes to escape?"

"Yes."

"Why?"

Gorecki raised his reddening face to sneer at the warden. "She knew it was all finished. She knew you would shut us down. It was her last chance to free them."

"Can you explain why she was holding a snake hook, then?"

the young warden asked. "If, as you say, she was intent on releasing as many snakes as possible before she was arrested, why was she trying to recapture them?"

Ted Gorecki's head dropped again as if his neck lacked the strength to support the weight of his massive brain.

"I have nothing more to say. My wife is dead. Isn't that enough for you small, selfish people?"

17

A week later, Bowditch and Volk were on patrol together. Volk was driving. He had the newer, nicer truck.

No more rattlesnakes had been sighted around the Sebago region, but reports had come in of feral pigs wandering over the state line from New Hampshire, where a small population had taken hold. Wild hogs could destroy entire ecosystems, and the department was in a panic to stop yet another invasive species from establishing itself in Maine.

"I've heard we're going to get to shoot them," Volk said merrily.

Bowditch kept quiet. They were approaching the Naples Causeway, where he had met with Melusine Gorecki.

Since the night of Fay's death, he had tried to convince Detective Finch and the district attorney's office to pursue a case against Naja Gorecki for using a captive rattlesnake to attack Jax Stevenson. They'd swatted down his request, saying there was no proven connection between the girl and the injured boy.

Bowditch refused to relent. "I spoke with Jax in the hospital, and he claims to have had sex with Naja last month and that she reacted badly when he told her it was just a onetime thing."

"But can you place her at the party?" Finch asked.

"Not yet."

Bowditch tried to make the point that Naja Gorecki had motive to plant the second rattler in his truck—because she'd heard he was searching for a link between her and Jax. She'd then returned to the farm ahead of the police and set to work smashing tanks in the serpentarium. This theory, he argued, had the advantage of explaining why Fay Gorecki had been trying to recover snakes she'd allegedly just liberated.

"Warden Volk has come to a different conclusion that agrees with mine," Detective Finch said.

"Warden Volk is wrong."

At which point, Bowditch had been shown the door. On his way out of the office, the DA had called to him, "You can overthink these things, Warden. Don't let the habit become a vice."

That same day, Mike Bowditch had filed his application to become a game warden investigator. Shorey and his committee might reject him, but he would just keep applying until they gave him the job or ran him out of the service. The brass already thought he was stubborn; he would demonstrate how much the bureau needed an investigator who was the embodiment of persistence.

As he and Volk crossed the causeway now, Bowditch realized that his driver had been yammering on about the best rifle caliber to use for feral pigs. It was a ninety-degree day, freakishly hot for the end of June, and tourists were queued up to buy sodas and ice cream cones while opportunistic gulls circled overhead, waiting for dropped morsels.

"Stop the truck," he said.

"Why?"

"Just pull into that space and wait for me. I'll be right back."

"I'll have a hot dog with mustard and grilled onions," Volk called. "And a coffee shake!"

But Bowditch wasn't making for Mainely Burgers. Instead, he

darted to the bench where he'd spotted the two young women sharing a basket of fries.

Volk didn't know that his fellow warden had been persistently visiting the causeway, sometimes twice a day, in the event fortune smiled on him, as it finally had this afternoon.

Melusine and Naja didn't see Bowditch coming until he spoke their full names.

"Oh, hello," said Melusine, looking up through dark shades. "Fancy meeting you here."

"Oh, hello," echoed Naja, behind similar sunglasses.

"You two look happy."

"Why shouldn't we be?" asked Mel.

"Your mother's dead and your father's in jail awaiting trial. I was also under the impression that you two were estranged."

"The ordeal brought us together," Mel said with a perfect deadpan. "I'm applying to be Naja's guardian."

He rested his hands on his gun belt. "You think the state will ignore your criminal record and grant you custody?"

His reference to her past didn't give Melusine a moment's pause. "It was a *juvenile* offense, dude. Meaning you shouldn't even know about it. Look, we're trying to have a sisterly outing here. So why don't you go hassle some Jet Skiers and leave us in peace?"

"We have a lot to catch up on," Naja added.

Bowditch couldn't help but smile. "I doubt that's true. I think you've remained close since Mel was shipped off to the Long Creek Youth Development Center. I believe you cooked up this whole scheme together, in fact."

Melusine burst out with a laugh. "For real, dude?"

"What makes you think we care what you think?" Naja snarled.

"I know you both have a low opinion of game wardens. But it was underestimating me that was your big mistake."

"We didn't make any mistakes," the younger, less guarded sister said.

Mel glared at Naja, then grabbed her hand and dug her nails into the pallid knuckles.

Bowditch paused to unsettle them before he spoke again. "This all started with an anonymous phone call I received from a woman claiming to have seen a rattlesnake on Black Cat Mountain. Her voice didn't resemble yours, Mel. Not your usual speaking voice, at least. But she did use some of your favorite expressions. The way she punctuated her statements with 'for real.' She also accused me of 'gaslighting' her when I said rattlers were extinct in Maine."

"That's not an obscure word," Naja snapped.

Mel dug her claws deeper into the back of Naja's hand.

"No, but your sister has a history of trying to get people to believe crazy stories. People have a habit of accusing others of their own worst tendencies, I find. A liar won't believe anyone else."

"You've been in the sun too long, dude," Mel said, faking a laugh.

"Coincidentally, that mountain was where I met Jax Stevenson. I don't know if that was intentional or not—but it doesn't matter. You only wanted to plant the seed with a game warden that escaped rattlesnakes were on the loose. And it was imperative that this call come before the keg party at which Jax was bitten. I spoke with him in the hospital, by the way, Naja. Jax tells me you stalked him after he ghosted you. You wanted revenge, and so you reenacted your sister's stunt with the copperhead."

"Jax was too drunk to remember anything," said Naja, then caught herself. "Or that's what people are saying."

Her sister spun on her. "Shut up, Naja! He can't prove any of this. He's just trying to provoke us so we'll say something he can twist in court."

Bowditch continued to smile. "Answer me this, then, Mel: Why were you so single-minded about us searching your parents' farm? After I spoke with your mom and got her side of the story, your only response was to text me asking if we'd secured a warrant. Hours later, someone put a rattlesnake in my truck. I don't think the timing was a coincidence."

"That was Fay," said Naja.

"Why would she do that, though? That snake was too small to kill me. And I can't think of a reason she would've lingered at the scene in her Subaru—not unless she *wanted* me to chase her back to Casco. The stunt only makes sense if it was you, Naja, driving your mom's car. You were trying to force us to search the farm when we didn't seem inclined to do so."

Mel had been listening with her lips clenched. Finally, she said, "No one's going to believe we wanted Fay dead."

"Maybe you did, maybe you didn't. You couldn't have anticipated she would be struck by a stray bullet. I will say that neither of you seem broken up about what's happened to either of your folks."

Naja looked ready to leap from the bench. "You're delusional."

"If anything, the tragedy only helped accomplish your real goal here. From the start, your plan was to stage-manage a scenario where the authorities would discover your parents' criminal activities and have no choice but to remove Naja from their home."

"If you're expecting a confession," said Melusine, "then you're only gaslighting yourself. For real."

She'd thrown out those words with relish, as if she enjoyed their taste in her mouth.

Behind him, Volk, oblivious and impatient as always, leaned on the horn of his truck.

Bowditch loomed closer to the sisters, but he could see they

were not intimidated by his size or his status as a law enforcement officer. "You haven't gotten away with anything yet."

Melusine raised her wrist to show a still-bloody pattern encir-
cling it. "What do you think of our new tattoos?"

Naja did the same, holding her arm parallel beside her sister's.

The design was identical: It depicted an ouroboros, the serpent
that swallows its own tail.

"What is that supposed to symbolize?" he asked with genuine
curiosity.

"Transformation, among other things," said Naja.

"I don't think either of you have been transformed by this
scheme," he said, "at least not the way you think. I believe you
two have always lacked consciences. And that's what I intend to
tell the Department of Health and Human Services. The district
attorney might not be ready—yet—to pursue an investigation
into your crimes. But I think social workers will be more recep-
tive to what I have to tell them. I think that after they read my
full statement, they will have grave reservations about placing
Naja with a sister who has a history of violence and deception.
So enjoy your reunion. I wouldn't count on it lasting."

Bowditch didn't care about having the final word, but Melusine
Gorecki did.

"They really were crazy, dangerous people! The world is better
off without them!"

"I'd be careful saying things like that," he called over his
shoulder.

"Why?"

"Because someone might say the same about you someday."

As he climbed into Volk's truck, the other warden—who'd had
a clear view of his confrontation with the Gorecki sisters—had
only one question for him.

"Where is my hot dog?"

"I forgot it."

"You forgot it? You're shitting me. I'll never understand how you got a reputation for being such a know-it-all, Bowditch. Sometimes I doubt you could think your way out of a wet paper bag."

"That's why you'll never find me inside a wet paper bag."

"What?"

"Never mind, Tommy. Just drive."

Sheep's Clothing

I

The Withams were one of those families you find at the dead ends of dirt roads in the far reaches of the Maine woods. To meet them—and God knows why you would have wanted to—you'd have to disregard the signs they'd posted about dangerous dogs and trespassers being shot and not care that your car would be scratched by the shrubs and saplings that reach their thorny fingers into the trail as if the forest doesn't welcome your intrusion here, either.

To meet the Withams, in other words, you needed to be one of two kinds of people—either someone with no concern for your personal possessions and safety or a game warden whose job was to look in on reclusive misfits whether they wanted your attention or not.

I had just been busted back to patrol from my position as a warden investigator because of some trouble I had gotten myself into up on the Quebec border. The move had been made to placate the Canadians and, to a lesser extent, certain bureaucrats in my own state who felt that a sworn officer who had violated so many rules and regulations, never mind international law, by chasing a fugitive into another sovereign nation, needed to be made a public lesson.

"*Don't be a reckless idiot like Mike Bowditch if you value your career*" was the statement my demotion was supposed to send to my fellow officers.

The truth was, I didn't entirely mind being back in uniform and on the road ten hours a day in my duty truck. During my years as a detective for the Maine Department of Inland Fisheries and Wildlife, I had missed regular interactions with the Withams of the world. *Missed* might be too strong a word, but I enjoyed the daily surprises that came with being a beat cop.

Patrols in the bleakest woodlots and buggiest swamps also helped remind me of certain uncomfortable realities about the place I inhabited. The foremost of which was this: No one knows more about rural poverty than conservation officers.

The Withams, for example, lived in a tar-paper-and-Typar shack *that was lacking an entire wall.* John, the husband, had backed his pickup through the house on one of his late-afternoon beer runs. Still drunk, he had first tried to patch it with plywood and then, after a blizzard blew the sheet to Timbuktu, had tacked up several vinyl tarps that flapped like the walls of a Bedouin tent. The frequently detached curtains admitted drafts, but not just drafts—the chickens that Martha kept for eggs and soup had immediately spotted an opportunity in the missing wall and rejected their henhouse for the relative warmth of the Withams' living room and began laying on the sofa pillows and armchairs. The birds were safe from foxes inside the house, although Martha did tell me of a particularly brazen vixen that had snatched one of her best layers—a Plymouth rock—from the recliner before John could get out his twenty gauge.

John Witham was a scruffy and big-bellied man, with an expression at once as baffled as begrudging, whose laziness was legendary in Waldo County and best illustrated by a story told to me by the warden who had patrolled the district before my reassignment.

John had, by some rare stroke of good luck, won the state moose lottery, granting him permission to shoot one of Maine's iconic beasts. Instead of having the animal butchered and the cuts of meat wrapped in wax paper or plastic for the freezer, he had hung the carcass from a cross pole in the dooryard, where, after a warm autumn and a slow-arriving winter, it had eventually frozen solid. Whenever John craved a steak or a roast, he'd send Martha out with a cleaver to hack off several pounds of ice-hard meat.

"It's just aged is all," Martha had told the nurse in the ER when they showed up at the hospital with food poisoning. "And I been meaning to lose a few pounds anyhow."

The last remains of that rotten moose were long gone on the hot August day I discovered their own dead bodies.

I'd been getting myself a cup of coffee and a molasses doughnut at the Kentville General Store when I heard that John Witham hadn't been in for a week to get his sheet of scratch tickets or, more crucially, his daily suitcase of Natty Light beer.

"You need to check on them!" the normally dour clerk insisted. Her name was Becca Bray, and she had broad shoulders, an unfortunate underbite that made her jaw seem larger than it was, and hair the color of wet straw. "Someone needs to see if they're OK."

Normally, I might have put this request low on my list of priorities, but I had never seen Becca in a state of excitement, let alone agitation. And so I offered my services, if only to assuage her worries. Because the Withams had no landline or cell phone, I told her I would drive out to pay the couple a welfare visit.

The road to their property was public, but the privacy-obsessed Withams had kept taking down the signs the state erected at its intersection with the paved way until eventually the department of transportation had stopped bothering to reinstall them. The state had given up grading the dirt, too, and no longer sent a crew to prune the raspberry brambles that clawed the paint from every vehicle that tried to bump and squeeze its way down the lane.

Another house—a trailer, actually—was the only other residence on the Witham Road, and it belonged to their son, John Jr., who was known locally as "Bottle Johnny" because of his vocation of collecting returnables from the roadsides for miles in all directions. I'd once seen him riding his bicycle, towing a cart laden with bags of cans and bottles, two counties distant.

He happened to be at home as I passed by that morning, and he came out and stood on his doorstep wearing nothing but boxer shorts with hearts on them: a scrawny man with bulbous elbows and knees, whose rangy body was topped, incongruously, with one of the handsomest faces I had seen on a person who didn't model or act for a living. Johnny Witham had smoldering eyes, full lips, and the hard jawline other, wealthier men requested from plastic surgeons.

"Whatcha want down here?" he called to me, his high voice at odds with his dashing profile.

"Just checking on your folks," I said through my open window. "Becca Bray at the store tells me she hasn't seen your dad in a week. Do you know if they're OK?"

"We ain't on speaking terms these days."

"But that doesn't mean you'd miss him driving past in his truck."

"I don't pay them any notice. The shrink at the VA says I shouldn't let those two live rent-free inside my head. Hey, I heard you own a pet wolf."

This aspect of my life, I had quickly discovered, was the main cause for notoriety in my new district. "Actually, he's a wolf dog."

"Ain't they illegal in Maine?"

"Yes, but I have a special permit to keep this one."

"A freaking wolf! That's so metal, dude. Whoever tries to rob your house is in for a wicked surprise. I hope someone tries and gets ripped apart. Wouldn't that be cool?"

And without another word, he turned and disappeared inside the mobile home, leaving the door ajar as if in invitation to any of his mother's free-range chickens that might be wandering about.

2

The forest was desiccated, the leaves papery and yellowing. It had rained three days earlier but been dry ever since. The last puddles had shriveled up, and the mud had cracked and hardened into high ridges and deep grooves.

There were no recent tire prints to announce that the Withams had recently driven in or out, but I spotted faint tread marks that had mostly washed away (meaning they predated the storm) but showed along the edges of the road. The tires were far too thin for a truck. The driver of the unknown vehicle had tried to avoid the protruding rocks and gaping potholes that John Witham simply rolled over as if he had a noodle for a spine.

I passed by the menacing signs now, including the ones warning trespassers about the resident watchdog. In fact, my last visit to the Withams' had been to put down said animal, a Lab-husky mix that had tangled with a porcupine and swallowed several quills, which became infected, causing sepsis. Becca Bray had mentioned that John was too distraught to do the deed. But when I arrived at the house, I found that Martha had dispatched the suffering animal and was engaged in the act of burying it while her grieving husband was passed out inside.

"I'm sorry you had to do that," I'd told the beefy woman. Martha had red, rough hands and hair like a ball of cobwebs, and she possessed all the vitality her husband lacked.

"I never liked that dog, anyways," she'd said, "and it's one less mouth to feed."

I remembered her determined and baleful stare—a queen's unspoken dismissal—as she'd returned to her digging.

A quarter of a mile in now, I came to the three-walled house.

John's pickup, a Ford F-250 purchased (it was rumored) with the proceeds of a fraudulent insurance settlement, was parked in its usual spot in the weedy clearing beside the door. Its hood and cab were powdered yellow with pine pollen and splattered with bird shit. From the dust and droppings, I recognized that the truck hadn't moved from that spot in days.

I paused a moment, idling behind the wheel, waiting for Martha Witham to come boiling out to confront her uninvited guest, as inevitably occurred when I paid them a visit, because she didn't acknowledge the state's authority to drive on its own roads.

Already my nerves were beginning to jangle with the suspicion that Becca Bray might have been right to worry.

Because the chickens were missing.

It was midday and the height of summer, and not a single hen was to be seen in the dooryard scratching for seeds or pecking at ants.

There was no breeze that morning, and when I stepped down from my GMC and called their names, my voice died in the air like a poorly hit baseball.

The tarp had come loose again, revealing a gap large enough for a person to slip through, and so I didn't bother with the door but reached for the hanging sheet of blue plastic. Immediately, my nose and mouth were assaulted by a smell that has no analogue in nature; even the drowned deer I came across after ice-out lacked the putrid foulness of a human corpse that has begun to rot.

Or two corpses, in this case, because as I clamped a handkerchief to my lower face and peered into the shadows, I saw the remains of John and Martha lying side by side on their backs on the carpet where their chickens had recently nested. Their faces were swollen and gray in the glittering shaft of sunlight that peered over my shoulder. Flies buzzed up from their liverish lips and purple eyes. The Withams had been dead long enough for their maggots to hatch, I was sure.

I fought down the coffee and half-digested doughnut surging up my throat.

Through streaming eyes, I took in the scene.

Martha had a ragged black hole in the center of her forehead. From the periphery of the room, I couldn't see John's fatal wound, but the Kimber pistol near his hand made me guess the medical examiner would find that Witham had fired his last shot through his temple. He had killed himself after shooting his wife and lying down beside her corpse and clasping her right hand with his left in a parody of the scene at the church or courthouse where they'd been married decades earlier.

Even if I'd still been a warden investigator, I wouldn't have entered the house. Murder-suicides in Maine belong to state police detectives. And on the off-chance that this tableau wasn't what it seemed, I didn't want to disturb potential forensic evidence that might point to the involvement of a third party.

Instead, I returned to my truck, gulped down a liter of water, and called the communications center on my cell—this wasn't news I wanted going out over the radio—and reported what I had found.

The dispatcher was professional and impersonal for the most part, but she couldn't help asking, "Have they been dead long, do you think? It's been so hot this past week, and . . ."

"I wouldn't try to imagine it, if I were you," I answered.

3

It was my bad luck that Bottle Johnny wandered bandy-legged down the road before the first police cruiser arrived. The Withams' estranged son had pulled on a T-shirt and jeans and was accompanied by a ponderously pregnant young woman who must have been inside the trailer during our brief conversation.

I would have put her age at somewhere shy of twenty. She had big, soft, brown eyes and the face of a child beauty queen. Her flushed and sweating complexion emphasized the auburn in her hair, and expecting or not, she weighed significantly more than her man, despite being half a head shorter.

Jack Sprat and his wife were based on real Maine people in my experience.

It wasn't even nine in the morning, but the younger Witham was carrying an open pint of peppermint schnapps.

"Hold up a minute, Johnny," I said advancing toward them, my hand mimicking that of a traffic cop.

"Why?" the woman asked in a voice at once girlish and autocratic. "What's happened?"

I ignored her and focused on Johnny Witham, who had lost all his brashness and seemed to be regressing in age in the company of his companion; in posture and attitude, he seemed the younger of the two, although he must have been a decade older than the woman.

"I just need you both to stay where you are."

Johnny took a long, desperately thirsty pull from the bottle of schnapps. He clenched his eyes as if the liquor had scalded his throat.

"How come?" the woman asked with more belligerence than curiosity. "What is it you don't want us to see?"

No law enforcement officer enjoys doing death notifications, but there are days when all the straws you draw are short ones.

"They're both dead, ain't they?" she said, saving me from having to speak the words. "That fat bastard finally killed her, I bet. And then killed himself out of cowardice and grief. Tell me I'm wrong."

"Who are you, ma'am?"

The woman took hold of her own belly, one hand on each side. "Lyla Duncan. I'm Johnny's fiancée, and he has a right to know if his mom and dad are dead—because this would legally be his property now."

I looked past her, into the vacuous and uncomprehending eyes of her man.

"There's no easy way to say this, Mr. Witham, but your mother and father are dead. I found their bodies inside the house."

He began to raise the bottle to his lips again but then let his arm go slack.

Lyla Duncan didn't reach for him, just raised her reddening face and barked, "I told you he was going to do it, Johnny. Didn't I say the situation was escalating? Didn't I say it was just a matter of time until your old man snapped?"

The expectant silence that had greeted me was no more. Dozens of dog-day cicadas whined now from the trees, making a high-pitched and otherworldly buzzing loud enough to pierce your eardrums. Down in the cedar swamp, a lone sparrow pipped once and went quiet.

"Ms. Duncan, I think Johnny might need a moment," I said, hitching a hand in my gun belt.

"I know what he needs and doesn't need."

I wiped the back of my hand along my sweaty forehead without taking my gaze from the mismatched couple.

Neither of them has asked how the deaths occurred.

I might no longer have been an investigator, but my thoughts continued to run in their old, familiar channels. In all the years I'd attended fatalities, I had never come across a family member who didn't want to know the details of how his or her relative had died.

She was giving me no choice but to interrogate her. "What makes you think John Witham Sr. killed his wife?"

"Because of the escalation, like I said. We could hear them shouting at each other all the way to our trailer. She said she knew he had a girlfriend, and I bet he did, knowing how the old sleaze looked at me when he was shit-faced. 'You're a fertile one, Lyla,' he used to tell me, and I swear he had a boner. There was no missing that thing of his."

A girlfriend? John Witham?

The man had always struck me as too shiftless to muster a vice like lechery, but I hadn't seen him around a woman other than his wife (and the epicene Becca Bray), and if he did become a goat when he drank, it partly explained Lyla Duncan's callousness—although why her disgust extended to Martha remained unanswered.

The thought of that slothful, unkempt man attracting a girlfriend was absurd, I decided. And yet someone had visited the Withams recently. The washed-out tire marks I'd spotted testified to the fact. It was a shame the rain had made identifying the mystery car's treads such a long shot.

I heard a heavy vehicle, likely a Ford Interceptor driven by the responding state trooper, scraping down the narrow road, trying and failing to preserve its paint job from the bushes.

The pint of schnapps slipped from Johnny's fingers and shattered on a rock at his feet.

"Damn, Johnny!" Lyla said. "Damn."

He covered his face with both hands and began to sob, or rather, his body shook like a person overwhelmed by grief, almost to the point of collapse. And yet, he made not the faintest sound.

"There, there, Johnny. I know your heart is hurting, but you always said how nice we could fix this place up. Think of how happy everything will be when we're settled here and the baby comes."

Still shaking, he turned away from us both, seeming to shrink in size as he did. His shirt was dark with perspiration between the shoulder blades.

Lyla made a vague, huffing sound as if in disapproval or embarrassed on his behalf.

I hadn't had the tarp open more than two minutes and, thankfully, could not detect the smell of death, but a shadow swept across the dooryard now, and when I looked up, I saw the first of the dozen turkey vultures that would eventually assume a holding pattern above the scene of the crime.

4

The state police detective assigned to the case was an old friend of mine, Sergeant Steve Klesko. Because he lived less than forty-five minutes away, he was one of the first officers on the scene.

Steve was a former college hockey star. Even in middle age, he had the stocky body of a brawling defenseman and a beetling brow that suggested an abundance of Neanderthal chromosomes in his genome. Had he lived in the Ice Age, he would have been the best-looking caveman on the tundra.

He pulled me aside when he'd heard I had been the one to discover the bodies. By then, the forensic techs had appeared, along with half a dozen deputies and troopers, and word was that the chief medical examiner herself was interrupting a hike up distant Mount Blue to inspect the corpses.

"What do you know about these folks, Mike?" Klesko asked.

"Calling them *dirt poor* would be an insult to dirt."

"Beyond the obvious, I meant."

We were both watching the techs mask up to enter the noisome house. I had encircled the building with crime scene tape while I'd waited for the forensic investigators.

I removed my cap and wiped the sweat from my hairline again. "John didn't poach—or poach much, I should say. Not enough for me to watch him. He drove drunk a few times a week to get supplies. Martha wasn't above shoplifting a few items from self-pay farm stands, I've heard. In extremely relative terms, I would have described the Withams as upstanding, law-abiding citizens."

The vultures wheeled in gyres in the bright sky above.

"The sheriff told me none of his deputies had ever been called out here on a domestic," by which Steve meant an altercation between husband and wife. "That's kind of odd, don't you think? A couple with no history of police visits are found dead in an apparent murder-suicide?"

"No *reported* history," I corrected him.

Klesko checked his notebook. "This Lyla Duncan claims she and her boyfriend, the son, heard something last weekend—an argument. The wife was accusing the husband of having a girlfriend on the side."

"So she claims."

"You don't believe her? Why not?"

"Because John Witham would have made a sloth look hyperactive."

"You're full of colorful metaphors today, Mike."

"I'm just trying to paint you a picture."

At that moment, Steve's partner and the medical examiner both arrived, and the three of them left me to begin their inspection of the rancid house. I didn't envy them the smells or the sights. On the other hand, this was the first time since I'd been busted down to district warden that I found myself relegated to the sidelines of a major crime, and I didn't like it one bit.

I was frustrated enough with my circumstances that I decided to head out.

Along the way, I stopped to inspect one of the washed-out tire tracks that seemed less eroded than the others. To avoid a pothole, the driver had veered halfway into the brambles. It was the only reason the other vehicles hadn't obliterated the marks.

Aside from the narrow width of its tread—16.5 millimeters, give or take—there were no identifying details. Maybe one of the forensic techs would find a usable print somewhere along the road. But that was unlikely with so many police vehicles having crushed the baked mud to dust.

I decided to return to Kentville Village to inform Becca Bray personally of what I'd found. I didn't imagine that asking questions at the general store would count as meddling in an active investigation. My superiors might disagree. But what were they going to do? They'd already demoted me.

5

Becca managed the Kentville General Store for her elderly parents, who had run the place for half a century, still resided on the second floor, and made surprise trips downstairs to double-check the register and to determine whether the pizza slices had gotten leathery from spinning all day in the warmer.

The daughter endured their micromanaging with more stoicism than I would have shown in her place, but you only had to look into her tired, prematurely aged eyes or watch her restock the beer cooler with all the exacting indifference of a robot to appreciate the cost of the job on her soul. I liked to think she had resigned herself to enduring the situation until her overseers shook off their mortal coils. But it was more likely that she simply didn't care—about the store, her parents, maybe her own drab existence.

Her voice, normally thick and monotone, broke when she saw me backlighted in the doorway.

"Is it true? Are they dead? Both of them dead?"

She already knew, had already heard from one of the deputies who frequented the store for the free coffee given to first responders. But I answered her anyway. "Yes, I'm afraid so."

"It's unbelievable. I mean, I literally can't believe it."

Despite her height and big bones, Becca carried no extra flesh: On her feet all day, scurrying back and forth from the loading dock to the sandwich counter, she burned every calorie she consumed. And there were other days when in her busyness she seemed to forget to eat at all.

"I'm having trouble believing it myself," I said. "But I didn't know John Witham well enough to be surprised."

"The man didn't have a murderous bone in his body."'

She wore a gingham blouse and high-waisted jeans and thick-soled sneakers made for nurses and restaurant servers and other workers whose jobs do a number on their feet.

"What about Martha?" I asked. "I know she had a nasty streak."

Becca's eyes, which tended naturally to squint, narrowed farther. "If the gun had been in her hand, I might have believed she'd killed him. But it wasn't, I heard."

I wondered who'd disclosed this information to her, which officer. It didn't matter that Becca Bray was no gossip. He shouldn't have confided details about the scene of the crime.

"How well did you know John?"

"My whole life. I get that he rubbed a lot of people the wrong way, but he was always nice to me. Most people, paying for their things, don't even say hello or treat you like a person nowadays."

The odor of frying oil wafted from the back of the store, where the man who made the pizzas and worked the sandwich counter was preparing for the lunch run. He was a former navy cook named Pee Wee.

"What would you say to the idea of him having a secret girlfriend?" I asked.

Her tired eyes widened, and she almost smiled. "He didn't use deodorant!"

This aspect of his personal hygiene, or lack of hygiene, didn't impress me as being dispositive, but Becca obviously thought the idea of him having a woman on the side was ridiculous.

"Did the Withams have enemies the police should know about?"

"There's a difference between people not liking you and being your enemy."

"What about the son, Johnny?"

"No," she said, almost too forcefully. "No."

"He stands to inherit the place."

"It's a swamp!"

People had killed for less.

"You must know Johnny's fiancée, Lyla Duncan," I said.

A laugh exploded from her thin mouth.

"I guess that's my answer," I said.

"That girl is the most selfish, reckless, unthinking person I've ever met." Red spots appeared on her cheeks, almost like an allergic rash. "She's . . . she's . . ."

"What?"

"Reckless."

That had certainly been my impression, as well. I went to the cooler now and removed a liter of Gatorade from the slot and came back and stood at the counter and drank it.

"Is Lyla from around here? I don't recognize the last name."

Her shoulders became rigid, the muscles defined like cables in her neck, but she did not raise her eyes to mine. "The family moved to town last year from somewhere up north. Greenville, I think. Mr. Duncan was a timber cruiser. Frye Mountain Joinery, that's his business. He runs it with his sons. I have to sweep up sawdust after any of them comes in for beer and ciggies."

I knew the farmhouse with the sign out front and the cinder block building with never fewer than four pickups in the yard, but that was all.

"She's a feisty thing," I said.

"Some people, you can tell they're the babies in their families. That's Lyla. She's the youngest and the only girl. And because she's pretty, she's always gotten what she wants."

It occurred to me that Becca knew more about the Duncans than I'd expected, but in small towns, a store clerk, if they are observant, stands as a witness to many of the residents' secrets and vices. She sees who is first in the morning to buy booze and who comes immediately from cashing their paychecks to buy lottery tickets.

I moved a thumb under my ballistic vest to get some air circulating. "She and Johnny Witham make for an odd couple."

Becca bit her lip. Her gaze roved around the store, touching on the wire racks of chips and the humming refrigerator with its door frosted into opaqueness.

"What?" I said lightly.

"I guess Johnny's good-looking," Becca said, her nostrils flaring. "But she ought not have trapped him that way. I don't know why she had to do that. He's a sweet guy, but not too bright, and why she had to go and get pregnant—she's going to make him do everything for that baby, and it's just so sad, especially after what happened with his folks. I feel like I just want to go into the back room and cry my eyes out, but I can't, because who's going to mind the store?"

Despite the outburst, she didn't strike me as being on the verge of tears. I would have said she seemed more frustrated, even a little mad, than overcome by despair at the tragedy that is the human condition.

I heard a car pull up outside and park in the gravel. Through the screen door came the sound of its muffled stereo: Johnny Cash singing "Hurt" by Nine Inch Nails. The driver was waiting for the song to end before they came inside for whatever was needed.

6

At the back counter, I ordered an Italian sandwich from Pee Wee, who seemed to have some private, indecipherable issue with officers of the law, based on the false friendliness with which he greeted us, and whom the Bray family didn't trust to tend their register, I had heard.

Becca seemed preoccupied when I cashed out and did not meet my eyes or say more than to wish me a good afternoon.

I attempted to eat my messy lunch in my truck while I listened to the police radio. There was no chatter about the Withams; the urgency had passed, and the cops had mostly dispersed.

My personal phone buzzed on the console. I'd asked Steve Klesko to call me after he had interviewed Johnny and Lyla. But it was still too soon for that, and he wouldn't view informing me as a priority.

It was my wife, Stacey. She was driving the ambulance today— she and her partner took turns—and must have been on her lunch break, too.

"I heard about the Withams," she said. "Everyone's been talking about it at the hospital. Neither the husband nor the wife ever came in, but the son is locally famous since people see him everywhere on his bike, pulling that cart of his. And I guess his girlfriend is a frequent visitor to the ER."

I sat up in my seat. "Really?"

"It's not what you're thinking," Stacey said. "She's never showed up injured or anything. She's just one of those people who misuses the emergency room. Anytime she needs prescription cough medicine or has a medical question, she shows up, expecting to be seen personally by the physician on duty. Every nurse here has had a run-in with her ladyship, Lyla Duncan."

I smiled as I dabbed at my mouth with a napkin. "She must really have rubbed people the wrong way if they're willing to break confidentiality."

"It's more like each of them wants to warn us. Now that she's pregnant, they think we EMTs will get calls to the house to rearrange her couch pillows and massage her feet."

"Technically, it's a trailer, and it belongs to Bottle Johnny. I'm still trying to wrap my head around the idea of gentle John Witham murdering another human being. On his moose hunt, I heard he was crying too hard to shoot the animal. Martha had to grab the gun and bring it down."

"People are mysteries, Mike. Isn't that what you're always telling me?"

I contemplated my own faux wisdom for a moment as I rolled down the window a bit more to admit the breeze.

"How are you feeling in all this heat, by the way?" I asked.

"I ride in an air-conditioned ambulance to an air-conditioned hospital. I haven't been in direct sunlight for more than fifteen minutes. I've told you not to worry about me."

I couldn't help myself, though. Couldn't help but imagine the worst.

"Are you at home now? How's Shadow?"

"On his best behavior," she said of the wolf dog.

"You bring that out in him." My voice sounded a little petty and jealous in my own ears, resentful she had managed to tame him.

She seemed not to notice. "Honestly, I think we should try taking Shadow more places now. Not where there are crowds or anything. But he did so well on that hike up Beech Hill last month."

"He was on a leash."

"He's not going to run off on us, Mike. He sees us as members of his family pack."

I was going to respond, but just then, the strangest thing happened.

I saw a hand flip the sign in the window from OPEN to CLOSED. And Becca Bray stepped onto the porch, locked the door behind her, and turned toward the parking lot, clutching her car keys in her hand. She was halfway down the steps before she spotted me in my truck.

She stopped as soon as we made eye contact. The look on her face was one of shock and fear. She might have been a gazelle on the savanna that has just noticed a lion and hopes that if it doesn't move, if it becomes motionless, the hungry predator won't see it and give chase.

"Mike?" Stacey said over the speakerphone. "Are you there?"

The sound of her voice broke the spell. Becca gave a weak smile and waved at me before hurrying back inside the store.

I saw her disembodied hand turn the sign in the window back to OPEN.

"Is something happening?" Stacey asked.

Becca never closed the Kentville General Store during business hours. Her parents, who were still upstairs, judging from the Buick in the lot and the ribbons fluttering from the air conditioner, would never permit such a thing.

"Yeah, but I'm not sure what. I'll call you back in a bit, Stace."

I wadded up the wax paper in which Pee Wee had wrapped my sandwich and stuffed it back into the oil-stained paper bag. I thought I would use the excuse of throwing away my trash to ask Becca what she had been doing.

But I hadn't taken more than a few steps before I caught sight of the lemon-yellow Fiat backed into the space between the rear staircase and the dumpster. It was Becca's car. I sometimes passed her on the road after a twelve-hour shift. Fiats were unusual enough in rural Maine to be notable. They seemed almost ludicrously small among all the pickups and SUVs that thundered along the roads.

A thought occurred to me, and I turned from the trash can beside the door to use the dumpster instead.

I didn't need to bend down or inspect the Fiat to notice two details about the tiny vehicle.

The first was that its sides were heavily scratched from having driven often down a narrow, thorny road.

The second was that the tires were quite thin. Sixteen-and-a-half-millimeter treads seemed about right by my quick estimation.

If this wasn't the car that had driven down the dirt road to the Witham place, it was its identical twin.

What had Becca Bray been doing down there? And more importantly, why hadn't she told me she'd paid John and Martha a visit before their deaths?

As I returned to my patrol truck, I knelt and pretended to retie the laces to my boots. It gave me a chance to glance at the store to see if Becca was watching me through the window.

She was.

7

An hour and a half later, I was at the boat launch on Lake St. George, checking the licenses and catches of the fishermen departing and returning from the water and inspecting their hulls for milfoil.

The early-afternoon sun was merciless, and so I took refuge in my truck and thus happened to be facing the road when a familiar maroon Ford F-250 went speeding past, doing seventy in a fifty-mile-per-hour zone.

Maine game wardens enforce all laws, not just those pertaining to fish and wildlife, but I rarely chased speeders unless they seemed particularly reckless or obnoxiously defiant. This one, I decided to pursue. I could scarcely believe that hours after I'd discovered the corpses of Johnny Witham's parents, he had had the gall to take their pickup out for a joyride.

I hit the switch on my dash to turn on the blue lights, but the maroon Ford only accelerated, heading east.

Unlike the SUVs built specially for police departments, my GMC Sierra was not equipped with a turn-on-a-dime drivetrain and a four-hundred-horsepower engine. I had to push the pedal to the floor just to keep up with Bottle Johnny.

It was my understanding that Witham Jr. had lost his license for six years because he was a habitual offender—hence his daily excursions by bicycle—and I wanted to nip this new criminality in the bud.

Just across the Liberty town line, however, he pulled a familiar stunt, one of the favorites used by speeders: he slammed on the brakes and turned sharply into the gravel lot of an old building and came to a stop, cutting the engine at once. He wanted it to seem as if he had arrived at his destination without ever having seen me. It was always the same conversation after that.

"No, I don't know why you stopped me. No, I don't know how fast I was going. I was watching the road. There are lots of dangerous drivers out there and you can never be too careful!"

I pulled up at an angle behind the Ford to prevent him from backing out. The dust kicked up by its wheels was still swirling and hard to see through, like a sandstorm in miniature. But I was out of my truck with my hand on the grip on my service weapon before the cloud could settle.

The driver's door opened and out dropped Lyla Duncan.

Johnny Witham emerged from the passenger's side a moment later. His eyes were as red as cherry tomatoes, and his shoulders were slumped as if he would never be able to square them again.

"Gee, Warden," the pregnant woman said with no particular friendliness. "If I didn't know better, I'd think you was stalking us."

"I was trying to pull you over, Ms. Duncan."

"Guess I didn't see you in the rearview. I was focused on the road."

"License and registration, please. And proof of insurance."

She reminded me of a silent film star in her exaggerated mannerisms. She rolled her eyes.

"That's what we was on our way to do—get all the paperwork transferred over for the vehicle. And we needed a license, too, before the town office closed."

"License?"

Lyla Duncan made a hitchhiking motion with her thumb at

the decrepit old building before which we had come to rest. Only then did I notice the sign out front. The dusty, clapboard-sided building was the home to the Mysteries of the Spirit Pentecostal Church.

"Johnny and I are getting married."

They were dressed as they'd been at the crime scene, and Johnny had even acquired a new stain—mustard?—on his Ozzy Osbourne Farewell Tour T-shirt.

I turned in disbelief to the slump-shouldered man. "Your parents haven't even been autopsied."

His voice came in even more of a mumble than usual. "Life is for the living, Lyla says."

"That's right. That's what I always say. With his folks gone, there's nothing stopping us anymore, and neither of us want this baby born illegitimate. You ain't going to ruin our happy day with a ticket, I hope," Lyla said as if daring me to write her up.

"Your happy day," I repeated.

But she seemed immune to my sarcasm.

"You want to be a witness?" said Johnny out of nowhere. "We need two people to swear we took our vows. And Lyla's brother Andy is running late."

How I kept from laughing, I did not know. "I didn't realize you were religious, Johnny."

"The pastor's the only clergyman we could find who would hitch us before God on short notice," Lyla explained. "You'd think marrying people would be more of a priority among so-called preachers. Ain't they always saying the world is going to hell?"

And that was how I found myself in a cushioned chair in the front row of the church, seated beside the pastor's wife—my fellow witness—while Johnny and Lyla took their abbreviated vows and became husband and wife in less time than it would have taken to boil an egg.

Lyla was glowing even more than usual throughout the

ceremony. Not once did Johnny crack a smile, and when he kissed his new bride, his tears didn't particularly strike me as joyful.

It wasn't mere perversity that motivated me to take part in this circus act. I knew I'd be retelling the tragicomic story well into my retirement. But mostly, I felt a duty to observe and listen to the Withams in case they said anything that might affect the state police's inquiry into the recent killings.

I was watching Johnny especially, as he seemed the more transparent of the two, but I found his general dimness harder to read than I had hoped. His runny eyes might have been from guilt or from grieving or even from the purple loosestrife he gathered from the edge of the field when his new wife remarked that she needed a wedding bouquet to throw.

It was bad enough, she announced, that he hadn't gotten her a ring.

"I haven't had a whole lot of time today . . ."

"You could have given me your mom's."

"It's evidence," I said, not adding that Martha's hands were so swollen that the medical examiner surely would be forced to amputate the ring finger to remove the cheap silver band during the autopsy.

A green pickup turned in to the lot, pulling a cloud of exhaust behind it. On its door were the words FRYE MOUNTAIN JOINERY. A man with a terra-cotta complexion and a coppery crew cut got out. He was a heavyset guy in his early twenties who would only get bigger with every cheeseburger he ate and every barbell he lifted, and his overalls were so covered with sawdust the canvas cloth appeared beige rather than their original forest green. He looked at me through sunglasses, which he did not remove, but I could sense the suspicion behind the darkly polarized lenses.

Lyla's brother Andy, presumably, arriving late to the shotgun wedding.

His sister didn't acknowledge him—although she was staring

into his unreadable face—but continued on the subject of her ring.

"Yeah, well, we'd better get it back soon or I'm going to file a complaint with the state. I don't see why I should be punished for someone else's crime. 'Only the guilty shall pay,' the Bible says," she added, citing an imaginary verse from a book I doubted she'd ever read.

8

"You did what for them?" Steve Klesko asked when I called him afterward. "You witnessed their marriage?"

"I signed the wedding album, too."

"Why, Mike? Why?"

I was seated in my truck on the pullout above the lush green wetland between Knox and Daggett Ponds. A slow, looping stream flowed through the green marsh, and red-winged blackbirds perched on cattails or ducked down into hidden nests to bring their chicks meals of spiders and mayflies caught on the wing. Every now and then, I scanned the channel with my binoculars for the secretive rails that croaked constantly from the rushes but might as well have been invisible.

I directed myself to the speakerphone. "Because I'm getting a feel about these two. Lyla Duncan might be the biggest narcissist I've met. Killing another person to her would be like stepping on an ant."

"Unless she was perched on a stepladder, I doubt that happened. One of the few things we've been able to determine so far is that the shot that killed Martha was fired at a downward angle—almost certainly by someone taller than she was."

"Maybe she was standing on tippy-toes."

But Klesko didn't catch the sarcasm. "Two people died violently, Mike. It's too soon to make light of it, in my opinion."

"I was trying to make the point that there are other explanations that reconcile the entrance wound with the idea of little Lyla Duncan as shooter. Her brother Andy acting as her surrogate, for example."

"Who's this Andy?"

"A tub of a man who showed up after the nuptials. I don't think he found the idea of me being a member of the wedding particularly amusing, either."

Klesko sighed, as many people in my life did—especially those who had to listen to my half-baked theories and unjustified suggestions.

"You remember that most criminals are impulsive idiots," he said, "that alcohol usually plays a part, and that sadly, most murdered women shared a bed with their killers. The odds highly favor John Witham having shot Martha, and you need to accept that. Just because we might never know what was going through his drunken head doesn't make it a mystery with a twist ending."

A van raced past along the paved road, raising dust that sparkled in the sun as if the sand had been sprinkled with glitter. Some of it settled on my windshield. The speeding vehicle belonged to a diaper delivery service. I didn't realize such businesses still existed, let alone in the patchwork farmlands of Waldo County.

"I get it, Steve. But I think you should take a look at the Kentville deeds."

"Why?"

"The Withams might have been cash poor, but Martha told me once that their land extended down to Knox Stream."

"Isn't it all swamp?"

"Mostly swamp, but my point is that most murderers are dimwits, like you just said. Their property doesn't have to be worth a damn. What matters is that the killer or killers thought it was—if they stood to inherit."

"I know you miss being an investigator," my friend said. "You pretend you don't, but I know you better than that."

"I'm just taking an interest is all."

"Please don't make me regret having told you so much about the case this morning."

I brought the binoculars up again after Steve signed off.

Two common mergansers had just rocketed up the stream, startling the blackbirds as well as a few swamp sparrows also nesting in the marsh. I had never taken a canoe up that brook; never seen anyone do so. But it occurred to me that it offered a fresh perspective on the Withams' land.

I restarted the truck, deciding to return home to fetch one of my several canoes. Stacey would be gone by now. But our conversation about Shadow had made me miss the beast and wonder if she was right about him being ready for excursions beyond our property.

Heading east, I came upon a simple roadside produce stand, and I remembered something I'd told Klesko: that Martha had a reputation for stealing from these unattended farm markets.

A big old willow draped its long branches over this one, creating an umbrella of shade for me to park under.

I was examining the ears of corn, pulling back the husks to check that worms hadn't been at the cobs, when I noticed that the cashbox had a padlock on it. Someone had bolted it to a metal post, too. And they had also inked a big warning on the side in permanent marker.

NO CHANGE GIVEN!
WE ACCEPT CHECK OR CASH.
WE ROUND UP TO SUPPORT OUR VETS.

I must have looked suspicious crouching down to inspect this lockbox because a white-haired woman appeared from nowhere—as if she'd been lurking behind the willow to spring out at petty thieves.

"Just slide payment through that slit in the top, Mike. We had to get rid of our old cashbox because someone kept looting it. Not that I would ever speak ill of the dead."

I looked up into the sun-freckled face of Denise O'Dowd. She was a tanned, stocky woman, dressed in a cotton blouse and dirty denim, whom no one would ever have called a beauty, and yet she continued to fascinate certain men, even at the age of sixty-five, due to the enormity of her bosom.

Some guys never grow out of baby's first fixation, I thought as she flashed the cleavage exposed between her opened shirt buttons.

"Hey, Denise," I said. "I take it you're referring to Martha Witham."

She pushed her broad-brimmed straw hat back from her forehead. "She cleaned me out of two crates of duck eggs one day! I know it was Martha even though I never saw their truck. It was because she left a single egg behind to taunt me. That was Martha Witham all over."

"She wanted to provoke you?"

"She loved nothing more than getting under people's skin. I've lived here twenty-eight years, and she always chided me for being 'new to town.' She wanted me to know I would never belong here because I came from New Jersey. The woman took pleasure in being nasty. When I heard John had finally shut her up once and for all, I said, 'What took him so long?'"

I hefted an heirloom tomato that I felt obliged to buy at this point.

"What about John? Did you ever have run-ins with him?"

"Not personally. But I'm sure you heard the stories about him being a Peeping Tom."

What did Klesko just say about most criminals being impulsive idiots?

"What I don't get," Denise continued, "is how those two people produced a son as sweet as Johnny. He helped me with my raking once and wouldn't accept a dime. With his good looks, he could have been on television—if his parents hadn't destroyed his self-esteem. Maybe he'll be liberated by their dying and finally become the good, independent man he was meant to be."

Doubtful, I thought, *with the former Lyla Duncan at his side.*

"I have a random question for you, Denise. You wouldn't happen to know if Knox Stream is navigable up to the Withams' land . . . ?"

"I suppose it might be."

"Can you ever remember seeing a fisherman take a canoe upstream of the bridge?"

"By 'ever,' do you mean in my entire life? I suppose once or twice."

I was thinking about the canoe waiting for me at home and how quickly I could load it onto my truck and get back to the bridge and launch it, and how much daylight I would have paddling into the swamp, because it was late August, and the days weren't as long as they had been. After that crazy wedding, I wanted to sneak back onto the Withams' land and watch them and maybe even eavesdrop on their conversations if I could get near enough.

"Thank you," I said.

"For what?"

"For the tomato," I said. "I don't suppose you can break a five."

"Those Cherokee purples are five apiece."

"In that case, you can keep the change."

"Don't you be a smart-ass, too," she warned me, as if there were still time to mend my ways.

9

Shadow rushed expectantly from the leafy cover of his pen to the gate—as excited and tail-wagging as any domestic dog when his owner returns after hours of absence. The difference with my "pet" was that he weighed 145 pounds and had a coat as black as the devil and eyes the color of saltpeter. His fangs were as long as my little fingers. The wolf hybrid had been raised in a home but had later lived in the wild for a couple of years. As an escapee, roaming Maine's Boundary Mountains, he had preyed on deer, beavers, and random livestock (I knew for a fact that he had killed and eaten at least one poor donkey). He'd been stand-offish and inscrutable when he'd first come to live with me, but Stacey's moving-in had awakened his inner puppy.

I pressed my palm to the wire so he could lick it.

"Sorry to disappoint you, buddy, but I'm just making a pit stop before I go out again."

The wolf waited for me to unlock the gate, and when I didn't, he began to whine.

"We've been through this before. You can't come on patrol with me. No one's going to be fooled into thinking you're a trained police dog. I still have a career in the Warden Service I'm hoping to salvage."

He rose onto his hind legs, pressed his massive front paws

to the chain link, and continued to plead his case with deep-throated appeals. Standing, he was nearly as tall as I was.

Shadow had never chased squirrels—even the kamikazes who entered his pen—but I was less sure what he'd do if he scented a deer in the woods. Stacey was insistent the wolf wouldn't bolt on us. Maybe she was right. He might not come immediately at my call, but I wouldn't lose him in the woods again, I tried to persuade myself.

Perhaps I was feeling punchy from the utter weirdness of my day. But I was only going to paddle up Knox Stream, right? We had microchipped him and purchased a GPS tracking collar.

Why not give him a chance?

I should have known how things would go when he refused to enter his crate but insisted on riding inside the truck cab. I threw down blankets to keep his claws from tearing apart the state of Maine's upholstery, but he seemed to take perverse pleasure in digging aside the protective layers of wool.

When we set off up Knox Stream, he seemed relaxed enough in the bow of the canoe. As I dipped the paddle and pushed against the slothful current, he twitched his ears and sniffed loudly.

I began thinking that my idea of bringing this half-wild animal for a boat ride was the kind of harebrained scheme I should have outgrown years earlier.

From the bridge, the stream flowed in shallow loops through a bottomland of speckled alder, willows, and sheep laurel. Blue, green, and red dragonflies bothered the sullen air with the rapid rustling of their cellophane wings. Bullfrogs burped from the lily pads until the canoe drew near and then dove for cover in the muddy depths. It was easy paddling, but the sun was hot on my neck, and I began to perspire heavily again.

I wondered who the last person had been to approach the Witham property through this blooming, buzzing swamp.

Maybe Denise O'Dowd's assessment of John and Martha as

miserable humans was all the explanation anyone needed for their tragic ends. One of my failings as an investigator had always been looking for complicated schemes and unexplained contradictions in crimes that couldn't have been any more cut-and-dried. Alcoholic husbands killed their wives with depressing regularity. Given the absence of any motive, and the deterioration of the physical evidence in the August heat, Klesko would probably close the case within the week, and rightly so.

About two hundred yards north of the bridge, the brook rounded a bend and came to a peninsula where an anonymous trickle flowed in from the east. There, on the raised point, stood a cluster of trees invisible from any road or hillside. It was a shady thicket of old, untapped sugar maples.

I dug the paddle into the stream, stirring up mud-brown clouds as I drove the bow onto the hummock.

Shadow leaped out before the keel even touched, and for an instant, I feared Stacey had been wrong about him: that he was going to run off and probably find some way to escape that GPS collar, that I would have to explain to my wife how I'd come to lose our "tame" wolf.

Instead, he waited for me.

Keeping my center of gravity low, I walked up the canoe and hopped onto the shore. Then I dragged the boat up behind me, even though there was zero chance of it being swept away by the sluggish stream.

Shadow was sniffing around the fallen, decomposing leaves at the base of the old maples. I didn't know why—canine noses have mysterious preoccupations. Then I saw the carvings in the trunk of the biggest tree. Someone had recently chiseled off strips of bark to reveal the living wood beneath.

I assumed it had to have been John or Martha. But why had they taken an interest in sugar maples they'd ignored for nearly half a century? Surely, they would have tapped them for syrup by now if they'd ever had a mind to do so.

I used my fingernail to scrape into the chipped places and saw some dimples in the wood where the grain appeared twisted.

"Bird's-eye!" I said aloud.

Not *bull's-eye* but *bird's-eye*.

Suddenly, it all made sense. Or almost made sense.

John and Martha Witham might have been as poor as field mice, but they were—unknowingly?—sitting on a stand of the most valuable trees in Maine.

Shadow and I made eye contact, and of course, he saw what I was thinking—that I needed to return him to the truck and call for backup before approaching Bottle Johnny's trailer—and of course, seeing what I was planning, he took off into the woods as if his tail were on fire.

Damn it!

The wolf didn't care about human trails; he made his own path through the underbrush. But I had to shoulder my way through the willows along the banks. I got whipped across the face by sapling branches I tried to push aside. And attacked by mosquitoes that had been resting as if in anticipation of a hot-blooded human stumbling into their kingdom.

Eventually, I located a trail. It was the secret passage someone had used to cut through the alders and shadbush out to the point. It was how the unknown person found the sugar maples.

I thought Shadow might be making for the shack, as pungent as it still must be. But there were no signs of him at the crime scene with its sagging cordon of yellow tape. I almost reached for my GPS dog tracker.

Then I heard screams. Not one woman but two, coming from up the dusty road in the direction of Bottle Johnny's trailer.

Car doors slammed. But the screams continued, muffled only slightly from the screamers being inside the vehicle now, insulated behind steel and glass.

I took off at a sprint, feeling the weight of my bulletproof vest with every stride. The baked road didn't show Shadow's tracks, but it was no longer a mystery where he'd gone.

Now the car began to honk: a pitiful, high-pitched tooting.

It took me less than two minutes to cover the quarter mile: not bad in this early evening heat and weighed down with my twenty-pound gun belt and ponderously heavy boots.

Through the breaks in the cedar boughs and maple leaves, I saw the maroon Ford pulled up outside the mobile home. The yellow Fiat didn't reveal itself until I was nearly upon it.

Shadow sat motionless in front of the tiny car while Becca Bray, in the driver's seat, leaned on the farcical horn. His tail wasn't twitching, nor were his hackles raised. He displayed no aggression whatsoever. But to the women inside the car, the wolf must have looked like he'd just come from devouring someone's grandmother.

"It's all right!" I shouted to Becca and the former Lyla Duncan, who was seated beside her. "He's not going to hurt you."

Just as I spoke those words, however, Johnny Witham stepped from the trailer with a rifle. It was a cheap, thin-barreled .22 but more than capable of killing a man, let alone a wolf hybrid.

Shadow's good fortune and mine was that Bottle Johnny's hands were shaking so hard he couldn't draw a bead.

Not having a target didn't stop him from squeezing off a shot, however. Fortunately, Shadow recognized what guns portended. He had broken for the foliage the second Johnny showed himself with the weapon.

I waved my arms, trying to attract his attention. "Stop shooting, for God's sake!"

Inevitably, he swung the rifle around on me.

Tears were streaming again down the handsome face. In addition to his nerves getting the better of him, I doubted he could focus with his eyes welling up like that.

"Put the gun down, man. You're going to hurt someone."

He laughed at that—not the response I'd expected. But he did lower the barrel. And a moment later, he collapsed on the ground like a marionette that'd had its strings cut.

"I'm not an evil person," he sobbed. "I swear I ain't."

Now another man appeared behind him: Lyla's brother Andy, toting a can of Coors and smiling like an overgrown boy watching a cartoon.

"Stop being a wuss, Witham," he said. "Get on your feet. The warden's got nothing on you or any of us."

Mindful of the rifle, I slowed my steps as I approached the sobbing, broken man.

"I can't," he said. "I can't take it anymore."

"Take what?" I asked as gently as I could. I desperately wanted to get ahold of that weapon.

"Shut up, Johnny!" It was his new bride, who had emerged from the car. "Don't you say another word."

With my peripheral vision, I tried to keep track of her and Becca. Nor could I ignore Andy Duncan while I got close enough to Witham to take the rifle.

"What are you doing here, sneaking around?" Lyla continued, as bold as ever. "Was that your wolf? It almost scared us to death."

I stood above Johnny now. He had his head on his knees and his arms wrapped around his naked, bug-bitten calves. I squatted and picked up the rifle. I slid the bolt back twice to eject the last two rounds.

"Lyla, honey—" said the sobbing man.

"Not a word, Johnny. What did I tell you?"

"Listen to her, wuss," Andy growled.

Now that he was out of sight, I gave a thought to Shadow, praying to heaven he was watching nearby. But I had more pressing issues to address.

I looked at the pitiable form of Bottle Johnny. "I know you shot them. I know she put you up to it."

"It's eating me up inside," he said. "Like literally! My heart feels like something's chewing at it."

"That's a coerced confession," Andy said, still smirking like a man who knew he had nothing to fear and so was taking pleasure in the desperation of his companions. "You used the wolf to scare him, and now he's unnerved. It'll get thrown out in court."

My gaze moved to Becca, who had turned deathly pale beneath her ashen hair and seemed to be trying to will herself into invisibility again. I had suspected I would find her here. What I hadn't suspected was that she would be weeping nearly as hard as Johnny Witham.

"Do *you* want to tell me what's going on, Becca?"

"No!" said Lyla.

"It's done, baby," Becca Bray said sweetly.

"Don't you call me that. I ain't your girlfriend, bitch."

I rested the rifle on my shoulder. "I knew from the scratches on your car, Becca, that you had driven out here recently. And at first, I thought it might have been on account of Johnny. But then I got to wondering how you knew so much about Lyla—about her father's old job as a timber cruiser—and I remembered how you described her as 'selfish, reckless, unthinking.' From the anger in your voice, it sounded like she'd hurt you, too."

Lyla spun on the other woman. "You think I'm selfish?"

Becca covered her face with her hands. "Please don't."

"I found the maples, Becca," I said. "I know what this was all about. I just need to hear your part in it."

"When she came into the store a couple weeks ago, I thought Lyla was just talking about what might *eventually* be hers. She said the Withams were just letting those valuable trees go to waste. She wanted my advice, it seemed. Like a friend or . . . No one else pays attention to me. But she's always been open and confiding with me." Becca turned to me, with the most imploring expression I had ever seen. "I only said, 'If they won't give you and Johnny the land with those maples as a wedding present,

I wish they'd just hurry up and die already,' I didn't mean it! I never imagined . . ."

"That's not true," I said. "Or you wouldn't have driven out to check on John and Martha last week. Maybe you hoped to warn them how badly Lyla wanted the land. But you didn't warn them, did you?"

She shook her head. "No."

"But then, when John didn't come into the store for a week, you began to worry. That's why you asked me to check on them—because you'd already sensed what had happened."

"It's true," she sobbed.

"You people are such crybabies," said Andy. He hadn't lost his superior, self-excusing grin.

"Why were you going to close the store this afternoon?" I asked. "Was it because you needed to hear Lyla say she had nothing to do with their deaths, even though you knew she was responsible? Because that was what always happened, right? She took everything too far: romancing Johnny, getting pregnant so he would marry her, plotting to get the land with those maples."

Still seated on the ground, Johnny rubbed his runny nose and gazed up with empty eyes at his new wife.

"What's he talking about?"

"He's only a game warden. He don't know shit."

"I know Lyla tried to convince you that your folks were denying you your rightful inheritance, Johnny. She pressured you to confront them, right? Ask for a piece of their land to help pay for the baby expenses? The two of you went to their house last week, and that's when it happened."

"I didn't mean to do it." He began crying and trembling again. "But my ma just kept getting madder and madder, and then she brought out that pistol and—"

"You took the gun away from her, and in the scuffle, it went off."

He bowed his head. "Yeah."

Andy crumpled the beer can and tossed it aside. "My God, you people are such idiots."

I addressed the brother now. "You were the one who found the maples. You came out here with your sister to visit Johnny, and because you're a logger, you had to have a look around at the timber. I know that's what you guys always do in the woods—appraise all the trees. Am I right? And high-quality bird's-eye is worth how much? Five grand a log?"

"More or less," he said with an amiable shrug. "Depends on the week."

"And all that stood between the Duncans and tens of thousands of dollars—maybe hundreds of thousands—were two old rednecks and their gullible son."

"Five thousand for a tree?" Johnny was struggling to get the gist of our conversation, but I sensed that he might finally be wising up to the notion he'd been played for a dupe.

Lyla very nearly spat at me. "He can't testify against me anyhow. Now that we're married. A husband can't testify against his wife."

"I knew there was a reason why you were in such a rush to get hitched."

"I didn't do a damn thing," said Lyla, cradling her pregnant belly.

"There's such a thing as conspiracy to commit murder."

Now it was Lyla's turn to gape. It had never occurred to her—having only been the instigator, Lady Macbeth to Johnny's Macbeth—that she might be liable for her new husband's crime.

Andy, too, lost his amused swagger. "Don't say another word, Lyla, not until we talk to a lawyer."

"I was just an innocent bystander," she said in her most babyish voice. "There ain't no crime to being an innocent bystander."

Even as an infant, I doubted the former Lyla Duncan had ever been innocent.

"But covering up a double homicide is a felony," I said.

Lyla, flushing crimson, thrust a finger at the other woman now. "It was all her idea!"

I had never seen disbelief take total hold of a person as happened with Becca Bray in that moment.

"Me? You're saying I had a part in this?"

"I was just pretending to like you and be your friend. As if I would ever—"

"Oh, God," said Becca. "I need to throw up."

And in front of all of us, she did.

While she retched and Johnny melted further into the ground, and the Duncans whispered conspiratorially with each other, I put in a call to Steve Klesko and told him I had solved his case. I said he was more than welcome to make the arrests, given that I had supposedly stepped back from investigations.

Under the circumstances, I preferred that my friend the detective be the one to get the glory.

10

Shadow was waiting for me in the canoe after I finished hand-ing over my suspects to the state police. I already knew that was where he would be, having nervously checked the GPS tracker and seen his signature blip on the screen.

What I hadn't suspected was that his muzzle would be ruby red with blood. He was still licking at it with his long tongue. I hoped it was the last of Martha Witham's wayward chickens he'd eaten, but I thought not.

The current in the stream wasn't strong enough to carry me back to the bridge where I'd parked my truck. As I paddled, I recalled the complaints Lyla had leveled at the state trooper who tried to handcuff her.

"What kind of sick man handcuffs a pregnant woman? It's brutality! What's your name? I'm going to make sure everyone in Maine knows you're a cop who likes to rough up helpless little girls."

The trooper, who had been trained in shrugging off these sorts of threats and should have known better, had acquiesced and let her ride to the jail, unrestrained.

Lady Macbeth, indeed, I thought.

Johnny Witham had confessed again to the detectives and would continue to do so, I had a feeling, for the rest of his life, never finding expiation for his role in his parents' deaths because he was incapable of perceiving where his guilt ended and that of the others began.

Andy Duncan would likely skate unless more evidence appeared to implicate him. But his arrogance would catch up with him eventually. It always did with unscrupulous men who weren't as smart as they thought.

I'd asked Steve what the district attorney might charge Becca Bray with, and he said it depended on Lyla's testimony—she was hardly a trustworthy witness—but he doubted that local cops and firefighters would continue frequenting the Kentville General Store once word got out about Becca's criminal associates. It might be punishment enough to have her heart broken and to lose the only job she'd ever had after her parents decided her presence behind the cash register was a drag on their business.

"For what it's worth, I believed her when she said she didn't mean for John and Martha to die," I said.

"That won't bring them back, though, will it?"

It was an excellent point.

Stacey's Bronco was parked in the dooryard as I pulled up to the gate of Shadow's pen. My wife came out with a beer for me and a lemonade for herself to hear the story firsthand. We sat on the porch and watched the satiated predator sprawl on the raised ledge that served as his throne.

In the summer heat, Shadow preferred sleeping outside, especially when the moon was full. And while it is a myth that wolves howl during periods of maximal lunation, something about those nights did seem to awaken the primal wildness within him. I felt some of the same pull—was conscious of my animal self in the company of my own pregnant mate.

When she'd entered her second trimester, Stacey had started wearing my T-shirts. Soon, though, even those wouldn't be big enough to cover her belly. But she had that special radiance everyone talks about; some clichés are real that way.

"You were right about Lyla," I said. "I've never met a woman who was better at using her pregnancy to get her way with men. I hope she gets a female judge at her bail hearing who sees through her act. It would be a travesty if she walks free on the street while Johnny waits for trial in a jail cell. Do you find men easier to manipulate now that you're beginning to show?"

"I haven't tried," she said. "But I can't blame women who do. For some, it's the first time any man ever really notices them, being pregnant. The first time they feel any kind of power." Then she took my hand and placed it on her stomach. "Lyla Duncan isn't the first woman to weaponize this."

Feeling the life growing inside her, the baby we'd created together, I knew that my own wife could have convinced me to do anything.

Murder?

Yes.

Maybe even murder.

Acknowledgments

M ost of the research I do for my novels and stories comes from spending hours in the woods hunting and fishing and birding and from riding along with game wardens, listening to their stories and meeting the people they encounter on a daily basis.

But occasionally I need to crack a book.

That was the case with "Rabid," especially since I knew so little about the disease when the idea for the story first came to me. The passage that is quoted on pages 66 to 67 comes from an invaluable and highly readable work titled *Rabid: A Cultural History of the World's Most Diabolical Virus,* by Bill Wasik and Monica Murphy (Penguin Books, New York, NY, 2012).

I use the quotation anachronistically since *Rabid* the book was published *after* the events of the story. But if there is one thing a fiction writer learns early in their career it is to never let facts get in the way of a good story.

About the Author

Kristen Lindquist

Paul Doiron, a bestselling author and native of Maine, attended Yale University, where he graduated with a degree in English. *The Poacher's Son*, the first book in the Mike Bowditch series, won the Barry Award and the Strand Award for Best First Novel, and has been nominated for the Edgar, Anthony, and Macavity Awards in the same category. He is a registered Maine guide specializing in fly-fishing and lives on a trout stream in coastal Maine with his wife, Kristen Lindquist.